One Month of You

Suzanne Ewart

ORION

First published in Great Britain in 2021 by Orion Fiction,
an imprint of The Orion Publishing Group Ltd
Carmelite House, 50 Victoria Embankment
London EC4Y 0DZ

An Hachette UK Company

1 3 5 7 9 10 8 6 4 2

A CIP catalogue record for this book is
available from the British Library.

ISBN (Paperback) 978 1 4091 9437 8
ISBN (eBook) 978 1 4091 9438 5
ISBN (Audio) 978 1 4091 9450 7

Typeset by Born Group
Printed and bound in Great Britain by Clays Ltd, Elcograf S.p.A.

www.orionbooks.co.uk

For my family

Rules

1. Do not fall in love

2. Stop thinking about men altogether

3. See as much of the world as possible

4. Save money for travelling instead of wasting it on magazines and tops

5. Stop pretending to like Prosecco; just drink wine instead

6. Keep going out, even when I don't feel like it

7. Never miss doctors' appointments

8. Tell no one else

9. Keep smiling

Chapter One

One more drink and the weekend will have to begin. Fifty-eight hours before my alarm goes off on Monday morning and the weekend is over.

If I were a doctor or a restaurant manager or a trapeze artist, weekends would not apply. Time would be evenly spread throughout the week. Small pieces of time between ward rounds or circus shows, I could handle. Huge chunks are much harder. Every Friday, whilst my colleagues switch off their computers early, tidy their desks and gather up their belongings, ready to shoot out the door like racehorses the moment Jane, our office manager, releases them, I curse the poor decision-making that led me to a nine-to-five in admin.

At least there are the after-work drinks to look forward to with Olivia at the pub across the road. But that's all it is. A few drinks. Not a plan for the weekend, rather a tag-on to the week before we part, and Olivia's real plans begin to unfurl.

When it's her round, she's good enough to buy us each a large white wine, but once we've drunk them, she'll pull on her coat, kiss my cheeks and be gone.

I won't ask her, I promise myself.

We sit side by side on our usual bench at the back of The Wishing Well, and she's laughing as I tell her about the row I interrupted this morning between our senior partner Mr Lewis and Jane, who also happens to be his wife. My glass is on the table, but she keeps hers to her mouth, the rim of it brushing against her lips in between sips. She nods along in agreement with my prediction that the argument must have been about her insistence he take up a personal trainer again because I'm sure I heard him say, 'six pack, my arse', when I walked in, but all the time she's working on her wine. My time with her is nearly up, but I won't ask her to stay.

Instead, I force myself to ask about her plans. 'Where's he taking you tonight?'

She groans. 'Bowling. Bloody bowling. I tell you, there's no surer sign you're getting too comfortable in a relationship than when your dates change from Michelin-star restaurants and hotels in the Lakes to bowling with his mates.'

'Absolutely. You're going straight there, are you?' I look under the table at the leather trousers and stiletto boots Olivia changed into in the loo before we left the office. 'You're going to fit right in.'

'Don't. I've told him I'm there for the beer and nachos and nothing else. What a waste of a night.'

She's not really annoyed. Maybe bowling's not her thing, but Rick is, and I can't believe she's not looking forward to spending the night with him. She does this, making out Rick's failed to please her or there are problems with their relationship, when we both know she adores him. Pretending otherwise is another blanket of kindness she likes to lay over me, like these Friday-night drinks, only this one is so thin and covered in moth holes, there's no point it being there at all.

'I don't know; it might be fun. You should get going,' I tell her, giving her permission to get up.

'I should.' Underneath heavy stuck-on lashes, she studies me. 'What about you? Are you going to be OK? You can come along, if you like.'

'Nice try. You're on your own. Come on, I'll walk out with you.' I grab my parka and my bag, and Olivia and I file out past a group from the accountants' office next to ours. I wave at a few people I've come to know from sharing the same Northern Quarter street over the years and turn towards the door. Olivia pulls me back.

'You know, it's not that busy in here tonight. Why don't you sit at the bar and have another drink? I'm sure Alec will be pleased. Alec, you don't mind Jess keeping you company for a bit, do you?' she shouts to the barman.

'I'd be delighted,' he says, smiling briefly at me, showing just a hint of the gleaming white teeth Olivia and I have had countless discussions about; our latest thinking being that they are definitely veneers. 'Are you off?' he asks, turning to Olivia.

'Oh, she's got big plans tonight,' I tell him. 'Bowling.'

'Sounds good,' he says. I'm sure he means it.

'It won't be. But I can go now, knowing at least you two will be sitting here having fun.'

She thinks I don't see her wink at Alec before she turns to me and leans in. 'Love you,' she whispers.

I shake my head before saying, 'You too. Have a nice weekend.'

A wrinkle of worry blots her otherwise smooth face. 'Are you sure you're going to be OK?'

'I'll be fine. Now go.'

'OK. Alec, get her another drink, will you?' she says before kissing my cheek and leaving.

She'll be pleased with her handiwork this evening. For two months, she's been trying to push Alec and me together, ever since he started working in The Wishing Well, and she declared him the second-most handsome man she'd ever seen. If it weren't for Rick beating him to the top spot, she'd have been after him herself. Instead, she went for another second best: setting him up with me. This is her finest work yet. Or it would be, if I were at all interested.

Alec's section of the copper-topped bar is free from empty glasses, dry and polished. Further down the bar, near to where the crowd of accountants have gathered, the bar is strewn with the detritus of some serious drinking. But that's not Alec's domain. That belongs to the barman in a matching grey shirt to Alec's, with sweat marks growing rapidly under the armpits like spilt ink.

'How are things?' he asks once he's put another white wine down in front of me and has begun polishing the already gleaming beer taps to my left, his gaze on the job in hand instead of on me.

'Fine. Don't you need to help out your colleague? He looks like he's floundering over there.'

'Mike? Nah, he's fine. Anyway, I couldn't, even if I wanted to. You've got to keep to your section, otherwise the system fails and anarchy breaks out over who gets what share of the tips. You keep your own space and your own tip-glass. Rules are rules.'

I can't imagine many of The Wishing Well's customers thinking to tip. Tipping is reserved for restaurants and the odd swanky bar if you order a cocktail that has a sparkler in it or froths with liquid nitrogen, not a back-street boozer.

'Who am I to argue with such a solid system? Any joy on the flat?' I ask.

'Lots of joy,' he says, looking up at last. 'I got the keys on Wednesday. I've moved in.'

'That's great. I've been wondering all week if you were in. Congratulations.'

His eyes widen a fraction like I've surprised him.

'Thanks. It's so nice to have my own space and not to be crammed in that damp house with three other barmen anymore.'

'I can imagine. Actually, I can't at all, but I'm still so pleased for you. When's the flat-warming, then?'

'Not happening. I fully intend to keep it as pristine as it is now. All the walls are white, you know. I can't be inviting any old lush from the pub back to it.'

I hold my hands up. 'Fair enough. Nothing worse than a lush round white walls.'

He laughs before turning away. He's not able to keep my face as the focus of his attention for more than a few seconds tonight. Whilst he's not looking, I run my fingers over my eyebrows, under each eye and around my mouth, in case something's gone hideously wrong.

The ten-pound note I put down for my wine is still beside my coaster. I'm about to tell him when the pub door swings open and a group of lads come in, walking to the bar with such pace that there's no doubt of their intent to get hammered tonight. Alec steps away from me, ready to serve them. I sit back in the stool and watch him set to work, ignoring the looks my way and the nudges a few of them give their mates to alert their attention to the lone woman at the bar.

I try to enjoy the wine, to squeeze out a final few moments of enjoyment before I leave. A thrum of music weaves in and out of the heavier beat of conversation, and I focus on following it until the lads get their drinks and Alec returns to me.

'Hey, you forgot to take my money,' I tell him. I try to place the note in his hand, my fingertips skimming his marzipan-smooth skin, but he recoils.

'No, I didn't.'

He's managing to look straight at me now. Olivia's right; beard aside, he really is incredibly handsome. But his looks aren't his best asset. There's an openness to his manner I've never come across in anyone else before. Every truth is imprinted on him. It's startling, really, how easy it is to read him.

It's how I know he's getting ready to make a move. The flush in his cheeks, the glint in his eye, the slight movement of his lips as he tries and fails to find the words. It's not been so long that I can't remember what it's like. The complicated tangle of panic and delight in the pit of my stomach hasn't changed.

I sink it with wine.

Alec may be about to find his courage, but he won't need it, and there's certainly no need for any alteration to my normally sturdy constitution. He might be ready to try his luck, but he won't be getting the chance.

It's time to go home.

Chapter Two

It's his weight I notice first – the warm pressure of a calf sprawled across both of mine. Still half asleep, I find myself enjoying the feeling and its gentle tug back into a past where I would often wake under a limb.

Glossy memories of long mornings spent dozing in a muddle of arms and legs emerge and I stretch out in them happily. Until I wake enough to remember whose body the calf belongs to and I'm flung forward into this moment, this bed.

Ever so slowly I start to wriggle out from under him, stopping every other second to make sure he doesn't wake at the movement.

Jess, how could you? I berate myself once free.

Turning my head on the pillow, I can just make him out in the charcoal light. He's on his back with his head turned away from me. The leg not tossed over mine stretches to the other corner of the bed, and, like a child, his arms are stretched out above his head. He lies in the middle, his body held in the memory-foam ditch he's created for himself, whilst my bum hovers uncovered over the edge. Despite the company, he's not relented an inch.

God, he's selfish.

I let out a long gust of breath and pull another one deep into my lungs. Pleased to have found a bad thing about him, I begin to search for others. Might as well get a list going.

There's the smell, for a start: stale and acidic. Good. That'll be all the wine he sunk last night after closing, seeping back out through his mouth and his pores as he's slept. OK, so it's not like he was the only one knocking it back, but the smell, I'm certain, is all his.

It's a shame he's not snoring or making clicking noises in his throat or any other noise from the orchestra of gross sounds men are capable of creating in their deep sleep; I could have been repulsed quite easily. Instead, he's absolutely silent. A little odd in itself, I suppose, but I can hardly dislike him for it.

In the gloom which the winter's morning and his blackout blind have colluded to create, it's hard to find anything else to fault without getting a closer look at him.

Most of his body is hidden under the duvet, which finishes high on his chest. Carefully, I shuffle up to him, hook the duvet with my finger and gently pull it down. He stirs at the movement, but it's not enough to wake him. It does, however, make him turn his head on the pillow, his face landing inches from my own.

And there it is: the flaw of flaws. The reason I'd given Olivia time and time again for not finding him at all attractive. The beard. Not a bit of fuzz, but a full-on, can-be-measured-in-centimetres shock of black hair covering the bottom half of his face. I hate beards. Unless the man in question is a cast member of *Game of Thrones* or is without access to running water or a razor, there's really no excuse for them.

I wince when I remember the hours I spent with my face enmeshed in that thing last night. When I press my fingertips to my chin, it tingles, and I know that when I look in the mirror I'll find a beard-shaped patch of irritated, pink skin.

Still, lucky for me he has it, because, aside from that, there's very little to dislike. A tumble of thick, black hair sprawls across his smooth forehead. Around his closed eyes, the skin is tight and untroubled. He has a narrow, straight nose with the slightest of points at the end and high, round cheekbones that begin to jut out from his slender face before being swallowed by the beard. His eyelids are closed, covering the stars of his face.

I run my index finger lightly over the tips of his hair, thinking about Olivia and what she'd say if she knew where I've woken up this morning. And not just Olivia; all of the girls in the admin pool at McAllister Lewis Glenn would have something to say about it. Since Alec started working at The Wishing Well, the department has skived off so much at lunchtime and returned filled with so many units of alcohol that if someone in HR did a chart, they'd find a direct correlation between Alec's arrival and a fall in productivity in the firm.

With one exception. My productivity has been as average as it ever was, thank you very much. Three years ago, maybe I would have seen past the beard and lusted after him too, but not anymore. Now I've got my rules, and I don't let myself fancy anyone. Apart from the odd Joe Wicks daydream, not thinking about men has helped streamline my life, to get rid of all the silliness and wasted energy. Or at least it had.

It's OK, though. Somewhere amongst the bottle we shared after he'd called last orders, I must have looked into his eyes and experienced a moment of forgetfulness. It won't happen again. I've got my list together, and I'm perfectly safe. No chance of love developing here.

A small laugh sneaks out my mouth at the ridiculousness of the idea.

'What's so funny?'

Before he opens his eyes, I quickly spin my body away from him and return to my edge of the bed, hoping I can feign sleep and he'll think I'm one of those jolly people who laugh even when they're dreaming.

It doesn't work. He shuffles up next to me and leans right over, resting his hand on my hip as he does so. I open my eyes to find his are examining my face.

'You know, Jess, waking up to the sound of you cracking up next to me isn't the most reassuring way to start the day.'

'Sorry.'

'Come on, what is it?'

'I was, er, I was thinking how much fun last night was.'

A grin pushes his cheekbones towards his eyes. 'Yeah, it was. Not funny, as I remember, but certainly fun.'

Without any hesitation, he presses down on my hip to make me turn enough so he can kiss me. All traces of shyness from the night before wiped as he's slept.

I'd like to let him. Every time he kissed me last night, he would look at me before our lips met with an expression on his honest face that made me feel like I was the only girl he would ever want to kiss from now on. I'd like to see that face one last time.

'I should go,' I say, rolling away from him and dropping my hands to the floor to retrieve my underwear. When I find it, I silently congratulate myself for following Mum's advice of buying everything black so it always matches and never looks grubby. She always said you should give as much consideration to your underwear as the clothes you put over them, because it's never a given when leaving the house in the morning that they won't get seen before you get home again.

I grab the duvet off Alec and wrap it around my shoulders in a re-creation of my schoolgirl method of keeping a towel round me as I dressed after swimming so the other girls couldn't see my bits.

The downside to preserving my dignity at this late stage is that it takes far too long to hook my bra back on whilst keeping the protective canopy of the duvet in place. I'm sure he'll be smirking as he watches the show, but when I'm finally decent and turn back to check, I find he's frowning. He tries to hide it with an arm stroke and a smile, but it's too late.

How much did I tell him? What I do remember of last night was lustful and light and happy. Could there have been a point when I felt compelled to share more with him than my body?

From the way he looked at me, I must have told him something.

'OK. Let's get moving,' he says, interrupting my alcohol-sodden memories.

He presses a button above his bedside table, and the blind begins to retract, revealing the most miserable of Manchester mornings.

'Looks Baltic out there. I'll give you a lift home, shall I?'

'You don't need to do that. I can get the Metro.'

'You could, but if I remember correctly, you didn't arrive at mine last night wearing much more than a dress and a pair of high heels. No, you'll only end up getting soaked, you'll come down with a horrible cold, and I'll have to watch you shuffling to and from work next week looking dreadful. That's just going to make me feel bad. You don't want that, do you?'

'Right, OK,' I relent, because it is miserable out, and he makes a good point about my lack of attire. 'But you can stop pouting like that, thinking it makes you look all cute and irresistible. It really doesn't.'

'Worked a charm last night,' he counters with a wink.

'Well, it won't work again.'

'That's a shame. I thought last night was pretty amazing. If you're not interested, though, guess I'll have to find someone who is. Hey, don't suppose you could put in a good word for me with Maureen?'

Poor Maureen is sixty-three, has four children and eight grandchildren and is by far the biggest wreck of all my co-workers when around Alec. Last week, after work, she dragged me to The Wishing Well for their cocktail night, and I had to go up to order all her drinks because she was terrified she'd accidentally end up asking him for a Penis Colada.

I launch a pillow at him, which lands, satisfyingly, over his arrogant face.

'Right, that's it.' He lunges towards me, fingers outstretched in an attempt to tickle me.

In as haughty a manner as I can muster in my bra and knickers, I stand up and move out of his reach.

'Wow. What a sight,' he purrs.

'Just get moving and give me this lift, will you?' I bend down to grab my completely creased work dress from the floor and wriggle back into it.

'OK, OK. But I'll need some breakfast first. You want anything?'

'Coffee would be good.'

'Coffee isn't food, Jess.'

'It is in my world.'

'Fine, I'll put on a pot.'

He stretches his body rigid before springing out of bed, his nakedness as irrelevant to him as the hairs on his legs.

He grabs a well-worn navy bathrobe from the back of his door and puts it on, tying it loosely so that most of his broad chest remains on show.

'Instant is fine,' I shout to him once he's left the room.

'It's not in my world,' he shouts back.

Now alone, I walk over to the full-length mirror he's placed across from his bed to assess how dreadful I look.

I'm twenty-eight, but the ink-blue semi-circles underneath my eyes tell a different story. Without my make-up bag, there's not much I can do about them, so I turn to the next most pressing problem: my dress, a maroon chiffon shift that can't even get to lunchtime without starting to resemble crumpled toilet roll, let alone make it through a full working day, drinking session and night in a heap on the floor intact. I rub my hands over the front of it as fast as I can, hoping that, in lieu of an iron, the heat from the friction might rub out a few of the creases. When it becomes obvious it's not going to make the slightest difference, I tug it down a few times and put my black tights back on, which at least eradicate the ugliness of the dress against my mottled legs.

A quick run-through of my hair, and I've done the best I can. It's not like it matters how rough I look in front of Alec anyway, I remind myself before opening the door.

I hear him in the kitchen, rattling around to get my coffee ready, and decide to wait for him in the lounge. Aside from the black L-shaped sofa that dominates the room, there's a half-empty bookcase and a small, cheap-looking wooden table in the corner. That's it. I'm surprised he's created somewhere so soulless, somewhere so at odds to how I thought he was. There are no pictures on the walls, no photo frames filled with groups of friends, not even a token feature wall to spruce the room up. The old me would be all over this, grilling him until I had a satisfactory answer as to why he lives somewhere so bland.

As it is, I remain silent when Alec comes in laden with cups and a stainless-steel cafetière. I expect he'll sit down and move to join him at the table, but he retreats straight back into the kitchen, returning a few seconds later with a box of croissants and a jar of posh jam.

'Croissants?' I ask, taking a seat and helping myself to the coffee.

'Yeah, I just happened to have some in. Would you like one?'

'Alec, no one just has croissants in,' I say, laughing.

'I do. I make a point of it. Nothing more important than a good breakfast, young lady.'

He's grinning as he sits. Underneath the cramped table his knees press into mine. He doesn't move them away.

That's when I know: this wasn't a mistake for him.

'Can you take me home now?' I ask bluntly after a few sips of much-needed coffee.

There's the tiniest pause before he abandons his breakfast and stands.

'Sure. You had enough?'

'More than enough.'

'Let me get dressed, then, and I'll take you.'

If he's disappointed, he does a good job of hiding it. When he comes back in, looking far too pulled together in a grey wool jumper and dark jeans, he extends his hand to help me up from my chair, and in a deep, rumbling voice declares, 'Your chariot awaits.'

It's bitter outside, the kind of cold that burns your skin if you're in it too long. His car is parked at the other corner of the sprawling development of new flats he lives in.

'Here, put this on,' he says, taking off his luxuriously thick wool coat and handing it to me.

Tempted as I am, I refuse. I've already accepted the lift. Accepting anything more would be leading him on.

Once we get to his car, we throw ourselves inside, and he turns the heater up as high as it can go. I gratefully press myself back into the seat as the first waves of warm air reach me. I watch the sleet dribble down my window, tracing its patterns with my finger as we wait for the car to defrost. Alec turns on the radio, flicking stations until he finds a countdown of the best Christmas hits of all time before setting off.

'Go on then, thoughts? Who's going to be number one? Surely, it's got to be Mariah Carey.'

I focus more intently on following the icy beads of water as they're thrust off their paths when the car speeds up.

'Hello? Jess?'

'I'm not really in the mood. Could we turn it off, please?'

'Sure.'

Just as we get out of the city centre and are heading south on the ring road towards the suburbs, thick snow descends. It's hard to see anything other than the tumult of heavy drops. Alec's silence changes from one of awkwardness to one of necessity as he tries to navigate the car through them.

It's only when he's turned into my street that he tries to speak to me again.

'Which one is yours?'

'I'm at the bottom,' I say, pointing to the end of a row of almost identical neat three-bedroomed semis, 'but you can drop me here. I'll be fine.'

He's about to object but stops himself. 'OK.' He pulls over and waits for me to open my door. He's not thought to stop the engine, and I'm grateful.

'Thanks for the lift.'

'No problem. Listen, I meant to say earlier, I don't want you to think last night was only about sex. I'm aware I might have got a tad carried away after we first kissed, but I'd hate for you to think I saw last night, saw you, as a one-night stand. I'll be at the bar tonight, if you want to come in to talk or whatever.'

'Maybe,' I reply, giving him a smile before jumping out. I didn't tell him anything. Any worry he has is entirely of his own making. I let myself feel a smidge of pride for keeping my lips closed, if not my legs.

Drops of snow blotch my dress and melt down my neck. 'Bye, then,' I say cheerily.

'Bye, then.'

I shut the door. His gaze moves from my face to the wing mirror, and his left hand grips the handbrake. I stand back on the pavement in case he makes an arse of setting off on the slippery road, but instead of pulling away, he changes his mind and opens the passenger window.

'Look, I can try and swap my shift tonight, if you'd like.'

'No, don't do that. I'm tired and I've plans anyway.'

'OK. I'll see you soon.'

'You will,' I lie.

I stand in the snow, watching him drive away, letting myself imagine for a little while what it would be like to carry this on. But as soon as his car's smoothly disappeared round the corner, I turn away, fold my arms around my body and shuffle through the snow to home.

Chapter Three

It's silent when I let myself in, and the dining-room door is shut. I tiptoe down the hall past the lounge where the undecorated Christmas tree stands accusingly in the corner. I must ask Mum where she keeps the decorations and get them out this weekend. Last year we couldn't have a tree; it was too much of a hazard. Now she's less able to get about by herself, and there's less of a risk of her stumbling into it, I thought it might be nice for her to see. On Thursday night I went to the monumental trouble of dragging the thing down from the loft and painstakingly slotting each branch into the plastic trunk before giving up, knowing I'd never be able to do such a good job as Mum. Her trees were always so perfect, I'm sure she used a ruler to measure the space between each carefully selected bauble.

I keep walking to get to the kitchen at the back of the house. As expected, I find Debs, bent over the black-marble island cradling a cup of tea.

'Hi, sweet,' she whispers in her Gallagher brothers' Mancunian accent, giving me a wan smile before straightening up. 'I was just thinking about you.'

I put my arms around her and kiss her on the cheek, noticing as I get closer the strands of hair that have erupted from the bun at the nape of her neck and the loose bronzing powder on her cheeks that has done nothing to stop her looking washed out.

'Debs, I'm so sorry I didn't tell you I was staying out. There were drinks after work, and one thing led to another. You know how it is with that lot. Everything OK?'

She considers her response. 'Yeah, we're doing all right.'

'That's good. And last night? How was she?'

'Not too bad. She was restless again, didn't manage more than three hours' sleep all night, but she took all her medicines and was perfectly content. It means she'll be tired today. Don't expect you'll see much of her until evening.'

'It also means you'll be absolutely knackered. Go on, you get some sleep. I'll take over.'

We've only known Debs for six months, but in that time she's come into our tiny family and stretched us out like we were a pair of tight-fitting jeans. She's made herself fit, and I couldn't be more grateful.

Debs isn't the only carer we have; Mum's needed day carers for over a year to allow me to keep working, but she's the first we've hired ourselves, selected by us to be with Mum at night ever since her sleep became so erratic. She loves Mum, calls her 'her dear friend', and, as a mother of three, she treats me like I'm another one of her grown-up-but-still-troubling offspring.

After looking me up and down, she crosses her hands over her large bust and tuts. 'There's no way you can let your mum see you in that state. Go and have a kip, get sorted and I'll stay on.'

'Absolutely not. All I need is a quick shower and a day catching up on the soaps. By the time she's awake, I'll be right as rain. We can spend the evening watching films together in our pyjamas. It'll be nice.'

'You sure?'

'Yes,' I say, ignoring the part of me that wants to cling to her like a little child and beg her not to leave me alone for the rest of the weekend.

'Right, then. I'll get back. Got the grandkids this afternoon, God help me, so I'd best get the house sorted.'

'Forget the house. Get some sleep, will you?'

'Yeah, you're right,' she agrees with a long sigh. After putting her cup in the sink and straightening the tea towel hanging from the oven door, she picks up her bag.

'See you Monday, love.'

She gets to the door before turning back.

'Anyone special, was he?' she asks, hopefully.

'No, it was nothing like that. I stayed with a friend.'

'Oh. There's me thinking you'd come back from a night of hot sex.'

'Debs!' I'm mortified. Mum would never say such a thing.

'Don't look so offended. A bit of a fling would do you good.'

'I've got a bit too much on my plate right now to be bothering about flings.'

I mean it to sound light-hearted, but the look she gives me is entirely full of pity.

'I know you do. I'll be back Monday, OK? Call me if you need me.'

Debs lets herself out after checking in on Mum one last time, and I spend the rest of the day in bed with the TV on. I try not to think at all about Alec and instead focus on the *Coronation Street* omnibus.

It's dark by the time I hear Mum stirring. I rush down to her, knocking gently on the dining-room door before entering.

'Hi, Mum. Good sleep? I'll put the light on, shall I?'

I hover in the long moments of silence, willing myself not to fill them, waiting for her to answer for herself. Now her voice is fading, having people speak for her is something Mum can't stand. Debs and I know we have to give her time to organise her thoughts and make words from them but most people don't.

'Yeah,' she says eventually.

I press the switch and the golden chandelier lights up, casting shards of warm light over us.

I hate the dining room. It's the only room downstairs that her bed can fit in and gives her enough privacy, but I wish she could be in another, cheerier room. When used in the way Mum intended, the dining room was elegant, with midnight-blue walls, a mahogany wooden floor and gold fixtures. When people came round and she lit the candles on the golden candelabra, it was a little bit magical. Now it's depressing.

'It's been snowing out. Didn't amount to much more than a spattering really, but the girls next door were still out making snowballs. Well, until the big one started screaming, and it turned out that the little one had thrown a handful of gravel in her face. Eloise dragged them inside before the big one had a chance to get her own back,' I prattle on, hoping the thought of snow will cheer her, as I move her from her bed into her chair. Mum was always a child herself when it came to snow. When I was little, I'd be pulled out into the back garden at the first flurry. We'd do our best to have snowball fights with a thin spattering of snow, and, when there was enough, we'd build snow creatures. Never men. Snow teddy bears, snow dogs, snow aliens.

I grab my childhood flowery blanket from the bed and lay it over her legs. Mum is so thin these days her being cold is a constant worry. She's gone from a snug-skirt, loose-cardigan, scarf-wearing size sixteen to a tracksuit-clad size eight.

When the weight first started to come off her, she'd joke about it, saying she could now eat a packet of Jaffa Cakes a day and still lose the pounds that years of Slimming World hadn't been able to budge. Her silver lining, she called it.

Mum would never want to look the way she does tonight, though: elbows protruding out of her wasted arms, the faded skin on her face covering her skull like gauze. She hates the way her head constantly bobs because of the involuntary movement of her muscles. Chorea, as it's officially called.

I kiss the top of her head and reach for her brush.

'I thought I'd make us some soup, then we could have a movie night, if you like. Maybe *Titanic*?'

I tidy up her thin auburn hair, hair that not long ago was as thick and unruly as mine, and moisturise her face as I wait for her answer. No matter what time she wakes, I've learnt she still likes to follow the same morning routine she's always had.

'It sinks, you know,' she whispers.

'Bloody hell, Mum, you've gone and ruined it now,' I say, bursting into laughter.

I pull in a chair from the kitchen. We have our tea and watch *Titanic*. Once it finishes – and I've recovered again from the ending – I check the time. It's almost ten, but Mum's nowhere near sleepy. I remember that Leo and Kate made another film together, and manage to find it on Netflix. After it ends, I declare that whilst *Revolutionary Road* isn't a patch on *Titanic*, the chemistry is still there, and it's a pretty decent film. Mum agrees.

She's finally getting tired, so I move her back to the bed, cradling her as gently as I can, trying not to think about how light she is now, and I move to her chair to doze until she needs me again.

Unbidden images of Alec leap out of nowhere as I curl up. I've tried to shake him off all day, but he's still here, turning up uninvited. I wonder what he'll be doing now, who he'll be with.

The bar will probably be winding down, and he'll be chatting to his last customers. If he's been unlucky, a bladdered group or two may have strayed from the busier streets of the trendy Northern Quarter and wound up in The Wishing Well. He'll put on his most charming act to get them out and hope it's enough. If he's having no luck, he'll have to resort to calling in the security guards from Drenched, the tiny cocktail bar on the corner of the opposite street.

He must be as tired as I am after last night, desperate to lock up and go home to his lumpy mattress and blackout blinds.

Unless he's with someone.

He could be at the bar right now, sharing a drink with another woman he's made feel special by letting them stay on when everyone else has had to go. He's probably sharing the same hilarious stories he told me last night. They'll be laughing together until there's that same shifting moment when suddenly he stops and everything goes a little fuzzy. He'll lean into that moment and the woman will find herself leaning in too, wanting nothing more than to meet his lips with hers.

Let them get on with it, I think, sick of how pathetic I'm being.

Whether he's on his own feeling wounded by how rubbish I was this morning or working his way through a different woman each night, it makes no difference. Alec isn't part of my life. Mum is.

I look over to her and smile. What I said to Debs earlier turned out to be true.

Today's been fine, nice even.

We're making this work. We don't need anyone else. We're fine as we are.

Chapter Four

Mum's shouting slaps me awake.

The lamp next to her bed is always left on in case she needs anything during the night. Now it's shining over her distress, making it painfully clear to see. She's thrashing on the bed, her tear-covered face contorted in anger. I rush to her side, grabbing both her shoulders to still her before she hurts herself.

'What is it? What do you need?'

I know she won't answer. This worked up, it will be impossible for her to find her words. Instead of waiting, I grab the laminated sheet off the bedside table and thrust it in front of her.

'What is it, Mum? Point to what you need.'

I take her hand in mine and direct it to the sheet I made up for her a few months ago. It's covered with pictures of the things she's most likely to want, so whenever she gets frustrated or angry like this, she has a way of showing her carers or me what the problem is.

She's so upset that she won't look at it at first and bats it away. After a few times of picking it up, placing it in front of her and directing her hand to it, she begins to look. Eventually, she spots the picture she wants to show me and is able to jab at it a few times with her finger.

The remote control. Mum likes to have it next to her bed so she can turn the TV on herself whenever she wants.

I search for it on the table, under the bed, between her sheets, before spotting it on the TV stand. Shit. I must have put it there last night after we finished watching our films.

'I'm so sorry. I'm so sorry,' I tell her after placing it in her hand. But she has no need for it now; she's in no state to focus on anything other than the mistake I made. She's sobbing because of it. Huge waves of grief for the remote control, and for the lack of control she will have felt when it wasn't where it should be, toss her body around the bed. All I can do is lie next to her and hold her in my arms until she wears herself out and falls asleep.

Once she's still and snoring lightly, I unwrap myself from round her. The upset has made candyfloss of her hair; thin, tangled tufts sit in a wispy dome on the top of her head. After doing my best to smooth it down with my palms, I take the chance to get her tablets and some water from the kitchen, so I'm ready to give them to her as soon as she can take them.

The rest of the house is blissfully dark, and I leave it that way as I pad from the dining room to the sink. I fill Mum's plastic cup and let the tap keep running so it flows over my hands, the icy nip of the water a welcome distraction.

Once I get back to the dining room and place the anti-psychotic and muscle-relaxant pills next to her bed in readiness, there are no distractions. Just Mum and the crushing reality of what the rest of her life is going to be like.

I lean against the doorframe, watching her. She always looks stronger when she sleeps; the chorea makes her blurry when she's awake, whereas sleep solidifies her, brings her back together.

I hope she sleeps for hours, dreaming of a life that's not this one for as long as she can.

As often happens in these moments of stillness, my mind flicks back to the day Huntington's disease officially entered our lives.

Mum had been going to the neurology department for tests, having been referred by our GP after a series of falls. Without a full family history – Mum's parents died in a crash when I was a toddler, and she never knew her grandparents; her mum and dad had fallen in love young and married without their families' approval – the neurologists could only examine her symptoms. Symptoms, we realised when the doctors probed into her life, had been present for years, without us ever thinking about them as symptoms of anything. Irritability, clumsiness, a struggle to stay organised. Apart, they were easy to ignore. Taken together, they began to fit into a horrible jigsaw, revealing a picture we never wanted to see.

It took a few appointments for their suspicions to develop and a simple blood test to confirm it. The morning we came to get the results, we were shown into a small, vanilla-scented-candle office with magnolia walls and cheap, self-assembled furniture to be greeted by a senior neurologist we hadn't met before. Dr Hoddert's concern was even stronger than the cloying smell of that candle, and I can't imagine she would have been expecting our calm reaction at all when she said the words:

'You've tested positive for Huntington's disease, Mrs Hyland, a neurodegenerative disorder.'

I wanted to launch a thousand questions at Dr Hoddert. What did that mean? What was going to happen to Mum? Was it fatal? But as soon as the first words came out, Mum squeezed my thigh, like she always did when she judged it best for me to keep my mouth closed. Trying to argue with a teacher after a bad parents' evening report: squeeze of the thigh. Starting to flirt with the waiter in Turkey, who had been coming on to me all week despite his wedding ring: squeeze of the thigh. I sank back down into silence to let Mum take charge and do the talking. Only she didn't. She nodded once at Dr Hoddert, before smiling and thanking her for getting to the bottom of it. A flicker of confusion pinched the skin in between Dr Hoddert's eyebrows before she also smiled and, following Mum's cue, turned back to the comfort of her computer to make a follow-up appointment for when we'd digested the diagnosis.

Mum's diagnosis. There it was, finally. A puzzle solved, the bad guy revealed. We could move forward now. Into what, we had no clue, but the weight of uncertainty falling from us made us freer than we'd been for months.

We didn't know anything about it. When the tests began, and it became clear there was something potentially seriously amiss, I'd made a promise to Mum to stay off Google, to resist the temptation to check her symptoms. The doctors would tell us what we needed to know, she'd said, and I was to put my trust in them, not the Internet.

My plan was to make the promise to her face before breaking it behind her back. Of course I was going to look. To think of the hours I'd spent searching the Internet for answers to ridiculous questions like best hangover cure and best hairstyles for unruly hair; now there was something I desperately needed to know, there was no way I was going to stay off.

Mum knew exactly what I'd be thinking. It's why she sat me down and told me how important it was to her that I didn't make things worse for her by coming up with my own theories, how she couldn't stand the idea of me getting upset about what we didn't know for sure and how much she needed me to stay positive because she was more frightened than she'd ever been. I promised I would do whatever she wanted and stuck to it.

So when I heard neurological disorder, I hadn't a clue what it meant. I thought it didn't sound too bad. Disorder wasn't that frightening a word. Hey, at least it wasn't cancer. That was where my fear belonged. I knew cancer, had seen it in action, whereas Huntington's was a stranger. A stranger I presumed I'd much rather get to know.

It was only at the follow-up appointment that we really began to understand what Mum was facing. I left that appointment with my arms around Mum, my handbag crammed with the leaflets Dr Hoddert had given us about the support we'd inevitably come to need. Support we needed much sooner than we'd anticipated, as the disease began to develop and all of the symptoms we never really believed would show in Mum invaded her body one by one, leaving her as she is now.

I creep forward to her hospital bed with its sides up to place a kiss on her head before returning to the chair, folding myself up like a fossil to counteract the cold that's spreading through the house now the heating's off for the night and fishing out my phone from my pocket. Knowing exactly what I'm looking for, I open the browser and type in 'Machu Picchu Travel Blogs'.

When Mum is awake, I'm all hers, but in the empty hours when she sleeps, it's hard not to think about what comes after this, about what the rest of my life is going to be like once she's gone. I've started making a list of what I want to do, and top of that list is to travel to South America.

Most of the links when they load up are coloured purple instead of blue; I've read them all before. Although I shouldn't, I click onto my favourite blog, called 'Finding Love in Peru'. It's written by a couple, Andy and Dess, who fell in love when they met travelling and charts not only their travels but their growing relationship as they travel from one jaw-dropping site to another. It was written four years ago, and they never carried it on when they got back to England. They really should have done. I imagine I'm not their only reader left feeling short-changed by the abrupt ending. Did their love perish after Peru? Or are they still together, their relationship fuelled by the memories of their shared experiences? I did try to get some answers by finding them on Facebook, but neither of them accepted my friend request.

I reread the bit about them sharing their first kiss at dawn with Machu Picchu spread out below them and the sun rising on the tall mountain of Huayna Picchu before hitting the home button to make Andy, Dess and South America disappear from my screen. I throw the phone to the floor and close my eyes, cursing myself for doing it again.

If I were really preparing for my own trip, I'd be researching the best hiking boots to buy or reading up on the best tour operators in Peru, not losing myself in the story of two people I've never met, who really don't include anywhere near enough detail on the practicalities of hiking through the Andes.

And if I were really preparing for my own trip, I wouldn't be wasting my time finding out what it's like to travel as a couple, because when I make my trip, I'll be making it alone.

Unlike Andy and Dess and their confident belief that life is always going to be light and fun and easy, I know much more. I've seen suffering first-hand and it's taught me a good lesson: you've got to prevent exposure to it where you can. Alongside this list of things I want to do with my life there are my rules. And the most important one of all is not to fall in love.

Chapter Five

Sunday mornings in the Hyland house ran to the same routine for nearly twenty-four years. Lie-in, fried breakfast, fresh air, roast. Occasionally, a guest would come over for the afternoon – one of Mum's friends or a boy I liked enough to bring home – but mainly it was the two of us.

These were our favourite days. When I was a child, Sunday was our one day of calm in a week of precision planning to allow Mum to work enough hours at the optician's and to make sure I was always where I should be and suitably looked after until she could get back to me. When I was an adult, that sense of calm never left. Sundays were a day to pause and enjoy each other before the bustle of a new week. I used to be the one to wake first. I'd hover over Mum, demanding she get up and make my breakfast, listening to her groaning under the duvet before she emerged, always with a smile and a kiss for me. From my teenage years onwards, the role reversed, and Mum would drag me out of bed with the smell of bacon wafting under my closed door.

This Sunday morning, it's the pain of being curled up for too long that makes me stir. I pull myself out of the chair and get to work stretching the aches away, otherwise they'll stay with me all day. The dining room is still in the half-darkness of early morning, and Mum is sleeping. It takes a strong sun to get past the navy velvet curtains, and this paltry morning light won't push its way in for a few hours yet.

I retrieve my phone from the floor and leave Mum to it. Eight-thirty-two, my display tells me, an ungodly hour for a Sunday. But I'm not the only one awake. My phone vibrates with a new message:

Hey, Jess. Hope you don't mind, but Olivia was in here last night and gave me your number. Meeting some friends this afternoon near you in The Rose. Was wondering if you fancied joining us. 1 p.m.? Let me know, Alec xx

I had been planning on going to bed for a few hours, but I hover on the bottom step of the stairs, far more awake than a fitful few hours of sleep should have left me. I go to the kitchen instead, automatically pulling the Cath Kidston mug Mum got me off the draining board and switching the kettle on.

My first instinct is an old one: delight. A boy I like has texted me. He wants to see me. I'll get to be close to him again.

But I have to fight those instincts. I take a few measured breaths and change tack to anger.

What is Alec thinking? Yesterday I couldn't have been clearer in saying that I wasn't interested. So what is he doing texting me at eight-thirty in the morning to ask me out on a date?

And then there's Olivia. If it wasn't so early, I'd be straight on the phone demanding to know exactly what made her think she had the right to give my number out.

Unless Alec told her about our night together.

Great.

I've started to compose my sweary reply to Alec when the kettle clicks off. I put the phone down, choosing caffeine over him for now.

I sit at the small glass table in the bay window. It's been snowing again overnight, transforming the familiar lines and angles of the garden into soft mounds and curves. The branches on trees buckle under the fluffy weight, and the dark, sagging sky threatens to drop even more.

It's pleasant inside the cocoon of the kitchen. I slowly sip my coffee, staring at the Christmas-card-worthy view and imagining seeing that lustful expression in Alec's eyes again as he cups my face with his hands.

Unable to ignore the tug of guilt for spending so long doing nothing when I'm meant to be caring for Mum, once my cup is empty, I go back to the dining room to check on her. From the other side of the door, I hear the familiar thrum of the TV.

'Good morning, Mum. Cup of tea?'

She doesn't look at me and turns the volume up. She's not forgotten last night, then. I know enough of Mum's moods to know if a day starts like this, chances are it will end in the same way. Mum's not lost any of her stubbornness and can wear a bad mood like a fur coat, wrapping it around herself, stroking it repeatedly to remember how it feels.

Without trying to bring her round, I give her the medicine and make the tea, embarrassed to have to present it to her in a toddler's cup with a spout on top to control the flow. Mum takes it and continues to ignore me, flicking from channel to channel, never landing on anything for more than a minute.

The best thing to do is to leave her to it for a little while. I keep the door open to the dining room and put on the TV in the lounge, channel hopping distractedly like she is before eventually dozing off.

I'm jolted awake by the doorbell. Looking down at my worn cat pyjamas with a bleach mark across the top, my first instinct is to ignore it to avoid anyone having to see me in such a state. Only I can't do that; it might be a delivery we need or even Debs calling in to check up on us. I run my fingers through my hair a few times and try to pat it down before answering the door.

'Hello, darling. Did you forget?' asks Auntie Sarah, running her bright, dark-circle-free eyes over me. She's perfectly presented, as always, in a tomato-red jacket so bright against the dull day, I can't look directly at it.

'No, not at all. We're running a bit late this morning. Come in, come in.'

The second Sunday of the month. Auntie Sarah's visiting day. I normally spend the days before looking forward to it, so I'm surprised it's arrived this month without my having thought about it once.

Auntie Sarah isn't my real aunt. She is, or was, Mum's best friend. The two of them worked for decades together as partners at their optician's practice in Cheshire. Auntie Sarah was a regular fixture in our lives and in this house. Most Fridays she would come back after work with Mum, and the two of them would sit round the island in the kitchen with a bottle of wine, shrugging off the week as they drank and ate giant packets of crisps, which Mum poured into a gold serving bowl to make their bingeing seem classier. At some point, one of them would always decide it was time for music, and they would have tipsy kitchen discos. More often than not, they would rope me into them. We would throw ourselves round until the early hours when Mum would suddenly remember – or be reminded by a thud on the wall – that we were not in a nightclub but a semi-detached house with children on the other side.

Even though Auntie Sarah is married with a son eleven years younger than me, she always made us feel like we were her family too. Occasionally, Mum and I would go to family events at her house, and once a year we'd sit through Freddie's birthday parties at the cricket club, but the best times were always at our house. Just the three of us.

But then Mum got sick, and Sarah couldn't cope.

She began to remove herself. Gradually, of course. Disappearing all at once would look far too rude. That's what she's done, though, over the last few years. As Mum got worse, Sarah got busier. Freddie, now a teenager, needed her more than he ever did as a child. The Fridays stopped, the invitations dried up, and all we're left with is a monthly visit. The best she can do.

'Are you sure it's a good time?' asks Sarah, hovering in the doorway. 'If it's not, I can always—'

'No, it's fine. You go in and see Mum, and I'll run up and get dressed, if that's all right.'

'Oh. Right, OK.'

I watch Sarah shuffle towards the dining room as though an invisible hand were pulling at her, trying to get her back out the house.

'Susan, you're looking wonderful,' she says, her voice as bright as her jacket.

Mum turns the volume up even higher on the TV.

I'm grateful Sarah's here. Now she's keeping Mum's bad mood company, it gives me extra time to take a long shower and properly dry my hair, even put on some make-up. Eventually, I'll have to go down there and join them, but I certainly won't be hurrying.

Once I'm dressed in a pair of grey jeans and black jumper, with co-ordinating grey eyeshadow and black, flicked-out eyeliner that's taken four attempts to get right, I return downstairs to check how the visit is going. I've not heard

Mum speak once since Sarah arrived. I suppose I should make the effort to catch up with her. I should ask the questions Mum would have asked her best friend after not seeing her for a month. The only problem is the answers. How can hearing about work or Sarah's upcoming holidays or the latest adventures her young, free son is enjoying help Mum? How can it help either of us?

I don't find Sarah in the dining room. When I peer in, there's only Mum, sleeping again, most likely faking it to escape Sarah's high spirits.

Sarah's pacing the kitchen floor. Her mouth is pursed and in constant motion. It's a new habit of hers, and I wonder if it's a nervous tic she has all the time now or if it's reserved only for when she's here.

'Everything all right?'

'Oh, I'm fine. It's just, it's just she seems much worse today. To think of the live wire she was. Seeing her like this, it's awful,' she says. Her eyes are covered with a thick film of tears.

'She has her good days,' I say. 'Today's not one of them.'

'Have you read the article I sent you yet? You know you really can get the most amazing results by trying some of these diets. It's got to be worth a go, hasn't it?'

'I'm not sure how much kale I'm going to be able to get Mum to eat, to be honest.'

'Well, we've got to try, Jessica. Anything's worth a shot, isn't it?'

We've got to try. I feel anger push up my throat like vomit and am unable to stop it coming out my mouth.

'Believe me, I'm trying every day to keep Mum from suffering, giving her pills and making sure she eats enough, but, hey, if you think you can show up once a month and make her better, be my guest.'

Instead of looking at her, I stare at the oversized clock on the wall. It's almost half twelve.

'I'm sorry,' I say, ashamed to have got so angry and frightened at how little control I had over the eruption. 'Do you know what, Sarah? I've completely forgotten I'm meant to be going out this afternoon for a few hours. I only arranged it because you were coming, and I knew you wouldn't mind giving me a break. I've got to go.'

Before there's a chance for her to voice any objections, I grab my jacket, phone and bag, pull on some boots and leave.

Outside, the air is so bitter it makes ice of my breath, but I hardly feel it. The excitement – and guilt – of an afternoon off is enough to heat me from the inside. I send Alec a message to tell him I'll be right there, turn left out of the house and start walking towards The Rose.

When my phone pings, I expect it will be Alec, but it's not, it's Sarah. I slow as I read her message, the cold air taking its chance to close in.

I'm sorry, Jess. You are doing a fantastic job, and I'm mortified I made it sound like I thought differently. I'll try to help more. It's just my heart breaks whenever I see your mum. And it pains me even more knowing this is going to happen to you too.

Chapter Six

Three years earlier

'Are you sure you want to know?' Kal, my genetic counsellor asked me for the final time.

'Quite sure.'

'OK. Here are your results. I'm going to hand them to you, but it is entirely up to you to decide what to do with them. If you change your mind, you can leave the envelope as it is. It's your choice.'

It had taken three mandatory counselling sessions and a blood test to get the results now lying in wait in the brown envelope in his hands, and still he was giving me a chance to turn back.

Turns out Mum being diagnosed with a fatal neurological condition wasn't enough for us to deal with. After Dr Hoddert told Mum about her own diagnosis, she went on to deliver the news that Huntington's disease is hereditary, and any child of a person who has Huntington's has a 50 per cent chance of inheriting it. Fifty-fifty. The toss of a coin.

Dr Hoddert gave us another leaflet at Mum's follow-up appointment, but Mum refused to take that one with us. It was the leaflet that explained about the genetic blood test the children of those with Huntington's disease could take to find out if they too possessed the faulty Huntington gene that would cause a breakdown in the nerve cells leading to catastrophe and death.

Mum was sure a positive result would ruin my life. She was every bit as sure of it as I was sure I had to know. We took our opinions on the matter and glued them to ourselves. My choice to find out if I had a future with Huntington's was the cause of some terrible arguments at a time when we should have been pulling together. But I had to know. The other option, of not knowing, of spending my life wondering if it was inside me too, lurking in the dark recesses of my brain, waiting to strike, wasn't even a consideration.

I tried to cajole her to my way of thinking by reminding her I'd always hated surprises. Like the time when I was ten, and the magic of Santa had been replaced with the magic of Mum going out and buying me a stack of whatever I wanted, and I snuck into her room whilst she was downstairs, not to look for the presents but to open her wallet and trawl through her receipts, so I knew exactly what to expect on Christmas morning. It didn't matter. Mum would never make her peace with my decision, and it would be a wedge between us, no matter what the result.

But Mum having to grapple with her new future, as well as contemplating her daughter's future, was too heavy a load. She would veer off into dark, silent moods that would take her away from me for days. To help ease her burden, I made an agreement with Mum: I would take a year to think about it.

I thought of nothing else but Huntington's that horrible year and, aside from Mum's deteriorating health, nothing changed. Twelve months after Mum's results, I went to meet Kal for the first time.

Mum hid my front-door keys that morning and refused to reveal where they were, such was her desire to keep my future from me. I had to leave by the French window at the back of the house. No matter what she did to stop me, no matter the life-changing consequences of a positive result that I was obliged to consider over three sessions with Kal, I didn't budge an inch; I had to know. Now, three months after meeting him for the first time, there was a result. All I had to do was read it.

'Jess?'

'Yes,' I told Kal. 'Yes, I'm ready.'

He handed me the envelope, and I snatched it from him so he wouldn't notice my shaking hands. I had to admit I wasn't quite as ready at this critical juncture in my life as I'd professed to be. Oh, I was going to open the envelope, there was never any doubt, but I needed a little longer to steady myself before my future was laid out.

Kal shuffled forward in his chair and crossed his legs. His trainers were scuffed and his socks were odd. I wondered how much Kal was being paid to guide people like me through such an ordeal. Not enough for matching socks and a decent pair of trainers.

'Remember, whatever the result, there is support available. We can meet again if you'd like, or there are support groups I could put you in touch with. Whatever the result, you're going to find yourself experiencing all sorts of feelings once you open that envelope, and it's important to remember that everything you feel is perfectly valid. There's no wrong or right way to handle this. You have the envelope now. You take your time opening it.'

I tore it open and roughly pulled out the paper from the gouge in the envelope I'd created, the need to know suddenly overpowering anything else. For a second, the words on the page wouldn't form, there were too many of them crowded on the page in one meaningless pile I couldn't decipher. But then I saw it: positive.

'Thank you,' I told Kal, pushing the paper off my knee and onto the floor. 'I'd like to go now, if that's OK.'

'Jess. I really think—'

I didn't stay to hear more. I left the results in his tiny office and walked out of the clinic, past the hospital, past the university and all the way home. I didn't know how I felt, if I felt anything at all, only that I needed to tell Mum.

But when I got home, Mum was crying. She had burnt herself with the iron. The week before she'd switched on my curling tongs and left herself with a nasty trail of blisters on her arm. The week before that it was a cup of tea over her hands. Clumsiness was part of Huntington's, we'd been told. I'd seen plenty of clumsiness over the years, but this, I knew, was something else. Mum was hurting herself on purpose.

It was her way of shutting off the horrors of her future running constantly through her mind, she admitted when I pressed her for an explanation. She needed a break from them. The courage required to hurt herself, the act itself and the pain after weren't about Huntington's. Those things belonged to the present and gave her something else to focus on for a while. She told me this in her normal voice, like it was the most rational course for her to follow, given the circumstances.

'Well, then, did you get the results?' she asked once I'd bandaged her arm, and the painkillers had set in.

I almost lied. It would have been so easy to tell her I'd chickened out and never got them. That would have been that. I could have made her happy with that lie. She could have carried on without worrying about the pain I would feel seeing her as she got worse and worse, knowing the same was coming my way. But I had to tell her. We'd always been truthful; it was the only way our relationship worked. When there are only two of you in a family, honesty matters.

'Yes, I did. I'm sorry, Mum. It was positive.'

'I'm so sorry, my love. So sorry.' She wrapped me in her arms, ignoring the pain of her burn to hold me tight, and I let her stroke my hair whilst we both wept. She didn't say anything else, and I was grateful. There was nothing else to say.

After tea, I helped her upstairs to bed. I took a bottle of vodka out of the freezer once she was asleep and went out into the garden. Sitting on a bench at the edge of the rockery that had always been well tended but was now beginning to be blurred at the edges by creeping moss, I drank and I cried and I mourned. The next morning I switched all of that off. Both our futures were to be twisted and torn at by Huntington's, but Mum's future was more pressing than mine, and it was the only one I was going to let us focus on.

Chapter Seven

The Rose is packed. On Sundays it does these roast dinners served up on a wooden board with a little copper saucepan of gravy on the side, and it has recently been awarded the *Manchester Evening News*'s coveted top spot for the best roast in Manchester.

Every other day of the week, its slightly scruffy interior, plasma screens and cheap ale entice mainly students, but on Sunday it becomes filled with well-dressed groups of friends sharing bottles of wine and trying to justify the cracked tiles in the toilets as a shabby in-joke. To get a table at 1 p.m., Alec must have booked weeks ago; there's no way he could have arranged it today because it happens to be in Didsbury village, round the corner from where I live.

I imagine I'll be early and plan to have a quick drink at the bar before Alec arrives. But as soon as the door closes behind me, I spot him sitting alone at a table next to the fireplace. His back is unnaturally straight and his head swivels from side to side every few seconds. He looks like a well-dressed meerkat.

If it weren't for the large party that's followed me in, I'd be backing out the door right now. Only they make such a drama of taking off their coats and moaning about the weather, that I know Alec's head is going to flick in their direction any second, and there's no way I can get out without him seeing me.

The last time I met a man in a pub, it was my former boyfriend, Liam, over four years ago. He sat at a table like the one Alec is sitting at, by a similar fireplace. Mum had just been diagnosed and I came to meet him after telling him the news with the expectation of a stodgy meal and some sympathy. Instead, I was told I was piling too much on him, that he wasn't looking for something so heavy, and I was dumped.

I take another look at Alec. He's bobbing slightly in his seat because of the way he's tapping his foot against the chair leg. He's nervous. Liam was never nervous with me. Not once. It's sweet, really. Even from the little I know of him, I'm sure Alec would never lure a girl to a pub with the promise of steak pie and chips only to break up with her.

Not that it matters if he would, I remind myself. He won't be getting the chance with me.

When Alec spots me, I'm weaving through tables to get to him. A huge grin spreads over his face.

'Hi. You're early,' he says, half rising from his chair to greet me before sitting back down when I pull out my own chair and sit in it before he can kiss my cheek or hug me or whatever kind of physical contact he'd been considering.

'And you're alone,' I say, taking in a faint whiff of aftershave and wishing, despite myself, that I had taken the chance to sit closer to him.

'Yeah, you missed them, I'm afraid. There was a bit of an emergency, and they had to take off.'

'Missed them, eh? Even though I'm twenty minutes early?'

He catches the smirk I can't hide quickly enough and laughs. 'OK, on first appearances I can see that it might look like I've made up some mates to lure you into coming

42

out with me, but if you look at the evidence, you'll realise that's not the case.'

After a huge swig of a disgusting-looking cloudy ale, he points to the mess on the table. 'See, exhibit A: a pile of screwed-up napkins on top of a still-wet table. And exhibit B: a high chair. Exhibit C: a bib hastily left behind in the chaos.'

'So your friend was a messy child?'

'Well, kind of. His parents are old friends from Leeds, who'd driven over for the day. It'd been planned for ages, and they were very much looking forward to meeting you. But then Sam poured a glass of blackcurrant juice down himself and it happened to be Tom's turn to pack the baby bag. Poor Tom forgot pretty much everything you'd need in a juice-related emergency. No spare clothes, no wipes, but five books and about a dozen boxes of raisins. If you'd arrived ten minutes earlier, you'd have seen Hannah marching out a child wearing only a nappy and a coat, and Tom slowly following in her wake, knowing the row he's going to get when they are back in the car.'

'Hmmm.'

'Jessica, are you implying I'm making this up? How insulting. If you need them, there are plenty of witnesses. Would you like me to disturb the lovely couple to your left to ask them to concur with my version of events?'

I narrow my eyes and pretend to examine his face. 'That won't be necessary. I believe you. Although, it's a shame; without your friends, it's the two of us again.'

He tips more ale into his mouth, and when he lands the glass back on the table, it's almost empty.

'It is a real shame. Well, we'll have to make do. Shall we order?' he asks before picking up a paper menu with only four items on it and studying it intently.

I can feel my carefree afternoon off slipping out of my hands like melting snow. Much as I want to stay here in the warm bustle, eating and drinking and laughing, I'm not sure I can. It may not have been his intention, but this has become a date for him. A date with potential.

'Actually, I think I should go too.'

'Don't, please,' he says, putting the menu down, his wide eyes meeting mine. 'This really wasn't deliberate. I promise this isn't all a ploy to get a repeat of Friday night. I remember what you said about it not happening again. Today was meant to be mates hanging out. I thought you'd like Tom and Hannah. They're always nagging me about meeting the new people in my life and making sure I'm OK, so you would have been doing me a favour by getting them off my back, that's all. You'll at least stay for a drink, won't you?'

'OK. I'll get it, though. You want the same again?'

'No. Tom got this for me, and it's bloody awful. Could you get me the sweetest, most sugar-filled cider you can see to make up for it, please?'

'Sounds good. I think I'll have the same.'

I sneak glances of him over my shoulder as I stand queuing at the bar: he's leaning back into his chair now, staring into the fire. On his thumb, he's wearing a silver ring a little too large for him, and he spins it round and round. He's shortened his beard since yesterday morning, making it easier to spot the muscles twitching around his mouth that he's working hard to control.

For all he said about this being casual, he's on edge.

'Right,' I say, dumping the brimming glasses on the table before I spill them. 'You need to tell me more about Tom and Hannah, so I'll believe they're real. Let's start with you explaining what you meant when you said they wanted to make sure you're OK?'

He watches me intently as I sit back down and pull my glass towards me. His hands are on the table. He turns his attention from me to them. He must decide they're in the wrong place, as he quickly puts them onto his lap, interlocking them over a jiggling knee.

'OK, I can do that. I meant they worry about me much more than they need to, especially Tom. We've been mates since we were five. He hates not being able to check up on me all the time now we're in different cities.'

'How come you moved away from them?'

He laughs. 'This is going to be an interrogation, isn't it?'

'It is. Now answer, please.'

'Yes, m'am.' He takes a sip of his strawberry-lime cider and winces. 'If you want the short story, it's that I broke up with my girlfriend, who happened to be friends with all my friends, and decided to make a clean break so I could properly move on.'

'Sorry, I'm actually looking for the long-drawn-out, no-holds-barred story,' I say, giving him my sweetest smile.

He angles his head, and I try to ignore how sparkly his eyes look when they're filled with intrigue. 'It's funny, I'm sure you said you weren't interested in me.'

I shouldn't be. The more I find out about Alec, the more I know I'm going to like him. And I like him too much already. It's just that keeping Alec talking about himself is the only way to avoid talking about me.

'OK, if you must know, I made the mistake of moving in with my girlfriend when things were pretty shaky with us. A few weeks after setting up home together, she decided to break up with me.'

'Why did she do that?' I ask, surprised. I can't imagine why anyone would want to break up with Alec.

'You really want to know?'

'I do.'

'You'll be disappointed to hear it's nothing sensational. No cheating, no huge rows, no clothes thrown out of a window. It was all very decent and polite.'

'Shame.'

'I know. We were one of those couples who stayed together longer than we should have. We broke up plenty of times but always remained friends and would see each other constantly. Eventually, we'd end up back with each other, vowing to make a fresh go of things. But the fact that we had nothing in common never disappeared. Nor did the lack of passion.'

'So this time it's for good, then?'

A hand pops back up and reaches across the table to cover mine. 'Don't worry. I'll never go back,' he says in a very serious voice before smiling.

I'm meant to laugh, but it's not a joke. Alec's been itching to touch me ever since I arrived, and I've given him the chance. His palm presses firmly against my skin, warm and heavy. I don't dare look at his face. Instead, I look at our bare hands and try to ignore my whirling stomach.

'So that's why you moved to Manchester?'

He removes his hand and tucks it back out of sight where it belongs.

'Yeah. It was such a relief when we broke up that last time, I had to make sure it was final. If we'd have kept seeing each other and hearing about each other it would have made it really tough to meet someone new. I needed to make something change – for the both of us.'

'That was a brave move.'

'Not really. I went back all those times before because it was comfortable. If I was brave, I wouldn't have done that, I wouldn't have wasted so much time on something

I always knew wasn't right for me. I'd have started looking for someone else.'

'Is that what you're doing now, then? Looking for the right girl?'

'Right now, I'm pretty much trying to get through each day without giving up and going back to Leeds, but, yeah, amongst everything else, I guess I am looking for someone.'

'And what would this someone be like?'

'Let me think. Red hair, cute smile, a bit short.'

'Very funny,' I say, hoping my cheeks aren't as red as the hair he likes. 'Come on, I'm serious. Maybe I can help.'

'I don't know. I can't say what she'll be like, only that she'll be someone I can really love, not half love like I did with my ex. Someone I can give everything to, be a little crazy about, even be heartbroken by, you know?'

He's good enough not to look at me when he says it, so I don't need to worry about going any more red under his gaze. I don't think any woman could have Alec staring into their eyes whilst saying that and not blush.

'Yeah, I do,' I lie. 'I get why you had to move away.'

'I'm glad. No one else does. My parents thought I was ridiculous to give up a solid job and weekly meal out with them at their local Italian in favour of working in a bar. They're still mad about it. Whenever I ring them up, we speak very formally and they never ask me about my new life. We mainly talk about the football and how my grandparents are doing. Really, it's only Tom who gets why I did it.'

'What about Hannah?'

'She doesn't like it. Our group is all out of kilter now I'm not in it. Apparently, Ellie's always arranging to go out with the girls, and the lads have started up a Friday-night drinking session. If it weren't for Tom telling her not to, she'd be trying to persuade me to go back so it could be like it always was.'

'Yeah, people can be arseholes when things stop going their way.'

I think back to the friends I used to see every weekend without fail. Girls I went to primary school with, who one by one dropped away once Mum became sick and my life became more than going out with them on the pull on Friday night and meeting in Nando's for lunch the following day to share hangovers or intimate details about the night before.

'Bit strong. Hannah's not an arsehole. I think it's human nature to want what's best for yourself, and me leaving hasn't been the best thing for her.'

'Sorry. You're right. I don't know her. I shouldn't have said that.'

'Don't worry. God, that looks good,' he says, his eyes following a roast being served to the table next to us. 'Are you sure I can't tempt you to stay for food?'

'It does look amazing. OK, but only if I get to ask you more questions and we move from cider to wine.'

It's a mistake, I know, but today's been like seeing an old photograph of my life. I can't remember the last time I did anything as nice as this. I'd completely forgotten about the pleasure of wiling away an afternoon with good company and good food. I want to linger in the past for a bit longer before I have to go back.

'Deal,' Alec says. He holds out his hand for me to take and I shake it.

'So, now you know all about me, what about you? Tell me one of your stories,' he says once he's been up to the bar to order two roasts and a bottle of Merlot.

'My stories?'

'Yeah, tell me something about you I don't know. It can be anything you like, something small or something, I don't know, life-changing and inspirational like mine.'

It had been nice until now. Suddenly we're moving towards dangerous territory. I hesitate, frantically searching around my brain for something that isn't tinged with Huntington's, something that's frivolous or funny, but there's nothing. There's only one image in there, and it plays on repeat, refusing to stop: Mum in her bed and Sarah standing over her in her red jacket.

'Nope. Sorry, we're sticking with you.'

'Me again? Go on, then.'

I think of my next question, and plump for the one I most want to know the answer to. 'Do you ever get lonely?'

'All the time. Until I moved here, I was surrounded by people. Every day was filled with friends or family. Now, there's work and that's pretty much it. I miss everyone like crazy.'

'You don't know anyone here, then?'

'Now I do. You,' he says smiling.

'True. But me aside?'

'No one.'

'That's really brave of you,' I tell him again. 'To have given up so much to find happiness.'

He laughs. 'You're making me sound much better than I am. I like it.'

'Any time.'

We move to lighter territory as we wait for our meals to arrive and devour them whilst Alec makes me rank my favourite films and TV shows of all time. I laugh at his fixation with putting things into neat lists. When the waitress takes our plates, our conversation stalls for the first time.

'I've got to get back,' I tell him.

'OK.'

He stands, putting on a quilted navy jacket and tartan scarf. Both look expensive, much more than a barman could afford, and I wonder what career he gave up to come here.

'I've not got the car, otherwise I'd have given you a lift. Do you want me to walk you home?'

'That's very chivalrous of you,' I say, patting his arm, 'but it's the middle of the day, and I live round the corner. I should be able to get back OK. But, hey, keep that stuff up. Girls go mad for that kind of crap.'

He pulls his mouth to one side and nods, remembering, I hope, the shift in our relationship from two people who shared a one-night stand to friends.

At the door, he gives me a quick hug and starts to walk towards the Metro station. I've already started walking in the opposite direction when I feel a hand on my shoulder.

'Hey, I just wanted to say that I know you only want to be friends, and that's fine. I like hanging out with you, Jess. It's weird, but when I'm with you, I feel like I've done the right thing by moving here. Sorry, that sounds far too mushy, doesn't it?'

'Horribly mushy,' I say seriously, pretending it isn't the nicest thing anyone has said to me in a long time.

'Sorry, but I mean it. I'm glad I've met you. It would be nice to think we could get together from time to time. Is that OK?'

'As friends?'

He nods. 'As friends.'

He briskly kisses my cheek – no lingering – and walks off again. As he's leaving, a surge of wind whips around my ears. I can't be sure if it wasn't just the wind, but I'm sure I hear the words, 'for now'.

Chapter Eight

Debs arrives at the house at seven, and the weekend draws to a close.

As soon as I returned to the house, I apologised to Sarah for running off and leaving her with Mum. Sarah cried a little, and we laughed at how Mum would take the piss out of her for being so teary all the time now when the two of them used to think themselves the toughest opticians in the north-west. It was nice talking to her properly for once, and, when she left, I went in to Mum to tell her that Sarah was planning on coming round in a couple of weeks to see us again. Mum didn't register the good news. I couldn't tell if she was angry at me for leaving her with Sarah or still annoyed about the remote control fiasco, but either way she was cross, and spent the rest of the day in silence, watching TV.

Once I catch up with Debs, I opt for an early night, turning in at the childlike time of eight o'clock. I fall straight asleep and don't wake until six the next morning.

I enjoy getting ready for work, taking my time, knowing I'll get in early and have a precious half-hour or so reading emails with a coffee before Jane arrives and the day properly begins. I've always been one for routine, was always the kid who felt a bit lost during the school holidays. I leave the house certain that a day doing the payroll and sorting out the Christmas bonuses with Mr Lewis is exactly what I need to reset myself after such an unusual weekend.

Mum's the same. Much as she loves me, she's more at ease in the week with the comings and goings of the carers, the scheduled hours and the security of knowing exactly what the day will look like. Debs is always the reward at the end of her day.

When I get back from the office at seven, she's sitting in her chair, with Debs painting her nails. I go in to see them and Mum manages to ask about my day. I give her a detailed account of the outrage caused by Mr Lewis's scaling back of all the directors' bonuses this year, and Mum listens with her eyes closed, her head bobbing slowly in what I take to be agreement with my point about the directors needing to do more sodding work if they want to get more money.

Debs suggests Mum settles down earlier than normal to try and get her back to sleeping regular hours, as her sleep has been so erratic of late. After staying with her to watch the soaps, I say goodnight and head upstairs, happy to leave her for the rest of the night knowing Debs will be watching over her.

She sleeps for four hours straight on Monday night, followed by another two before dawn. By the time I'm leaving for work on Tuesday morning, she's the best I've seen her in weeks, and there's not even a smudge of the weekend's upset left over in the house.

The timing of her improvement is perfect. Tuesday is the long-awaited day of the Christmas party. With Mum so content, there's a slim chance I might enjoy this year's party instead of enduring it and waiting to go home like last year. To mark the occasion, we're allowed to leave work at three to give us enough time to get ready and return into the city centre for the party to start at six. Mum's physiotherapist is finishing up helping Mum with her exercises when I get in.

My room is a slightly bigger-than-average box room at the front of the house. Then there's Mum's room, now sitting abandoned next to mine. I know she wouldn't mind, but I would never dream of setting up in there whilst she sleeps downstairs. Or ever.

Truth is, I need my room and its whisperings of a happy childhood. When I lie in bed, I stare at the ceiling and remember when I tacked an A1-sized poster of Kian from Westlife up there so he'd be the last thing I saw before I closed my eyes. I look at the orchid on my windowsill and recall a time when, in its place, I kept my troll collection, my most prized possessions for years. Now my wardrobe is perfectly organised into categories: work clothes on the left, occasion wear on the right, a shelf for T-shirts and jumpers, one that houses my jeans folded in a pile going from lightest shade to darkest, and the racks on the back of the door for scarves. It wasn't too many years ago, though, that it was chaos, and 'my look' was generally whatever I could find that was clean.

I smile to myself as I leaf through its contents now, recalling some of the mad outfits of my teenage years, often backless, strapless and covered in glitter. For tonight, I pick out two potential outfits: a shimmery-silver body-con dress I bought last year, that even then was borderline too young for me, and a black jumpsuit that's starting to become shiny with overuse.

'What do you think?' I ask Mum, holding up the two outfits by their coat hangers when the physio's gone and she's sitting propped up in bed with her iPad on her lap.

The wrinkles round her eyes deepen as she smiles; she always liked helping me get ready when I went out with the girls or on a date. We both loved nothing more than the evenings we'd go out together, when she'd be in and out of my room, borrowing my make-up or lending me a necklace she thought would look nice on me.

'I like both,' she says before changing her mind. 'No, the dress.'

I agree with her, although I'm worried about how I'll manage to pull off the rubber ring of flab around my waist in what is essentially a sparkly piece of elastic.

I quickly top up my make-up and run the tongs through my hair whilst Clara, Mum's least-favourite carer, sees to giving Mum her medicine. I hear Mum protesting and switch off the tongs. Clara's meant to stay until five, but I come back downstairs a few minutes after four and tell her she might as well get off early seeing as I'm here.

'Beautiful,' Mum says, holding out her hand for me. I sit next to her on the bed, and she strokes the tips of my hair while I pretend to moan about what a pain it is having to go back out again tonight.

Debs arrives just before I need to leave. She tries to shoo me out of the house but can't get rid of me. Mum's laughing at my attempts to cover up the bulge, first with a cardigan, then with a pair of control tights, which, for some reason, push the flab down to my thighs, both of which she's dismissed as ridiculous. Once I go, I'll be taking the laughter from the house with me, and I want her to hold on to it for a bit longer.

'Take a picture,' Mum tells Debs. I grab my phone from my bag, give it to Debs and go and stand against the wall, one leg crossed over the other, my stomach pulled in as much as I can manage.

'No, not there, go over and sit next to your mum.'
I do as I'm told.

'OK, everyone say spandex.' Debs takes a picture of me with my arms wrapped round Mum's waist, our heads pressed together, both laughing.

'Eh, you, look at the time,' Debs says. 'If you don't go now, I'm going to put on my own tight silver dress and take your bloody place.'

'OK, OK. I'm going. Have a nice night, ladies.'

'You too,' Mum and Debs say together. I leave them feeling light and giddy.

Under Jane's rigorous guidance, Maureen's undertaken the task of organising tonight, so of course it's The Wishing Well we're to meet in, not any of the other several hundred bars in Manchester. I take the Metro back into town, arriving horrendously late and finding the bar mobbed with my already half-cut associates.

From his place behind the bar, Alec spots me as soon as I walk in and waves me towards him.

Funny. I thought I'd want to avoid him tonight, to make sure I don't give him any further encouragement. Maybe I'm still in the afterglow of everything being so lovely with Mum, but I'm happy to see him. I give him a little wave back, and make my way towards him.

'There she is,' he shouts over the racket.

'Hi,' I say uncertainly, taken aback by his obvious delight in seeing me, a complete deviation from the usual play-it-cool attitude of the boys I used to know.

'I was beginning to think you'd swerved tonight and left me with your impeccably behaved workmates,' he says, nodding in the direction of two swaying interns next to me.

'No, just running late.'

'What'll it be?'

'A glass of champagne, if you've got it.'

He raises his eyebrow. 'Well, we don't normally do it by the glass, but for you I'll make an exception. What are you celebrating?'

'Christmas,' I tell him, thinking of the good cheer back home.

He moves away to the end of the bar to get my drink, and there, tucked away in a corner, oblivious to the raucousness surrounding them, I notice a couple sitting on bar stools, gazing at each other. As the woman reaches across the few inches between them to stroke her boyfriend's cheek, I imagine doing the same to Alec. They begin to kiss, and I find myself longing to feel Alec's lips pushing against mine.

Thankfully, Olivia appears behind me, bringing me back to my senses.

'You look amazing,' she says, wrapping her arms around my middle. 'Love you in that dress.' Then, spotting Alec, she adds, 'Don't you agree, Alec?'

'Yeah, she looks great. You all do.'

After handing me my glass, he moves off to serve another customer, and Olivia grabs my hand to take me to the area of the bar that's needlessly been cordoned off for our use, even though almost everyone in here is from the office, and we've filled the whole place rather than our few assigned tables.

Olivia lets me say hi to everyone before loudly announcing she needs the toilet and pulling me along with her.

'You and Alec,' she squeals once the ladies' door has shut behind us. 'You and Alec! I could not be more excited if this was happening to me.'

'Er, what about Rick?'

'Screw Rick!'

'Really?'

'No. I'm joking. No one compares to my little Rick. But lucky you. I couldn't believe it when he came over asking for your number the other night. I hope you didn't mind me giving it to him. I know you insist you're happy being single and all that, but I thought, seeing that it was him, you'd be pleased.'

'No, it's fine. But, just so you know, there's nothing going on with us.'

'Sure about that? You should have seen him creeping up to me the other night all bashful, barely able to look at me, stumbling over his words. He really likes you, Jess.'

'No, he doesn't. We're friends. Honestly, that's it.'

'How could you only want to be friends with that god? Guys that good-looking don't stay around for long. You should get him while you have the chance. It doesn't have to be serious; it could be a bit of fun.'

'Much as I appreciate your advice, you've got it wrong. Ask him, if you want. He'll say the same as me: we're mates.'

Olivia sighs and rubs my arm. 'OK. I know you have your rules, and I get them, Jess, I do. It's just that he's not only so good-looking it makes me want to cry, but he's also a good guy. If you were thinking about breaking your rule, he'd be the one to do it for.'

I don't regret telling Olivia about my rules or telling her about testing positive for Huntington's. At first, the plan was to tell no one, but I couldn't keep it up. One morning she caught me crying at my desk and took me to the ladies to help me calm down. When she asked what was wrong, the words left me in a rush, like air escaping from a popped balloon. I needed to speak about it to someone who wasn't Mum or a medical professional to stop me going mad with all the thoughts I had. I also needed someone to cover for me at work when I needed time off for Mum. Telling her has been the best mistake I've made, but, that said, there are downsides to Olivia knowing, and her insistence to disregard my most important rule is one of them.

'You're right. He's great, but nothing's going to happen, so please let it drop.'

'OK. Come on, then, let's get back out there.'

'Don't you need the toilet?'

'No. I needed the gossip about you and Alec. Now I've got it, or not got it, rather, we might as well join the others.'

We sit with a few of the admin lot and a couple of paralegals we're friendly with, as well as Eric McAllister, the CEO, who, wildly drunk, slurs his annual speech about how he thinks of his three hundred and ninety employees as his children. I sip my champagne and nod politely, trying to control the urge to ask what time he wants us all round for Christmas dinner, then.

The tiny bubbles slip down far too quickly. As I'm standing to go to the bar, Alec appears by my side with another glass.

'I thought you might fancy another one. And seeing that you made me open a bottle when no one else is drinking the stuff, I need to get rid of it one way or the other.'

He disappears back to the bar as soon as he's delivered it, but it's too late. Only Mr McAllister is oblivious to what's happened – although even he senses that something's shifted and stumbles to the group next to us. Once he's gone, everyone turns to me.

'What. Just. Happened?' demands Jane, leaning as far forward as her halterneck will allow. 'You and him? Him and – you?' She sounds put out, like she can't believe that Alec's deigned to go for one of us and has picked me, not her, despite the sparkling diamonds reaching up to her knuckle on her ring finger.

'What? No. Like he said, I asked him to open a bottle of champagne, and he's trying to finish it off so he doesn't lose money. Given the face he pulled when I asked for it, he'll be making damn sure I pay for it before leaving.'

Olivia's gone stiff in the seat next to me.

'In fact, I think I'll go and pay for it now, so I don't forget.'

I bend to get my bag from the floor, turning to Olivia as I do so, shooting her a warning glance. It's killing her not to say; her lips are pressed so tightly together, the skin around them has gone white. But she nods once, and I know she'll keep quiet.

'Thanks for that,' I say when I get to Alec.

'You're welcome.' He's grinning at me, pleased with himself.

'No, not for the champagne, thanks for making me the subject of office gossip.'

'Huh?'

'You coming over personally to deliver me a drink when you've never once done that for another customer, it makes it a bit obvious. I could have done without being the focal point of the party for the rest of the night.'

'What are you talking about? I didn't think there was anything to be obvious about. You've made it pretty clear that there's nothing going on between us. I was just trying to be nice.'

'Yeah, well.' I can't think of a reply. He's right. I've got nothing to be angry about.

'Right. Well, here's the money for the drink anyway. Thanks.'

He snatches the money out of my hand and turns straight to the till. 'See you later,' I shout to his back, but he doesn't turn round.

There's nothing else to do but to return to the party. Reluctantly, I take my seat amidst a conversation that's still about Alec.

'Wouldn't it be lovely, though,' Maureen says, turning to me. 'I bet he'd treat a girl real proper. He's a romantic type; you can tell by looking at him.'

'You don't know that,' Olivia counters, squeezing my leg. 'He's got to be charming here, hasn't he? It's his job. Everyone knows bar staff rely on tips, so he's going to pull out his best act. But behind closed doors, he might be a right knob.'

'And arrogant to boot. He's told me he's single, yet I've lost count of the amount of times I've seen him brushing off beautiful women. You don't do that unless you think you're something special,' Jane says, her words tipped with pointy ends. Olivia and I exchange a look, confirming what we'd already suspected: Jane must have tried and failed to get together with Alec.

'Or you care about more than the size of a woman's boobs,' argues Maureen.

'I'm not talking about boobs,' Jane snaps back. 'All the women who come in and out of here, and he's never taken an interest in any of them. Charming or not, he thinks he's above everyone. You can see it a mile off.'

'Rubbish,' Maureen tells her. 'There's no act about him. Just because he isn't interested in the women in here doesn't make him arrogant. I reckon he's lovely. You can fake some things, but not the eyes. They tell you everything you need to know, and his are full of kindness.'

She's right, of course. I could tell her about the night we spent together, how, as soon as he'd got his breath back after we'd slept together, he insisted I spent the night before jumping out of bed to get me a drink and to find a spare toothbrush.

60

'He's nice enough,' I agree, trying to put an end to it. 'But we don't know him, not really. I reckon we stop worrying about him and start worrying about getting to this restaurant. I'm starving.'

I manage to herd my lot out before the rest of the firm have even thought about moving to get to our eight o'clock reservation at Zicco's, the swish Italian a few streets away.

Olivia links my arm with hers, pulling me slightly back from the others. 'You all right?'

'Fine. Why wouldn't I be?'

'I don't know. I thought I might have annoyed you banging on about Alec in the toilets, then when he came over and the piranhas started circling you, I was worried you were getting upset.'

'There's nothing to be upset about, I told you. Thanks for checking, though. Now come on,' I say in the most upbeat voice I can find, 'before that lot get there and work their way through the money McAllister put behind the bar. It's only two thousand pounds, so we'd best be quick.'

Olivia laughs and races ahead with me, overtaking the others so we burst into the restaurant first, flustered and high-fiving each other to the alarm of the diners, who clearly weren't warned about the incoming party.

Amongst the noise and clamour of the restaurant, it's easy to pretend to be having fun. I'm careful not to talk to Maureen, Jane, or even Olivia, in case they mention Alec again. I spend most of the night with the Human Resources lot, who I sometimes work with and have never really bothered to get to know. They met us at Zicco's, and I've never seen them in The Wishing Well, so they're a safe bet.

It's only in the taxi on the way back that I let the aching muscles around my mouth sag. Hot tears arrive without warning, and I press my hands to my eyes to stop them falling.

'Boy trouble, eh?' asks the taxi driver.

'Excuse me?'

'I've been doing this job fifteen years now, and I can tell you there's only one reason girls like you finish up your night all upset. Whoever he is, he's not worth it, love. Trust me.'

But he's wrong. It was easy to pretend that Alec isn't special with Olivia and the others. But now there's no need to lie.

'That's the problem, I think he is.'

Chapter Nine

Nothing gets done at McAllister Lewis Glenn in the three days following the party before we finish up for Christmas. One of my favourite things about where I work is that, even though they're now one of the most successful corporate law firms in Manchester, they've still held true to the habits they formed when they started off with only five employees. And favourite of all those habits is shutting down entirely for two weeks until after New Year.

In the wind down, I'm able to spend extended lunch breaks getting my shopping done, followed by afternoons wrapping presents and writing cards from Mum and I with what I hope to be the same well-thought-out sentiments she would have included in each one.

On the Friday, it's barely worth turning up. We spend the morning swapping secret Santas – I acquire a packet of neon eyeliners and a ball of fluff on a key ring – before gathering in the conference room at noon to hear the Christmas speech from the partners. After a morning of working their way round the numerous conference rooms in their seven-storey offices, by the time they get to us, their festive cheer is on the wane, so they give us the briefest and best Christmas message we could have hoped for: pack up and go home.

Jane suggests going back to our desks and opening the bottle of her favourite Sauvignon Blanc she suspiciously managed to bag herself in the secret Santa. I firmly decline, telling her I couldn't think of anything worse and am thanked for my honesty by a huff and some very lacklustre Yuletide well wishes. I race to the lift before she realises the rest of the team have bolted whilst she's wasted her time on me and she tries harder to persuade me to stay.

The rain that's been coming down mercilessly all week is beginning to ease off when I get out, although the sky is still a solid sheet of steel cloud. I can either make a dash to the Metro station and try and get home before the rain begins again or stay around the city centre a bit longer, taking shelter in a coffee shop with a giant hot chocolate. I could even go into Felters, the bookshop round the corner and treat myself to a Christmas read.

Mum's got Jeanette coming in today. They rub along well enough together, and it's not like she'll be expecting me home anyway. I decide to stick around.

Once I've been to Felters and the pimply youth behind the counter has persuaded me to buy a Christmas thriller from a few years back about an assassination attempt on a president on Christmas Eve, which he assures me is an absolute classic festive read, the rain's started falling with serious intent. There's a Starbucks in the Arndale centre I could take refuge in, but it would mean wading through a hopeless throng of last-minute shoppers to get there. If I walk back in the direction I came in, I could be at The Wishing Well in a minute, which should be opening up by now.

Alec won't be working. Last night when I was leaving work, I saw him in there chatting to two women whilst clearing a table by the window. If he's done the evening shift, he surely won't be back the following morning. Why pass up spending a few hours in The Wishing Well's fairy-lit warmth when he won't even be there?

The door opens with such a thud when I push it and enter with a lunge to get out of the heavy downpour that the half-dozen or so early drinkers already there snap their heads up to watch my soggy entrance. Behind the bar, a man smirks. Ginger, beardless and not at all Alec. After ordering my drink and politely laughing when he asks me if I want a towel to go with it, I take the table by the window and open my book. I'm a few pages and one attempted murder into it when the barman brings my drink, apologising when the whipped cream sloshes over the sides as he places it down. I tell him not to worry, that a drink overflowing with cream is never a bad thing. Without thinking, I ask, 'Is Alec working today?'

'Yeah, he's just come in. His shift starts in half an hour. I can go and get him, if you want me to.'

'Oh no, don't do that. No, no, it's fine. Thanks,' I reply, my cheeks bursting into flames.

'OK, I'll leave you to your drink.' He laughs. A nasty little snigger he doesn't see the need to conceal from me.

I gulp down a few sips of the painfully hot chocolate before deciding to abandon it. The barman goes straight from my table to a concealed black door at the end of the bar. He holds it open with his bum and begins talking to someone in the room beyond. Right now, he'll be telling Alec that some stupid, flustered girl's been asking for him. I watch as he guffaws, his head flinging back with the sheer force of the hilarity, before he shuts the door and returns to his post, quickly glancing my way before serving his waiting customer.

There's no way I'm going to let Alec know I'm that flustered girl, no chance I'm going to let him laugh at me like his friend did. I toss my book into a bag full of presents I'd been storing under my desk at work and make a bolt for it before he comes out.

Now the magic of the afternoon has been switched off, I go straight to the Metro station, ready to start my break from work – and everything else in its vicinity.

It's only in the evening when I get round to putting the presents under the tree that I realise my mistake: I left the office with two bags and returned home with only one. My first thought is to give the presents in the other bag up as lost, to make do without them. But with a wave of nausea I recall Mum's present is in that bag.

I'd spent weeks racking my brain, wondering what to get her before realising she'd given me the perfect hint a few months ago. In a rare nostalgic mood, she'd reminded me of the set of friendship necklaces she gave me as a child. I kept one half of a heart dangling from my thin chain, and she had the other on hers. For years we both wore them. Until I became embarrassed about it, didn't want anyone at school to laugh at me sharing it with my mum instead of an actual friend and insisted we both take them off.

I went to the jeweller's hoping to find something similar to give her this year, and there it was: the exact same one we had, all these years later. The exact same one now sat in the bottom of a bag in The Wishing Well.

I could go back and get it, but it's already gone seven when I notice the bag's missing. By now the bar will be mobbed with workers beginning their perilous journey into Black Friday, the messy, drink-fuelled final work night before Christmas. Someone must have found the bag by now, handed it in or taken it for themselves. I'm not sure I can face either result.

Ringing to check or returning to the bar and gingerly asking Alec for the bag will only confirm what an arse I was this morning, running away from him like a schoolgirl running away from boys in the playground. I can already picture his face, his chestnut eyes lit up with amusement as he listens to whatever explanation I manage to get out of my mouth. And if the barman from this morning is there, I know they'll exchange a look, and they'll both try to hide their smiles whilst feigning concern about my lost present situation.

That would be devastating enough, but to go back down there to face Alec only to be told that they've seen no bag, that Mum's necklace has gone, would be even worse.

Sulkily, I go in to see Mum and get her ready for bed. Debs has finished for Christmas, taking a two-week break from us whilst I'm at home. Mum asks what's wrong with me tonight, and I tell her everything's fine. She knows I'm lying; my face is scrutinised inch by inch, as she tries to find the truth on it. It's almost nice, an echo back to a time when I would carelessly lie to her about all sorts of trivial things, like where I'd really gone out to, or who with, and she'd fix me with her glare until I caved and confessed the truth.

It would be so good to admit it all, to tell her about Alec. I'd explain my reluctance to see him, because every time I do, I end up liking him more than I should. She'd nod sympathetically and reach for my hand. Only, I can't have Mum worrying about me on top of everything. Instead, I plump for the lie, telling her I'm tired and ready for a break.

'Bedtime,' she orders, and I comply, skulking away to my room, my stomach aching with disappointment.

Outside my window, the heavy, sodden clouds have finally passed. A half-moon sits high in the sky, its crisp line so perfectly straight it looks like a cut-out stuck onto the sky rather than the real thing. Its bright light makes the sky silver, lessening the glare from the golden lights the house opposite have wound around their bush.

I throw open the window, needing a sharp pinch of the air on my face to revive me enough so I can come up with a plan to get Mum's present back.

Just as I've decided that tomorrow I'll have to ask Jeanette if she minds keeping Mum company for an hour after she's finished getting her sorted for the day whilst I go back to the jeweller's and buy another necklace, my phone bleeps.

Hi. By any chance, were you the mysterious redhead in the bar earlier asking for me before disappearing? If so, you left a bag here. Will drop it off, if you want. Let me know, Alec x

I type back immediately, telling him I've been at home all day so it couldn't possibly have been me. It's only when I get to the end of the text and am deliberating whether or not to add a kiss, that I work out if I send this, I'll be saying goodbye to ever getting my bag back and will have to fork out on another necklace I really can't afford.

It doesn't matter if he knows. Nothing is going on with him. It doesn't matter.

Deleting the message I've typed, I write a new one: *Hey. Yeah, it was me. So glad you found my bag. If you don't mind, that would be great.*

Getting Alec to come here means I won't have to leave Mum and trek across a city of drunkards, but it also means Alec is coming here. To my house.

If he comes in, he'll see the medical equipment stacked up in the hall, he might disturb Mum, and she'll wake wanting to know who's in the house at this time. I'll go from being the 'mysterious redhead' to the girl from the house of illness. And, worse, Mum could find out about him.

She hates the idea that I'm going to stay single all my life. I made the mistake of telling her about that particular rule once she'd got help to stop her hurting herself and had started questioning me about how I was planning to handle my future. She was livid. That's why she didn't want me to get tested in the first place, she said, because she knew I'd let it strip away all the good things I should have had.

We fought about it for months.

Mum never used to treat me as a child, even when I was a child. All the other kids I grew up with had almost every aspect of their lives controlled by their parents until well into their teens, but not me. Most nights, Mum would pick me up from the childminder, bring me home, throw open the fridge and ask me to decide what we were having for tea. If I said pancakes, that's what we'd eat. Sandwiches, no problem. Not the healthiest of lifestyles, but it certainly made teatime special.

When I was seven, she handed me a holiday brochure of cottages in the UK and told me to choose wherever I wanted. We went to Anglesey in Wales and had the most wonderful time.

All my childhood, I was brought up to think my decisions were valid, but with this, she told me off. Told me I was plain wrong.

I knew I wasn't. By the time I'd decided to create my rules, I'd spent hours researching Huntington's. Mum stuck to the leaflets and information given to her by the doctors and the specialist nurse who came out to see us not long after she received her results. I scoured Google and YouTube for as much insight as I could lay my eyes on. I knew more than she did about both our futures, yet she would not accept that I had made an informed choice.

'You've not met the right man. Those other boyfriends of yours were just that: boys. You wait until the right one comes along,' she'd say.

'I don't want to meet the right one,' I'd answer. 'Right or wrong, I'm not going to be responsible for bringing another person into this.'

'Don't be silly. If someone loves you, they'll want to care for you.'

'No,' I would say. 'No, they wouldn't. They'd have to, Mum. No one in their right mind would want to.'

'Oh, you mean how you have to care for me?'

'I'm your family. We're in this together. It's not the same thing at all.'

'You sure about that?' she'd ask.

Each time we'd have the conversation it would end in sulking and silent days between us. Eventually, it was easier to stop talking about it.

If she sees Alec tonight, she'll think I've changed my mind. It would be the best Christmas present I could give her, but I can't let her have it.

I send him another message: *Mum sleeping. I'll meet you at the end of the street. Text me when you've arrived.*

It's a bit mean, I know. After coming out of his way, the least he'll be expecting is a drink for his efforts, and here I am refusing him admittance to my house. His reply doesn't come straight away, and I wonder if he's so annoyed, he's trying to get out of his offer. When my phone does bleep, I'm reluctant to pick it back up.

So you want me to pull up at your street corner to hand over a package late at night? This is all getting a bit shady, Jessica. Should I dress in black? Turn off my headlights? Cover my face?

A bubble of laughter pops out of my mouth. I fire back my reply: *No more questions. Come alone. Tell no one.*

I go downstairs and wait in the lounge, determined to watch the rerun of the Christmas panel show I saw last

70

year and not go back upstairs to put on more make-up or change my clothes before he arrives.

An hour after his last message, he sends another one to say he's here. I check in on Mum before pulling my coat on and tiptoeing out of the house.

When I tap on his window, he opens it enough to push out my bag before revving his engine, pretending to leave.

'Hey, don't do that, you'll wake the whole street.'

He puts his window fully down and turns to me, grinning. 'Sorry, I was getting into my new criminal life.'

'Very funny. Thanks for this, though. You're a life saver.'

'No problem. Heard you left the bar in a bit of a rush this morning.'

'Yeah,' I say, wishing he couldn't see my face in this glaring moonlight. 'Had to get back all of a sudden. Shame I didn't catch you.'

'It's all right. Everything OK?'

'Yeah,' I say, glancing over my shoulder to the house, hoping he's not going to invite himself in.

'Good.'

'I, er, should get going.'

'Yeah, of course. You'll freeze standing there.'

I've got all the way to my front gate when I hear his engine thrumming quietly next to me.

'I forgot – Merry Christmas,' Alec says quietly through the window of the passenger door, leaning across the seat. 'And I was wondering, seeing that I'm all alone in a big new city for Christmas, would you maybe want to meet up at some point?'

'You're not going home for Christmas?'

'No. I volunteered to take on extra shifts. If I went home, it would only end in too many nights out and everyone trying to find ways to get Ellie and me back together. Can I rely on you to take pity on me instead?'

'I'm sure there are plenty of people who will take pity on you, Alec.'

'Maybe,' he concedes. 'But I can't think of anyone I'd rather spend time with than you.'

'Thanks. I don't get why but thanks.'

'What do you mean you don't get why?'

'You could spend time with anyone. You could be out meeting this new someone you can fully love. I don't get why you're so fussed about making something out of our pissed one-night stand.'

'Bloody hell, Jess. You really don't remember that night, do you? I knew you'd had a few, I never realised you'd sunk enough to forget the whole night. You don't remember how we laughed so much together that wine came out your nose at one point? Or how you leant into me after that first kiss and closed your eyes like you'd found something in me you needed? Or the sex? The mind-blowing sex that was so good we couldn't stop laughing at the end of it. Why wouldn't I want more after that? Even if it's to be your friend and pretend the sex never happened, it's worth it.'

I busy myself checking through the contents of the bag. It's easier to pretend I was too drunk to recall than to have him know I remember it all.

'So? Meeting up?'

'I can't. I'm sorry. Merry Christmas.'

I don't wait to hear what he'll say in return; I turn away, walking up the short path to the door so that I can throw myself inside and go straight to bed before I say anything else today to make me more of a liar than I already am.

Chapter Ten

Eight years earlier

'Come on, Jess, you've missed half the day already.'

At the sound of Mum's voice, I reached for a pillow and pressed it over my head. The close smell of my breath brought back a pile of memories, almost all of them involving shots of tequila. I had been nervous leaving the house the night before and thought about cancelling, but Gregg had been adamant I meet his friends. Everything had been so perfect between us since the moment we met in a nightclub six weeks before when he grabbed my hand and spun me around on the dance floor to some song by Swedish House Mafia; I didn't want to let him down. It meant I had to forgo my usual Christmas Eve ritual of crap films and sherry with Mum for a night at Gregg's local, but she was happy to let me go, as long as it was only a quiet drink and not a session.

Lying in bed, I assessed the damage. A pounding headache, a protesting stomach and a sore throat. Had it been worth it? Well, Gregg had been stuck to my side all night, proudly showing me off to his friends. That was nice. They were a fun bunch too, from what I could remember. There was a vague memory of pelting out Adele's 'Hometown Glory' with another girl's arm around my waist, passing the microphone between us. But the cost of it had been steep: Christmas morning wasted, and a throbbing hangover on my favourite day of the year.

'Oh dear,' Mum said, when I came into the kitchen in my dressing gown. 'Look at the state of you.'

'Sorry. I know what you're going to say, and you're right. I was an idiot last night. What time did I come in?'

'Well, I heard a lot of fumbling at the front door around two, which I presumed was you. Good night, was it?'

'I guess.'

'I hope this Gregg didn't end up in as much of a state as you did.'

'I can't remember, to be honest.'

'Bloody hell, Jess,' Mum said and began to smile. 'Well, if you think you're skulking around here all day feeling sorry for yourself, you've got another thing coming. Here.' She handed me a Buck's Fizz and picked up her own. 'Happy Christmas, love.'

'Happy Christmas, Mum.' I took a sip from my glass and leant forward to hug her.

'My God, the fumes on you. Go and get yourself showered and dressed up, then we can open the presents,' she said, singing the last word in her excitement. I smiled at her, all dolled up in a new red velvet off-the-shoulder dress, her face done up, and her shoulder-length auburn hair clipped back off her face. I didn't know anyone who loved Christmas as much as Mum, and I decided to hide the hangover from her for the rest of the day.

'OK, but I think it would be best if we did the presents now.'

'Oh, you do? Go on then, but only because I'm desperate to see your face when you open them.'

I followed her into the lounge and burst out laughing. There, in front of the couch, was the same sack that had been holding my Christmas gifts since I was a child, as full as it always was. And just as she always did, she had covered the room in balloons and fake snow and that glitter confetti that got everywhere.

I went straight to the presents and sat before them, eyeing up the wrapping paper and making a mental inventory so I knew where to start.

'Do you want yours now or after we've eaten?' I asked.

'After. Watching you opening yours is my favourite bit of the day.'

'Can I?' I asked.

'One second.' She went to the CD player and picked up *Christmas* by Michael Bublé from the shelf above it. When she dropped the CD on the floor, she swore under her breath and bent to pick it up, stumbling as she bent down.

'Bloody hell, Mum, how much have you had?'

'You can talk. It must be my age. I swear I'm getting clumsier by the day.' She was right. The last few months had seen more broken glasses and dented food packaging than ever. She tried again to insert the CD. This time the opening notes to 'It's Beginning to Look a Lot Like Christmas' began to ring out.

'Perfect,' Mum said. 'Now, dive in, love.'

Chapter Eleven

For the two nights before Christmas, Mum's sleep solidifies into long, restorative hours, bringing colour back into her face and a calm, cheery mood. If it weren't for the guilt of letting Alec down, I'd be calm and cheery too.

When I go down to her on Christmas morning at nine, she's already awake and sitting up in bed, waiting for me. A troubled look flashes across her face as I sit next to her, but she removes it quickly and wishes me a Merry Christmas. I've already been in the lounge to fish out the necklace from the small pile of presents under the tree, and I place it in her lap at the same time as wishing her a Merry Christmas. She spends so long admiring the wrapping, which I had to redo after getting the bag back from Alec to find the paper torn and the bow crushed, I eventually take it from her and tear it open. She gasps. Old Mum would scold me for being so reckless ripping off paper that could have been folded neatly and used again if I'd have been more careful. But Mum's gasp now is for the red jewellery box, and she puts out her hand for me to give it back.

Seeing the two necklaces lying side by side on the black velvet, Mum closes her eyes and nods.

'Do you remember, Mum?' I ask pointlessly. Course she does. 'You gave me a set exactly like it for my tenth birthday. The idea was that I'd share it with a friend, but

I gave the other one to you. You wore it every day until I turned into a brat and demanded you take it off for fear one of my friends would notice it and laugh at me for being so uncool.'

'I do.'

'Well, seeing I'm past the brat phase now, I'd love it if you'd wear one again.'

She nods, and I put the necklace around her neck. I hadn't reckoned for the upset of seeing it rest upon the jut of her collarbone. I turn away to put my own necklace on, only turning back when I've attached the clasp and can muster a smile.

'Ta-dah.'

'Lovely,' she says, although her brow creases at the sight of me.

I go into the kitchen to get us a cup of tea and some cereal. After moving Mum to her chair and helping her with breakfast whilst we sit and watch a *Songs of Praise* rerun, I take myself upstairs to get sorted, trying very hard not to think of past Christmases as I do.

Before, Mum and I would always dress up for Christmas. We'd both come down for the day as though we were going to be spending it in some fancy restaurant.

Seeing me this morning with my matted hair and faded Harry Potter onesie must have been a blow to Mum, another reminder of the distance we've travelled from our normal life. I resolve to make the rest of the day as similar as I can to the many happy Christmases before Huntington's.

Hair curled and jumpsuit on, I go back down. I show her the silver cardigan I've picked from her wardrobe. She shakes her head and turns away from it, and I curse myself for not considering how little she'll want to get trussed up like a bloody foil-wrapped turkey when she's in so much discomfort. A carer we haven't met before comes in for twenty minutes to help Mum in the bathroom, and when they reappear, Mum is still in her pyjamas. She lets me do her hair and make-up like normal, but nothing more.

All morning she paws at the necklace round her throat, the worried look still there.

'You're sad,' she utters, matter-of-factly, when I appear with two champagne flutes filled with orange juice.

'I'm not sad. I love Christmas Day. How could I be sad?'

'You are,' she replies, suddenly looking weary and closing her eyes.

I leave her to sleep, and I roam the house, entering rooms and leaving them without having done anything, not feeling like I'm in the home I've known since I was a child, but, rather, as if I'm a stranger trying to get to grips with these new surroundings, not having a clue where to put myself.

I always thought I spent every Christmas doing nothing, but I was wrong; I spent every Christmas having fun with Mum. Now I'm really doing nothing, and the shock of loneliness is so great I go back to bed to hide under the duvet.

The beep of my phone rouses me from a light, miserable snooze.

It's a picture of Alec. He's sitting in his bare lounge with a Santa hat and Christmas jumper on, a gormless grin on his face.

I have to laugh at him. Throwing back the cover and sitting up, I compose my message. *Very fetching. Happy Christmas. Please tell me you're not sitting on your own like that all day.*

I hit send, and, instead of going downstairs, wait for his reply. For weeks, I've been thinking about getting the most out of today for Mum's sake, thinking of ways to make it nice for her. Alec's given me a tiny pocket of the day that's mine, and I'm grateful. In a few minutes, I'll go down, and I'll be all hers.

My phone beeps again.

Yep. All on my lonesome until the pub opens tonight, but you can't have Christmas without a festive jumper, right? I hope you've got yours on too. x

Of course, I reply, looking down at my jumpsuit. *It lights up and everything. X*

As I'm waiting for his reply, there's an unexpected knock on the door. When I open it, I find the best present I ever could have wished for: Debs.

'Merry Christmas, love.' She gives me a kiss and whisks past me to the dining room, calling Mum's name. Winking at Mum, she turns to me, hands on her hips, looking as serious as anyone can do wearing a reindeer jumper with a flashing nose stretched across their paunch.

'Right, lady. I've left Ray in charge of Christmas dinner, and I reckon I've got about an hour until I need to get back to rescue it. There're presents to be opened. Let's get down to business.'

Mum's as giddy as an elf now Debs has arrived and can't stop giggling. I join in too, not knowing what I'm laughing at but so happy to be laughing with Mum at all, it really doesn't matter.

Debs marches out of the room to turn on the lights on the tree, a rather key job I'd forgotten to do.

'Back in a sec, Mum,' I say, following Debs into the lounge.

She's already on her knees, organising the presents from under the tree into two piles.

'Listen, Debs,' I whisper so Mum can't hear, 'as amazing as this is, you know you don't need to be here. You should be with your own family today. We're fine.'

'I know I don't *have* to be here. I *want* to be here. Flipping heck, Jess, you sound like Ray.'

'Sorry,' I say, not really knowing why I'm apologising for sounding like Ray. 'But he's right.'

'Look,' she snaps, 'it's entirely up to me where I spend my day. With the amount of work I've put into getting everything organised, making sure that the grandkids all have the same amount of presents, that lunch will be ready at two for Samantha's lot, that the buffet will be ready at five for when Mark and his brood arrive, and that there'll be enough for another round when Lauren's boyfriend and his family come round tonight, you'd think I might be allowed to have an hour off to check up on you. They know how much you mean to me. It shouldn't be such a big deal for everyone.'

'OK.'

Debs finishes organising the presents, chewing the inside of her cheek like it's a boiled sweet. She pushes a small pile of presents towards my feet.

'Who are these from?' I ask.

'They're from your mum. Who else do you think they're from? Some secret admirer?'

I laugh off the suggestion and go to get Mum. When I've moved her back to the bed, dragged her chair in from the dining room, gone back to carry her in and we're all set up in the lounge, I turn my attention to the pile of presents. They're not in the usual red tattered sack this year, but, as I wasn't expecting anything, I can't be too disappointed. Underwear, a new e-reader to replace the one that broke a few months ago, a bottle of perfume and chocolates. Blissfully ordinary presents. Nothing sentimental to hint things have changed and may be coming to a close. This is what I should have done for Mum.

Debs gives us a few presents each from her, and we polish off the chocolates Mum bought me between us. Then it's time for her to return to her family to try and salvage the turkey dinner she's meant to have ready for the first influx of her family. She's reluctant to leave us. I wonder if there's more to her coming here today than she's letting on, something that's nothing at all to do with her patient and her patient's daughter, but rather something in her own family that's made her want to escape it.

When she comes to kiss me goodbye, I pull her in for a tight hug.

'Thank you. You've made Mum's day.'

'Nonsense. I've done nothing. It looks like you were doing a pretty good job all by yourself. Now, get to work. At least one of us needs to end up with something decent to eat.'

Once Debs leaves, the sparkle of the day disappears too. I ask Mum if she wants to play Monopoly like we used to do, but she's too tired. I put on *Home Alone* and leave her to doze in front of it while I set to cooking the beef joint and ready-prepared veg I picked up from Marks & Spencer.

'How was it?' I ask later, looking at Mum's untouched plate once my own is empty.

'Lovely. Sorry I couldn't manage it.'

'Don't be daft. It's fine. I'll clear the plates and then we can do something nice, eh? What do you fancy? Another film? Or we can play cards, if you want?'

'I'm tired,' she says, apology in her eyes. 'I think I'll go to bed.'

Once I've settled her, loneliness creeps back into the house, and I return to my room, retrieving my phone. The reply from my earlier conversation with Alec is waiting for me.

Send me a picture. Seeing you in a light-up jumper is exactly what my Christmas needs.

I consider replying with something witty in an attempt to start up another chat, but it's hours since his message. He'll be at the pub by now, and I can't rouse myself to come up with anything funny. I put the phone down, pick up the book I bought on Friday and read until Christmas is over.

Mum's mood changes when she wakes in the dark on Boxing Day morning. She's tucked herself into her own mind and doesn't want my company. Apart from the brisk in-and-out of the morning carers, we have no one coming to the house now until New Year's Eve. I'm happy to look after Mum for a while; it makes me feel better to know I'm being useful. It would be nice if Mum felt the same, but she'd rather the briskness and chatter of her usual daytime carers over my constant lurking. Once everything's been done, there are long hours to fill, and I begin to crave company other than the TV.

By the time Clare, Mum's occupational therapist, arrives on New Year's Eve, I'm so desperate to have a conversation with someone that I insist she stays after Mum's session for a glass of wine. I lead her into the kitchen and ask question after question about her Christmas, ignoring her clock watching and increasing glances at the front door. An hour later, once she's convinced me she can't possibly stay a second longer, and I've finally released her coat and scarf from my custody, she's feeling so sorry for me, she invites me on her night out.

'No, God no,' I protest. 'That's so kind of you, Clare, but I'm fine here.'

'OK,' she says, not pressing the matter, 'but will you do me a favour? Go for a walk for half an hour when your mum's asleep or get some of your friends round. You don't need to keep vigil at her bedside.'

She doesn't say it, but we both hear the extra word: 'yet'.

'I will. Happy New Year.'

She gives me a brief hug, the kind that's more of a body press than an arms-around-each-other type. Mum's asleep by midnight, so that hug, it turns out, is the only contact I have with another person to bring in the New Year.

I'm more than ready to get back to work the following Monday morning. I must be the most well-rested employee stepping back into the doors of McAllister Lewis Glenn. Everyone else in the office looks like they've come out of a coma, and there's lots of talk about needing at least the first week of January off to recover from the chaos of the holidays. I, however, set to work with such a vigour, Jane remarks that my New Year's resolution should be to get more of a life so that I look as knackered as the rest of them coming back to work.

I take the chance to get out in the air at lunch instead of sitting in the staff room listening to everyone sharing their festive stories, trying to outdo each other with tales of five-star hotels, fireworks and parties lasting until dawn. It's one of those fresh, windy days that are just the right amount of cold if you wrap up properly.

I see him the moment I step out of the lift into the glass porch at the front of the building. In amidst the purposeful bustle of the suited men and smartly dressed women, he stands perfectly still, wearing a khaki jacket and jeans, sticking out like a schoolboy who's got the date wrong for non-uniform day.

'There you are!' he shouts across the lobby when he sees me, making the heads of my nosier co-workers snap round to gawp at me.

I freeze. Since Christmas Day, I've heard nothing from Alec. The time at home has given me a chance to rebuild the wall around my heart. Seeing him now, my heart's pounding so hard in my chest that my careful construction comes crumbling down.

Part of me wants nothing more than to go to him, to start talking, to look into his eyes as he drinks in my face, making me feel like I'm the most important person in the world. It's what he's expecting me to do. Why wouldn't I go to him? We're meant to be friends, and now he's standing there grinning at the prospect of spending his lunch hour with me. I've not forgotten that he's been every bit as alone as I've been over the holidays, probably more so. I've been on my own, but I had Mum, whereas he's been surrounded with crowds at the bar but had no one around who really cares for him. He probably wants a little company from someone who isn't a punter. But I can't give it to him. I've got my rules, and right now, they are closer than ever to being broken. So I do the only thing I can come up with to make sure there's no scene and make myself move. I saunter straight past him, as though I've not seen him.

'Hey, wait up,' he calls after me.

I ignore him at first, only turning back once I'm away from the office entrance.

'What do you want, Alec?'

'What do I want? Er, to say hello, to see if you fancied getting some food so we can catch up. What's going on?'

'Nothing apart from you hovering around my office like a stalker. You need to back off. I've told you nothing's going to happen with us.'

'Yeah, and I heard you. But then we became friends. Remember?' He speaks slowly in an attempt to get his words into my thick brain.

'Look, I've got enough friends. And none of them turn up at my office unannounced. I think we should forget it.'

His shoulders curl in around his frame, and he crosses his arms. 'You sure about that? From what I've seen, Jess, you have Olivia and that's it. I've never seen you with anyone else, never even heard you speak about anyone else.'

I breathe out, trying to sound exasperated. 'Think what you want. I've got to go.'

I run into Lettuce and Loaf, the artisan deli next to the office which I usually shun in favour of the more reasonably priced Co-op, and join the queue. Thankfully, it's still early enough to be able to shut the door behind me instead of having to line up in the street. A few seconds after I've come in, Alec walks past the shop without looking in. Even so, I make a point of keeping my arms by my side, not wiping away my tears until he's turned the corner and is out of sight.

Chapter Twelve

Three and a half years earlier

The bang from downstairs made me jolt the mascara wand in my hand, creating a thick black smudge over my gold eyeshadow.

'Coming,' I shouted.

It was as I expected. Mum had fallen. She was sitting on the bottom step, rubbing her ankle, swearing under her breath.

I touched the top of her hair, as I came down and sat next to her.

'What happened?'

'Nothing happened,' she snapped. 'I was walking upstairs one minute; the next, I wasn't.'

'Oh.'

'Shit,' she shouted. There were tears in her eyes, which she rubbed furiously.

'Hey, it's OK, Mum. It's OK.'

'No, it's not. Thanks to this fucking disease, I can't get up my own stairs. Nothing about that is OK.'

I winced at Mum's swearing. As far back as I remember she'd been a regular in the lower divisions of swearing – her conversations peppered liberally with arses and bloody hells – but the last few months she'd gone up to the top flight.

'What can I do?' I asked quietly, once she'd taken a few deep breaths and shaken her head to rid herself of the anger.

'Right now, nothing. You go and enjoy your night out. But we're going to have to think about what to do about these stairs before too long.'

'I know,' I said, before changing the subject, as I'd grown accustomed to doing whenever hard conversations came up. 'Come on, you go back to the couch, and I'll get you some tea.'

'No, no. You'll be late. Where are you meeting them again?'

'I was going to go to Alison's first and then meet the others in town later, but I can cancel. It's not a big deal.'

'No, don't do that. I'm fine, and if you cancel any more nights out, you're going to find yourself with no friends left.'

'Honestly, it's fine. They get it. I'm not in the mood anyway. I'll nip up and text Alison, and then I'll see about that tea. OK?'

Back in my bedroom, I wiped off my ruined make-up, took off my skinny jeans and top, changed into my pyjamas and reached for my phone.

Hey, Ali. So sorry, but I can't make tonight. Need to look after Mum. If you're all meeting for lunch tomorrow, I'll join you. Let me know. Have a great night.

I should have left the phone upstairs. That way, I'd have been able to sort Mum's tea and bring her bedding downstairs for the third night in a row without listening out for its ping. I would have been able to enjoy *Gogglebox* without checking the screen every few minutes.

Midnight came and went without a word from Alison. In the morning, when Mum seemed fine and a few hours out of the house would have done me good, there was nowhere for me to go. Ignoring the signs of desperation I must have been giving off, I text Alison again.

Hey, hope you had a great night. Mum fine today. Would love to hear the gossip if you're meeting up. Let me know when x

The reply came at ten past seven that evening:

Hi Jess, it was a good night. No one was up for meeting up today. Hope your mum is better x

I read the message again and again, my throat constricting, until I found what was wrong with it. What the glaring omission was.

There was no mention of the next night out. There would already be one planned. There always was. Only, I wasn't invited.

Chapter Thirteen

Alec doesn't return. I pay nearly a tenner in Lettuce and Loaf for my sandwich and drink and rush back to the safety of the seventh floor.

I take one bite of the baguette, but it congeals into a tasteless lump in my mouth, and I throw the rest of it away. Maureen comes into the staff room and offers to make me a coffee. I take it from her gratefully, but it tastes sour. I can't stomach a thing.

Giving up on lunch, I go to the toilets to rest my head a little against the cool, cream, marble wall. Despite the privacy of the cubicle, guilt finds me, flooding under the door and rising round my ankles until I'm soaked in the stuff. When it comes to Alec, all I seem to do is lie and disappoint, constantly worming my way out of perfectly nice situations. Only this time it's worse. This time I've hurt him. I should have come up with something better than that ugly scene downstairs. It's not his fault, after all. I really shouldn't have told him it was.

Soggily emerging from my cubicle twenty minutes later, I know what I need to do. I can't have him around, but I can't leave it like this. I sit at my desk and pull out my phone from the top drawer.

Sorry about my terrible behaviour before. Forgiven?

He replies straight back. *Why don't you come to mine for a drink tonight? JUST FRIENDS!*

I don't reply. Instead, I make my way to Olivia's desk.

'Hey, what you doing tonight, Liv?'

'Trying to keep my eyes open long enough to make myself some tea and watch *Corrie* before crashing out.'

'How about I save you the job of cooking and you come to mine for tea after work?'

'That sounds good. You sure your mum won't mind?'

'No, of course not. She'd love to see you. What do you think?'

'OK. As long as what you make is an improvement on my planned meal of beans on toast, I'm there.'

'Great.'

There's no sign of Jane after four, so we take the chance to sneak out of the office early. I'm surprised it's so dark when we leave and shudder against the cold and the January grimness. When we get to the house, Mum's awake and in her chair with Jeanette by her side. Her face lights up when she notices Olivia come in behind me. What started as a way to cover my back by making plans with Olivia tonight, meaning I couldn't possibly face Alec and his questioning, has turned into a good idea in its own right.

'Hi, Susan. How are you?' Olivia asks, going over to place a kiss on Mum's cheek.

'Good,' Mum replies, holding on to Olivia's hand.

'You look good. Better than me. I'm knackered.'

'Too much partying,' Mum says.

'Tell me about it. Then again, a holiday's not a holiday if you don't feel worse coming back then you did going.'

I catch Mum glancing my way as she laughs with Olivia.

'OK, you two,' I say. 'I'm going to fix us something to eat. Pasta anyone?'

'Great. I'll be through in a minute,' Olivia says, choosing to stay with Mum.

'Thanks,' I tell her when she comes into the kitchen to join me. 'You'll have made her day having a chat with her.'

'It's OK.' Olivia picks at the last of her purple nail varnish. 'She's struggling more, isn't she?'

I know she means her speech. 'She is. It's such an effort for her, I worry that the time's fast approaching when she's going to stop speaking altogether.'

'Oh, Jess.'

I shake off the upset. 'See, this is why I can't be getting involved with anyone. Alec's still trying, you know.' It wasn't my intention to bring him up, I was hoping Olivia being here would help keep him pushed away, but there's a need to say his name, to talk about him I can't suppress. 'I wish he'd get the message.'

'You sure about that?' Olivia asks, still hopeful.

'Yep. I told him so today. A little harshly, I admit. But you know what his reaction was? To invite me round to his for a drink.'

Olivia gives me one of her stares. 'You're tempted, aren't you?'

'If it was really just as a friend, yeah, but it's not, is it?'

'I don't think so,' she admits.

'Me neither. If I can't get through to him that nothing's happening, I can't see him at all.'

'Maybe you should tell him, then.'

'What?'

'Tell him about your mum. And you. At least he'd understand your reasons for not wanting to get involved. And I think it will do you good to tell someone else, Jess. It's not a dirty secret. You're allowed to talk about it.'

'I know that.'

'Well, then, be honest. And if after that, if he's able to see you as a friend and nothing more, you'll have another person in your corner. That can't be a bad thing. Unless it's *you* who can't see *him* as a friend.'

I stop twirling the pasta around the pan. 'That's the problem.'

I arrive outside Alec's block of flats a few minutes before eight, but it's twenty past by the time I'm ready to knock on his door.

Over an especially watery penne arrabbiata, Olivia tried to convince me I needed to see him. One way or another, putting an end to things was the kind thing to do, if that's what I really wanted, she said. I insisted that it was and reminded her yet again of my no-dating rule.

It was the point she made whilst putting on her coat as she was leaving that got me in the end.

'Tell him or don't tell him, it's up to you. But remember, this isn't someone you'll never see again. It's Alec from the pub across from work. Your options are to end it properly or spend your life avoiding bumping into him.'

I closed the door to her and went to my phone, texting him to tell him I'd come round as soon as I could.

When he lets me in, I'm relieved there's no music playing or candles lit or any other attempts made to make this romantic. Quite the opposite: the main light is on in the lounge, its stark light making it feel more like a doctor's waiting room than a home, and there's a smell of fried onions he's not bothered to mask. I sense Alec's trying to make a point when he doesn't offer me a drink and sits down on a dining chair rather than joining me on his leather sofa.

I don't blame him. I hurt him and now it's time for me to make up for it.

'I'm sorry for today,' I begin. 'I didn't mean to be so cruel; you caught me off-guard and I . . .' I trail off.

He says nothing, just continues to look at me, waiting for what I'm going to say next. His eyes are bright, but there's a coolness to them I've never noticed before. He's not going to give me anything until he hears me out.

I begin the speech I practised on the way over. 'Thing is, I can't be your friend. It's not that I don't like you, it's more that I like you too much, and saying we're friends is really me pretending there's nothing more going on.'

'I'm doing exactly the same, Jess, pretending to be your friend so I get to see you. If we both feel the same, that's great, isn't it?'

'No, it's not. See, I can't like you that way. Much as I want to, I can't.'

'Why not? We're both single and we both know there's this huge impossible-to-ignore attraction between us. I don't see what's stopping us.'

'You wouldn't.' I intended to stay calm, serene even, tonight, but my words come out as knives, attacking him again for his lack of understanding.

'OK. So tell me.'

I want to. Now I'm in front of him, all the words I planned to give him fall away. Instead, I want him to have the truth. He's looking at me with his concerned, kind face, and I want to tell him everything, because I know he'll be OK with it. More than that, I know he'll be kind, not just tonight but every time I see him afterwards. Olivia's right: there's no one better I can think of to have in my corner than Alec.

'It's my mum. She has something called Huntington's disease. It's bad. The disease is attacking the nerve cells in her brain, and it's affecting pretty much every part of her. There's the physical side of it, with her body failing her, but it also affects her behaviour and her memory. They say it's like a combination of motor neurone disease, Parkinson's and Alzheimer's. We don't know how long she has left, but it's progressive, and it's going to kill her.'

'Jess.' The pain for me as he says my name takes the breath from me. When I told Liam about Mum, the pain was only for himself and his bad luck in having been lumped with me. There's a comfort in Alec's sadness, especially when he moves towards me, not away. He joins me on the sofa, and we both watch him tracing the blue veins on the top of my hand with his finger until he can find the next thing to say.

'I'm so sorry. Is she, is she bad now or is all this to come?'

'It's getting pretty advanced now. Mum had early symptoms for years before she got diagnosed – clumsiness, becoming forgetful and having mood swings – but now it's attacking her brain more, her muscles are failing her. She's struggling to move by herself and her speech is going. Her memory is OK right now, but it's likely to deteriorate. She needs a lot of care these days.'

'Your poor mum. Do you have family to help out or is it just you?'

'Just me. My grandparents both died when I was little, and Mum was an only child like me. But there's a whole host of carers who come to the house to help out.'

'That's good.'

We fall into a silence. He's still holding my hand. I don't want to look at his face in case all the sympathy on it makes me cry, but I need to know what he's thinking.

'Alec?'

'Yeah?'

'Do you understand now why I can't see you?'

He takes his time to answer. 'Honestly, no. I'm struggling to see the link between what you've told me and us being impossible.'

How could he understand? He has two perfectly healthy parents living their life in Leeds. Plenty of people are walking around every day with sick loved ones at home, or in the hospital, and they still carry on. More broken than they once were, but they don't stop living. It's me I need to tell him about. There aren't quite so many people walking around knowing how they are going to die and how bad it's going to be. It'll be harder for him to argue against that.

If that's still not given him enough reason, I'll have to go on. I'll tell him about the rule I've made myself that I'm going to do this on my own, how I don't want to bring anyone else under the shadow of this horrible disease. How, after watching Mum suffering, I can't let myself get involved with someone, knowing, if things worked out, that's what they'd end up doing with me.

But I can't do it. I try to get the words out, but they cling to my gums, my teeth, hold onto my tonsils for dear life. Telling Alec about Mum isn't nearly as hard as telling him about me. Once I do that, I'll become a sick girl, and he'll start to pity me. I can't let him see me that way. Right now, Huntington's disease is tucked away in a dark corner of my brain, unseen and unheard. It won't always be – there'll be a time everyone sees it – but, for now, it's the most private piece of who I am, and I want to keep it hidden away, especially from Alec.

'Listen,' I say, ready to put an end to this and get out of his flat. 'You're lovely, and I am attracted to you, but it's not going to work. If it makes you feel better, it's not personal. I've made it a rule to stay single. My mum comes first. It would be great if you were fine with that.'

'OK.' It's all he can say. 'I will be fine with it. Not now, maybe. Now, I'm pretty gutted, but I will be.'

'Thanks.'

After a few strange minutes of holding hands in silence, I get up, and Alec follows me out. It occurs to me that this might be the last time I see him on his own. I'm sure there'll be plenty of run-ins at The Wishing Well, but it'll never be the two of us alone again.

'You won't tell anyone about this, will you? Aside from Olivia, I've made a point of not sharing it with anyone at work.'

'Of course not.'

We stand in his narrow hallway staring at each other. He has the key to the front door in his hand, but he makes no move to open it. Instead, he suddenly lunges towards me, wrapping his arms around me and squeezing my face against his chest.

'I'm sorry, Jess.'

I notice the movement in his throat as he tries to swallow down whatever he really wants to say to me. It's an effort not to make his case for us carrying this on, despite Mum being ill, but he's good enough to master it.

'It's fine,' I tell him. 'I'm glad I told you. At least you won't be thinking the reason I couldn't go out with you was entirely about the beard.'

'Excuse me? Why would I think it's the beard? Everyone loves the beard.'

'Do they?'

'Shit, Jess. You can't tell me this and leave. I'm going to have to rethink everything now.'

I laugh. 'Not everything. Goodnight.'

He opens the door and pushes his body back against the wall to make space for me. The hallway is so thin I have to shimmy past him to get out. Crushing myself against him is a mistake; I look up at his face, and all the control I've gathered for tonight falls away. His mouth, now smiling gently at me, is too lovely not to touch. I want one more memory of him to take away.

I spring upwards to meet his lips with my own, kissing him with such ferocity, I push his head back into the wall.

There's a terrible first moment when it's just me kissing him, but then he pushes back. My fingers trace the bones in his face, run down his neck before moving up to find his hair. There's a particular pleasure in pulling it off his face, ruining the careful style his hair wax has kept in place all day. His hands are less curious, they stay firmly round my waist so he can pull me into him so tightly not even a dust mote could fit between us.

I'm the one who pulls back first, apologising as soon as my lips leave his. 'I shouldn't have done that. I'm so sorry. I came to tell you there's nothing between us, and then go and do that. You must think I'm completely messing with you.'

'I wasn't thinking that at all. I was actually thinking it's the first time I've ever been pounced on. I kind of like it.'

'Oh God, it was a proper pounce, wasn't it?'

'Yep,' he agrees, and laughter erupts from us both. We try to contain it, but it's impossible. As soon as one of us manages to stop, the other starts and off we go again. We remain in the doorway clutching our stomachs until finally Alec gets himself under control, and I'm able to follow suit.

'Apparently, I have no willpower, so I should leave before I jump on you again.'

'Please do.'

I shut the door, only walking away once the laughter on the other side fades to silence.

Chapter Fourteen

Olivia is late for work three days in a row. It's not like her to dangle her sloppiness like bait in front of Jane, who loves the drama of a disciplinary hearing and is always on the lookout for new prey. We've all become experts at undercover skiving, especially Olivia.

But when she comes in on Wednesday at a quarter to ten swinging a Co-op bag and unloads a five-pack of jam doughnuts on her empty desk before taking off her coat, it's clear someone needs to get to her before Jane has the chance.

'Bloody hell, take off your coat and sit down quickly before Jane gets back. If she knows you've been to the shop before coming in, she'll have you on a written warning and doing the five o'clock post-office run for the rest of your life.'

'Don't worry. She's not even here. She'll be too busy planning this birthday party of hers today to worry what any of her lackeys are up to.'

'Or not up to, in your case. At least turn on your computer, throw a few files around your desk.'

Olivia's not listening. She's too busy ripping open the doughnuts in a way that'll make it impossible to reseal the pack and keep the others for another day; they'll be stale by lunchtime. If they're still around by then. If the way she's shoving the first one into her mouth is anything to go by, it doesn't look likely.

'What's with the sugar fix?'

'Here, you want one?' she asks through a solid lump of dough in her mouth.

'I'm good, thanks.'

'Tell you what,' she says in a break between mouthfuls, 'I could do with a morning out of the pit. Feel like making up some emergency filing so you can join me in the records room?'

The records room can be found in the basement of the old bank McAllister Lewis Glenn bought five years ago. The millions they spent refurbishing the place to be befitting of a top Manchester firm ran out before they got down to the basement. Damp, dark and with a vermin problem, it's the worst place the firm could keep their records, and spending time down there is usually the part of the job the girls and I try our hardest to avoid.

I look back at my desk, at the drawers stuffed with old case notes that should have been filed away months ago. At least if I deal with them now, I'll have some company that isn't of the four-legged kind for once.

'Go on, then.'

'Great. Let's have half an hour at our desks looking busy, and then I'll meet you there.'

At the allotted time, I grab my coat and scarf, both of which I'm going to need. Olivia's already in the basement, slumped on the only chair with her bag of doughnuts on her lap, her fur hood pulled over her face, obscuring everything but her sugary mouth.

'Come on, then, spill.'

'What do you mean, spill?'

'I mean you've been acting strange all week. You're never normally late and you never normally eat like you're in training for a boxing match. What's going on with you?'

99

There's a pause. Under her hood, her frosted bottom lip begins to wobble.

'Oh Jess, it's a mess.'

'What is?'

'I'm pregnant.'

It's cold down here. I pull my unbuttoned coat together until it's tight around my body.

'Oh wow. Wow! Congratulations. I mean, it is congratulations, isn't it?'

'Yeah. No. I'm not sure yet. I've only been with Rick for three months. Three months, and now we're going to have a baby. I'm not ready for a baby. Am I?'

She doesn't look ready. Right now, she looks like a frightened teenager. Despite the dirt on the floor, I kneel in front of her and put my hands on her knees.

'Of course you are. You'll be a great mum.'

I've never actually seen Olivia with a child, and she certainly doesn't display many of the traits most people would deem necessary for motherhood when she's arsing about in the office or out on the lash. But there's another side to Olivia, one she's shown me almost every day since I decided to tell her about Mum and me. She cares about people. She wants the best for them. Isn't that what being a mum boils down to?

'You think so?' she asks.

'Yes. This is what you wanted, remember? Before you and Rick finally got together, all you'd ever talk about was wanting to be with him and to have a gaggle of little Rick babies running around.'

She laughs. 'Little Rick babies. I did say that, didn't I? He's been brilliant about it, Jess. The moment I told him, he's been so supportive. It's what he wants. He's not stopped grinning since.'

'See. There's nothing to be worried about, is there? Unless *you* don't want the baby?'

'No, I do. I can't stop stroking my stomach. It's just this is massive, life-changing stuff, and I don't normally do massive life-changing stuff, do I?'

'Well, now you do.' I pull her forward into a hug. 'Congratulations,' I say through a mouthful of fur.

Olivia leans into me. She'd keep this hug going if I let her, but I need to be out of it. I let go and give her a stern glare. 'If you are doing this, you're going to need to stop inhaling cakes and start looking after yourself.'

She nods. 'I know. This is my fourth one. I'm totally gross, but I feel so shit. My head hurts, I've got old-man's heartburn and the only thing that helps is stuffing my face.'

'Fair enough.'

'It's horrible, Jess. I've never felt so crap in my whole life. I hope when it happens to you, you'll be one of those lucky ones who only finds out they're pregnant a few months down the line, and gets to tell everyone how fabulous they feel right until the baby pops out.'

'Yeah, sounds good.' She doesn't realise her error. She's too upset, and I don't correct her. This moment should be about Olivia, not me.

'God knows how I'm going to get on this afternoon. Knowing Jane, you'll all be on the champagne whilst I'll have to make do with sipping water. And there'll probably be nothing else on offer but prawn canapés and caviar on Melba toast. I'm going to have to sneak something proper up there to eat.'

'Do we really have to go?'

'To Her Majesty's rooftop birthday shindig? I'd say so.'

Aside from the initial stomach drop of dread when Jane's e-invite landed in my inbox at the start of last month, I haven't bothered to think about the party. It's all Jane's droned on about for weeks, but I'm more than adept at zoning her voice out, and, anyway, there've been more important matters to deal with.

Between Mum's stomach problems starting up and the constant bad weather that's made leaving the house every morning an endurance test, January has passed in a blur, and now February has sprung up under its coat-tails to grip me with a series of celebrations for Jane's fortieth I'll never be able to wriggle free from. Especially not a rooftop party at the office during working hours.

Never mind us being in Manchester not New York, it being February and pissing down; since the idea popped into her head, she's run away with it entirely. Rumour is there are going to be fire pits to keep us warm, a jazz band and even a specially designed cocktail named 'The Jane'.

'You know,' Olivia says, 'I think the best thing for us to do is to get back up there and make ourselves look snowed under with work all day. That way, when four o'clock comes, we can make out that we've got far too much to get through to break off for the party. Jane can hardly be annoyed with that, can she?'

'Please. There's no way she'll fall for that, knowing what we're like. Especially what you're like.'

'Maybe not,' Olivia admits. 'Worth a shot, though. And anyway, being down here's making me feel even more terrible than I felt before. I'm going back up. You coming?'

'In a minute. I do actually have some filing that needs to get done.'

'Meet you up there?'

'Sure,' I say.

'Don't forget to look rushed off your feet.'

'OK.'

Once the heavy metal door has shut, I take Olivia's empty seat and lean forward in it until my forehead is inches from my knees.

It hurts. It hurts so much I think I might be sick. But it's not sick that comes, only fat, pointless, stupid tears. I press my fingers against my eyes so hard it sends shooting pains into my forehead, but they still don't stop.

I haven't cried in weeks. Not when Mum's had a bad day, not when I've woken sweating with fear from one of the nightmares where I'm in Mum's place, where it's my body failing and all I can do is look out helplessly at a world that, increasingly, doesn't apply to me. Not over Christmas, when the loneliness was so intense I would press my ear against the wall to listen to the chatter of next door as an escape from the silence. Not even over Alec.

And now they come when there's no need for them.

I don't want children. The pain in my stomach isn't a pang for them. It's not the pang of knowing I'll never have my own moment where I get to pat my stomach and tearfully announce I'm with child. It's not the pang of knowing I'll never have the moment Olivia had, where, stick in trembling hand, I discover that I'm going to have a baby with the man I love. The one Huntington's sacrifice I've not struggled with is this one: having children.

It makes no sense to be this upset. Why break my heart over the thousands of moments Olivia's going to get and I'm not when I've never wanted them in the first place?

I make myself sit up. The black trousers I'm wearing are filthy from when I kneeled in front of Olivia. I concentrate on picking off the bigger specks of dirt and brushing away the dust until nothing remains, and the tears begin to slow down.

Once I've reached for the pile of folders at my feet and rearranged them into alphabetical order, the tears have stopped entirely. I set to work filing, slotting folders into their rightful place where most of them will rest, untouched, for decades to come. The light work does me good and starts to lull me back to a suitable state of calm.

Back in the office, Olivia is chatting to Maureen, the dough-nuts are out of sight and it's as if nothing has happened at all.

Most people clear out before four. Olivia and I stay logged on to our computers, and Olivia pulls out a stack of gossip mags she bought earlier. We stay in the office reading them behind Manila files until Maureen comes back down from the roof with hair twice the size it was before she went up there, telling us she's not going through with this on her own, and we're to get up there now.

The wind is so strong at the top of the building that it takes the three of us to push open the fire door to the roof. When we get outside, far from the scene of urban glamour Jane was hoping to achieve, it's one of absolute calamity.

Silver stools lie on their sides, and fairy lights against the railing droop morosely to the floor. Horizontal rain pelts the guests, forcing them to huddle under the sheet of corrugated steel usually reserved for smokers. Amongst them, a few young men in tuxedos try to weave through, carrying full trays of wet canapés that no one would dream of touching. A long trestle table, presumably set up to be the bar, stands empty. Boxes of Prosecco and lager have been dragged under the shelter and remain unopened.

On the other side of the roof, under a golfing umbrella, stands Jane wearing a black leather dress, gold sequinned Christian Louboutins and a man's suit jacket. She flails her arms in front of Mr Lewis, who is out of the circle of protection the umbrella offers and remains with his head dangling between his shoulders in a now-see-through white shirt. I turn away before I spot his nipples showing through. If I saw them I'd never be able to look him in the face again.

The best course of action would be to shut the fire door and return downstairs before we're spotted, only Maureen grabs our arms and frogmarches us to join everyone else.

'Everyone having a good time?' I ask. Maureen jabs me in the ribs.

'Sssh. Poor Jane,' she whispers. 'She must be devastated.'

'She doesn't look devastated. She looks like she's about to kill Mr Lewis.'

'Oh yeah, she's livid at him. Still, it's not nice for her, is it? She came up to the roof all dolled up, expecting a grand welcome and saw the lot of us huddled like sheep under here. Not even her Botox could hide the panic. "Don't worry," she told us, "the Manchester weather's not playing ball today, but there's no reason not to bring the party inside." Only there was a problem: Mr Lewis told her there was nowhere to go. All the conference rooms have been booked until six. Well, they've been arguing ever since. She wants him to free up a room for her, but he won't hear of it, says he can't interfere with his solicitors' work for the sake of a party.'

'And what? We're meant to wait around for him to change his mind? Fat chance,' Olivia says.

'I know. She'll never get her own way,' Maureen agrees, 'but what can we do? We can't leave without her seeing, and if she thinks we're abandoning her party because it's so awful, there'll be hell to pay in the morning. We're trapped.'

'Sod this. The only thing we'll need to liven up at this rate is the circulation in our legs. I'm out of here,' Olivia declares.

As soon as she's said it, Jane strides over, a fake smile glued to her face.

'Thank you all so much for coming. You'll be pleased to hear that my Harold's just got off the phone to Alec at The Wishing Well, and he's agreed to let us have the place for the next few hours. And, what's more, my darling Harold has put five hundred pounds behind the bar, with the clear instruction that Alec makes sure we all have a fabulous time. I told Harold we should have gone there all along, but you know Harold, nothing's too much for his princess,' she says, giving a high-pitched empty laugh before adding 'chop chop,' and sauntering off. Mr Lewis has already left the roof.

Olivia perks up at the new, drier plan and pulls me forward to join the rest of the guests vying to get off the roof. The rain washes my weak protests away.

I'm quiet as we make our way back inside, happy to let Maureen do the share of the talking as we line up in front of the sinks in the ladies, trying to calm our bouffant hair and wind-smacked faces. The vertical line between my eyebrows is deeper than ever.

Nothing to worry about, silly, I tell my reflection.

Alec isn't a problem. All I need to do is to remember that last time together, Alec shutting the door to his flat and us both laughing on either side of it. He's not going to be awkward or nasty. He's going to be the same as he's always been: perfectly lovely.

He's busy with a group of girls when we arrive, a solid smile on his face that doesn't move up or down despite the frequent rise of their laughter. His whole body is oddly solid, in fact. The girls sway on their stools, flick their hair, throw their heads back with laughter, touch the jewellery dangling from their ears and necks whilst Alec remains unmoveable.

I tell Olivia I'll get us both a drink and sit on a stool at the end of the bar whilst I wait for him. Within a few minutes, the girls grow still enough to finish the rest of their drinks, put on their coats and leave.

As they pass me, I'm covered by a strong waft of flowery perfume. A few of the girls are particularly beautiful – far more groomed and sleek than I am. Yet Alec was a statue before them. It's as if he didn't even notice. Something approaching smugness creeps in when the memory of my night with Alec leaps into my mind. Back then he was all movement.

'Hello,' he says, coming over, a little waver of uncertainty in his voice. 'I wasn't sure if—'

'It's good of you to let us have the place,' I interrupt. 'We really appreciate it.'

Alec nods. If we're going to have to see each other like this, it's really for the best to pretend there isn't this elastic attraction between us pulling us back to each other, no matter how far we try and stretch out from it.

'Oh yeah. No problem. To be honest, I'm still shocked you all deigned to come in here at all after the grand heights of a rooftop party. Take it you'll be making light work of my Prosecco stock?'

'I'm not sure it's going to be that kind of do. We're all absolutely freezing. The plan is to stay for a drink and get off as soon as we can, preferably in time to get our normal trams home.'

'Oh, OK. What can I get you?'

'What I really want is a cup of tea, but I'll settle on a lemonade. Two please.'

'Coming up. So how are you?'

'Good, thanks,' I reply automatically. 'The beard?'

He strokes his clean-shaven jaw line and smiles, revealing boyish dimples his mane had hidden. 'Yeah. I saw Tom last week, and he had a word with me about it. You were right – it turns out not everyone's a fan. In fact, he told me I'd long passed over from the cool side of bearded men to the skanky side.'

'You look funny without it. Naked.'

Shit. Of all the words I could have reached for in that moment I've gone for the one that catapults us back to the memories I've been trying to banish for the both of us. Memories that keep showing up like an outbreak of acne.

Whilst I'm shrinking into my bar stool, he laughs briefly, and grabs a glass from the rack above my head. Jane slinks over at the perfect time, wraps one arm round my waist and pulls Alec forward by his shirt to air-kiss both his cheeks. 'Alec, my darling, my saviour. What would we have done without you? What a joke those party planners were. They swore they'd deliver sophisticated chic al fresco, whatever the weather. Well, Harold's sitting back there now, writing the most ghastly review he can on their Facebook page. We'll show them,' she laughs.

Noticing Alec pouring lemonade, she turns to me. 'Nothing stronger? Come on, it's a party, for heaven's sake, and we're making up for lost time. We'll have three bottles of Prosecco, Alec. Jessica, help me with the glasses, will you?' When Alec returns with her order, she grabs a bottle and a single flute off the bar before returning to Harold, leaving me to the rest.

'I can't believe you have to work for that woman,' he says, shaking his head. 'Here, you want a hand?'

'No, it's fine. Give me a tray and I'll manage.' I slide off the stool and gather our drinks and as many flutes as I can.

'You'd best hurry up. She looks determined to get that stuff down your necks.'

'She will be. Heaven forbid we don't celebrate her birthday in a fitting manner. I'm sure she'll have ordered Maureen to propose a toast in her honour. Can't miss it. I'll see you later.'

'OK. Erm, I was kind of hoping to ask you something whilst you're here. How about you deliver those glasses, I'll make sure everyone's been served and we'll meet outside in five minutes?'

I should protest, remind him that two people who mean nothing to each other don't need to meet outside to talk, but I can't bring myself to. It's so good to see him, to relax into conversation with him. And without the beard, he's launched himself to model levels of handsomeness. Instead, I remind him that it's freezing outside, and he changes the meeting place to the stockroom.

Olivia's been watching our exchange. When I walk to the table, she's already smiling, no doubt wanting a recitation of every word of our conversation. Despite the understanding she professes to have about my rules, she still wants Alec and me together. I should join her, but, instead, I deliver the tray and veer off to the toilets for a few minutes of peace.

Alec's waiting for me when I emerge. He opens the black door at the end of the bar and holds it open for me to step through. Immediately, I regret handing Olivia my coat on the way in. The stockroom is every bit as cold as outside.

'Here, put this round you,' Alec says, taking his navy wool coat from the coat hook and handing it to me. 'I should have warned you that we were meeting in what is basically a fridge.'

'Thanks.'

The air is damp and close, and there's a smell of stale beer and something putrid I can't identify. I make a mental note never to eat food from here again. I walk over to the back of the room, past the shelves of wine and beer, to a pile of empty crates next to a freezer. Turning one upside down, I sit on it and pull the coat around me. 'Go on, then, what was it you wanted to say?'

'You sure you're OK? Warm enough? You know, if you'd rather, I could give you a ring later,' he says, running his fingers over the bottom half of his face, stroking a beard that's no longer there. Not ten minutes ago, he needed to talk, and now he's putting it off. I don't get it.

'Alec, whatever it is, just say it now, please.'

He clears his dry, phlegm-less throat. 'OK. Well, I've been thinking about our last conversation a lot. I really am sorry about your mum, Jess, but—'

'There's a but?'

'There is.'

'How can that be? Let me get this right: I tell you I can't be with you because I need to look after my mum, and you come back at me with a but. Most people would show some bloody understanding and accept that as a pretty good reason, Alec.'

'You're right. I do understand, really, I do. I've been doing some reading about it. It's awful what your mum's up against. I can't imagine how hard it is for her – and for you.'

I jolt as he says it. If he's been reading up on Huntington's, it won't have taken him long to find out about the chances of me inheriting the faulty gene from my mum. Is this what he wanted to ask? Does he want to know whether my life is going to turn out as horribly as Mum's?

'But,' I make myself say for him.

'But I can't pretend I agree with your logic about you and me. How looking after your mum means we can't see each other.'

Maybe he hasn't read enough. Still, I can't be relieved. Who the hell does he think he is? He doesn't have the faintest idea about my life, what it's like to watch Huntington's peeling off layers of my mum, knowing it won't stop until she's nothing more than a body in a bed, before finally taking her.

I jump up from the crate, letting the coat land in a crumpled heap behind me, and he puts his hands up defensively.

'Hear me out, OK? I know your mum comes first, and I know there'll be times you won't be able to think about anything else but caring for her. I'm OK with that. Now you've told me everything, I think we can make it work.'

'Listen to yourself,' I shout, storming past him and grabbing the handle on the door. 'A few Google searches and you think you're in a position to help me. You might think you know how it is now you've read about the shaking, the irritability and all those other symptoms you'll have found in a neat little list, but you don't have a clue.

'A person with Huntington's can change beyond recognition, do things that they would never imagine doing before the illness hit. That's why it's such a hurtful disease to watch. My poor mum. It's been the two of us since I was a baby. My dad was this waste of space, and she finally realised we were better off without him. After that, she had the odd boyfriend, but, really, she was happy being single, content with it being the two of us. Then, before any of the falling or slurred words showed up, months before we had a clue there was anything wrong, that began to change. She became obsessed with finding a boyfriend. She signed up to all these dating sites, and every waking hour she'd be consumed by trying to meet someone. This is a woman who would normally get dressed up a few times a month for a meal out with me or friends, suddenly going out until all hours, bringing back a constant stream of guys to the house. It was horrible. I'd wake up to strange men at the kitchen table and would have to watch Mum fawning over them. When they were there, she'd be cold to me, scornful even, making it clear I was in the way. And when those men didn't call her back, I was to blame. No man would want to shack up with a woman living with her grown-up daughter, she'd say; I should get a place of my own and give her some space.

'The more men who came and went, the more desperate she became to hold on to them. She'd try to keep them with money, buying them aftershaves and watches, taking them away for the weekend. There was this one man she met in our local supermarket, whom she took to Paris after one date.

'When she'd been diagnosed and the point came when I needed access to her accounts to help her manage the bills, I found out she'd been spending thousands on them. Not one of them stayed; they must have been pissing themselves, this woman throwing herself and her cash their way so easily. That's what Huntington's really looks like, Alec. If that sounds like something you can *make work*, well, good for you, because I don't have a fucking clue how to make it work, none of it.' I can feel the tears arriving, and I swing the door open, wanting to get out before he sees.

I've shocked him. His mouth is a perfect circle, and he's looking down at his shoes. There was no need to be so brutal with the truth. Only part of me needs him to understand. I need him to be horrified by it. If he's not, it raises too many questions, questions about him knowing about me, about whether I'm right keeping him away. Questions I can't allow to be answered.

'You're totally right,' he admits, disarming me enough to make me pause. 'Sorry. I don't know anywhere near enough to dare tell you you've made a mistake. I'm getting this all wrong. The plan was to run an idea of mine past you, and I've gone and messed it up.'

'An idea?'

'Yeah. So you've got this rule about staying single, right?'

'Right.'

'I get that. When your mum gets bad, you'll of course want to be with her all the time. The last thing I'd want is to be a distraction for you. But right now you're able to spend nights at the bar with Olivia, you were able to come back to mine that night. It makes me think there could be some room in your life to fill. I wondered if this logic of cutting out men might not be necessary quite yet.'

'Alec, I don't want a relationship. I can assure you I've absolutely no room in my life for having to dump someone further down the line when it gets too much, or for hurt feelings, for more bloody pain.'

'I know that. But I'm not talking about further down the line. I'm talking about now. You deserve to have all the good bits of a relationship, even if it can't last. All you need is someone who knows the situation, who you can enter into an agreement with about time limits and so on and, most importantly, someone who believes that whilst it won't be a long-term thing, spending any time with you is better than spending no time with you.'

I release the handle from my grip and step towards him, an amused smile sneaking out, despite my best intentions to remain outraged. 'And I take it you're that person.'

'I sure am. So here's what I wanted to ask: Jess, will you go out with me? For one month?'

Chapter Fifteen

The house is dark and full of sleep when I enter it, even though it's not yet eight. Mum's door is open a fraction, and I peek in to see her on the bed, her face turned away from me. Debs is snoring in the chair, a book open on her lap, her glasses fallen to the floor. I'd go in and retrieve them to prevent Debs stepping on them like she's done before when rushing to Mum, but I imagine Debs would rather have another pair of smashed glasses than Mum disturbed, so I leave them to it.

Exhausted, I pull on my tartan pyjamas, rub my toothbrush over my teeth a few times and use a baby wipe to get my make-up off. Once I've made sure I can't hear Mum, I collapse gratefully into bed.

Rather than spending a restless night hovering between fantasies of being with Alec – of the dates we'll go on, the time we'll spend hidden away in his flat, just the two of us, our legs tangled like spaghetti – and internal lectures about the importance of keeping to my rules, I force myself to make up my mind before I go to sleep.

Alec didn't expect an answer straight away. I thought I knew what my answer was and had agreed to wait before giving it to him only because turning him down flat seemed unnecessary. But replaying the conversation on the tram on the way home, my firm 'no' began to shrink and whither. He had only asked for a month. I'd never thought about dating someone for an agreed period of time, of having an expiration date to make sure all the bad stuff would be avoided. There's no rule for that. And a month with Alec is a tempting offer – until my phone vibrates on the bedside table, and I roll over to find a message from him.

Hey, just wanted to say thanks for not shutting me down completely. Even knowing you're thinking about this makes me happier than I've been in ages. A month together. Can you imagine? Well, that's all I wanted to say. Let me know when you decide. Xxx

Bad move, Alec. It's been hours since he asked me out, and he's already piling on pressure. How does he expect me to reply to that? To agree to his proposal, no doubt, forgetting the few days he insisted I have to mull it over. Just because he's capable of saying he understands my situation and appreciates there's a lot to think about doesn't mean he really does. I'll bet he's no intention of keeping it to a neat month. He probably thinks that once I agree, one month will become two, then three, and he'll have me for as long as he wants.

I make my decision. In the morning, I'm going to have to tell him I can't. I close my eyes, lulling myself to sleep with the thought that, come tomorrow, everything's going to go back to the way it was.

I've nearly convinced my brain to stop thinking about Alec when there's a knock on my bedroom door.

'Oh, sorry, love. I didn't think you'd be asleep yet. I've brought you up a hot chocolate.'

I shuffle up the bed and take the drink out of Debs's hands. She sits on the edge of the bed, in the exact spot Mum would so often sit when I was little and she'd read me a bedtime story, or when I was a teenager and she'd fish out the truth about whatever latest problem was causing me to be impossible to live with before deciding with me how I could fix it.

'Thanks, Debs.'

'What happened to the party? I thought it'd be the early hours you'd come crawling in.'

'There was a change of plan. We ended up in The Wishing Well, and I needed to get back out of there as soon as I could.'

'Why's that? I thought you loved it there.'

'I did until the barman asked me out.'

It's the weight of her on the edge of the bed, the way she's pulling the covers tight by sitting on them. I can't help but tell her, to see if she can do what Mum managed to do all those years, making me feel better by listening to me as I shared my latest bother.

'Oh.'

'Exactly. Well, to be precise, he asked me out for a month.'

'Eh? Why would he do that?'

'Because I told him about Mum and my rules, and he thought this was the best way to get me to agree to seeing him.'

Debs laughs. 'Sneaky bugger. Still, that's brilliant you told him everything. The Jess I first met six months ago couldn't even say Huntington's out loud. I'm proud of you, love.'

'I didn't tell him everything,' I admit, pulling the covers away from her and further up my chest. 'I told him about Mum, not me.'

'Why ever not?'

'Come on, Debs. You don't really think he'd have come up with this proposition if he knew everything, do you?

If he knew about me, he'd be running in the opposite direction, thinking what a lucky escape he's had.'

'You don't know that,' Debs chastises with every bit as much firmness as Mum would have if she were sitting here. 'You can't be deciding what people are thinking all the time. He's given you no reason to doubt him, has he?'

'No, but knowing about Mum and knowing about me are completely different. Anyway,' I say, handing her back the almost-full cup of hot chocolate. 'I'm not interested, so it doesn't matter. I'm tired and ready to forget all about it. Goodnight.'

'Night night.'

I turn on my side and pretend to sleep whilst Debs hovers in the doorway. Mum never hovered. She had no need to. When Mum was by my side, I would never be allowed to sleep until she was satisfied I was going to be OK.

Olivia's not in the office when I arrive at work the next morning. Neither is Jane. Knowing her, she'll probably have taken the day off to nurse her hangover, treating herself to a morning in Harvey Nichols to buy something designer and to eat eggs Benedict in the café rather than staying under a duvet eating crisps and watching *Bargain Hunt* like the rest of us in the office would prefer to be doing right now.

At eleven, when I've still not seen Olivia and have checked the toilets and basement to make sure she's not in hiding, I begin to grow worried. I ask Maureen if she's heard from her. She tells me she called in sick first thing this morning, a clear note of disapproval in her voice.

This is the first time I've ever known Olivia to call in sick. Normally, if she's unwell, she goes for the heroic approach of dragging her illness into the office and doing nothing all day apart from complaining how shit she feels.

It must be the morning sickness. When I left her last night to run for the tram, she looked dreadful. I imagine her sitting on the floor of her bathroom, curled up around the toilet.

My face a mask of concern, I approach Maureen's desk again. Without Jane, Maureen is in command and much more likely to grant my wish.

'Maureen, can I ask you a favour?'

'Course. Here, have one of these as well.' She hands me a near-empty pack of digestives, and I gratefully pull out half a biscuit.

'I'm really worried about Olivia. It's not like her not to come in. I think I'd best check in on her to make sure everything's all right. Would you mind if I took a longer lunch today? I'll stay later to make up for it.'

'Are you sure she's not off because she was so pissed last night?'

'No, she wasn't even drinking.'

'Oh.' Maureen has pale, freckled skin, the kind that flashes pink at the first sense of heightened emotion. Right now, her cheeks are magenta. 'In that case, absolutely. Get going now and, whatever you do, don't rush back,' she says guiltily, her doubts about Olivia being genuinely sick having been proved unfounded.

I knew her answer before I even asked, but still I give her a hug, accidentally crushing the biscuit in her hand against her white shirt.

'Look what I've gone and done,' I say, reaching forward to brush the crumbs off her.

Maureen bursts into laughter, a long line of bubbly giggles coming from her mouth. 'What are you like?' she manages to ask before batting me away with her hand and coughing very loudly to calm herself down while she brushes the crumbs off her shirt.

I wonder how much Prosecco she had last night, and, more importantly, how much of it is still in her system.

Too nice for her own good, Maureen. We all know it. With her sharp brain and eye for detail, the seasoned solicitors often choose to go to her to help with their cases instead of the paralegals, much to their chagrin. Technically, the admin department isn't meant to get involved with legal work. We're more like the boiler room, keeping the ship running smoothly below deck. Yet, Maureen's desk is often covered in cases she's been given to work on instead of file away. Like me, there was once a plan for her to work her way up the firm, but doing that would mean that eventually she would have to take on managerial responsibility. Everyone, including her, knew that she would be a terrible manager, far too soft and compassionate.

Thankful now for her softness, I grab my coat and leave my work abandoned on my desk.

It's strange being out of the office this early. The pavement outside, usually crowded with suits coming and going from the office, is empty apart from two women pushing prams and a group of tourists ogling over a guidebook, hoping that by straying off the beaten track they'll discover the real Manchester. I feel a thrill, like I've stepped into a parallel world I've never experienced before: the world of the un-workers.

The thrill fades when I notice the lights are on inside The Wishing Well; I'll have to pass it. I tuck my face deep into the cashmere scarf belonging to Mum I'm wearing. On my way out this morning, I accidentally picked it up from the coat stand. I shuffle past as quickly as I can without breaking into a run.

Eventually, I'll have to tell Alec his deal's off. I know that. Only, I couldn't face doing it this morning when I checked my phone. He'd sent me two more text messages. They sat there on my screen, his words waiting to be read, nice words that could make me waver. I deleted them without reading them.

Tonight, I'll send him a message, brief and polite, explaining that I can't possibly be with him, even for a month.

But for now I'm meant to be on Olivia duty. I shrug Alec out of my mind and enter the health-food shop on the corner of Felix Street. Ten minutes later, I come out armed with a paper bag full of supplies.

Olivia lives near to Alec's flat in the trendy Green Quarter, near Victoria station. There's just a hint of warmth in the February morning to make being out not an entirely miserable experience. I walk through a thin stream of shoppers near the Arndale centre and past the high-rise offices at the top of Ancoats Street, bag of goodies in one arm whilst stroking Mum's scarf with the other, feeling light and celebratory with the unplanned change in the day's events.

Arriving at her block, I find the door open. Instead of ringing her buzzer, I go directly to her front door, knocking on it loudly, expecting to wait whilst she hauls herself up from whatever surface she's lying on and makes herself look passable enough to greet her visitor.

Instead, after a few seconds, the door swings open and I'm greeted by a perfectly quaffed, well-muscled man wearing a hoodie and shorts.

'Hi.'

I must stare at him a fraction too long. Cautiously, he adds, 'Can I help?'

'Hi. You must be Rick. Olivia's told me lots about you. It's a pleasure to meet you,' I gush once I've got over the shock of it not being Olivia. It's nice to meet the man Olivia's so wild about. If it weren't for caring for Mum at the weekends, I'd have probably met him long before now. I expect he'll be pleased to finally meet me too.

'Hi. Olivia's not feeling too good right now. Is there anything I can do for you?' he asks in a neutral voice.

'Oh no, no. I know she's not well, that's why I came. I brought her these. To make her feel better.'

Rick takes in the paper bag I'm wafting in front of him but doesn't budge. I'm beginning to get the impression Rick has no intention of letting me in when Olivia emerges from the bedroom.

'Jeez, you look dreadful,' I say, trying to bend my voice round Rick's huge frame to get to her.

Rick turns to Olivia and gives her a puzzled look. 'This is Jess,' she tells him. 'You know, Jess from work, the one who has been covering my back these last few days so I don't get the sack.'

'Ah, of course. Hi, Jess. Come in, come in,' he says, finally relenting his position by the door and handing my bag back to me. 'Can I get you a drink?'

'No, nothing for me, thanks. I'm not staying. I only popped by to see how Olivia is.'

Rick disappears into the kitchen, and Olivia and I sit next to each other on her much-too-firm IKEA sofa. Far from it being the pigsty I've seen before in the few times I've been to her flat, her lounge is spotless. A small pile of magazines have been neatly fanned out on the coffee table, the carpet has been freshly vacuumed, the cushions are perfectly angled on the sofa, and I count four scented candles burning around the room.

'Yeah, Rick's been busy,' she says, smiling at my open mouth. 'He took today off to look after me, bless him. There's me thinking we'd curl up and watch daytime TV in between my trips to throw up, but he can't keep still. If you think it's clean in here, wait until you see the bathroom. Every time I'm sick, he's in there after me with his mop and a bottle of bleach.'

'That's nice,' I reply.

'Suppose so. I'd rather have gone for the duvet day, to be honest, the smell of pine isn't exactly helping with the sickness.'

'Ooh, here, this might,' I tell her, remembering the bag at my feet.

'Yay, you brought gifts. Give me.'

She empties the bag onto the sofa. Out tumble the box of raspberry tea, brown rice crackers, organic apples and packet of crystallised ginger.

'I went to that health shop on my way over. The woman there swore these were the best things for morning sickness, and she should know; she has four kids and was as sick as a dog with all of them.'

'Oh, great. Thanks, Jess.'

We both look down at the little pile between us, the contents of the worst goody bag I could possibly have brought her.

'Come on, what is it? Don't you like crystallised ginger?' I ask seriously before beginning to laugh.

'Love the stuff, especially with a nice raspberry tea to go alongside it,' she answers before bursting into laughter too.

Rick comes in to see what all the noise is about. As he stands there smiling at us, a flicker of irritation crosses his face. I have no idea what job Rick does, but I reckon he'd much rather be at it right now.

'I should go,' I tell Olivia, standing up. 'I'm only here because Maureen's in charge, and she agreed to let me check up on you. Best not take the piss.'

'So Jane was too wrecked to make it in, was she?'

'Yeah, I guess so.'

'Damn, that means we missed all the fun last night. I'd have loved to have seen what state she was in when she left The Wishing Well. Hey, you could ask your man for the gossip.'

'My man?'

'Yes, Alec. I saw you two sneaking off into the stockroom last night. Deny it all you like, but there's definitely something going on there.'

'How many times? There's nothing between us.'

'You sure?'

'Never been surer of anything,' I tell her.

She goes from jiggling with excitement on the end of the sofa to throwing herself back against the pillows, as if she's the one being rejected.

'Look, I'll tell you about what happened with him over lunch tomorrow, OK? You'll be back tomorrow, won't you?'

'We'll have to see,' Rick says in place of Olivia. 'If she's too sick, she's too sick.'

'Of course,' I answer.

'Yeah, *I'll* have to see,' Olivia replies pointedly at Rick. 'Come on, I'll show you out. Rick, put the kettle on, will you? Let's test this herbal stuff Jess has given me.'

Rick follows orders and returns to the kitchen without saying goodbye, and Olivia drags herself off the couch with an 'oof', putting both hands on the small of her back when she's vertical.

'Sorry about Rick. He's not normally so, well, rude.

Since I told him about the baby, he's developed this protective alpha-male thing. Drives me mad. He'll think the office has sent you over to check up on me, to make sure I'm really ill. Once I explain to him you're only here because you spotted a chance to bunk off for an hour, he'll be nothing but charming next time you meet him. Promise.'

Just before we get to the door, her face turns even greener, and she dashes to the toilet. I leave them to it, Olivia to her retching and Rick to his mop and bucket.

Walking back to the office, I replay the scene I've left.

She might have said she was sorry about his behaviour, but she wasn't. Not really. Instead of dust covering every surface in her flat, like I imagined, there was something else all over the place: happiness. I can't expect her to apologise for that.

Olivia and Rick. What I saw today isn't a blip; it's her future. I could have that too. I could have it right now.

If I said yes to Alec, I could have my own someone looking after me for a little while. I could have a little taste of not having to think about everything myself all the time. And Alec knows about Mum. Our time together wouldn't be based on a lie. Not entirely, at least. I could talk to him, properly, genuinely talk, without my teeth having to be clenched shut, guarding my mouth, making sure words that aren't allowed don't pass through.

I lean back into the idea. The warm, comforting idea of Alec's arms around me, of waking in his bed in the morning and lazily following him through to the lounge for his croissants and posh coffee.

For one month I'd have someone to eat with, someone I could watch a film with at the cinema, maybe even someone to go away with for the night. It would all make a dent in the savings fund, but I'll just have to budget more when it's time to go to South America. It'll be worth it.

Lunchtime has come and gone. By the time I turn onto Fletcher Street and the office comes into view, the glass entrance is deserted. Maureen will be starting to fret by now, growing panicked in case one of the bosses notices the empty desks around her and asks where all her staff have disappeared to.

I'll make up for it. I'll stay later tonight and let Maureen see me diligently working away when she picks up her coat to leave. That'll make her feel better. But before I do, there's one more errand I must run.

One that must be done now before I have another chance to think myself out of it.

I push open the door of The Wishing Well. It's quiet, and Alec's offering table service, taking down a late lunch order from a bustling table of half a dozen women so absorbed in their meeting they barely glance at him as they fire off their orders.

Without waiting for him to finish, I march up to him, my mouth at his ear before he's even had a chance to turn to me, and whisper, 'Yes.'

Chapter Sixteen

'This can't turn into love, you do know that?'

'Yeah, you've mentioned it a few times now.'

I can hear the clatter of the bar through the phone. It must be starting to fill up with the post-work crowd. Soon he'll have to go and see to them. It's a shame; I've become rather attached to this conversation.

'So what's next?' I ask.

'You mean there's more? What else can we possibly plan for?'

'Excuse me, it's important we get this sorted before the month begins. You wouldn't want to waste time during our dates going over the ground rules, would you?'

'No, I suppose not. Go on, then, hit me with the next one.'

'Hmmm.' We've already agreed to have six dates in the month, to have none of them at The Wishing Well and to each get to choose alternate dates. Oh, and that none of these dates can lead to love, so easy on the big romantic gestures. What else? I don't want to take the fun out of our arrangement completely, but then again, it is better to be prepared for what's coming.

'Oh, got one! What do you think we should do about other people?'

'Other people? Look, I'm a pretty liberal guy and all, but it might be a tad premature to consider introducing a third party into the mix.'

I let out a loud, snorting laugh, which earns me a few curious glances from my fellow tram passengers.

'No, you clown. I didn't mean that. As you well know. Do we keep this month for the two of us, or do we have dates that include meeting up with other people?'

'I think it should just be the two of us. Are you OK with that?'

'Yeah, that sounds perfect. Give me a sec.'

The tram is pulling into my stop. I gather the two Tesco bags stuffed with ready meals and wine and make my way off the tram.

'OK, I'm back. Anything else?'

'Well, there is one thing I've been thinking about.'

'Go on.'

'Sex.' The word wobbles out from his mouth like jelly. A sudden image of an awkward teenage Alec navigating his way through his first time with a girl appears, and I smile at it.

'Sex?'

'Yeah. See, normally that would come after a few dates, right? But as we've already been there, I was wondering whether we should pretend it never happened and build up to it again, or if we should, well, just crack on with it.'

'Crack on with it. What a delightful way of putting it. Oh, I don't know. Maybe we see what happens as we go along. Let's have that as the one thing we don't decide on before we start dating.'

'OK. Good plan. If we organise that side of it too much, there's the potential for me to end up feeling like your male escort.'

It's hard to hear him above the rapidly growing noise in the bar. I'm just about home so, reluctantly, I suggest we leave it there.

'One last thing,' he shouts above the din. 'When are we planning for this month to start?'

'I'll let you know.'

I let myself into the house. Mum's engrossed in an episode of *Pointless* and doesn't turn to me when I say hello, and Debs sounds busy with something in the utility room. I unload the bags, making sure to put the white wine in the freezer for express chilling, and head upstairs to my room.

I perch on the end of the bed and reach for an old cuddly dog an ex-boyfriend bought me to make up for kissing another girl in our sixth form. He went but the dog stayed. Squeezing it now for moral support, I get out my phone and type in a message, ignoring the sensible voice in my head asking if I'm sure this is a good idea: *Monday night. Your turn to choose first xx*

I lie back, putting my hands over my heart, enjoying the long-forgotten feeling of it thudding quickly in my chest.

Downstairs, Debs is still clanging about. Once my heart rate has reverted to normal, I return downstairs and find her in the utility room, head in a cupboard.

'What are you doing?'

'Shit. Bloody, bloody shit,' she shouts and emerges with her face screwed up, rubbing the top of her head. 'You gave me a fright. I didn't even know you were back.'

'Sorry, I didn't mean to scare you. Are you all right?'

'Yeah,' she says, her features returning to normal. 'I've lived through worse.'

'Good. What are you doing, though?'

'I was looking for the dustpan. Something must have been broken in your mum's room before I arrived; there's bits of glass everywhere.'

'Oh no. That'll be my fault. I left a few photo frames on the table next to her bed. I thought her jerkiness seemed to be calming down recently, so it might be nice for her to have a few reminders of her happy times near her. Was I wrong?'

'No, I don't think so, love. I've noticed it too – she's not been as restless this last week, and her arms especially have stopped jerking so much.'

'Exactly. I wonder how the frames got broken, then.'

'It could have been anything. It might not even have been your mum. There's nothing in the file about her getting worked up at any point today.'

With Mum having multiple carers, it's important that information gets shared amongst them and with me too. In the hallway on the table where Mum used to keep fresh flowers in a vase, there's a red A4 folder which each carer updates on a daily basis to record when medicine is taken, what Mum's eaten, how her mood has been and any other detail of her life they deem necessary to share.

When the carers first started, I would pore over that folder every night, telling myself that I needed to know everything because, essentially, I was in charge. Really, I was looking for clues that Mum wasn't as bad as the doctors had made out, that her case was milder. I wanted to discover that the carers weren't really needed, that Mum was doing pretty much everything herself and I'd been wrong to bring in help. But every entry proved that wasn't the case. When it became clear that there would never be anything in that folder to comfort me, I stopped obsessing over it, and it became just another thing we needed to help Mum.

'You're right, they could have been smashed by one of the carers.'

'Exactly.'

Debs finds the dustpan in the back of the last cupboard she searches in and passes me, squeezing my arm as she does. I should let her get on, should leave it at that, but I can't help myself.

'It's good about my mum, right?'

Debs freezes in the doorway, her back to me, and instantly I regret asking. Like with the folder, nothing good will come out of this.

'In a way, yes.' Turning back to me, she lowers her chin and smiles at me before continuing, in the same way she always does before telling me something hard.

I really shouldn't have asked. Mum isn't the first lady with Huntington's Debs has cared for. She looked after a woman in her sixties with the disease a few years before joining us. Aside from the warmth she brings into our home whenever she enters it, it's one of the things that made her so perfect for the job.

'It'll be a relief for her, yes, but you should know, Jess, it's really a sign of the disease progressing. As she moves towards the advanced stage of Huntington's it's common for the chorea to stop and for the Parkinson's-like symptoms to begin. Have you also noticed your mum's hands bending at the wrist towards her stomach? That's because of her muscles freezing. It's been a while since the doctor came out, hasn't it? Maybe we should schedule another check-up, just to see what's what.'

'Yeah, OK. I'll sort it.'

'Good. Better to know everything, right?'

'Right,' I force myself to agree.

'Anyway, you're back late. Have you eaten yet?'

'No,' I tell her, remembering the toad-in-the-hole I'd planned to have tonight and, more importantly, the wine.

'I've been to the shops, though. Got some wine. Fancy a glass?'

Debs shakes her head after an unusually long struggle over the answer. 'No, not when I'm working. Thanks anyway.'

I should let her get back to work, to the broken frames she needs to take care of. Yet the way she bit her lip before refusing the wine snags on me. She doesn't look quite right tonight. Looser, somehow. Her hair is down instead of in a bun, and her trousers are definitely crumpled, despite it being the start of her shift.

'Are you all right, Debs? Everything OK at home?' I ask lightly, feeling awkward for asking, even though I probably should be intruding a little more upon her life. Here's someone I see nearly every day, and I can't remember when I last asked her how she was.

'What, me? I'm fine. Don't be worrying about me. Go and get your tea sorted, have that wine. All's in hand,' she says, but her eyes do this strange darting thing where they can't stay fixed on me or anything else.

She shuffles past me to get back to Mum, a weak smile on her face, and I know she's just lied to me.

Chapter Seventeen

Our first date is to be a surprise. Despite my attempts to persuade him otherwise, Alec tells me nothing aside from our meeting point – at the tram stop where usually I get off for work.

I have no idea what we'll be doing. Unless he intends for us to walk any distance, whatever the date is it will be in the Northern Quarter. There are so many bars, restaurants and quirky shops, it's near impossible to come up with a good guess. After spending the weekend fretting over what to wear, I decide surprise dates aren't exciting but annoying.

I opt for dark-blue jeans, my nice cream chiffon top from Zara and a leather jacket. It's too cold out for the thin jacket, and I spend the tram journey with it pulled tightly around me, trying to stock up some warmth for when I have to get off at my stop.

It's not hard to spot Alec as I get off the tram. Monday nights are quiet in the Northern Quarter, most people opting for a night off the booze after the weekend, but even if the street was crowded, I'd still have noticed a man standing perfectly still on the pavement with a red rose held between his teeth.

'A good start on the no-romance plan,' I say, pulling the rose from his mouth.

'Come on, you've got to let me be at least a bit cheesy on our first date. Hi,' he says, and as he bends down to kiss my cheek, I catch the faint scent of the cut rose. 'This way.'

He sets off, and I try to keep up with his wide strides. In my heels, I've no chance to match his pace and end up walking behind him, unsure whether to shout for him to slow down or to continue to walk in a line until we've reached our destination.

'God, I'm nervous,' he says, eventually slowing down to let me get into step with him.

'You're nervous?' I begin to laugh.

'Why's that funny?'

'It's just you don't normally come across as the nervous type.'

'I'm not normally, but tonight I'm a mess. I caught myself shaking when I was waiting for you. I had to have a little pep talk with myself to force myself to stay put.'

'If it helps, I'm exactly the same. It's so stupid, though. I know you. I've never been nervous in your presence before, so I've no idea why tonight I've been feeling sick at the thought of seeing you. In a nice way, of course.'

'Of course. Nice sickness.'

He takes my hand as we turn left down Key Street, towards a row of restaurants.

'Ta-dah.'

We stop outside Viva Viva, and my heart sinks. I think of the cream top I'm wearing and how hard I'm going to have to try not to spill Brazilian barbecue on it. Should have gone for black. Always play it safe, I remind myself.

'Brazilian, lovely,' I say, looking up at him and smiling.

'That's not why we're here. We can grab something to eat later, if you're hungry, but we're wanted upstairs first.'

'Upstairs?'

133

Alec leads me through the half-empty restaurant, weaving through the tightly packed wooden tables until we're at the back of the restaurant. He nods to a waiter, who pulls aside a curtain next to the bar, revealing a narrow staircase. Still holding my hand, he leads me up into a small, dingy room, with walls painted red and yellow to compensate for the lack of natural light.

'We're here,' Alec calls out to a woman in the corner of the room with her back turned to us, her thick black hair in a plait running down her back.

'*Olá, olá.*' She comes towards us with an iPhone in her hand, the thin chiffon of her black dress swaying as she does, showing off her toned body. Alec leaves my side to kiss both of her cheeks. He only kissed one of mine.

'Jess, this is Marta. Marta's boyfriend, Jack, works with me at the pub. She's kindly agreed to give us a samba lesson.'

They both wait for my reaction. 'Fantastic,' I say when it's anything but. I'd hoped Alec and I would have a chance to talk tonight, not to fling ourselves around an airless room with a beautiful woman called Marta watching over us.

'Let's get going.' Marta returns to the corner of the room, plugs her iPhone into a speaker and loud, Latin music with a scarily fast beat fills the room.

'OK, you two. Let's learn the basics, shall we? Get you two moving. Alec, place your right hand on Jess's back and take her right hand with your left. Jess, you put your left hand on Alec's shoulder.'

We step towards each other, and underneath the naked bulb in the middle of the ceiling, I can see the colour change in Alec's cheeks. I bet he's wishing he still had his beard to cover it.

'Closer than that,' Marta says. She steps behind me and pushes me towards Alec, so our hips are almost touching.

'Better. OK, you're going to do some steps now. Samba is all about movement, the rise and the fall. Each time you move, you need to bend your knees. Alec, you put your left foot back, and Jess, you put your right foot forward. Now put your feet back together. Alec right foot back, Jess left foot forward.'

She teaches us a simple four-step routine and, at first, all I can think about is getting it right, so I won't look completely unco-ordinated in front of Alec. I'm concentrating so much my eyes don't leave my feet. Only once the moves are starting to feel a little more natural do I dare look up at Alec. He's still too busy looking at his own feet to notice. He doesn't need to, though, his body is moving to the music with a natural rhythm I don't possess, and I realise he's been leading me throughout.

'You're good at this,' I tell him. 'Much better than me.'

'What can I say? These hips don't lie.'

'Oh dear.'

At this, even Marta stops pretending she's not watching us to look at Alec and shake her head. 'I'll take that as my cue to leave,' she says. 'I've a class in here in half an hour, but you two can keep dancing until then.'

'Thanks, Marta,' Alec says.

Before she goes, she plugs in a disco light and turns off the overhead light. The track we've been dancing to finishes and the next song on Marta's playlist starts. It's much slower than the first and Alec slows his step to try and match it. I should be worrying about matching his speed and bending in a light, sexy manner, but all I can think about is the heat of Alec's hand on my back, the unchecked moisture on his lips, his breath on my neck when he moves in even closer.

Now we're alone, we could be laughing or making conversation like most couples do on a first date, but we stay silent, our bodies inches from each other, following our little routine diligently, aside from our roaming hands, until the overhead light switches on and a middle-aged woman in a red tassel dress apologises for interrupting us and switches the light back off.

'Drink?' Alec asks. We leave the room and file past a row of similarly clad middle-aged ladies lining up on the staircase until we're back in the restaurant and have the eyes of the diners and waiting staff on us. I smooth down my top and pull down my hair, trying to erase the evidence that Alec's spent the last half-hour exploring my body.

'I'm curious, what made you go for samba dancing?' I ask him once we're sitting on two bar stools next to the tiny bar in the corner of the restaurant and have ordered two glasses of wine.

'Seeing as you like all things South American, I thought you'd enjoy it.'

'I did,' I tell him, touched that he'd remembered, although the enjoyment didn't come from the music or the dance moves but being pressed against him.

We each take a sip of our wine, and I wait for Alec to say the next thing, but he remains as tight-lipped as he was upstairs.

'You're still nervous, aren't you?'

'You got me.'

'Why?' His idea to dance together has worked perfectly; I don't feel anything aside from the longing for him to touch me again.

'I think it's because it's our first date out of six. It kind of needs to go well, doesn't it?'

'It doesn't *need* to go well. This is like any other first date. If at the end of it you don't want another one, that's fine. You're not locked into anything, Alec.'

'I know. Only, I want this month to be perfect for you, and it starts with tonight.'

'Let's take it a date at a time, OK? And, for what it's worth, so far, this is the best first date I've ever been on.'

'Me too.' He puts his hand on my knee. 'OK, no more nerves.' He squeezes his thumb and forefinger together and twists them round like he's turning a switch. 'I'm turning them off.'

I take a huge swig of the delicious cold wine. 'Good. Shall we continue?'

'Yeah. So on a normal first date, this would be the part when I'd be asking you all sorts of insightful questions about where you live, what you do for work. Given that we're way past all that, I reckon we jump straight into the snogging section of the evening.'

I giggle. Feeling light with the wine, I lean into him, and we share a lengthy kiss. When finally I pull away, three girls are watching us from the table next to the bar. They quickly look back but not before I catch the longing in their eyes. I lean away from Alec and pick up my glass. It doesn't do to be smug.

When we've finished the wine and shared some olives, chicken croquettes and chargrilled halloumi whilst sitting at the bar, Alec offers to take me home if I don't mind the short walk back to his to get his car. I happily agree. We get to his flat building, and he doesn't invite me up.

The drive to mine feels much shorter than it did the last time he drove me home after I woke up in his bed. Without the snow or awkwardness, we're outside my house far too soon.

Instead of getting out of the car, I stay where I am, continuing to chat to Alec until I run out of anything to say other than goodnight. Before I go, I shuffle towards

him and kiss him one last time. He kisses me more passion-
ately now than he did in the restaurant. His hands begin
to explore my body again, my neck, my waist, my breasts.

'OK, I think that's enough for a first date,' I tell him,
pulling away.

'You're right. First dates should be proper and polite,
and here I am feeling you up like a horny teenager.'

'It's all right. I quite liked it.'

Alec grins and moves towards me again, but not before
I notice the time on his display.

'Sorry, that's your lot. I've got to be at work in the
morning. Tonight's been great, Alec. A perfect date – I'm
very impressed.'

'You should be. And now it's your turn.'

'It is,' I say, winking at him before getting out of the car.

The TV's on in the dining room when I get in, and
my light, frothy mood begins to ebb. Mum's not had the
telly on so late for months.

'Only me,' I shout.

Debs comes out of the dining room immediately, holding
a tray with an untouched glass of water and a bowl of
scrambled eggs.

'Mum not hungry?'

'No, she won't have anything. Says her throat is sore.
I'll keep an eye on her and try her again in a little while.
You going in to her?'

'Yeah, I'll just get a drink first,' I tell her, feeling the
saltiness of the olives and the wine merging. I go straight
to the tap without turning on the light and find a glass by
the sink. Debs follows me in, puts the tray on the island
and waits for me to finish gulping down the pint of water.

'Thought I heard a car out there. Was that Alec?'

'Yeah, it was.'

She flicks on the light and marches to the table, taking a seat and pulling out one for me, beaming as I sit down.

'Well, how did it go?'

'Great. We went dancing, and it was lovely.'

'How wonderful. I'm so glad you agreed to go out with him.' My bit of news has done more for her anti-ageing regime than any of the make-up she's piled on her face tonight.

'It was. And now it's my turn to come up with the next date. It'll be hard to find something to top tonight.'

She takes both my hands in hers. 'You'll come up with a lovely date, I'm sure. Oh, I'm made up for you, I am. Wait till you tell your mum. She could do with a bit of nice news.'

I pull my hands away. 'Absolutely not. I've told you I don't want Mum to know anything about it.'

'Why not, Jess? Look how happy you are coming back tonight. She'll be delighted for you.'

'I know. That's why I can't tell her. And you promised not to either.'

'I know I did, but it's such a shame for her not to know.'

'It's not a shame at all. This isn't long term, it's just a bit of fun.'

'You say that now, but you never know what might happen.'

She's still smiling, talking to me in the same way she would with one of her own children when she spots a mistake and gives them a nudge in the right direction.

'I know exactly what will happen. I'll go on five more dates with him, and we'll go our separate ways. That's the arrangement we've made, and we'll be sticking to it.'

Debs shakes her head and looks away from me out to the garden, despite not being able to see anything past our reflections in the window.

'I won't say a word. Not my place. But, Jess, I think you should consider telling her, even if it's only to say you've gone on this date. It's been a long while since real life ran through this house. Your mum's days are always about her illness, and your time with her is always about it too. Sharing this with her would do the both of you the world of good.'

Until it ends. If I tell Mum I've been on a date, she'll be delighted, of course she will, but she'll also think I've changed my mind, that I'm ready to share my future with someone. The disappointment she'll feel when I tell her it's over won't just be the disappointment any mother would feel for a daughter who has been unlucky in love, it will crush her, like it did when I first told her my intentions.

'No,' I tell Debs firmly. 'Mum isn't to know.'

Chapter Eighteen

It's snowing. Half-arsed flakes that dissolve the moment they hit the ground. All morning I've watched them from various windows in the house, waiting to see if they're going to get their act together or not.

There are two types of people when it comes to snow: those who panic at the sight of the first flakes dropping from the sky, cancelling plans, making sure their cupboards are stocked, and those who use the chance to show how tough they are, treating it like an enemy to be conquered, no matter what amount of devastation it creates.

It's just gone twelve now, and my phone hasn't bleeped once. Guess Alec belongs to the heroic, yet ridiculous, latter group. I'm meant to be picking him up in an hour for our second date: a trip to the Lake District.

As a firm member of the abandon-all-plans-and-milk-the-chance-to-do-bugger-all-in-front-of-the-telly group, I'd been hoping that Alec would be the one to suggest postponing today or at least bringing our date inside. I can't be the one to do it, not when this was my plan in the first place, designed to show Alec another string to my bow aside from drinking in bars. Mum and I would go to the Lakes at least twice a year when Mum's work was taking over a little too much and we'd been spending less time together. Mum would plan a walk beforehand and we'd set off in our walking boots, chatting for hours before we descended on a country pub for a stodgy meal before coming back home. I wanted Alec to see that side of me, and for me to have a chance to have a day like that again. But not in the bloody snow.

His cancellation message never arrives, and the time comes to collect him from his flat. I find Mum's car keys in the kitchen drawer. Mum used to love her gold Volvo, but it's been almost three years since she last drove it, ever since the chorea made it unsafe for her to do so. I used to borrow it all the time, but now, aside from the odd trip to the supermarket, I don't use it either. But this is my date, and I can't very well have Alec doing the driving.

I nip into the dining room to say goodbye before leaving.

'You look nice,' Mum says when I lean in to give her a kiss.

I feel my cheeks flush. 'Do I?'

'Different.'

'Yeah, well, I've arranged to go out for a walk with Olivia. I need to get rid of this post-Christmas blob somehow,' I laugh in an unfamiliar, pitchy tone.

'Lovely,' Mum says, smiling, most likely relieved I'm not spending a Saturday afternoon watching the soaps for once. 'Take a scarf.'

I turn to Debs to tell her I won't be long and to thank her for coming to sit with Mum whilst I'm out, but the look she gives me lodges the words in my throat. I've never seen her pulled so tight; she's piled all her features in the middle of her face. Her small mouth is so puckered it looks like a raisin.

I'm caught off-guard. I know she's not happy with me keeping Alec from Mum, but it's not that I'm seeing. Lurking underneath her disapproval, there's something else. Disapproval doesn't make you jittery, it doesn't make you wear creased clothes and have only one side of your hair straightened. It's not my lie that's squeezing her face together like that but something else.

I turn away from her, mumble a goodbye and bolt out the door.

It was a big favour I asked of Debs, to give up part of her day off to come to work, that's why I offered to take the Sunday-night shift instead. When I asked her yesterday before she left, she sounded perfectly happy to do so, telling me not to be daft giving her the Sunday off, she was happy to help out.

Maybe I should never have gone to her for this. Maybe I should have been clear with Alec that our dates need to be on weekday evenings only, when Debs is already here.

What if she doesn't want to be here at all anymore? What if she's had enough? Enough of the unsociable hours. Enough of us. All she does for us and still I ask for more, ignoring any advice she gives me to boot.

I shake my head, feeling the shame of my mistake and pick up my trusty sausage-dog-printed brolly next to the front door before setting off.

Alec is waiting for me in the small entrance hallway in his block. He looks like he's stepped out of a page of *Country Life* magazine with his khaki waterproof coat left open to show a navy-and-maroon tartan shirt, dark-blue jeans and tan walking boots that look a little too new.

'Hi. You been waiting long?'

'Oh, I'm sorry, there must be some mistake. I'm expecting a girl called Jess. You are?'

'Oh, ha ha. Very funny.'

'I know,' he says as we walk to Mum's car. 'You look great, by the way. The casual look suits you.'

I rub the sleeve of Mum's borrowed Barbour jacket self-consciously. 'Well, I can't very well go for a walk in this weather in a frock, can I?'

'Good point. It's bloody horrible out.'

'Yep. Do you still want to go, then?' I ask, hoping that he'll say no, and I can drive back home and let Debs get back to her family.

'Absolutely,' he says. 'A little bit of snow never hurt anyone.'

We get into the car and immediately he leans over for a kiss. The benefit of a second date. No need to wait around until the end of the date to decide if it's gone well enough before making a move.

By the time we reach Grasmere, the snow is falling with malicious intent. The narrow road wrapped around Windermere, Rydal and now Grasmere is clogged up with cars having to navigate carefully over increasingly dangerous terrain. I'm petrified.

Alec stopped trying to talk to me once we came off the motorway and the mistake of our outing became clear. He switched off the radio, straightened himself up in the passenger seat so he was no longer facing me and let me get on with it.

I manage to park in an empty car park off the main road, the starting point for the three-mile walk around the banks of Grasmere I'd planned out.

'You OK?' he asks.

'Fine. What shall we do? Do you think we should do the walk?'

He shrugs. 'Your date, your call.'

It's madness to go walking out in this weather, as the empty car park testifies. The driving snow and a sky the colour of pencil lead obscure the romantic views. Even if they were still in sight, we wouldn't be able to look at them anyway as we'd have to be looking at our feet the whole time to make sure we don't slip over.

'Come on,' I say. 'We can always turn back if it gets too bad.'

Within ten minutes my hair is as drenched as it would be if I were to submerge it in bath water, my lips are quivering and my ungloved fingers are painfully tingling. I hold my sausage-dog umbrella by my side, it having utterly failed me against the rougher elements of the countryside.

'I'm sorry, Alec. This was a bad idea. I should have cancelled this morning.'

'No,' he protests before starting to laugh. 'Bloody hell, look at the state of you.'

'I know. I'm a mess,' I say, trying to straighten up. 'To think I want to climb to Machu Picchu one day.'

'Lucky for you, this is Cumbria not Peru. Come on, let's find a pub to warm up in.'

We find a hotel with a pub attached in the centre of Grasmere's quaint village and park outside. Alec takes my hand as we walk in and, for the first time all day, this date begins to feel like it was a good idea. The earthy smell of a real fire welcomes us, and I'm pleased to find the pub is as quaint and untouched by the world outside as Grasmere is itself.

'So how serious are you about travelling?' he asks once we've ordered two hot chocolates and are sitting next to each other on a studded leather bench running the entire length of the pub.

'Very serious indeed. Some people put their ambition into careers, some into money, I put mine into seeing as much of the world as I can.'

'That's good. I'd like to do some travelling too one day. It's embarrassing, but the furthest I've ever been is Tenerife with my mum and dad when I was a teenager. Ellie was terrified of flying and could only bring herself to get on a plane if the destination was less than two hours away, which was rather limiting, as you can imagine.'

'Yeah. I'm not great with flying either. Not without copious amounts of gin, at least, and even that doesn't completely block out the fear.'

He laughs. 'So how are you going to fare going to deepest, darkest Peru, then?'

'Probably not great, but I figure it's something that will have to be done. When the time comes.'

'And when will that be?' he asks bluntly before his brain has time to catch up with his words. 'Sorry, forget I asked that. I bet it's hard to plan anything with your mum right now.'

'It is.' The admission is alien to my lips. I never speak about this at home. How could I? I could never suggest to Mum or Debs or any of the other carers that I had plans to leave when the time was right. They'd all know straight away when that time would be: when Mum was no longer with us.

It's different with Alec. He doesn't know Mum, he just knows me. Instead of him tying Mum and I together like everyone else we know does, instead of looking at me as some future mirror image of Mum as she is now, and how she's going to be, I'm on my own in Alec's eyes.

'There's no way I could go now. I wouldn't want to. Mum needs me and I need her for as long as I've got her. Anyway, it'll cost a fortune to go. A fortune I'm way off having.'

'That sucks. I'd offer you my riches, but as a lowly barman, there's not much in the pot.'

I laugh politely, before diving in with my own question for Alec, one that's been on my mind ever since that morning in his flat.

'What did you do before you were a barman? It must have been something well paid for you to afford the new flat, the car, the nice clothes. What was it?'

'How do you know I wasn't a particularly well-paid barman in Leeds?'

'Come off it, there's no way that's what you did. No way you'd be able to set yourself up so comfortably on a barman's wage.'

'OK, you're right,' he relents. 'I was actually a chartered accountant for a big firm in the city. Started there after I graduated and qualified through their training scheme. I was very sensible for a very long time.'

'That sounds more like it. And now?'

'Now?'

'Yeah, why the dramatic change? I bet you could easily have found a job here as an accountant.'

'I could have, yeah, but I figured if I was going to make the break from Ellie, move away from everything, I should pluck up the courage to change my job as well. I never liked it, not really. Every time I put on a tie, I felt constricted; sometimes, I'd look up from my cubbyhole in the open-plan office and would feel like I wasn't breathing.'

I try to picture Alec in an office like mine, keeping his head down for hours at a time, but fail. He's too large, too bright for the landscape, and I can't make him fit.

'I get that,' I say. 'Doesn't explain why you went for a bar job.'

'Well, for a start, bar jobs are pretty easy to come by, there's no long wait before you start. It was a good option to get some money whilst I got my new life off the ground. I never imagined I'd enjoy it so much. So much so, it gave me a new plan: I'm going to save up and open my own place. Somewhere with good ale, a cosy atmosphere, regulars. Basically my own version of The Wishing Well.'

'That's great. Sounds like you've got it all figured out.'

'Almost,' he replies, bumping his hip against mine.

Outside the snow is coming down even more heavily. I'd been so busy enjoying being close to Alec, I forgot to worry, but seeing the covering of snow on Mum's car that's fallen in the last half-hour, the panic arrives.

'We need to go,' I say, standing up and walking out without waiting for him to put on his coat.

'OK, OK. Don't worry, we'll be fine.' He puts his hand on my shoulder as we walk out into the snow and we both look down to see how far up our boots it is.

'Are you going to be OK to drive, Jess?'

'I have to be. Debs is with Mum, and I need to get back.'

'OK. Let's get going, then.'

It takes us two hours to drive from Grasmere to Ambleside, the next town along. I fight back tears as we come against another snaking queue of traffic trying to make its way out of the Lakes. The M6 is miles away.

'Why don't we stop for a bit?' Alec's face is tight with concern. He's right. This is pointless. The snow is still falling; for all we know, roads could be closed up ahead, and we'll be queuing for nothing.

'I know you want to get back,' he says gently once I've parked in Ambleside, 'but it's not looking good. It'll be dark soon, and I'm sure your mum and Debs won't want you driving in these conditions in the dark. Why don't we see if there's a B and B with a room for the night, and we can head back first thing?'

There's the faintest pull of a smile on his face after he's said it. Concern aside, he knows what he's suggesting.

'Are you proposing we spend the night together on our second date?'

'Yes, I am. Only because of the weather.'

'Of course.'

He leans across the car and kisses me. His hands go up to my damp hair, and he pulls me closer to him so our lips are meeting over the gear stick. He wants more than my lips, I can feel it in every movement he makes.

'I say we find that B and B,' he says through jagged breaths when he pulls away.

We get out of the car and start to walk towards a row of terrace houses, all with lace curtains in their windows. All but one has a sign swinging outside its entrance saying: NO VACANCIES. We try the odd one out and are in luck. The owner tells us she has plenty of space, but we're lucky to have come in now, as it's just been on the radio that there's been a crash outside Lancaster and the M6 is shut southbound.

'How many rooms will it be?' she asks before adding, 'I never like to be presumptuous, you know.'

Alec turns his body to me but can't meet my eye. We both know what lies ahead for the rest of the evening. I want to bite my lip against the desire surging through my body, but before he can answer for us, I say, 'Two please.'

Chapter Nineteen

Ambleside is filled to the brim with cafés. I sit at a table in the window in the quietest one on the high street and wait.

The sky is cloudless and summer-bright. Inches of snow cover the edges of pavements and the sad patch of lawn outside the main hotel, but the council here have been busy this morning, out gritting the roads and pavements so normal life can resume after the chaos of yesterday.

A large group of walkers in cagoules of every colour congregate outside Fat Face and chat animatedly before a large man with a red bobble hat and laminated map claps his hands to bring order and begin the journey. I smile as two women exchange a look and hover at the back of the circle round him, thinking that would be Olivia and I.

My head snaps back to the door of the café when the little bell above it tinkles. Alec has to stoop slightly to get through it. Once he's in and back to his full height, he takes off his black hat and rakes through his hair with his fingertips. A stab of desire pierces me.

'Hi. Sorry I'm late. I wasn't sure what coffee shop you meant. There are so many, I . . .' he trails off and takes a seat opposite me.

'It's OK. Did you sleep all right?'

'Not bad. You?'

'Not bad.'

We drift into silence, and the waitress takes it as a sign to approach.

'Hi, how are you?' Alec asks her.

'Good, thanks,' the young waitress replies, barely able to look at him.

I listen to the friendliness in his voice, the inherent niceness of him as he orders a white coffee and a teacake. I want to stroke his arm to show him I've noticed it, but I stay where I am.

'What happened last night?' he asks once the waitress has gone.

I could tell him I had a headache or was tired from the driving. He'd understand that. I grapple between the lie and the truth under his gaze.

'Jess.' He prises my hand away from the label I'm peeling off from the ketchup bottle on our table and places it in his. 'Tell me.'

I do as I'm asked.

Last night was a close call. If I had gone into a bedroom with him, I'd have gone in as a liar. He isn't getting to know me like he thinks. We aren't getting closer. How can we be when I'm keeping a colossal piece of me from him? As I lay longing for him in my cold bed last night, I knew there would have to be a trade-off: the truth for him. More than my worry about telling him, more than the fear of seeing pity, or something worse, in his reaction, is the fear of not getting to spend the rest of this month with him in it.

'It's not that I don't like you. I do, I really do, but I couldn't share a room with you last night knowing where it would lead. It wouldn't have been fair to you.'

'Fair? What do you mean? It's not like we've not done it before.'

'I know, but that was a mistake.'

He recoils slightly from the sting in my words, and I rush on to try and take it back.

'That first night was the result of too much drink. Last night, if we'd stayed together, it would have been because of how much we like each other after these few dates. I couldn't go into that room with you knowing what would happen when I've not been completely honest with you.'

'About what? Jess, we have the most upfront relationship any two people could possibly create.'

'Not quite. I've told you some of the truth about my life and why I can't be with you, but not everything. I wasn't going to tell you more. I was going to have this month with you and then go back to the way it was before we spent that first night together. But the more I get to know you – to like you – the more I know that's wrong. You should know everything before we continue with this.'

'I'm listening.'

I take a deep breath and begin. 'One thing about Huntington's disease that makes it so devastating to families is that it's hereditary. A parent has a fifty per cent chance of passing it on to a child. There's a test you can take to find out if you have it, and I took it three years ago. It was positive. I'm going to develop Huntington's disease, just like my mum.'

His face darkens like an internal light bulb has been switched off.

'I should have told you from the start. I'm sorry.'

'No. Don't apologise about this to me. Or to anyone.' His voice is fierce. 'I knew it was a possibility ever since you told me about your mum, and I did some reading about it, but I promised myself I wasn't going to ask. I can't even begin to imagine what it's like for you. I'm only glad you felt you could tell me.'

Relief threads through my veins to my heart, slowing it down, steadying it. *It's OK, it's OK*, it seems to beat.

He leaves his seat and comes round the table, kneeling by my side. He wipes his eyes with the sleeve of his tartan shirt and pulls me into a hug. His shirt smells slightly damp from yesterday's snow but there's a stronger smell of soap, the same B-and-B-issued soap that's on my body after my shower this morning. He begins to place gentle kisses on my neck, on my earlobe, on my hair.

He knows and nothing's changed. For the second time, I've trusted him with my horrible truths, and for the second time he's rushed towards me.

I'm falling for you. The thought is so sudden and so unguarded, I push myself out of Alec's arms and excuse myself to go to the ladies before he can read it on my face.

I almost wish he'd been horrified like Liam, or flung a barrage of questions at me like Olivia. This immediate, unflinching kindness feels dangerous to be around. There's too much temptation to lean into it and never pull away again.

'What do you want to do now?' I ask, once I've calmed myself in the ladies and returned to sit down opposite him again.

'Now I know? I want to go back to my room and get into my squeaky single bed with you for the rest of the day, but checkout was at eleven, I've got work at five and you need to get back.'

'I do.' Debs's flat, humourless voice from last night's phone call when I told her I wouldn't be home comes back to me. 'Do you still want the rest of our dates, then?'

'The four more dates we have? Yes, I still want them. I want more, you know that, but this is what you agreed to. Four more dates with the most beautiful, least practical, loveliest girl I've ever met. Why wouldn't I want that?'

Because we're going to get hurt, I silently reply.

'Come on,' Alec says eventually. 'We'd best go.'

We get back into Mum's car, set the heater on full and wait for the snow to thaw enough so it's safe to drive. I let a long silence grow around us once I set off. By leaning forward over the steering wheel and squinting a bit, it's easy to pretend it's because I need to concentrate on the road. But I'm not doing it for that. If he talks any more, I'm going to blurt out the darkest of all my secrets, the one he really can't know.

I'm falling in love with him.

Chapter Twenty

Debs calls as I'm leaving work on Monday evening, and I do a strange thing: I don't answer it.

Looking at her name flashing on the screen, I know something is wrong, and I can't bring myself to hear it. Instead, I let Debs tell my voicemail whatever it is she needs to say. Once she's hung up, I force myself to listen to the message. Amidst much garbling and many profuse apologies is the let-down: she's not coming tonight.

If only she'd put on a hoarse voice or fake coughed and spluttered through the message, I wouldn't have been so worried. That she rang so late, didn't pretend to be ill and didn't give any reason, in fact, for not coming terrifies me.

I don't mind sitting with Mum tonight. Most likely, I would have spent the evening with her and Debs anyway, like most nights. What I do mind is Debs's disapproval of me impacting on the job we pay her to do. When I got back from the Lakes, she was in a foul mood, rushing off before telling me how Mum had been, and now this. I've never seen her as an employee before – I haven't needed to – but thanks to her skiving, we've been slotted into our true positions. As her employer, I want answers.

I make a decision. Clare, Mum's occupational therapist, is with Mum right now. I give her a call and ask her to stay on an hour longer if she can.

Instead of getting on the Metro, I take the bus to Withington. The journey is only ten minutes, but when the bus pulls away, leaving me at the entrance to a maze of terrace houses, it's obvious the next phase of my journey is going to take longer. I trail around hopelessly, trying and failing to find Poppy Avenue. I take out my phone to help, but it dies on me. Eventually, I have to bother a young mum pushing a pram with a crying toddler inside, who wafts her hand towards the direction from which I've come and gives me some rushed directions that don't help at all.

The bus journey and circling of streets before finding Debs's must have jiggled some of the anger out of me. Now I'm here on her doorstep, I hesitate, unsure whether I should have come. But here I am. I pull my rage back up like a pair of sagging tights and press the bell of number forty-two. It's a musical bell that plays a tinny version of 'Greensleeves' for so long that the door is opened before the final notes have chimed out.

A woman with curled platinum-blonde hair and a huge bust threatening to pop the buttons of her blouse greets me.

'Hi. Can I help you?'

I lean back to look at the door number on the wall, double-checking this is indeed forty-two, before asking if Debs is in.

'Yeah, I'll give her a shout. And you are?'

'I'm Jessica. Debs looks after my mum.'

A warm, wide smile breaks out on the woman's face, and it's clear then how much she looks like Debs. 'How lovely to meet you. I'm Lauren, Debs's youngest. God, Mam talks about you so much, I feel like I know you. She's always saying we'd get on like a house on fire and we should go out for a drink. I'll have to get your number before you go.'

'I'd like that,' I say, and I mean it.

'Come in, come in.'

I follow her into a dark, narrow hallway, which Debs has inexplicably painted maroon. Debs's house is made up of a row of rooms. First we enter the lounge – a formal room, also red, which, judging from the cool air, doesn't get used much – before going through to a much snugger sitting room dominated by a plasma TV above a fireplace with no fire; just a recess Debs has filled with a vase of artificial lilies. There's a final door in the corner of the sitting room leading to a small, square kitchen and, finally, at the back of the house, is an extension big enough for a dining table and a fridge freezer.

Debs isn't in any of these rooms.

'Can I get you a drink?'

'A cup of tea would be nice.'

'Coming up. I'll pop the kettle on and go and get me mam for you. Take it she's told you, then?'

'What's that?'

'About Dad. I'll kill him the next time I see him. He's never exactly been known for keeping a cool head, but this is ridiculous. Fancy packing up and leaving when things don't go his own way. He's like a spoiled child.'

'Your dad's left Debs?'

Lauren whips round from filling the kettle and stares at me, mouth open. 'Shit. I thought you knew. Thought it was why you were here. My dad walked out on Mam this weekend.'

'Oh no, I had no idea. When exactly did he walk out?'

'I thought you knew,' she says again. 'On Sunday, when she came back from yours. He'd been getting on at her a lot over the last few months about her job. God, sorry, this is awkward.'

157

'No, no, it's fine. I want to know. Carry on.'

'Truth be told, he'd never liked Mam working, full stop. She'd had so many years at home looking after us lot, I think Dad assumed it would always be like that. When I left home, though, Mam wanted to do something to fill her days. That's when she went into caring.

'Dad was used to having all his meals cooked for him, a nice clean home to come back to, and he didn't like the inconvenience of Mam being out the house. When her first patient passed away about six months after her starting the job, Dad thought that might be it, that she'd got it out of her system and all would return to normal, but then she got the job with your mam. She kept telling him how much she loved it, but that didn't matter one bit to Dad. When she got back, he told her he'd had enough. It was either him or the job. She chose the job.'

My hands fly to my face. 'Oh God, I'm so sorry, Lauren. If I'd have known there were problems, I'd never have asked her to come over this weekend. Is she, is she all right?'

'I'm fine,' says Debs, leaning against the kitchen doorframe. Looking at her, everything says the opposite. The skin around her eyes is puffed up and not far off the shade of her hallway, and her hands pull at a mangled tissue. Her hair is unwashed and falls in lank strands around her face.

I rush towards her, pulling her into a hug.

'I'm so sorry, Debs. I should never have asked you to work on your days off. I'm so sorry.'

'Don't be daft,' she says, pushing me gently away so she can take over the tea making from Lauren. 'It takes more than that to break thirty-two years of marriage.'

'But you should have told me things weren't right at home. You could have had time off, could have tried to fix things.'

'Listen, when you're married to someone who can't bring himself to be happy for you, can't conjure up the smallest shred of enthusiasm for the things you love, you realise there's not a lot to fix.'

'Don't say that, Mam. Dad needs to cool off. He'll soon be back.'

'I don't want him back,' she snaps at Lauren. 'I don't.'

'Cut it out, Mam,' Lauren warns. 'It was just an argument.'

'It wasn't just—' Debs begins, but Lauren is already walking through the back door, vape in hand.

Debs places a teapot on her well-worn wooden table, and we sit down together. It's strange seeing her in her own home, after all these months of her being in our house. Where Mum and I have always strived for tidy minimalism, Debs's house is overflowing with clutter – the fridge is covered with magnets and scraps of paper; an entire wall is given over to collages of smiling children; her work-tops are filled with appliances and jars, leaving very little room to prepare food, yet there's a well-worn-in smell of home-cooked meals.

I'd always thought Debs fitted in perfectly in our house, but seeing how she lives, I'm not so sure she'll have felt that.

'She's always been a daddy's girl, has Lauren. I think she's still under the impression Ray can do no wrong. This'll hit her hard.'

'Is it really for good, then?'

'I don't know. Truth is, there've been plenty of times we've come close to breaking up over the years, and we might have done it, if it weren't for one grandchild coming along, then another and another. The time was never right for it.'

'And you think now's the right time?'

'Maybe. I'll tell you what, though, no matter how often I've thought about it, the whole thing's still come as a shock.'

Debs unfathomably gulps down her scalding tea, and I busy myself picking non-existent threads from my coat.

'So you and your husband breaking up is nothing to do with me?' I make myself ask.

'You? Course not. Why would you think that?'

'It's just you looked so angry at me when I got back yesterday, and when you rang earlier, I thought you'd had second thoughts about looking after Mum, about being in our lives.'

'Jess, this is about a pillock who can't accept his wife wants to do more than cook his meals and wash his socks, nothing more.'

'OK. That's good.' If Debs wasn't sucking her bottom lip between her teeth, I'd be relieved.

'That said, I still think you're wrong not telling your mum about Alec. You're happier than you've been since I've known you. I can see it and so can your mum. I think you should tell her why.'

'Let's not get into this again.'

'Why not? Someone has to talk some sense into you, love.'

'I've got plenty of sense when it comes to Alec and me, thanks.'

'Have you?'

I don't want to get annoyed at Debs. This is her hour of need, and I should be nothing but calm and supportive. But she's getting into the wrong conversation.

'Yes. We've got a good plan, one that's working. I'm not telling Mum because there's no need to. I've no idea why you're sitting here encouraging me to make it more than it is, especially now—'

'What? Especially now my marriage is over? Before all this, Ray and I loved each other for a long time. At least there's that. But you? You're not going to squeeze a great deal of love out of six dates, are you? Not enough to last you.'

There's no arguing with this woman, and I can't summon the energy to try. 'Maybe not. Anyway, that's not important now. You should take the rest of the week off.'

'No, no, I—'

'I insist. We'll be fine. You'll need some time to deal with this, and you don't need to be worrying about us.'

'I think I'll always worry about you,' she tells me, rubbing the back of my hand.

I get up to leave, and she follows me through the warren of rooms to the front door.

'You'll be all right?' I ask.

'I'll be grand. Lauren's insisted on staying with me for a few nights. I wish she wasn't staying, mind. I'm going to need to get used to being alone.'

'You sure you don't need anything?'

'Just for you to get back to your mum and to stop fretting about me,' she says, smiling, looking in that moment more like herself than she has for weeks.

Chapter Twenty-one

Whenever Dr Baker has visited our house over the last two decades, it's always struck me, as I've watched him hopping from foot to foot in the hallway, taking off his coat but keeping his hat on, in what I always imagined was an attempt to keep any more energy leaking out of him, how ill-fitted he is for his profession. With his Peter Kay levels of joviality, he might well have enjoyed great success on the telly if he hadn't followed his calling into medicine.

Unfair, perhaps. After all, for many years he invariably would give good news, and for that he was very well suited: *'It's only a cold; it will clear of its own accord.' 'No need to go to hospital for that rash; it's nothing serious.' 'Here, drink this yellow medicine, and you'll be right as rain before you know it.'*

For the good news, Dr Baker was excellent. It was the bad he struggled with. Not because he was incapable of speaking it. He delivered his news calmly and clearly. The problem was that no one ever believed bad news could come from him, which made it far harder to digest.

When I hear his familiar heavy knock and open the door to his ruddy cheeks, tweed flat cap and red-and-blue-striped blazer, I let myself believe it again: the belief that something good is going to come of his visit. Happily, I lead him into the dining room, asking about his day and how many more house calls he has to make before offering to nip out and make him a cup of tea whilst he has a 'wee chat' with Mum.

Waiting for him in the kitchen, I don't allow myself to remember that any good news related to Huntington's could only ever be a pebble skimming the lake of Mum's illness before sinking out of sight. Instead, I hum the latest Little Mix song. Loudly. Determinedly.

At my insistence, despite her attempts to convince me she should be coming back, Debs has taken the last three nights off, and I've looked after Mum at night after work. Out of sheer exhaustion this morning, I decided to take the day off. I left a message on the office answering machine at six this morning, knowing no one would be there yet, explaining I'd been throwing up all night and couldn't possibly come in and spread my germs. In actuality, I'd been up all night watching *QVC*, bought a face cream and new handbag and drunk toxic levels of coffee to stay awake.

Seeing as I'm off on a weekday for once, it's a good chance to find out how Mum's really doing.

Dr Baker comes to find me in the kitchen less than ten minutes after going in to see Mum. I turn to him, beaming, waiting for the reprieve.

'I've left your mum watching TV. I trust that's OK?' he asks.

'That's great.' I hand him his tea and motion to the breakfast bar stools for him to sit. 'Did you notice it? The lack of chorea?'

'Yes. I agree; it seems to have calmed somewhat. Although, I did notice some dystonia – muscle contractions – in her wrists and hands. It's not that the movement problems have gone, Jess; it's that they are changing.'

'I know. Mum's carer noticed the same. But otherwise, how would you say she's getting on?'

Dr Baker pauses and studies my face, weighing up how to say what he needs to.

'Well, I have some concerns, predominantly about your mother's weight. It can be hard for family to see a difference when they're caring for someone every day, but it's been three months since I've seen your mum, and I would consider her to have lost a significant amount of weight. I also noticed that, for the first time, your mum wasn't communicative with me today. Is she still able to speak to you?'

'A little.'

In truth, hardly at all. These last few days her voice has been noticeably absent; we've needed the picture charts more than ever. I'd put it down to her being withdrawn because of Debs's absence. Or rather, I'd hoped that was why.

'OK. And how is she getting on with eating? Would you say she's finding it harder to swallow? Or that food is becoming a particular challenge in her life?'

'I don't know. She's still eating three meals a day and a few snacks, although the carers have been recording that it's taking longer, and she's giving up before they think that she's had enough. Do you think it might be worth her taking some supplements?'

'It might be worth getting in touch with the speech and language therapists. I think the muscles in your mum's mouth and throat have significantly weakened since I last saw her, which would be making eating far more of a challenge. It accounts for the weight loss and the decline in speech.'

How foolish to think this man could deliver anything but blow after blow.

'Do you think they can help? The speech and language therapists, I mean?'

'Yes, if they come and assess her, they'll be able to create a plan to help with the muscle decline. They can relieve symptoms, help make life more manageable, but they can't reverse the disease's progress or provide any sort of cure. You know that, don't you?'

'Of course I do. Anything else?'

Instead of answering, he strokes the top of his cap, which, frankly, looks bloody ridiculous on him when he's standing in the middle of a warm kitchen, and I take it as a sign that he's ready to leave. I hop off my stool in readiness to see him on his way, making a note to myself that next time I want an opinion on Mum, I will call anyone but him.

'There is one more thing,' he says in a low voice, making me turn back to him from the kitchen doorway. 'It's a little delicate, and I'd rather your mum not hear.'

Reluctantly, I step back towards him, hating that he's spoken the words that render my mum an incapable participant in her own life. I could demand that anything he say, he say in front of Mum. I should do that. Only I'm too scared of what he has to say and how much it could hurt her.

'What is it?'

'I think the time's come for us to consider the best place for your mother to be given the care she needs. If, as I suspect, your mum is no longer able to maintain an adequate weight, other artificial means of getting nutrition into her may need to be considered. If so, the best place for her may be in a specialist care facility.'

'Dr Baker, my mum is already in a specialist care facility. It's called her home. If needs be, I'll fill it with every kind of carer we need, round the clock, but she will be staying right where she is.'

'I understand,' he tells me.

'I don't think you do. My mum's request – her only one by the way – is that she remains at home. So I'll thank you not to bring up the matter again. If you could arrange a repeat on her prescriptions and for the speech and language therapists to be in touch that would be fantastic. Now, let me show you out.'

Once Dr Baker has huffed his way out of the house, I go to Mum.

'What a waste of time that was. I don't know what he told you, but everything's fine. I don't know why I bothered asking him to come round.'

Mum says nothing.

'Can I get you anything?'

When she doesn't answer I grab the sheet, and she points to the picture of the remote control.

I sit with her for a little while whilst she flicks channels, but she has no interest in being with me. I retreat out of the room, back to the kitchen, to explore the contents of the fridge for something to make for tea.

Just as I'm deciding between scrambled eggs for the third night in a row or pesto pasta, which I'd rather have but know Mum will struggle with unless I blend it, the idea of which turns my stomach, the doorbell goes.

I quickly take the eggs out of the fridge and leave them on the side for later. The most likely caller is Dr Baker, returning to collect something he's left. Or to deliver more bad news. I steel myself for round two as I answer the door.

'Hiya, love. Hope you don't mind me coming round, but if I have to stay in that house another night with our Lauren trying to persuade me to go out with her and her mates to Liberty's this Saturday to see what it's really like to be single, I'll end up getting back with her dad just to shut her up.'

'Debs! It's great to see you. Are you here for a visit or is this you ignoring me and coming back?'

'Well, if you won't be too offended, it's me coming back.' She pats her rucksack of overnight essentials as she says it, and I beam at the familiar sight.

'No, that's great. I'm making us something to eat, want something?'

'God no, all I've done at home is eat. Lauren did the weekly shop for me and you wouldn't believe the amount of crap she came back with: biscuits, crisps, two boxes of Sauvignon Blanc, pizzas. And, what's worse, we've demolished the whole lot. I'm half here to stop myself stuffing my face when Lauren gets back with the next load.'

'OK,' I say, laughing. 'You go in to Mum, and I'll bring her food through. Remind me to tell you what Dr Baker said once she's finished.'

As if to prove the good doctor wrong, Mum finishes all of her tea and half of mine besides. I toy with not bothering to tell Debs everything he said, just the part about the chorea. If I keep his advice about a specialist care facility secret, it would be as if he never said it. Share it with Debs, and there's the frightening possibility she'll agree with him, and the importance of Mum's wishes will begin to fade.

Debs follows me into the kitchen, takes the dishes from my hands and begins to wash them up.

'Go on, then.' Her command is so matter-of-fact, I know I can't keep anything from her.

I could kiss her when she tells me he's talking nonsense. She agrees with me: Mum doesn't need a nursing home with the support she has at home. She makes a point of reminding me that every time the disease has progressed, I've dealt with it, including hiring her. As long as we make sure we know where's she's up to, we can continue to make sure she's getting the care she needs.

Friday morning, I return to work, making sure not to wear any make-up and to enter the office clutching my stomach. Jane, who doesn't believe I've been ill for a second, makes an elaborate detour to my desk, insisting I go straight back home *if* I've been sick, as I shouldn't be in until forty-eight hours after my last *incident* to avoid spreading my germs. When I refuse by telling her I'll keep to myself but would much rather soldier on, she leaves me to it, tutting as she goes.

I avoid looking up from my computer all morning, forgoing my normal trip to the canteen for a mid-morning skive for the sake of looking conscientious. When the office has sufficiently thinned out and, crucially, Jane has gone to The Wishing Well for lunch with Maureen and a few others – I venture away from my desk, starving and busting for the loo.

In the ladies, I bump into Olivia, who, I'd presumed, was off with morning sickness, seeing as she's not been over to see me. By the looks of her, she should be curled up in bed, bucket by her side. Compared to her frightening complexion, matted, scraped-back hair and watery eyes, it's no wonder Jane took one look at my peachy appearance and knew I was faking being sick.

'Hi, Jess,' she croaks, her voice raw with all the barfing.

'What the hell are you doing in work? You look awful.'

'No, I'm all right. Honestly, I'm past the worst of it for another day. I always thought the morning part of morning sickness was a myth. Both my sisters were sick all day long for all three trimesters. I assumed it was a pointless name. Turns out, I could be the poster girl for morning sickness in its truest sense: sick until midday, perfectly fine after. Day in, day bloody out.'

'So why aren't you staying off until you feel better? I imagine if you spoke with Jane, she could arrange for you to start work later, when it passes, or work from home,' I say, not convinced that Jane would do any such thing.

'Because if I don't go to work, neither does Rick. He either takes holiday to be off with me or pretends to work from home. I mean, God love him and all that, but when you've got your head down the toilet, you don't really want an audience, do you? I'd rather pretend to him that I'm fine and come and hide in here for some peace. Anyway, speaking of being sick, heard that's what you were yesterday. You OK?'

'Yeah, I'm fine,' I say, opting not to bother my green-tinged friend with Debs's marital status and Mum's sleepless nights. 'I fancied a duvet day, that's all.'

'Fair enough. Seeing as you're nothing more than a lazy cow and not on your deathbed, then, that'll mean there's no reason for you not to see Alec tonight.'

'He's working. I wanted to meet up, but it's his turn to shut the bar tonight.'

'Shame. Although, the good thing about dating a barman is, when he's at work, you can still see him. You could sit at the bar, get a few free drinks, stick around until he clocks off.'

'On my own all night like a lemon, fawning over him to get a few snippets of his attention between him serving punters? No, thanks. Unless you fancy keeping me company?'

'You're joking. These days, if I'm not in bed by nine, it's a late night. Sorry.'

'Nah, it's fine. I'm sure I'll see him over the weekend.'

'Do you want to see him tonight?'

'Yeah, but—'

'That's that, then. Go and see your bloody boyfriend, have wonderful sex and try not to rub it in too much when I next see you.'

I told Olivia after the second date. Not the whole story, expiration date and all, more a loose, casual-as-you-like drop-in that Alec and I were seeing each other. Olivia, as I knew she would be, was ecstatic.

This is the nice thing about friends which I'd let myself forget. Whenever something good comes along, having your friends elbow their way into it with their questions, unasked-for advice about how not to fuck it up and their demands to know all the details can make it even better. Even bigger.

And it works the other way round too. When something bad comes along, something that feels like the end of the world, friends can make it smaller for you, can make you see that you can get through it, that it isn't going to entirely define you.

'You're right. I should go. Do you not think it might come across a bit desperate, though?'

'Course not. Bet he'll love to see you. You'll make his night.'

'OK. But I'm not turning up until late on.'

With that decided, I allocate the rest of the afternoon to planning my strategy. Tonight is date number three. It should be his turn to decide, but when he realises the end goal to this date, I'm sure he won't mind. In my previous experience, date number three is when, all going well, sex becomes a likely end to the evening. Add to that the not insignificant matter that tonight we'll be recreating the exact set of circumstances that led us into his bed the first time, and the odds of it happening again are pretty high.

For tonight's outfit, I'll go for my skinny jeans from Primark, the ones that push my bum up into a cartoon-looking peach, and my good black T-shirt tucked in. A total sex outfit, masking as a casual, no-effort look. Perfect. Let's face it, Alec probably isn't going to need too much persuading tonight, but I find I'm enjoying playing the seductress.

On the tram home, two teenage boys start sniggering at me, and I know I'm getting carried away. I catch my reflection in the glass: red and grinning inanely. For the rest of the journey, I focus on the much more practical matter of whether I should take my small clutch bag, which is far more Friday night but holds next to nothing, or take my roomy work bag. Boring as it is, at least there's room for a fresh pair of knickers and a toiletries bag.

When I get in, I read the red folder, say hi to Debs, who is here an hour earlier than normal, and ask Mum about her day. In her place, Debs gives me the same short, uneventful report I've just read. As an afterthought, I drop in the fact that I've got plans to go out tonight with Olivia, whom they don't yet know is pregnant, and we'll probably end up in a club until late, so I'll stay at hers.

Debs is in the middle of giving Mum a hand massage. Mum looks up to smile at me, but Debs keeps her head down, concentrating on rubbing Mum's blue-veined hands. I suspect she knows exactly where I'll be tonight, but is good enough not to let on.

I send Alec a text to let him know I'll be in later and to prepare himself for our third date. Then it's time to get ready and wait.

After long hours lingering at home, feeling increasingly nervous and uncertain, I set off again to the Northern Quarter.

The Wishing Well is surprisingly quiet for half nine. I thought I'd be clamouring to even get to the bar, let alone command any of Alec's attention. As it is, he spots me the moment I come in and rushes towards me to grab the door.

'Hello, you,' he says before kissing me on the mouth. His lips linger. It hasn't taken him long to work out what tonight might bring.

'Hi. God, it's quiet in here.'

'Yep. Thankfully, it's the dead weekend before payday, which means I get to spend time with my favourite customer.'

'Oh yeah. And who's that?'

'Bob, the guy over there with the fleece. Excuse me, will you?'

'Very funny.'

He takes my hand and leads me to a bar stool before going round the other side of the bar. 'So the good news is, if it stays like this, Hal says I can get off early, and he'll lock up for me. I need to give it half an hour or so to make sure no big groups arrive late, but, if not, we can get off. Do you want a drink whilst you wait?'

'White wine, please. So,' I say, daring myself to be flirtatious, 'where exactly will we be going when you finish?'

'Good question. Seeing as you've commandeered our third date, I think you'll find it's for you to decide.'

'Hmmm. In that case, I say we waste no time in getting back to your flat.'

He leans back a little in surprise.

'Can't think of anything I'd like more.'

Just as it looks like we're going to be able to leave early, there's a tumultuous crash on the doors as they swing open, revealing a group of at least a dozen women, all with bright pink feather boas wrapped in a number of creative ways across their matching skimpy black dresses.

'Shit,' Alec mutters, letting go of my hand and stepping to the end of the bar where they've gathered. 'Evening, ladies. How are we tonight?'

Three hours later, after turning down endless requests for him to take off his clothes as a treat for the bride-to-be, Alec is ready to go.

'You OK?' he asks once we're in the back alley, walking towards his car.

'More than OK. I had a great time watching all those women drooling over you, safe in the knowledge that I was the one going home with you.'

'That's good. Whenever I looked around to see you nursing that one glass of wine, I thought you might have been having second thoughts.'

'Not at all. I just didn't want to have too much to drink. I'd like to remember tonight, unlike last time.'

'Best make sure it's something worth remembering, then.'

Chapter Twenty-two

I wake with my head on Alec's chest, my leg and arm wrapped around him to keep him in place: next to me. My ear is burning from being pressed too long against muscle and bone; I sit up to ease the pain before lowering myself back to reclaim my position.

We're still in the true black of night, hours away from morning, but I don't want to fall back to sleep. I want to lie here, listening to the muted thud of his heart, tracing the outline of his arms, his stomach, his hips as he sleeps, savouring him for as long as I've got him.

Savouring too the calm that comes after hours of making love. A calm I'd almost forgotten about. It's so simple and uncluttered – so blissful – I begin to worry.

How many more times am I going to get to feel like this again? How many more times can we fit in nights like the one we've had before our month is up?

I shouldn't do it. I should let him sleep off the exhaustion of last night's frantic lovemaking, but as soon as I notice the sliver of grey under his door, I can't resist.

'Alec, Alec, wake up.'

He's sleeping so deeply, my soft voice does nothing. A rough shove in the side does more.

He throws a loose arm around my middle.

'Huh?'

'Come on, sleepyhead, it's morning.'

'Is it?'

'Yes.'

'OK.' He snuggles up closer. If I don't pull away from him, he's going to fall back to sleep.

I sit, pulling the duvet off him as I do so. The cold air hitting his naked buttocks does the trick.

'Crikey, Jess, it's the middle of the night. Why are you so wide awake?'

'Why do you think?' I ask, running a finger down his chest. 'Let's just say, if the first time I woke up in your bed I'd remembered so many of the finer details of the night before, I wouldn't have been in such a hurry to leave it.'

'Oh really?'

I shimmy back down the bed until I'm back at his neck and can punctuate each word with a kiss. 'Yep. Now I'm in. No. Hurry. At. All.'

He's wide awake now. He turns towards me, pressing the length of his body against mine. He looks into my eyes and laughs once before pointing his head down so he can explore my body with his lips all over again.

The next time I wake, it's to a beautifully clear late winter's morning. Alec has opened the blinds and hovers over me with a cup of coffee in his hand. He's wearing the navy dressing gown I remember from my first visit. Once he's handed me my cup, he shrugs it off. It lands in a heap on the floor as he clambers back into bed beside me. We lean against the headboard whilst we sip our drinks, his legs threaded through mine.

'You know, it's far more enjoyable waking up with you second time round,' he tells me.

'Why ever so?'

'Well, as I recall, last time you were here, you were dreadfully hung over, laughed at me, wouldn't look me

175

in the eye and couldn't wait to get out of my bed and my flat.'

'Oh that. I was a right bitch that day, wasn't I?'

'I wouldn't go that far. You hadn't got to know me well enough then. How were you to know what you were missing out on?'

'I knew you enough to know you were a vain sod even then,' I tease. 'But I was a cow.'

'Don't worry about it. This morning's more than made up for it.'

He kisses my cheek, and his mouth begins to move towards mine. I worry this kiss has an agenda. I can't fathom how it's possible for him to be hungry for more when my body is worn out. But it's OK; his mouth stays closed and, after a peck, he pulls back. The sex has been amazing, and Alec is every bit the attentive lover, but it's this moment, this peaceful intimacy, I've enjoyed the most, and I'd rather it didn't end.

'I'm glad,' I tell him. 'And I'm glad you and your thick skin didn't pay any attention to the many, many signs I gave you to show I wasn't interested in you. Think how much we'd have missed out on if you'd run a mile like you were meant to.'

'I know. Lucky for you I did wake up remembering how phenomenal that first night was and my blinderitis kicked in.'

'Blinderitis?'

'Yep. Putting the blinders on. I've got a severe case of it, my mum tells me. A wonderful, not at all annoying ability to only see what I want.'

Alec unthreads his legs from mine and shuffles to the other side of the bed to put down his coffee cup. His hand strokes the short hairs of his returning beard and, if I'm not mistaken, his cheeks have coloured.

'You OK over there?' I ask.

'Yeah, fine. It's just that, well, speaking of mothers.'

A swig of coffee catches in my throat and goes down as a hard, hot lump.

'I was wondering if, for our next date, seeing as it's my turn to choose now, if you would mind breaking one of your rules and doing something that might possibly, no, *definitely will* involve meeting my parents.'

I picture a small dining room with a table set for four, a home-cooked meal – shepherd's pie or something similarly hearty – warm white wine and an evening of conversation so intensely awkward I end up leaving with a headache. I'm about to object, to reiterate the importance of my rules to Alec, but he beats me to it.

'I know, as far as fourth dates go, it probably sounds horrendous, but hear me out. My mum is a patron for a children's charity in Leeds. Every year she organises a fundraising ball at a posh hotel in the city centre. Again, that might sound very unappealing, but really it's not. My mum likes to think she's a rival to Nigella Lawson when it comes to putting on fancy, indulgent, boozy, fairy-lit affairs, and, to be fair, she always pulls off a cracking night. It so happens that this year's ball is next Wednesday night, and I, well, I thought it would be a shame for me to go alone, when we could enjoy it together. What do you think?'

I shuffle further up the pillows, my unease increasing.

'I don't know, Alec. The idea of meeting your parents and answering a million questions about us—'

'It won't be like that. I promise you there'll be no grilling whatsoever. Mum will be so busy sorting everything behind the scenes, she'll barely have time to say hello, and Dad's not really the most gushing conversationalist. And, hey, Tom and Hannah will be there. I'll get to prove to you finally that I do have real friends. You'll love them.'

This matters to Alec; his wide eyes are pleading. If Alec's mum puts on this event every year, for a number of those years he'd have gone there with his ex-girlfriend, Ellie. If I don't go with him this year, he'll be alone. A position I'm guessing he really doesn't want to be in. He wants me there as a buffer, someone to shove in front of his parents' friends to help him save face.

It's something of a relief to realise his motives aren't pure and aren't anything to do with our quasi-relationship.

'OK, OK, sales pitch over. I'll go.'

'You will?'

'Yes.'

He throws himself on me, spilling coffee from my mug all over his white sheets and my naked chest.

'Shit.' He bends down to retrieve his dressing gown from the floor and starts wiping off the still-hot liquid, splashing it all over my stomach.

'Ouch. Get off, you clown. I'll do it.' I rip the gown out of his hands. Once I've dried off, a red mark replaces the spilt coffee.

'I'm so sorry, Jess.'

I'd laugh at his clumsiness if he weren't looking so sheepish.

'It's all right,' I tell him, stroking the worry off his face. 'It's my sensitive skin. The red will disappear in a few minutes. You've not ruined my boobs.'

He looks so adorable staring at my chest with his creased brow, oblivious to the state of his sheets.

'Let's move,' I say, wanting to rescue him from his embarrassment. 'We should make the most of the morning. What shall we do?'

I'm skull-thudding tired, but it doesn't matter. There are two hours left before Debs's shift ends, and I'll be needed back at home for the rest of the weekend. I intend to fill them up with Alec, to squeeze every ounce of enjoyment out of them to last me until our next date.

Alec shrugs, the sleepiness not quite eradicated from his brain. 'You decide.'

'We could go for a walk into Castlefield, maybe keep walking along the canal for a bit, or we could go shopping, come back and make a huge, disgustingly unhealthy breakfast.'

'Or we could do nothing but spend the rest of the morning in bed drinking coffee, eating the croissants I've already got in. We could even watch a film in bed. When was the last time you got to watch a film in bed in the morning?'

I decide not to divulge the frequency with which I watch TV in bed. Besides, watching TV nestled against Alec and watching TV alone whilst listening out for sounds of unrest downstairs are hardly the same experience.

'Your plan sounds much better,' I say, reaching out to stroke the hairs on his chest. 'Let's do nothing together.'

Chapter Twenty-three

Five years earlier

It was supposed to be laid-back. A coffee so Mum could meet my new boyfriend, Liam, before he took me away for the weekend to Wales. No big deal.

Under normal circumstances, it would have been just that, but Mum had been so agitated since the start of the year, I was desperate for it to go right, for her to like him. She promised there was nothing going on at work, but I'd watch her from the corner of my eye as we sat in front of the TV in the evening, fidgeting and shaking her feet while trawling those dating sites she'd joined, and was sure something was wrong.

I'd never thought all that much about Mum liking my boyfriends before. She always had, and they'd always liked her. This time, it mattered. I wanted to be able to give her some happiness by showing her how happy I was.

I selected the little deli in Didsbury village that Mum liked, and we waited at one of the tables outside for Liam.

'He's running very late,' she said five minutes after he'd been due to arrive.

'He's had to get the bus in. I'm sure he'll be along in a minute.'

His hands on my shoulder and a kiss on my cheek as he came up behind me announced his arrival a few minutes later.

'Hi, babes. Hi, Mrs Hyland.'

He stuck out his hand, and Mum turned to me, giving a little nod of approval before taking it.

'Hi, Liam,' Mum said, looking him over without any subtlety as he took the seat next to me. 'I'm so pleased to meet you. Jess tells me you're staying at your parents' lodge this weekend. That sounds lovely.'

'Yeah. It sounds lovely, but, as I told Jess, it's actually a bit of a shithole. The only good thing is it's right on the beach and has a great pub on site.'

'I see,' Mum said before taking a sip of her cappuccino. 'And apart from the pub, what other plans do you have?'

Liam turned to me, a gormless grin on his face. 'I don't think we were planning on much else, were we?'

'I'm sure we'll find plenty to do. Although, Liam is actually an avid reader. He'll probably have his head in a book half the trip.'

Mum brightened a little. 'Oh, what do you like reading? I used to love to read at your age, but I barely have the concentration to pick up a magazine these days.'

'All sorts. Just a sec, let me get this waiter over. Excuse me,' he shouted at the waiter at the next table, who was still speaking to his customer. I didn't dare look at Mum when he ordered his beer.

'Sorry,' he said, turning back to us. 'What were we saying?'

'I was asking what you like to read,' Mum said.

'Oh right. Anything going really, but since Jess has come along, I've only eyes for her.' He flashed Mum a grin before kissing me on the lips, trying to part my mouth with his tongue.

Mum didn't ask another question after that. Nor did Liam. As soon as he'd finished his drink and realised he wouldn't be getting my undivided attention with Mum sitting opposite pulling a sour face, he made his excuses to leave by saying he hadn't packed a thing yet.

'What was that?' I asked her once he was out of earshot.

'I could ask you the same,' she shot back.

'You were so rude to him. I don't get it. Could you not have tried to be nice?'

'I did try.' She leant forward to me, her elbows resting on the table. 'I'm sorry, Jess, I'm not sure about him.'

'After that? God, he was nervous, that's all. You could have helped him out, instead of making it perfectly clear you didn't want to get to know him. What must he be thinking?'

'I'm not sure I care all that much. I'm only bothered about what you're thinking, getting involved with someone like that.'

'You can talk,' I said, thinking back to the dates Mum had been on recently.

'Don't you dare speak to me like that. I can date whoever I want.'

'And so can I,' I said before standing up, wanting to be away from her. I took a deep breath and some of the anger left with it. 'Listen, I need to pack and get over to Liam's to set off before traffic hits. I know this isn't you speaking. It's the stress. You wouldn't normally be so mean. I'll talk to you when I get home.' I began to walk quickly, to outpace the tears that were threatening to arrive.

Mum stood too, and followed me down the street. A few shoppers paused as she reached for my arm, sensing a scene about to unfold.

'That boy isn't right for you. Don't you dare blame me for the way that went. Sooner or later you're going to see it. I'm telling you, that boy is going to let you down.'

'No, he's not. The only person who let me down today was you,' I said before shrugging her off me and walking away.

Chapter Twenty-four

A strong morning sun shines over Mum's neglected garden. The tree in the corner has already started blooming with pink flowers. I must remember to tell her, to help her get to the window to see it. I stare out of the window at it, thinking of Mum's old excitement for something as simple as a flower appearing, until Debs joins me in the kitchen to throw most of Mum's bran in the bin.

'Debs, how do you think Mum would handle meeting Alec when he picks me up for our next date?'

I have to ask her. The question's been pulling sleep from me these last few nights and won't let me rest until it's answered.

Debs knows better than to smile, but she wants to. She hides it underneath a gossamer-thin thoughtful expression.

'I don't think there's as much to handle as you imagine. She'll be fine. It'll do her the world of good.'

'You don't think she'll get carried away about what this might mean?'

'I think she'll see it as her daughter going out on a lovely date with a nice young man. She's got enough sense to know she's meeting a date, not your future husband. She'll be made up enough with that, knowing you're having a bit of fun for the first time in years.'

'That's what I've been thinking.'

After Mum's diagnosis and the creation of my rules post Liam, I haven't needed to worry about introducing another man to her. When Alec came along, I had been so sure Mum couldn't handle meeting him and that it would set off another avalanche of disappointments and remonstrations. But the more I get to know him, the more selfish it seems to have someone as bright as Alec in my life and squirrel him away. Mum would love him, and I so want to see her face light up because of a choice I've made. I can tell her it didn't work out, or that Alec and I are going to remain friends when the time comes, but tonight, I don't want to hide him.

'Tonight?'

'Yeah. I'd thought he could pop in to say hello.'

'Jess, that's wonderful. She'll be so happy. Shall I tell her?'

'No, I will.'

I'm dangerous levels of late, but I stop by the dining room on my way out. Mum's watching *Lorraine* and smiling at the screen. She's always had the idea that she and Lorraine would be best mates if ever they had the opportunity to meet. Lorraine's doing a piece on spring trends, and Mum nods along, heartily agreeing with Lorraine's notion that there's a floral skirt out there for everyone. I shouldn't interrupt this happy hour.

'Mum? I'm going out tonight. On a date.'

She turns to me.

'He's picking me up. Would you like to meet him before we set off?'

'Yes, please,' she says after the shortest pause she's had before speaking in weeks.

'Great.'

Seven on the dot the doorbell rings.

Debs emits a small squeal. Mum nods in approval of his punctuality. I leave Mum's side, pretending to be unfazed by this event, like it's an everyday occurrence to sit waiting for *The One Show* to come on wearing a cocktail dress and being interrupted by my for-one-month-only boyfriend popping round to say hello. Whatever. No big deal.

Only I fumble trying to open the dining-room door, sweaty palms struggling to grip the handle.

Alec looks smarter than I've ever seen him; he's wearing a beautifully fitted tuxedo with a white shirt and maroon bow tie. His beard has been shorn back down to a thin spattering of stubble, and his hair has been cut specially for the occasion. He carries a small bunch of pink and white peonies. Thoughtful flowers, definitely not bought last minute from a garage forecourt.

I reach out to take them off him. 'Thank you.'

'Excuse me,' he says, pulling them behind him, out of my reach. 'As stunning as you may be looking tonight, don't be so presumptuous. You're not the only woman in this house.'

'You're right, how rude of me.'

It occurred to me mid-morning that the only person I'd not considered in the plan to meet Alec was Alec himself.

Jane had been complaining all morning of a migraine. I'd popped out on the pretence of getting us all a chocolate éclair to cheer us up and took a detour to see him.

'What are you doing here?' he asked after leaning over the bar to kiss me. 'Oh no, don't tell me, you're here to commandeer this date as well, aren't you?'

'No, not at all. Well, maybe a bit. How would you feel about meeting my mum tonight when you pick me up? You don't have to, if you don't want to, but she wants to meet you. If it's too much, or if—'

'I'd love to meet her.'

'Are you sure?'

'Positive. It would be a pleasure.'

'Great. It's just I wouldn't want it to upset you – seeing what Huntington's looks like. If it's easier not to see, to keep it as a list of symptoms, I'd understand.'

'I'll see you both at seven,' he said.

I move aside now to let him in. He kisses my cheek before stepping back again to take in my dress. I bought it during my lunch hour yesterday, after Olivia insisted I couldn't go to a ball in my trusty black jumpsuit. Once she'd finished being sick for the day, she had marched over to my desk, picked up my bag and ordered me to get my arse over to Selfridges.

Normally I hate parting with my money for something I know I'm only going to wear once, especially when I'm meant to be saving (though, truth be told, I haven't thought about travelling half as much these last few weeks), but as soon as Olivia pulled out the dress, I had to have it. Emerald-green with a calf-length fifties-style skirt, high neckline and open back, it looked perfect swinging from its velvet coat hanger. I agreed to try it, not getting my hopes up in case the colour washed out my already pale complexion or the material pulled across my plump bum. But it did neither. It flattered, it sang, it elevated, and two hundred pounds was nothing to pay for the favours it did me.

Seeing Alec's expression, I know I made the right choice.

'Do you know how beautiful you look? I don't think I'm going to be able to stop looking at you all night.'

'That's fine by me.' I grin, taking his hand. 'You ready?'

'Absolutely.'

I open the door to the dining room, and Debs jumps out of her seat to rush to us.

She's a good one, Debs. Gracious enough to pretend the grilling I gave her about not telling Mum never happened.

Considerate enough to come up to my room as I was getting ready, to remind me that Mum knows this is just a date and I'm not unleashing a new version of my future in front of her.

'Would you look at the pair of you?' she gushes.

'Alec, this is Debs, Mum's carer.' If I let her, Debs would start throwing questions and compliments Alec's way until it's time to go. But it's not Debs Alec's here to meet.

Fortunately, he's more than aware of that himself. He shakes Debs's hand formally, tells her he's pleased to meet her and turns to Mum.

'Hi, I'm Alec. These are for you.' Instead of trying to hand them to Mum, he places them on the table next to her bed. 'Can I say what a wonderful daughter you've raised; I'm a very lucky guy.'

Mum smiles up at Alec from her chair, and I wonder if, despite my warnings, Alec's going to expect her to talk back. There's a short pause. When it's not filled by Mum, Alec tells her about the ball and the charity it's for – a charity called Whispers his mum set up herself to support parents of sick children after Alec spent the first year of his life in and out of hospital being treated for a heart defect. It's hard to believe Alec could ever have been small and vulnerable. Hearing he was works as another nudge, pushing me closer to him.

He talks carefully to Mum, making sure he doesn't ask her questions she won't be able to answer. Mum smiles at him the whole time, willing him to carry on. Debs and I stay silent. I turn to smile at her and give her a thumbs-up. In turn she raises her newly over-plucked eyebrows and mouths 'He's great'.

'Well, Mrs Hyland, we'd best be off,' he tells Mum after five minutes or so. 'The meal starts at half eight and my mum will sulk with me all night if I'm not there for it. I'll have Jess back by midnight.'

'She's not Cinderella, love,' Debs tells him, and we all laugh.

I give Mum a kiss goodnight and do the same to Debs. Alec tells Mum and Debs it's been lovely meeting them and, once I've shut the door, whispers to me, 'It really was.'

In the car on the drive over to Leeds, Alec is quiet. Despite his hand on my knee, his thumb stroking the satin dress, something's not right. Seeing Mum has upset him. It must have brought home what's coming my way. It was like I suspected. Until tonight, he hadn't understood the severity of Huntington's, what it does to a person. Now he does.

Was I wrong to let him meet her? When I'd suggested it, I was thinking about Mum, how she'd like to see me getting dressed up for such a nice event and how very much I wanted to make her happy. Alec meeting her tonight was a favour for Mum's sake. I'd let him convince me he was fine with it, because I wanted him to be. For me, for Mum.

'Stop chewing your lip like that. Everything went fine.' I turn my head away from the window to find Alec staring at me.

'Did it?'

'Yes, it went great. Stop worrying, will you?'

'If it went so well, why have you been silent for the last half-hour? Mum shocked you, didn't she?'

'No, I wouldn't say that. She was lovely, didn't stop smiling the whole time we were there. And the way she looks at you, Jess. You could tell she was so proud of you. Anyway, I knew what to expect. If you must know, I was thinking about our arrangement again, about your reasons behind it.'

'What about them?'

I expect him to launch into another speech to try to persuade me I've got it all wrong, but he surprises me by shaking his head.

'Let's not talk about it now. We'll be at the hotel soon. Let's just enjoy our date.'

'OK,' I say warily.

'OK,' he repeats, taking my hand and kissing it.

Chapter Twenty-five

The Ellesmere is a grand, elegant hotel in the heart of Leeds. Its bricks are illuminated with different-coloured spotlights, forming bright ribbons of light across the golden-brown facade. Inside, the lobby hasn't a single nudge towards the contemporary: it's unabashedly classical. We pass over the black-and-white marble floor to the mirrored lifts past the reception desk, where a hand-made notice board decorated with hundreds of diamantes directs us in swirly gold writing to Whispers' Annual Ball in the ballroom on the first floor.

Whilst waiting for the lift, I turn back to the lobby we've passed through. Amongst the tourists, tired businessmen and fellow guests in black tie and full-length gowns, I catch a few people abruptly turning away from my direction, having been caught staring. Alec and I must make quite the striking couple tonight in our finery. I look at Alec to see if he's noticed too, but his eyes are cast down.

The lift arrives, and a heavy silence gets in with us, the kind that doesn't want to be interrupted with light-hearted chitchat. Why did he have to bring up our arrangement in the car? We should be enjoying tonight, not worrying about any of that. It's the first time Alec's shown me this side of him, and, I have to say, I'd much rather be spending the evening with Charming Alec or Funny Alec or anyone other than Sulky Alec. I look up at him, hoping to see traces of his usual self, but his face is unreadable.

Once the doors open to the first floor, he walks out without waiting for me. I try to catch up with him, but he races ahead, swinging open the door to the ballroom and entering alone.

We should be arriving arm in arm, meeting his parents with matching broad smiles. Instead, I'm left to catch the heavy wooden door before it closes.

Even undecorated, the ballroom with its golden ceiling, art deco floor and marble columns would be spectacular. With the hundreds of candles in glass vases dotted around the floor and the dozens of heavily packed-in bouquets of white roses on the tables, it's breathtaking.

Alec's a few feet in front of me, greeting a small woman in a sleeveless black velvet cocktail dress, which hugs her slim body perfectly and finishes just below her knee, showing off her slim calves and gold court shoes. She would be the paradigm of elegance if it weren't for her short, spiky hair, the colour of which could only have come from a bottle labelled 'cherry red'. The contrast between the elegance of her clothes and her punk hairstyle works beautifully, making her by far the most noticeable woman in the room.

I sidle up to Alec's side, noticing how the woman beams at Alec, her hand running up and down his sleeve as she talks to him. Alec's face, in turn, is pinched together; his answers to her questions uncharacteristically curt, as though he's worried what might spill out if he doesn't keep himself pulled so tight.

'Hello,' I say when the woman turns her gaze from Alec to me.

'Mum, this is Jess.'

'Hello, Jessica. Lovely dress,' she says, but it's as though someone has taken a cloth to her face, rubbing away any trace of the warmth she showed her son. 'If you'll excuse me, those blasted waitresses are meant to be out now serving canapés. I must go below deck to find out what on earth the delay is.'

'Sorry about Mum,' says Alec once she's disappeared into the kitchen. 'She's stressed. Wants everything tonight to run perfectly.'

I'm about to tell him that I'm certain her coldness towards me has nothing to do with her ball, and that I'm more interested in why he's acting so strangely, but I don't get the chance. A ruddy-faced man in a tuxedo a size too small for him spots Alec from across the room and beckons him over.

Again, Alec sets off, weaving himself through tables, without thinking to wait for me.

'Dad, this is Jess,' he says when I catch up with him, his voice as flat as my enthusiasm now is for the rest of the night.

'Ah, how lovely to meet you,' Alec's dad gushes, pulling me into a tight, mouthwash-scented bear hug. 'Lovely. I was delighted when Alec said he'd be bringing you.'

'Thank you,' I say, smoothing down my dress.

'Now, how was it you two met?'

'Kind of through Alec's work,' I answer.

'Ah, lovely. So you work in the bar too, do you?'

'No, Dad. What Jess means is that she and her work-mates come and do the drinking, whilst I do the work by serving them.'

'Aha!' He begins to laugh, the kind of bellow that only a man in his mid-sixties with a protruding beer belly is capable of. 'Very good. Sounds like you've got the right idea there, Jess. Now listen, Alec, make sure you do a bit of mingling tonight before you set yourself up at the bar. Your mum's in a right state. I've told her there's no need to worry, it's the same people here who have been coming to this thing for the last decade, so they all know exactly what the drill is, but you know what she's like. Every year she needs to raise more money than the one before. If she sees you talking to some of the golf-club lot, giving the usual spiel about how cracking the auction is, it'll make her feel better. Oh bugger, I'm wanted. See you soon.'

In front of a small stage covered in cellophane-wrapped hampers, Alec's mum furiously signs for her husband to join her. I feel sorry for him as he puts down his pint and, face flushed, pushes his way towards her.

I'm also sorry he's leaving Alec and I alone. With him, Alec seemed to relax into the evening; now he's gone, his face is pulled tight again, and the distance between us has returned.

'Are you all right? You seem tense.'

He stares at the growing bustle by the doors as more couples arrive. 'I'm not tense at all,' he answers. Tensely.

'If you say so. Do you think we could get a drink now?'

'Sure, come on.'

Alec's mum has covered the entire length of the bar with tea lights and sprigs of rosemary and lavender. From a distance, it looks so pretty, but in front of it, with nowhere to put my elbows, let alone any drinks, it reveals itself to be an ill-thought-out idea.

'Rosemary with your pint, sir?' I ask Alec, picking up a sprig and wafting it under his nose. He isn't paying me any attention. His focus is further down the bar. Whatever he's seen has taken the colour from his face. I follow his gaze and find it's landing on a pretty blonde woman wearing a black floor-length dress with an elaborate organza bow on the shoulder reaching to her ears.

'What the fuck?'

He walks – no, storms – towards her, and I follow, certain I know who I'm looking at.

'Alec,' she says, feigning surprise at finding him by her side when she must have been waiting for him the entire time.

'Why are you here?'

'Don't be like that. Your mum invited me. She knows how much I love this event, and seeing as it's for charity and all, we hoped you might be a bit more charitable yourself. Clearly not.'

'Ellie, you've no right to turn up here,' he says, his voice unsteady with anger.

'She has every right,' a girl behind us tells him. Before I turn, I can feel eyes boring into my back. When I face her, her eyes zone in on mine, their expression so frighteningly hostile, my stomach lunges. Next to her is a man not dissimilar in appearance to Alec, aside from being slightly less handsome and looking like he wants the ground to swallow him up.

'Hannah, stay out of this,' Alec says to her.

'I will not! We're Ellie's friends, your family are like her family, and just because you've chosen to sod off and abandon her, it doesn't mean the rest of us are going to do the same.'

Ellie says nothing, just sips at her glass of Prosecco without the contents going down. She pulls Hannah towards her and squeezes the top of her arm to quieten her before leading her further down the bar where the two of them launch into an urgent whispered conversation. If Ellie's noticed me standing next to Alec, she's made sure not to acknowledge it.

'Good to see you, mate,' Tom says once a sufficient gap from Hannah's outburst has opened up.

'You too.'

The two of them launch into that double handshake thing you sometimes see presidents and other dignitaries doing when they want to show they like the person they're meeting so much one hand simply won't do the job.

'Hi, Jess. It's great to meet you at last. Sorry we couldn't stick around to meet you at the pub that time. If the baby had lasted even ten minutes, you'd at least have seen us making our blundering exit. You must have thought our Alec was a bit of a sociopath that day, luring you out on the pretext of meeting his friends only to find him sitting waiting for you all alone.'

'Yeah, that's exactly what I thought. I still wasn't sure until now if you actually existed or if he'd made you up, so it's really great to meet you. Here, let me get us all a drink. What would you like?'

'Doombar for me, if they've got it. You on the same, mate?' he asks Alec.

'No. Driving, I'm afraid. Got to get this one back at a decent hour for work tomorrow. Diet Coke, please.'

Hatred is still coming out of Hannah like steam from a kettle, but she is Tom's wife so I step towards her and Ellie and ask, 'Can I get either of you a drink?'

They don't reply.

'Hannah, you're being asked a question,' Tom says.

'I know I am. But I'm refusing to speak to the arm candy Alec's decided to parade around tonight as if Ellie doesn't even exist. You arrogant prick,' she says, directing the last bit at Alec.

'Sorry, mate,' Tom says in a small voice as Ellie and Hannah link arms and move across the room to the stage where Alec's mum is setting up. I watch as Alec's mum breaks off from her job to comfort Ellie and gives her a tight hug, looking over Ellie's shoulder straight at me as she does so.

Tom, a man caught between a pint and catch-up with his friend and the wrath of his wife, looks hopelessly from one to the other before following her.

'I'm so sorry,' Alec says. 'I promise you I had no idea Ellie would be here tonight. And as for Hannah, I've never seen her behave like that in my life, and I've known her for pretty much all of it.'

I take a large gulp of my gin and tonic before speaking again. When I take the glass away from my lips, I see I've polished off half of it in one swoop.

'Don't worry about me. I don't know them. I'm fine. It's you I'm worried about. You know, you've spent pretty much the whole night so far apologising to me or ignoring me and now that. What's going on?'

He sags onto a bar stool.

'Truth is, I've not been home for a while, not since before Christmas, and I think it might have been a mistake not coming here alone.'

'Got you.' My heart lodges in my throat. I down the rest of my drink to push it back down again. 'Well, I'm sorry if I've been such an embarrassment to you. That's easily solved, though. Goodbye, Alec.'

'Wait,' Alec says, reaching for my arm. 'You've got it wrong. You're not an embarrassment to me. How could you ever think that? I'm proud to be here with you tonight. That's not at all what I meant. Look, there are things I probably should have told you, things you really should have known before coming here. It's just that, with our short shelf life, I wasn't sure you'd want to know, if I should bother you.'

I sigh. 'Will you please tell me what you're talking about?'

'It's Ellie. You see, now I've moved on with my life and it's become clear I'm not planning on returning, Ellie's decided she can't bear to live without me. You know I'm completely over her, don't you? I'd never go back, only she doesn't believe that's the case. She thinks if she can show me what I'm missing out on back home, I'll come back to her.

'She's been very devious about it. First, she put an end to our mates going out as couples by making them take sides. Except for Tom, the lads have been on my back constantly, telling me to get back with Ellie and return to the good times we had. Anything for an easy life, eh?

'And as for the girls, well, she must have been working hard on them, judging by Hannah's welcome back there.'

'Don't pay any attention to what she said. There's nothing arrogant about moving on and trying to make a better life for yourself.'

'Thanks. I know. And I'm used to being called arrogant. Comes with the territory of being a barman who doesn't want to get laid every night. I just hate that Hannah's the one saying it when we used to be good mates.'

'In that case, she'll realise she's talking shit eventually, Alec. Don't worry.'

'Hope so. But if Hannah's not bad enough, Ellie's also been working on Mum. She's got back into her life, acting as a daughter-in-law-in-waiting, taking her out for lunch and visiting exhibitions together. Mum's always been fond of Ellie, and now won't stop badgering me to get back with her. I never thought she'd be so crass as to invite Ellie to this, though. I'm going to have to speak to her about that. The worst thing about it is I wanted Mum and Dad to get to know you tonight, to fall for your charm like I did, to see how I've moved on. With Ellie here, that's not going to happen. I'm sorry you got involved with all this crap.'

I should say something, only I have no idea what Alec wants to hear. I could tell him it's outrageous of Ellie to turn up, and he can talk to me about it anytime, or I could tell him the truth: none of it is meant to matter to me. This is our fourth date. Two more, and I won't be in his life. If, despite what he says, he chooses to go back to Ellie, he's perfectly free to do so.

I settle on kissing him on the cheek and skirting the issue.

'Don't worry about me. For the rest of the night, I say we make the most of this very beautiful venue, our very fine clothes and have some fun.'

The DJ has started playing his first song. Ignoring the empty dance floor and the dodgy acoustics caused by him being relegated to a corner of the room so the stage can hold the auction items, I take Alec's hand and pull him into the middle.

It's an eclectic set the DJ has gone for. Once Lionel Richie finishes dancing on the ceiling, Little Mix come out with their 'Shout Out to My Ex'. We stand opposite each other, awkwardly sidestepping and occasionally swinging our arms. I'm beginning to regret my decision when the DJ takes pity on us and abruptly cuts off the song, replacing it with an Ed Sheeran swooner. Alec steps towards me and puts his arms around my waist. I hook my arms around his neck and we begin to sway together. We start off dancing for our audience, or I do, at least. Ellie, Hannah and his mum are all watching us. I can see their open mouths from here. I want to help Alec show them all he's moved on. He didn't deserve to be railroaded tonight, to be bullied into getting back with Ellie. He deserves to have at least one person sticking up for him.

But taking in his clean smell, the warmth of him as his solid frame presses against my body whilst we circle around the dance floor, it becomes more than that. I hold him closer, not wanting to let go, because if I do, he might go to them. He might start talking to Ellie and realise he's glad she came. He's already said how easy it's been for them to fall back together in the past. What if the same happens tonight? I stop dancing and wait until Alec becomes still before leaning upwards and kissing him hard on the lips in front of the whole room.

We stay on the dance floor until it's time to eat. Following suit, other couples join us, and Alec and I try not to giggle at their dancing. It becomes obvious that we are by far the youngest people up here. Our fellow dancers are Alec's parents' age and all favour the identical, finger-clicking, shoulder-shrugging routine, no matter what the song.

When the DJ announces it's time to take our seats, I'm absolutely starving. Alec leads me to a table where his parents are already sitting. Ellie, Tom and Hannah are on a table near the exit. It's a mercy that his mum didn't place us all together. I'm seated next to his mum. I busy myself reading the menu to avoid looking at her.

There's no need. After watching us dance, her manner is completely different. Straight away, she offers me wine and proceeds to pour it into my glass until it's brimming. She turns in her chair to face me and begins chatting, as though she couldn't be more delighted to find herself next to me. No way would Alec have told her about our temporary situation or the reasons behind it, but her conversation is careful: never probing, light and warm, centred on the evening we're sharing and the man we have in common. When talking to others around the table, her eyes involuntarily flit back towards Alec. They lock eyes, and she mouths, 'I'm sorry.'

After a delicious starter of king prawns and scallops in garlic butter, I excuse myself to nip to the loo, glad of a break from the intensity of so much attention. The ladies are as I expected, filled with fancy soaps, a tray of designer perfumes and towels instead of a hand drier. I could happily spend some time hiding away in here, but I don't get the chance. A toilet cubicle opens and out walks Ellie, dabbing a tissue at her eyes, mascara halfway down her face.

'Hi,' I say.

'Oh. I thought I was alone.'

'I'm sorry; I'll leave you to it.'

'No, it's fine. I'm going. You've won.' Unlike her friend, there's no malice in her voice, just painful resignation.

'Won? I haven't won anything.'

'You have. You've won him. He's besotted with you. The two of you together . . .' Her voice trails off and she bolts past me out the door.

I don't wonder what she's going to say. She's seen it. His mum's seen it. I have too, though I've tried not to. Alec and I are perfect together.

And after two more dates, he's going to be out of my life.

Chapter Twenty-six

'Debs, I'm late, I'll see you later,' I shout into the kitchen.

She doesn't shout back. The patio door is open a crack, and I spot her in the garden, cradling a cup of tea between her hands. Thin ribbons of steam twirl upwards before being swallowed by the thick, low, morning haze.

Oversleeping has done nothing to lessen the aching tiredness after the ball. If I don't leave the house now, I'm going to miss the last tram that will get me to work on time. But there's something about seeing Debs out there that roots me to the spot. To my knowledge, Debs has never stepped foot in the garden before now. Why would she? With weeds springing through the cracks in the patio flags and its overgrown lawn, it's hardly a peaceful retreat.

It's more than that though. Her posture, the way she stands so still despite the cold, sends a shiver of panic through me.

'Debs?'

'Oh, hi, love. What you still doing here?'

'I'm on my way out now.'

Now she's facing me, I can see the red rings round her eyes and blotches down her face that only come from heavy, unrelenting crying.

I have to ask: 'Is everything OK with Mum?'

'Your mum? Yeah, your mum's fine. She's asleep. I, er, just stepped out for a bit of fresh air. Headache.'

It's an almost giddy feeling, the relief it isn't Mum but Debs's own problems making her weep. Here is Debs, covered head to foot in upset and I'm glad. When did I become so selfish?

'What's wrong? And don't tell me it's nothing, because I'll know you're lying.'

Fresh tears arrive then and stream down her face. They must sting as they fall over the already-raw skin.

'Nothing. Not really, not compared to—'

'Debs, what is it?'

'Well, if you must know, my marriage is over. I've left him for good.'

'Oh, Debs. Are you sure?'

'I am. When Ray left, I was angry. I couldn't believe he'd been so pig-headed over my job. Then he came back, and he was so apologetic and kind. He's been on his best behaviour for my sake, but it turns out it doesn't matter. Even with him trying so hard, I don't want him around. If he hadn't left, I'd probably never have noticed it, but we're strangers to each other.'

'I'm sorry. You loved him once, though. Isn't it worth trying to get to know him again, to see if the man you fell in love with is still there?'

She gives me a hard, teary laugh. 'Jess, no offence, darling, but I'm not sure you should be dishing out advice on love, given your present situation.'

She doesn't mean it to be malicious – in fact, she's grinning at me as she says it, grateful for the break I've given her in her misery – but her words are like rocks being flung at me.

'Excuse me?'

'C'mon. You know full well what I mean. You're telling me to keep going, not to give up on love and all that, yet, here you are with a handsome, polite, charming boyfriend, who is absolutely besotted with you, by the way, and you're about to bin him off.'

'That's different,' I say, my voice cold and low.

'I know, I know. Still, it might be worth listening to the advice you give out a little yourself.'

We stand side by side, looking out at the garden, both lost in our thoughts. Truth is, I've thought of nothing else but Alec all night and I'm not sure I can bear to start thinking about him again. I shake my head to close the matter and tell Debs I'm late for work before returning to the house, checking on Mum and bolting through the front door.

I enter the office with the tailend of arrivals just after nine. Jane is not happy. Gone are the days when I was the keenest worker, always in first to welcome her with a cup of coffee. She approaches me with a wobbly pile of files that 'urgently' need filing, and I'm sent down to the basement for the morning as a punishment for my lack of commitment.

Well, not long now, Jane, I think. *Soon everything will go back to normal.*

I have to hand it to her; she's come up with a fitting punishment. Filing doesn't require much in the way of brainpower, leaving my mind free to roam as I shove bulging files onto overflowing shelves. And there's only one place it wants to roam to: Alec.

Last night our relationship altered. It wasn't because of the dancing or the lovely meal or the prolonged groping in his car outside my house at the end of the night; it was because of all the things that went wrong. Seeing Alec so uncomfortable, acting like a knob at times and discovering the reasons behind it, allowed me to know him so much more. Before last night, our dates had been removed from real life, just the two of us, on a remote island of our creation.

Perhaps we should have stayed there. Perhaps last night was a mistake. Stepping into each other's lives was a forward step in our relationship we shouldn't have taken. I'm falling even deeper for him. And we've only got two more dates left.

At lunchtime, Olivia comes to find me.

'There you are. Fancy some fresh air and a vanilla slice?'

'Odd combo, but yes, I think I do.'

'Great.'

I follow her out, glad I'm behind her so she doesn't see the tears that have arrived in gratitude for her making the effort to come and pull me out of the basement. How much easier it would have been for her to take the lift down to the lobby and head out to get that vanilla slice on her own. The one day I need dragging out of my thoughts and here she is.

'Excuse me, I don't think so,' shouts Jane, elbowing people out the way to get to us when she spots us across the lobby making our exit. 'You can't seriously be going out for lunch given the time you turned up this morning. Go on, get back downstairs.'

I'm about to do as I'm told until Olivia pushes past me to get up close to Jane's snarling face.

'Jess has every right to her lunch hour, Jane, as you well know. It doesn't matter what time she got in this morning, she's still entitled to eat. And I'm sure if there is a need for Jess to work back a few minutes owed to the business, she will be happy to discuss it later and make suitable arrangements that don't involve starving and being shouted at across the lobby.'

I'm pulled outside by Olivia and daren't stop walking until she tells me I can.

'That felt good,' she says when we take our place in the queue outside Lettuce and Loaf.

'Bloody hell, Olivia, are you trying to get yourself fired?'

'She won't fire me. I'm golden,' she says, patting a stomach that looks no more than a little bloated. 'For the next six months, I've got it good.'

'Well, thank you and the baby for coming to my rescue.'

'No problem. We like to use our powers to take down evil office managers. Anyway, you look so shit today I didn't think you'd be able to stand up to her yourself. You look like you're about to fall over.'

'Do I? It was a late night.'

'With Alec?'

'Yeah.'

'Goodie. Let's get an extra vanilla slice between us and you can tell me everything.'

So much for escaping my Alec-filled thoughts.

We navigate our way through the close streets of the Northern Quarter until we reach Piccadilly Gardens. Gardens is a generous word for the few patches of grass in a concrete square, but it is an open space away from work and has plenty of benches.

'So why the suitcases under your eyes and the lank hair?' Olivia asks once we've sat down, and she's started to pick out flakes of puff pastry from her paper bag.

'Thanks for that. It was a late night, that's all.'

'A good late night, I hope.'

'I guess. We went to a ball thing his mum had organised.'

Olivia's hand pauses, a custard drip threatening to fall on her light-grey trousers. 'Wow. You're meeting the parents now. Sounds serious.'

'It was a little. More serious than I'd been planning on getting, if I'm honest.'

'You mean for so early on or more serious than you're ever planning on getting?'

'The second.'

'Oh no. You've been so happy these last few weeks.'

'I have, but it's meant to be a bit of fun. I don't want more.'

'That's sad.' Olivia pauses. We watch the pigeons approaching us, their target Olivia's fallen crumbs. 'Look, I get life's hard with your mum and this shitty disease. I just wish you'd see how good you and Alec are together. It would be such a shame if you let that go.'

'He's great,' I admit. 'Amazing, actually, but it was never meant to be a long-term thing. We had an arrangement to keep this short but sweet.'

'And now? Given how wonderful he is, will you not reconsider?'

'I can't.'

'But—'

'Enough, Olivia.' I'm snapping at a pregnant woman on a bench who sought me out to sit with her and eat vanilla slices.

'OK. I won't say anything else about it.' Olivia pulls out the remaining slice from the bag and takes a bite. I think that might be the end of it until she swallows and starts again.

'You've changed these last few months, you know? Maybe Alec coming along is a coincidence and you'd have changed anyway. All I know is that you're more open now than I've ever known you to be. Before you decided to let me in, you were like a ghost. We'd all see you, you'd come along to the odd thing outside office hours, but you weren't really there. You hardly ever talked. Then you told me and started to come out of your shell a little. Since Alec's come along, the trick's been shutting you up,' she says, giving me a playful nudge. 'Whatever's made you change, it's been a really good thing, Jess. I'm happy for you. If Alec's the cause of it all, I'd seriously consider letting him stick around.'

Chapter Twenty-seven

The list I make after lunch confirms what I already know. There's only one reason for not staying with Alec: Huntington's. On the one side of my notebook, there are all the reasons I want to be with him: gorgeous, wonderful sex, kind, makes me laugh, lovely to Mum, knows everything about me and still wants to be with me, is the first real man I've ever dated instead of the boys before, doesn't pretend to have everything worked out, brave, makes me feel brave, would always be by my side. On the other side, there's just the one, lonely word.

But words don't hold the same weight. Words like gorgeous and sex are feather light, whereas Huntington's carries the weight of a thousand rocks. Mum's shown me how heavy that word is, and I have to take steps to make sure I can lug that weight as best I can. Linking Alec with it is only going to make it heavier. But seeing all those lovely light words about him, so beautifully lined up, makes it harder to let him go.

My pen hovers over the page. I should scrub the words out, be done with the list, but I can't do it. I read it again and again, and as I do, the words start to become more significant. Kind: that's not quite as light as I first thought. He's been brilliantly kind about my disease, about Mum. Not everyone would have done that; many would have run. Makes me laugh: it's been so long since I've laughed and felt the happiness and lightness of doing so. I never imagined I'd feel light again, but Alec's given me that. And sex: being intimate with him has been the biggest gift of all. Pen in mid-air, the revelation comes: I don't need to erase these words. Not yet. One day, yes, I'll have to forget all about Alec and his substantial list, but there's no harm in holding on to him for a little while longer.

Say another month.

I send a text asking him to meet me at The Rose this evening. If I'm going to ask for more, I want to be close to home in case he doesn't agree to the plan, and I need to make a swift exit.

Politeness (and a need to keep my job) dictates I work late tonight. I can't leave before Jane does, and she makes damn sure she's in the office until half six. There's only an hour until I'm meeting Alec, and I can't turn up in the same clothes I've been wearing all day. Black leggings, a creased tunic and matronly grey cardigan aren't going to do much to help sell my idea to him. He's hardly going to be asking where to sign up to spend another month with a knackered, creased frump.

Mum's asleep when I rush in, and I'm glad of it. I'm in the bathroom piling on layers of Touche Éclat when there's a knock on the door.

'Jess, you got a minute?'

'Not really,' I tell Debs.

'Can you try and find one, please.'

I open the bathroom door, expecting her to be upset again, for this to be about her marriage, but there are no tears, just the red folder from the hallway cradled in her arms.

'Everything all right?'

'I'm not sure. I've been looking through the folder, and it seems your mum's not been too good today. She's not eaten at all and has been unusually tired.'

'Do you think she's coming down with something?'

'Maybe. We'll need to keep a closer eye on her tonight. Oh,' she says, taking in the make-up round my eyes and the rollers in my hair. 'You're off out?'

'Yeah, I'm meant to be meeting Alec. I can cancel, though.'

'No. Don't do that. You go have fun. I can always call you if I need you.'

The Rose is a mistake. The football is on and the place is packed. Every seat is taken. The only standing space is at the end of the bar where we'll be shoved and jostled all evening. What's worse is that it's his team playing in a European qualifier. A squeezed-in conversation during half-time isn't how I wanted to admit the depth of my feelings to him.

I order two bottles of beer and walk back outside to wait for him in the car park.

'Good evening,' he says, coming up behind me, snaking his arms round my waist.

'Good evening to you too.'

'What are we doing out here?'

'It's packed in there. Couldn't hear myself think. Fancy a drink in the beer garden?'

'You mean the empty beer garden with soggy chairs and no lights? Sure.'

It's a clear night, the Manchester sky allowing a few of the closest stars to shine through. I give Alec his beer, and he kisses me for a long time.

'Nice as this is, it's bloody freezing. Shall we go in?'

'In a minute. There's something I want to ask you first. Mum's not so good tonight,' I tell him. 'Debs is holding the fort and has strict instructions to ring me if there's a problem, but I shouldn't be out for too long.'

'Oh. Listen, if you want to do this another time, that's fine. I understand.'

'No, no. Honestly, it's OK. I would have cancelled if I were worried anything was really wrong. She's been very tired today and seems to be starting with something. It's probably no more than a cold, but with her not being able to speak much now, it's hard to know for sure what's going on. She was asleep when I left her. Fingers crossed, whatever it is will be gone in the morning.'

'OK, if you're sure.'

'I am.' I take a deep breath and begin. 'So, I know this is a pretty quick next date but I really wanted to see you.'

Alec pushes my hair away from my face and strokes my cheeks with his thumbs.

'I wanted to see you too. I've been thinking about you all day.'

'Same here. About you, I mean; I haven't been thinking about me all day.'

God, I'm nervous.

'Yeah, I got that.' He laughs kindly, squeezing my arm to encourage me to go on.

'Anyway, I wanted to tell you the dates we've been on have meant a lot to me. More than I thought they would. When you came up with your whole idea about having this month, I was so unsure about it. I'd promised myself I wouldn't get involved with anyone. The only reason I agreed was because I thought a month was nothing. I thought we'd have a bit of fun and that would be that.'

'That was the plan,' he says, a flicker of sadness passing across his face. 'I figured a month of being with you, of getting to know you, was so much better than nothing. And I was right. I've been thinking about this: if it weren't for your Huntington's diagnosis, I'd never have had this chance.

I reckon you'd have been long shacked up with someone, maybe even married by now. Even if you weren't, if you were still looking for love and a future with someone, I don't think you'd have taken one look at me.'

'Of course I would have. You're quite the catch, you know.'

'I don't know. Maybe you'd have seen me as a bit of eye candy, maybe we'd even have had that sordid first night together, but I doubt it would have gone further. In any other situation, we wouldn't have had *this* month together. I'm so grateful it happened, Jess. I needed it. Coming here, taking the job, was all well and good, but those were the practical sides of moving on. I needed to show myself I could emotionally move on too, and you gave me that.'

'I'm glad you feel that way. It's what I wanted to talk to you about. As I say, I've got something to ask you. I'd really like it—'

A buzzing at my feet interrupts me. I bend down to scoop up my bag and take out my phone. I swallow hard when I see the caller's name flashing on the screen: Debs.

'He-hello?' My voice is shaking. Despite her promise at my insistence to call if there was even the slightest change with Mum, Debs wouldn't ring unless something was wrong.

'Jess?' Debs shouts into the phone. There's a lot of noise behind her: voices and movement and urgency. 'Jess, it's me. I'm sorry, love, but it's your mum. We're in the ambulance on the way to hospital.'

Chapter Twenty-eight

The phone plummets to the ground. Alec leans forwards and runs his hands over the wet, uncut grass to try and find it.

'Jess?' he says, his face a mask of horrified concern once he's handed it to me and seen my face.

'I've got to go.' I stand up, shocked I can still do so with this ton weight of guilt pressing down on me.

'Of course.' He stands too.

'No!' I protest. 'You stay here.' The last thing I want is Alec coming with me. Somewhere in the back of my mind, I'm already registering my reaction as unfair, but, right now, I can't look at him without seeing this as partly his fault.

I was here, with *him*, instead of with Mum. I left her knowing she wasn't right so I could meet *him*.

Alec sits back down. I wait until I'm in the car park, away from Alec, then ring for a taxi. The air is bitter, slapping my cheeks in remonstrance for my poor choices.

Thankfully, Manchester Royal Infirmary is only a short distance from The Rose. The taxi arrives after five minutes, and the driver, upon hearing where I'm heading, nods once and speeds down Wilmslow Road at frightening speed.

I ask to be dropped in front of the A & E department, where I imagine Mum will be. Inside, the waiting room is overflowing into surrounding corridors with a mix of bloodied rugby players, frightened parents with their ill children and elderly men and women who stare into the middle distance, much more at ease with waiting than the others. I expect amongst the jumble I'll find Debs and Mum waiting their turn too, but there's no sign of them.

'Excuse me, I'm looking for Susan Hyland, my mum. She was brought in by ambulance,' I tell an intimidatingly hostile receptionist through the glass divide.

'One moment.'

She asks me a hundred questions, all of which I answer correctly but with increasing impatience before she's willing to give over even a scrap of information.

'Yes, got her,' she says after tapping some keys on an ancient block of a computer. 'She's been taken up to intensive care. Second floor.'

The blow hits me across the middle, punching all the air out of me. I have to hold on to the desk to steady myself.

Intensive care? I imagined I'd find Mum unwell, but intensive care isn't just unwell, is it? How could Mum go from being tired and a bit 'off' to needing the maximum level of care a hospital can offer in the space of a few hours?

I take the lift to the second floor and race down long corridors until I come across the inconspicuous sign pointing to the ICU.

To the left of the locked double doors to the unit there's an intercom. I press the button and in a small, shaking voice ask for Mum. There's a pause as the nurse on the other side of the door checks her patients. I pray when she speaks again she'll tell me there's been a mistake. Susan Hyland isn't here. Susan Hyland is just fine.

But the nurse doesn't say anything else. Instead, there's a buzzing noise and the door gives way.

The ward is smaller than I imagined with only six bays separated by papery blue curtains, but the noise of the dozens of machines working to keep these people going is overwhelming.

I must look scared; a dumpy nurse steps in front of me and immediately takes both of my hands in hers.

'Are you Mrs Hyland's daughter?'

'Yes. Is she OK?'

'She's in the end bay,' the nurse tells me, avoiding the question. 'The doctors are just finishing up with her.'

I follow her to the last bay, the only one with all its curtains shut, and, for the first time, spot Debs looking out the small slated window at the end of the room onto a view of the hospital's air-conditioning system.

'Debs?' I whisper.

'Oh, sweetheart,' she says, flinging her arms round me. 'She's OK. She's OK. It looks like she's got pneumonia. They're giving her a bit of help with her breathing, but they think we caught it early enough.'

'Thank God.' The relief breaks me, and the tears I've kept in since the pub finally arrive. Debs holds me, and I sob into her coat.

I only pull away from her when I hear Mum's curtains rustle. Two doctors wearing dark-green scrubs and crocs on their feet squeeze themselves through the small gap they've made between the curtains and immediately pull them back tight together.

After a whispered conversation I can't catch hold of and some tapping on their iPads, they turn to Debs and me.

They aren't smiling.

'Are you Mrs Hyland's daughter?' I'm asked again.

'Yes.'

'Hello. I'm Dr Bazra and this is Dr James.'

Forget the pleasantries and spit it out, I want to scream at him.

'How is she?'

'She's stable. It's a good job she came in when she did. The pneumonia had caused something called acute respiratory failure. Her lungs weren't able to release enough oxygen into her body, which is why she wasn't able to breathe properly. That caused the blue lips you noticed,' Dr Bazra explains, turning to Debs.

'My God,' I croak.

'We've put her on a ventilator to help her with her breathing and started a course of strong IV antibiotics to get rid of the pneumonia. We'll need to closely monitor her for the next few days to make sure the antibiotics are doing their job, and we'll keep her sedated and ventilated for the time being until we're certain the lungs have recovered enough.'

Both doctors look expectantly at me. This is the moment I should be thanking them for saving Mum, the moment I should be asking questions. Instead, I remain mute.

'Thank you, doctors,' Debs says, taking over. 'Can she go in and see her?'

'Of course,' Dr James says in a syrupy voice he must have learnt during his years of training. 'You'll see a lot of tubes and machines, but don't be alarmed. Remember, they're there to help your mum get better.'

We all exchange nods and the doctors move on to the next cubicle, the next patient.

'Wait,' I say. 'I don't understand.'

The doctors return to us, a tiny flicker of impatience shared between them as they do.

'How did my mum get pneumonia in the first place? She hadn't been unwell. She hadn't even had a cold. I don't get it.'

Dr Bazra steps towards me. 'I'm afraid the pneumonia is related to Huntington's disease. Pneumonia is a common

216

complication for patients in the end stage of the disease. There are a number of types of pneumonia and the most common for HD patients is a type called aspiration pneumonia. As it becomes more difficult for your mother to swallow and to eat, the chances of her inhaling food and saliva into her lungs becomes much higher. The harmful bacteria from these products can affect the lungs and cause pneumonia.'

'Oh.'

I hold on to Debs to steady myself. Dr Bazra's words are physical, pushing me over with the force of them. *End stage*. How can we be here so soon? How can he use the word *end* in a sentence about Mum? She's meant to have so much longer than this.

'What's important is that we've caught it and have brought it under control. Although, once she gets out, you'll want to speak to her healthcare providers about taking steps to prevent it happening again. If you'll excuse us, we've other patients to see, but we'll be back to check on her throughout the night.'

'Of course. Thank you, Dr Bazra,' I say, desperate to be away from him, to get to Mum and see for myself how wrong he's got it.

Dr Bazra enters the next cubicle, pulling the curtains shut, and I pull Mum's curtains open.

She looks so small and unfamiliar covered in a pale-blue sheet in the middle of the hospital bed, surrounded by machines, with wires and tubes and the ventilator obscuring her face. I sit on the plastic chair next to her bed. I don't dare touch her, not even to hold her hand.

It's true: it doesn't look like there's much life left in her right now. I can understand Dr Bazra's mistake now I've seen her, but, once the shock recedes, I calm down. This is temporary. Pneumonia is an illness she can get better from. This isn't the end, not at all.

Dawn arrives in haste the following morning, pushing out the soothing darkness on the ward and filling it with harsh light that lands on the machines and metal beds, on the mint-coloured walls and the Formica floor. Illuminating everything, hiding nothing.

The arrival of the new day marks no change in Mum, but reminds me that the last time I ate or drank anything was yesterday lunchtime. Not able to ignore the growing headache any longer, when Debs comes back in after a few hours sleeping on the waiting-room chairs outside, I suggest we find a café and refuel before the doctors' rounds at nine.

It's a large, school-style canteen we find, rather than a café, and it's packed with staff and visitors grabbing caffeine and breakfast at the start or end of their days. I spot an uncleaned but empty table in the corner and rush over to claim it whilst Debs takes care of breakfast.

She arrives twenty minutes later, by which point I'm close to passing out with hunger.

'I'm not sure it's a fry-up you were after, but it's pretty much all they had that was decent.'

She plonks down a plate heaped with scrambled eggs, beans, hash browns and sausages, and places a large paper cup of frothy coffee next to it.

'Right now, it's the most delicious thing I've ever seen,' I tell her before tucking in.

We're both so busy concentrating on demolishing our matching meals that we don't think to talk in between mouthfuls. It's only once our plates are scraped clean and our cups drained that we begin to notice our surroundings again, and Debs reaches for my hand.

'You doing all right, love?'

'I don't know. I think I might still be in shock. When I left the house I really didn't think it was anything serious. I promise. I wish I'd never gone out at all. I should have kept an eye on her, maybe I'd have spotted it earlier.'

'Spotted it earlier than I did?'

The accusation lies heavy between us, and I want to swallow it back.

'No, that's not what I meant. Of course I wouldn't have been able to do any more than you did. Thank God you were there and acted so quickly when she went downhill.'

'Good. Because it's like you say, she seemed fine when you left. One minute she's sleeping and I'm watching the TV with the volume down, the next she's gasping for breath and her lips are turning blue. There's nothing you could have done differently.'

'Maybe. Doesn't stop me feeling like a lousy daughter.'

Debs smiles, which is graceful of her given my suggestion she's not up to her job. 'Sweetheart, there isn't a lousy bone in your body. It's horrible but these things are going to happen with your mum, and, although you might feel a bit better being the one who's with her when they do, you'll never be able to stop them happening. Huntington's is a bastard. It's the disease you need to blame and to hate, not anything else and never, ever yourself.'

'You're right.'

'I know.'

The arms on the plastic clock nailed to the wall above the tray rack nudge round to eight-thirty. Customers are beginning to thin out, appointments and rounds waiting for them on the wards. I watch them leave, idly wondering who they are returning to, how happy their endings are going to be. Happier than mine, I'm guessing. When I turn back to Debs to suggest we return to the ICU so we don't miss Dr Bazra's update on Mum, Debs is no longer there. She's bent under the table, rummaging for something in the RSPCA cotton shopping bag she carries around with her everywhere she goes. When she sits back up, she's clutching an envelope.

'Before we go back up, we need to have a bit of a chat. I've been dreading this, but, after talking to the doctors and seeing your mum like this, I can't put it off any longer.'

She places the envelope on the table. The fingers of her right hand paw at it, pushing it towards me before snatching it back. Forwards and back, forwards and back, unsure where it needs to go until she forcefully shoves it towards me and sits on her hands. I don't want it, but it lies between us like a gun, and I know I need to take it from Debs, to relieve her of the burden of being in its charge. I pull it off the table and onto my lap. Debs nods. I catch a whiff of the coffee breath she releases.

'When you first took me on, your mum and I used to stay up together a lot during the night when you'd gone to bed and she couldn't sleep. You know we became close, and before long coming to work felt more like visiting friends.'

'I do know. It was the same for us.'

'And you'll know that your mum and I used to talk all the time those first months, when her voice was still hers and her mind still able to hold conversation. Well, it'll be no surprise to know that she spoke about you more than anything else: how proud she was of you with your job and the way you'd handled finding out you'd tested positive for Huntington's disease; how much she wanted you to travel and live a big, full life for as long as you could and how much she worried about you when she saw you shutting people out of your life without replacing them with anyone new.

'She also spoke about something else: her wishes when the Huntington's became bad. Whenever she did, the first thing I said was that she should speak to you about this, not me, but she didn't feel she could.'

'That's rubbish. We've always talked about everything. Nothing's off limits with us.'

'I know, love. There's no denying how close the pair of you are. But this was different. She wanted to protect you from this, to keep you young and unburdened by the decisions she'd had to make, so she told me instead. No matter how clear her instructions were, I had to keep telling her, it wouldn't be up to me when the time came; any decisions that needed to be made would have to come from you, not me. She understood that, although still she couldn't bring herself to have the conversation. Instead, she gave me this letter. I promised to look after it and only give it to you when I thought the time had come for you to start making decisions about what's best for your mum at the end of her life.'

I look down at my lap. My name is on the envelope, written in the almost-familiar loopy hand of my mum, with only the odd shaky letter to speak of her chorea. I put it back on the table and recoil. No matter how strong the pull is to see more of Mum's writing with its comforting jolt into the past, I can't bring myself to open it. This letter is about the future. A painful, terrifying future.

'Not you too, Debs,' I say with a sigh. 'You sound like the doctors. Mum will be fine. It's pneumonia. Tons of people get that, healthy people. It'll get sorted with antibiotics. I know it's been awful seeing her like this, and we've had a fright, but this doesn't signal the end of her life.'

Debs is stuck. There's a flash of panic in her eyes when I push the envelope back across to her. However she imagined this conversation playing out, I'm sure this scenario never entered her head.

'No. I'm very sorry, Jess, but I think it is the right time. She's ended up with pneumonia because she can't swallow, because her muscles are failing her so much that whatever food she's managing to get down her can't travel to the right place and is ending up in her lungs. I know it's hard to hear, sweetheart, but now this has happened and is likely to happen again, I really do think the time has come to have a think about what's going to be best for your mum.'

I know exactly what she means but still I ask, my voice venomous, 'I take it you mean putting Mum in a home?'

Debs reaches out for me, but I shove my hands under the table.

'I do. I'm so sorry, but I think your mum's going to need more care moving on, and I know, despite what she said about wanting to stay home, it was her strong wish that she doesn't want you to have to give it to her.'

'Enough!' I shout at her. I shove the table away from me, and bolt out of the canteen, smashing into a child carrying a tray full of crisps and fizzy pop.

'Idiot,' he calls after me.

I don't slow down. Once out in the corridor, I break into a run, forgoing lifts for stairs in my haste to be back with Mum. Only once I'm at her side, seeing her smallness, her frailty afresh, do I let myself crumple, curling over the bed, my head falling next to hers.

End stage. There's nowhere to run from it. In the daylight, it's glaringly obvious. I have so little time left with her.

'I'm so sorry, Mum,' I whisper to her.

Debs taps me on the shoulder when she returns to the ICU.

'Mum isn't going into a home,' I tell her through snot and tears.

'That's up to you, not me. Just promise me you'll open this envelope before you decide anything.' She places it gently on the end of the bed. 'Your mum needs you to know what's inside it.'

Chapter Twenty-nine

The heating hasn't been on in the house for days. When Debs went back to get me some supplies, she knew I wouldn't dream of coming home until Mum was out of danger and had the foresight to turn it off.

During one of her interior-design sprees, Mum ripped out the gas fireplace in the lounge, filled the hole and papered over it. Now, I turn on the light in the lounge and look at the Laura Ashley paper through hateful eyes.

Mum was moved down to the high-dependency unit this afternoon once her ventilator came out. The nurses assured me this was great news; the doctors wouldn't allow her to come out of the ICU unless they were sure she was past the worst of it.

It wasn't their fault. Sedated and under blankets, it was hard to see Mum's Huntington's. To the nurses who didn't know about the cruel way the disease would grasp a person and never let them go, Mum may have appeared to have been getting better, which would, of course, be deemed great news. Only, I couldn't wring more than a few moments' relief from her improvement. Yes, she was ridding herself of pneumonia, but in doing so, she'd only freed herself from one prison to be returned straight back to another.

When I shared this with a student nurse tucking Mum between worn cotton sheets in her new bed, I was smiled at, told I was tired, that I wasn't able to stay with Mum on this ward outside visiting hours and should go home to rest.

It's too cold to rest. I've cranked the heating up as high as it will go, but it's an old system, which has long developed an autonomy in selecting which rooms it fancies heating and to what degree. I run upstairs to make sure all the doors upstairs are open so at least any heat will spread through the house. I return downstairs to the kitchen, longing for the spread of alcohol through my blood supply. Jane's agreed to give me time off while Mum is in hospital, and I raise my glass to her, thanking her for giving me no reason to be up first thing so I can drink to my heart's content.

Mum's letter is folded inside the pocket of the coat I'm still wrapped up in. The more I drink and try to forget, the more I feel its pressure against my side. By the third glass of Shiraz, it's prodding me in my ribs, demanding my attention. I pull it out and place it on the worktop before returning to the table.

It's dark out, and, aside from the hob light to guide me to the wine, I've not thought to put the lights on in the house. The envelope lurks in the blackness. Waiting.

I'm just bringing myself to pick the thing up when there's a knock at the door. It's such a timid knock, at first I'm not sure if it was a knock at all or rather a gust of wind outside. I wait until I hear it again before getting up.

I discover Alec on my front doorstep, two plastic Sainsbury's carrier bags at his feet.

I'm surprised.

I'd have thought Alec would be the kind of person to bring his own bags to the supermarket.

Coming out of the hospital, I turned my phone on to a barrage of texts from Alec. In response, I raced out a text: *Mum better, on way home for a bit.* And now here he is.

'Hi, you,' he says, stepping out of the way of his shopping to pull me into a tight hug.

'Hi.'

'This is OK, isn't it?' he asks when I don't invite him in or say anything.

'Is what OK?'

'Me coming round. I figured you'd have been surviving on hospital food for days now and could do with a good meal. And some company?'

'Yes, it's fine. Come in.'

Alec picks up his bags and bounds past me to the kitchen like a dog that's been granted permission to enter the house.

Every light switch he passes on his way he flicks on, his very presence bringing light to my life.

'I thought I'd go classic, if that's OK with you. Prawn cocktail to start followed by chicken wrapped in Parma ham. I've brought wine too, though I see you've already got a head start on me there.'

I survey the scene as he makes his way around my kitchen, unloading the food over the worktop, landing an iceberg lettuce on top of the envelope, helping himself to one of the Vera Wang wine glasses Mum's work colleagues gave her to celebrate the ten-year anniversary of her opening the optician's. The more he makes himself at home, the worse it becomes.

There's no one I want more in this moment than Alec. If I let him carry on, I know he'll make me feel better. We'll eat, share wine and, at some point, he'll open those wide arms of his and let me fall into them. But I can't fall into them. Not anymore.

Mum has been dragged into the final stages of Huntington's. I can't waste any more of the time she has left chasing a dream that doesn't apply to me. Every second now needs to be about her.

If I told him that, he'd understand, but it's not as though we can pick up where we left off afterwards. When the disease is done with her, sooner or later, it's going to be my turn. The only life I can offer him from this point on involves boundless pain.

If only I'd stuck to my rules, he wouldn't be mixed up in this. He's standing in a house of suffering, and he thinks he wants to be here. There's only one reasonable thing I can do at this point: let him out of it.

'For God's sake, Alec,' I erupt. 'What the fuck are you doing?'

His back is to me. I can see his muscles harden, straightening him up to his full six-foot height.

'I thought I was being nice.'

'Nice? What's nice about coming to my house uninvited, trying to have a romantic dinner with me whilst my mum is in hospital? Talk about insensitive,' I shout at him, looking down at my feet as I do when calling him something he could never be.

He laughs. A horrible, incredulous laugh, designed to rip into me. 'Insensitive? What, worrying about you for days, hearing nothing and rushing round to look after you the moment I know you're home is insensitive? I'm pretty sure most people would say the opposite.'

He begins to pack up, storming around the kitchen, shoving his lettuce and tomatoes and a packet of chicken breasts back into the shopping bags. I let him carry on, staring at the floor and trying to keep my face from falling out of its indignant expression as he does so.

'I was worried about you,' he says once there's nothing left for him to do but go. 'I wanted to make sure you were OK. Sorry I've offended you so much.'

'You're not meant to be worrying about me, though, are you?'

'That's right. Our arrangement. We can date each other, have sex but can't care about each other. How silly of me to forget.'

A hand covers the bottom half of his face. That and the low voice he speaks in make it hard to work out if he's being sarcastic or not. Not that it matters.

'I wish you hadn't forgotten. It makes this much harder than it needs to be. I was hoping, given the circumstances, you'd realise that our month's up. The last thing I need is an argument from you, Alec.'

'Don't worry,' he says, passing by me into the hallway. The bags brush against my leg, and I feel the cold of the chicken. 'You won't get one.'

He's at the front door, hand on the latch, about to turn it, when his shoulders fall.

'I don't understand this. That night at The Rose, the night your mum went into hospital. Right before you got the call, I was sure you were gearing up to suggesting we become more serious. Was I completely wrong or did you want more?'

'You were wrong. I was going to thank you for showing me a bit of fun the last few weeks. That was all.'

'Huh. I could have sworn you were about to tell me something else. I was going to tell you something too. If we'd had longer, I'd have told you I was falling in love with you.'

A silence falls between us, as clogging and oppressive as car fumes.

'Good job you never got the chance,' I say, longing to be free from it, to let him be free from me.

He stares at me, trying to work out if my face matches my words, trying to spot any discrepancy. Finding none, there's nothing else for him to do but leave.

Job done.

I slide down the closed front door until I'm sitting on the wooden floor with my legs splayed out in front of me. I've no idea how long I stay like that, eyes firm shut, but when I open them again the heating has made the house sticky warm.

I'm ready to be consoled. I return to the kitchen and the near-empty bottle of wine, safe in the knowledge that there are another few bottles tucked away behind the cereal boxes. It's the height of rudeness to run out of booze when there are visitors round, Mum always said. I make a point of adhering to her wisdom and keeping a well-stocked kitchen.

After pouring another glass, I'm ready to make myself feel better.

It was the right thing. Where would honesty have got us, really? What point would the truth have served?

I could have told him how being with him has split me in two. As well as the Huntington's me, he helped create another me, young and healthy and happy. Being with him fed that other self to the point where it had become bigger than the self I'd known. For a short time there I thought I could look after Mum whilst waiting for her symptoms to become mine *and* live as though it weren't happening. I thought I could be with him, could love him and could let him love me.

And if it weren't for Debs ringing me about Mum, I would have told him this. I'd have asked for more and let him give it. After that, when would I have stopped? What would it have taken for me to realise I'd pulled him too far? A proposal? A marriage?

Everything I swore I wouldn't do to another person, I'd nearly let myself do to Alec. If there's one good thing to come from Mum's pneumonia, it's that it showed me how dangerously far I'd come with Alec, and it made me stop. It put my rules back in place, so no one else has to suffer because of this disease.

It was the right thing.

These thoughts are meant to soothe, to numb, but I'm left disappointed. Every thought I force into my mind is squashed by Alec's words: *I'd have told you I was falling in love with you.*

Grabbing another bottle of wine, I wander the empty house drinking straight from the bottle, looking for somewhere to go. Eventually, my feet come to a stop in the doorway to the dining room. I turn the light on and am assaulted by the sight of the empty bed, the sheets on the floor. I make my way to the chair where I've sat watching over Mum for so long. The sight of her absence is too much.

I quickly put the wine bottle down before the cracking begins.

Funny how most images of heartbreak are so neat. A clean line slicing the heart in two. But there's nothing neat or clean about my heart. It's shattered into a hundred different pieces. For Alec, for the life we're never going to get, for the hurt I've caused him, for all the love for him I've got nowhere to put, for Mum, for her life cut short, for my life cut short.

I curl up in a tight ball, my hands pressed against my chest in an effort to control the mess, and I cry until I fall asleep.

Chapter Thirty

I open Mum's letter the following morning.

Three things fall out of the envelope onto my lap: a handwritten inventory of Mum's savings, bonds and shares; a typed letter and a print-out of a care-home website.

I arrange them into a pile, the letter at the bottom. After scouring Mum's savings, reading about the facilities Henley Hall has to offer, taking two paracetamol for the Shiraz-induced headache and making myself a cup of tea, I sit back down at the kitchen table and place the letter in front of me.

I don't want to read it. There's a voice inside my brain screaming at me not to. Once it's read, it can never be unread, it says. Look away now, it warns me. But I have to read it. Mum's voice is here in these pages, and it's up to me to listen to what she has to say.

Dear Jess,

The strangest thing happened this morning. I woke up, and it was as if the last few years had been erased. Most days it feels like I'm underwater, but today it was as though I'd woken in fresh air on the calmest, clearest day you could imagine. I can't tell you how wonderful it was.

You thought I was asleep as you crept by the dining room on your way out to work, but I wasn't. I was watching you. Watching the way you've started to drop your head between your shoulders when you walk. Your hair was scraped back into a ponytail and you looked dreadfully tired, even though your day had only just begun.

I remember, when you first got your job, how you used to wake up at six to curl your hair and put your face on, only happy to leave the house when you looked like a character from Suits.

Seeing you this morning, I knew what I had to do. I called Debs into my room once you'd left and asked her for the laptop and a favour.

If you're reading this, it means Debs has decided the time has come when I'm going to need more care, that I'm nearing the end. I gave her instructions to pass this letter on to you and to make sure you don't ignore it.

What would we do without Debs? If we're to look for a positive to take from this whole thing, Debs has got to be it, right? It's such a comfort to know that you've got her in your life now, and such a relief that I can trust her to choose the right moment to give you this letter.

There are so many things I'd like to use this letter to tell you, my sweet, sweet girl. So many memories I have of you as a child, so many pieces of my life I want you to learn, because once I go they'll be gone forever. Only, I don't know how long this clarity will last for, nor do I know how long I'll be able to keep punching the keys on the laptop before it becomes too difficult. I'm going to have to focus on the things I think might help you the most. Before I do, let me tell you simply that you have given me the best life I could ever have wished for, and I love you with all my heart.

And now to business:

I don't want you to care for me when things get bad. I've thought about this a lot, Jess. I know you'll want to be there for me – you can be – but I won't have you nursing me to death.

I've done my research and found a lovely nursing home to take care of me. Debs has spoken to the manager for me, and they're happy to accept me when the time comes. You'll find a copy of the website with this letter with all the information you need to get in touch with them. They'll be happy to answer all of your questions. You'll also find details of all my finances. You've got power of attorney and will be able to access them when you need to pay for the home. It's not cheap, but there should be enough to cover it. To think I saved like a squirrel all these years, planning to spend it when I retired on cruises around the Med and lunch at Harvey Nics. Well, it is what it is, and I can't dwell on it too much. If spending that money prevents you being scarred by the memories of caring for me in these last months, it's worth it.

Come and visit me whenever you feel the need. No matter where this disease takes me, I'll always be happy to see you. But if you don't want to, if it's too hard, that's fine too.

The only thing I want from you is a promise you'll start living your life again. You won't admit it, but you've given up. You've done so ever since you got the results from the genetic test. The reason I didn't want you to get tested was that I knew it would stop your life unfolding the way it should do. You're the most organised person I've ever known, and I knew if the news was bad, you'd try to plan around it, would try to pack things into boxes to make it all as neat as you could.

Please be brave. Let your life get messy every now and again. I know it's hard when you're watching me fade

233

away. Harder still when you know the same thing might happen to you, but finding the bravery to live a normal life despite that will be the difference between having a good life, one, I hope, with as much happiness as mine, or waiting in the shadows, hiding away until illness comes calling.

I'm getting tired now, so I'll have to finish. If Debs has given this to you, it means it's time for me to do the last thing I can for you and spare you some pain. I want you to know how loved you are and how thankful I am I got to be your mum for so long. Everything is OK, my darling, so you can stop worrying.

Now go and be happy.

Mum xxx

I push it away before getting up and leaving the kitchen and the letter, wanting to be as far away from it as I can. The walls in my room are too small to contain my pacing, so I grab a coat and leave the house, walking aimlessly around the streets, careful not to stray too close to Didsbury village in case anyone I know comes across my fury.

How dare Mum make these decisions without me? How dare she effectively cut me out of the end of her life?

I'm angry with Debs too, for conspiring with her. For knowing for months what Mum was planning and never so much as hinting to me what was going to happen.

And to say my life needs to get messy. I could laugh at that one. After the mess I made of things with Alec, I'm going to be keeping my life as clean as it can be, thank you very much.

Once I've been walking for nearly an hour, I realise I shouldn't have left the house. If I'd have stayed in my room, I could have held on to this anger, kept it enclosed.

The more I walk in the cool, fresh air, the more the anger withdraws from me like a receding tide. I needed that anger. Without it, the letter is much worse.

I go back home and read it again, this time seeing in it the kindness in Mum's words and the love for me in them. More than anything I see her determination to be able to have some control over the last aspect of her life. God knows, I can understand that.

Suddenly, hot tears are splodging onto the letter, blurring some of Mum's words. Horrified, I run to get a tea towel and dab the letter until it's dry. The blurring remains, but the words are still readable, preserved for all the times I know I'm going to need to read them over the coming months.

Carefully, I bring the letter to my chest and press it to my heart.

'I don't want you to go,' I whisper, although the house is already empty and there's no one to overhear me.

Chapter Thirty-one

Seven years earlier

Once I'd finished packing my own suitcase, I started on Mum's.

The one proviso Mum gave me when she called to say she'd booked us a last-minute getaway to Barcelona was that I had to do her packing, as she was going to be working flat out to get through her appointments before we left on Friday lunchtime.

Her room was a mess. Clothes were strewn on the back of her chair and in a heap down the side of her bed. It amazed me how someone as professional as Mum, someone who had such pride in her house, had started leaving her room in this state. I stepped on a pair of those pointless, thin, skin-coloured tights she put on every day under her work dresses and winced. I wouldn't be packing any of those. At the back of her wardrobe was a plastic box labelled: *Summer Wear*. I pulled it open to find a pile of pale linen. Old, rumpled clothes that had seen her through years of summer holidays. Once I'd pulled out a few select pieces, the pile I'd made for her on the bed looked small and colourless.

With an hour to spare before the taxi was booked, I left the house. A new boutique had opened up in Didsbury the week before and Mum had admired the bright dresses in the window as we passed it.

A navy maxidress, a palm-tree-printed shirt-dress, a black camisole and a pair of hot-pink trousers later, I was ready to get home, finish the packing and go.

'Did you manage to find everything?' Mum asked on the way to the airport.

'I think so,' I said.

She pulled her dress away from her stomach and sighed. 'I'd be amazed if anything fits, the weight I've piled on recently.'

'I'm sure it will.'

We arrived at the hotel that evening in time to get ready and head out for a meal and drinks. I was in the bathroom when I heard the swearing.

'What's wrong?'

'I've only gone and picked up the wrong suitcase.'

'Are you sure?' I asked, coming out to see her holding up the pink trousers.

'Unless these are yours, yeah, I bloody well have.'

'I think you'll find they're yours,' I told her. 'A little present from me to say thanks for the holiday.'

'Oh, you gorgeous girl, you shouldn't have. How can you afford them?'

'Hey, I'm a worker now, you know.' I'd spent most of my second pay cheque from the marketing company I'd been working at as a part-time assistant on the clothes, and, from her face, I knew there was nothing better I could have spent my money on.

'I do indeed. Well, I love them. Thank you. And these dresses?'

'Yours too.'

She squealed. 'You shouldn't have,' she said, already laying out her new clothes on the bed. 'They're beautiful.'

'What are you going to wear first?'

'Definitely the pink trousers. What Spanish hunk would be able to resist these?'

'Oh God, you're not going to be flirting with the waiters all night, are you?'

'Of course not. In these, there'll be no flirting required. They'll be falling at my feet.'

She wasn't far wrong. As we set off from the hotel and walked down Las Ramblas arm in arm, I saw the heads turning, the prolonged glances at her. She'd have said it was the clothes, but it was nothing to do with them. It was her smile, her laugh, her delight in being there. It was all her.

Chapter Thirty-two

Mum has made a good choice. Henley Hall is a grade-two-listed former stately home boasting stained-glass windows, pillars guarding its front entrance and a turret at either end. It has a sandstone front, the clean, caramel-coloured kind, the kind that gets power-washed twice a year. If it weren't for the folded wheelchairs lined up in the porch and the two women wearing pale blue nurses' tunics, Henley Hall could easily be mistaken for an upmarket hotel.

Debs and I pull up outside. Mum follows in the ambulance, which the nursing home had arranged to collect her from the hospital. Leaving the suitcase I packed with her tracksuits and pyjamas, and a bouquet of flowers in the car, Debs heads through the open oak doors to the small reception area in the entrance hall to let them know we're here, and I walk towards a gated, formal garden to the right of the building.

Someone's placed a bench in front of the lily-covered pond. Attached to its back is a shiny brass plate. I bend to read the inscription: *In Memory of Maggie, who loved these gardens and this home. Missed by Frederick and Richard every day.*

I gently run my fingers over it. If Maggie can bring herself to love this place, there's hope for Mum. I start exploring the garden in a bid to discover more good things, like the weeded borders filled with colourful flowers and the towering pink rhododendron bush beginning to bloom.

Things to make Mum happy. Things I can cling on to when we drive away.

'Here's the ambulance now, love,' Debs shouts over the low hedges separating the driveway from the garden.

Mum's arrival brings out a small woman in a power suit and stilettos, her hair pulled so severely into a topknot, I can see the skin pulling around her hairline. She looks so polished that, instead of being impressed with her professionalism, I immediately conjure up an image of what she must look like when the costume comes off and she lets her hair tumble free. It's an unfortunate by-product of her efforts that when I go across to shake her hand, I'm picturing her in a dressing gown and bunny-rabbit slippers.

'Hello, you must be Jess. We spoke on the phone. I'm Nina Lew.'

'Yes. Hi.'

'Shall we go and help your mum settle in? You're welcome to stay with her as long as you want. We always recommend relatives seeing as much of the day-to-day life of Henley Hall as they can to put their minds at rest. You're more than welcome to stay for dinner with us, if you'd like.'

'That would be lovely, thanks.'

'See, told you they'd be nice, didn't I?' Debs whispers to me as the three of us make our way to the back of the ambulance to greet Mum.

Two porters also join us to help get Mum's wheelchair down from the ambulance and to carry it across the inconvenient gravel driveway to the entrance.

Mum looks tiny in her chair with the hospital blanket covering her body, finishing under her chin. Whilst I take in the grand entrance, Mum remains still. Whether she has no interest in her surroundings or isn't looking because it's too hard to swivel her head, I can't be sure.

'We'll take you straight to your mum's room. Once you've made yourselves at home, please feel free to come back down and explore our communal rooms. If I'm not available to take you around, one of our nurses will be more than happy to help. Lift's this way.'

A black mark. This Nina Lew should be talking to Mum, not me. If she can't even get this simple matter right, what else is going to get missed under her watch? I push Mum towards the lift, feeling with every step we're being swallowed further and further into a mistake.

Mum's room, when we get to it at the end of a long, wide corridor on the second floor, is bright and large. I suspect we've been lucky getting this room with its bay window overlooking the driveway rather than a smaller room at the back of the hall. If it were a hotel, this room would certainly be classed as Superior.

It's nice, I suppose. If only the bed cover on the hospital-style bed wasn't peach, if only the curtains didn't have a frilled trim.

There's more than a sniff of the elderly in this room. Of course, most of the people in Henley Hall will be old, decades older than Mum. At fifty-five, Mum's the youngest they've ever taken in. They refuse to take anyone younger. If Mum had reached this stage of her Huntington's last year, she would have been made to find somewhere else.

There's a snot-green armchair in front of the window, overlooking the garden. I perch on its arm, back straight as a rod. I'm sure it would do Mum good to see me settle in, might make it easier for her to do the same if she thought I was comfortable here, but my unease is deepening like fake tan, and there's no way I can scrub it off.

This isn't Mum. Mum is all about deep colours, big patterns, contrasting textures and soft lighting. Now she's ended up in a pastel box.

It's clear we've not brought anywhere near enough to make this place feel like home. Despite her best efforts, when Debs finishes laying out the photo frames, blankets and ornaments she thought to bring, it's still a bedroom belonging to a crinkly woman called Joan or Mavis and not to a formerly stylish, modern woman in her fifties.

'There,' says Debs, putting the bouquet of flowers she bought onto the dressing table. In the car, the flowers loomed massively in the back seat, filling the car with the sweet perfume of roses and carnations. In the vastness of this room they've shrunk into little more than a token posy and do nothing whatsoever to cheer the place up. I resolve to bring as much as I can from the house when I come back tomorrow. Not just trinkets. I'll bring the bookcase from the dining room filled with her favourite novels; her numerous Jo Malone candles, which she may not be able to light but I can still dot around the place; the Next rug from the lounge and the purple velvet cushions off the sofa.

'Thanks, Debs,' I say when she sits on the bed with an 'Ooof'.

'You're welcome. It looks good, doesn't it?' she asks Mum.

Mum's getting tired. Her eyes fall shut in long blinks.

'Where do you want to go, Mum?' I ask her loudly before she falls asleep in the wheelchair. 'To the armchair? Or shall we get you into bed?'

Mum points her finger to the bed, and Debs and I lift her across. Immediately I pull the covers over her in case she gets a chill.

Once settled, Mum's eyes start to close again. I perch on the side of the bed and tap her legs to get her to look at me before she sleeps.

'Are you OK here, Mum? Is this what you want? We can always take you home if you don't like it. It's not too late.'

'Jess,' Debs warns, 'your mum's made her decision.'

'I know,' I snap, but I need to hear her answer all the same. Otherwise, there's no way I'll be able to leave her here.

'I'm fine,' Mum says a few seconds later. I can see by the drop in her colour how much it's cost her to get the words out. She also manages to give me a small smile and to squeeze my hand. As soon as she's done it, she closes her eyes and doesn't open them again.

'She'll be worn out from all the toing and froing, I expect,' Debs says. 'Best let her have a good sleep.'

'It's dinnertime soon. We were meant to be going down together so we could check out the dining room.'

'I wouldn't worry about that too much.'

'Yeah, OK. Maybe they'll bring up a tray for her instead.'

'I'm sure they will, if she's awake.'

'Yeah, that's what they'll do.'

I place the old laminated sheet I've brought from home on the bedside table for when she wakes, so she needn't speak again if it's too hard, and walk aimlessly around the room.

'She'll be all right here. I know she will,' Debs tells me. From the sharp resolve in her voice, I suspect she's telling herself that too.

'Will she?'

'She will. This might not be home, but it's somewhere she's safe and will be well looked after. This is her choice, Jess, and we've got to make the best of it we can.'

'I know.'

'Good. Now, let's get going before the traffic gets bad.'

'Oh no. I can't leave her. Not yet.'

'You can, sweetheart. You need to.'

Somehow, Debs gets me to speak to Yolanda, Mum's nurse for the day, and run through the long list of instructions I've already emailed over about Mum's care. I even thank this woman for promising to look after Mum and ask her to give me a call in a few hours.

It's like I've become an infant again. With a bit of coaxing, I'm letting myself be torn away from my mother like a toddler at playgroup. With so many distractions and the quick pace with which Debs moves me, I don't even think to cry for her.

It's only when I get dropped off and enter our silent, terrifyingly empty home that the pain of parting begins to throb like an infected cut and the tears arrive. Back at Henley Hall, Mum was looking after me, like always. I'd been so relieved when she squeezed my hand, when she told me she was fine. I was able to leave her because of it. But now I'm home, and, for the first time, she's not. She's not here to tell me it will be OK, because we don't live together anymore. We never will again, and there's nothing I can find within these walls that will ever ease that pain.

Chapter Thirty-three

A bunch of flowers from Marks & Spencer are lying on my desk when I return to work for the first time since Mum was taken ill. Whoever bought them spent their money wisely; long stems of gladioli stretch over my keyboard and over the side of my desk interspersed with unopened lilies. When they bloom, the bouquet will look glorious and much more impressive than a few roses ever could.

There's a card attached to the cellophane wrapping written in Jane's overly large scrawl:

Thinking of you at this difficult time. We're all here for you.
Your friends at McAllister Lewis Glenn.

A kind thought, but, as is often the case with Jane, a little off the mark. This is a sentiment for the bereaved. I'm not bereaved; I'm pre-bereaved. No one makes cards for that. What will Jane do when it really does happen? There'll have to be another whip-round, another bouquet purchased in my honour. I just hope there's a suitable gap between the two; otherwise there's going to be a lot of grumbling over the expense.

When Jane saunters over, her face a mask of sympathy and blusher, I smile politely and keep quiet about the pointlessness of her gesture.

'There you are, sweetheart. Come here.'

I'm pulled into a light embrace at odds with the

mournful note in her voice. Fair enough. She's wearing her silk Jaeger shirt today; anything more than a light brush of her body against mine would leave the most gruesome creases.

I had to tell Jane about Mum's illness. With the two weeks I'd taken off visiting her in the hospital and sorting out her move into the nursing home, keeping quiet about it would have risked my job. There's only so many sick days you can get away with round here before the partners start sniffing around, getting HR on the case. Telling Jane was the only option if I wanted to have any more time away from my job and still have that same job to come back to.

A neurological condition, I told her. If I'd have said more, coming back to work today wouldn't have been a case of catching up with emails and fielding well wishes. There would have been stares, mutterings behind my back and diversions by some to avoid passing my desk. That would be just from the girls in the office. Further up the chain, there'd be meetings about what to do with me. I'd be called into occupational health, my competency to remain in my post examined. They'd have to let me stay on. They can't get rid of me for a disease lying in wait. But they'd be watching me – everyone would – waiting for the signs that it's starting.

It's what Mum hated most when her chorea became noticeable, all that attention. If people were nice, they'd stop and ask if she was all right, suspecting she'd had a few too many. If they weren't, they'd glare at her as she struggled to keep her body under her own control before averting their eyes. I couldn't bear it either. No, at work, the story ends with Mum. It has to.

Still, it's been a relief. Keeping Mum's illness a secret made my life harder, I see that now. It's the lies that do it.

The pressure of throwing a disguise over your life, always having to think about how to keep the truth concealed.

I expected Jane to press for more, but I was wrong. The way she stepped up to help, telling me I absolutely must not dream about coming back to work until I was ready, felt good. Tentatively, she asked if I wanted her to share the news with the girls in the office, as they've been concerned about my absence. Of course, I told her. Let them know too. If they react to the news the same way as Jane, coming into the office to their support every day might be the tonic I need.

'How are *you*?' Jane asks, taking a seat in my chair.

'I'm fine, thanks. It's a big readjustment, but Mum's settled in well, and I'm starting to accept it's the best place for her. Thanks for being so understanding.'

She dismisses my gratitude with a bat of her hand. 'Not at all. We're here to help, my darling. To think you've kept quiet about it all these months. If only you'd said, we could have been here for you.'

'That's very kind of you.'

'Don't mention it. Now, I expect Harold will be popping down at some point today to have a little chat with you. Just to make sure you're OK. When I told him about your poor mum, he was as distraught as me. Fifty-five and in a care home – you wouldn't wish it on your worst enemy.'

'No, you wouldn't.'

When Jane disappears, I remind myself it's not crass of her to say such things, so I have no right to feel prickled by the comment.

Pushing the flowers to one side, I begin to scroll down hundreds of unread emails. All will have to be opened, all dealt with. Deciding I'm only going to get through this with caffeine, I scoop up the flowers and head to the small kitchenette partitioned from the rest of the open-plan office, where I find Olivia making herself some awful-smelling herbal tea. When she turns to me, there's a new, neat semi-circle poking out from under her dress.

'Look at you,' I say.

'Jess, you're back.'

I'm in her arms before I know it. This time, it's a hug that could squeeze the life right out of you.

'OK, OK,' I tell her, wriggling free.

'I've been so worried about you. Well done for telling Jane about your mum. She's an arse, but she means well. I'm really proud of you.'

'Thanks.'

Olivia and I had spoken the night before I told Jane. I had to know I could trust Olivia not to tell anyone about Mum's actual diagnosis, about my own diagnosis. She assured me she wouldn't tell a soul, and I know she's been true to her word. Of all the hundreds of hours of gossip my announcement must have created, Olivia hasn't spoken a word more than she should.

'Why didn't you tell me how much worse things were getting? And why didn't you tell me your mum had gone into hospital when it happened? These last few months I've been feeling so sorry for myself, all I've done is moan, and you've put up with it all. I could have visited your mum or brought you food.'

'It's fine.'

'No, it's not. I could have helped you.'

'Sorry, I guess I shut down a bit.'

'Well, no more of that. You've got me and the whole office behind you now. We're all going to do our best to make life a bit easier for you when you need us to. Even Jane.'

I laugh. 'Who'd ever have thought it? Hey, you're looking less green than the last time I saw you. I take it the morning sickness is wearing off?'

'Yep. Here, smell me.'

'What?'

'Smell me.'

I lean forward and take a polite sniff.

'Go on, what do you smell?'

'I don't know. Deodorant. Shampoo.'

'Exactly. Not a whiff of sick. Three whole days now I've gone without throwing up.'

'Wow. Congrats. I take it that means Rick's off your case.'

'He is,' she says, smiling with her eyes closed. 'He went to work this morning without even saying goodbye. It's wonderful.'

'Great.'

There's a pause between us. I take it as a chance to fill the kettle and fish out my mug from the back of the cupboard, but Olivia hovers nervously, shuffling from foot to foot.

'There's something I need to tell you, only I wasn't sure if you'd want to hear it after you and Alec broke up.'

Alec's name catches me round the throat, and I swallow uncomfortably. I've not seen Olivia since Alec and I finished. Apart from the bare facts that I wouldn't be seeing him, we've not discussed him.

'Go on,' I tell her through closed teeth.

'Rick proposed,' she says simply.

'Oh.'

'And I said yes.'

'Oh. Well, that's great. I'm delighted for you. Why ever would you think I wouldn't want to hear that?'

'Thanks. It's just that you and Alec were getting pretty close back there. You know what it's like, when you're cut up about finishing with someone; the last thing you want is other people lording their own happiness around you.'

'Olivia, how many times did I tell you that Alec was a bit of fun? Really, I've barely thought about him the last few weeks. It's brilliant about you and Rick. I'm genuinely over the moon for you.'

'Thanks, Jess. You're the best. So you'll come to our engagement party, then?'

'Just try and stop me.'

She lets out a little squeal and grips my elbow. 'Brilliant. It's only a low-key affair. Can't exactly be partying too hard in this state,' she says, cupping her semi-circle. 'But I'll make sure it's lots of fun.'

'Sounds lovely.'

'Great. Catch up with you at lunch?'

'Yeah.'

She takes her disgusting-looking tea and leaves me alone in the kitchenette.

It's a good job she does. I grab on to the counter and lower my head between my shoulders. I search around for some more of the grit I poured into myself this morning before leaving the house. Between walking past The Wishing Well, hearing Alec's name and colliding into Olivia's news, there's hardly any of it left. And it's only ten past nine.

Chapter Thirty-four

'How about it, Jess? Fancy a drink?' Maureen asks on the way out of work on Friday.

'I can't, sorry. I'm off to see Mum tonight.'

'Silly me, course you are.'

'Just one, Jess?' Olivia chimes in. 'It's the first time I've felt like going anywhere but straight home in months. Say you'll come and mark the occasion.'

'I'd love to,' I say, and I mean it. Everyone in the office has been so supportive all week that I've left for the weekend with unusually high levels of admiration and warmth towards them all. It would be nice to spend a few more hours in their company. 'I can't, though. Mum will be expecting me.'

'You go,' Olivia says. 'Give your mum a kiss from me.'

'And from me,' Maureen adds.

'You've never even met Jess's mum,' Olivia points out.

'No, but she can have a kiss from me all the same.'

I walk towards the Metro with heavy feet, but before I let myself feel miserable, I tell myself not to be so ridiculous as I'll be seeing them tomorrow evening anyway for Olivia and Rick's engagement party.

I'd conjured up dozens of reasons not to go – most of them involving Mum, but every time I tried to share one with Olivia, she pre-empted me by telling me how pleased she was that I was coming, or how much work the party was turning out to be, how she'd lose her shit if something went wrong at this late stage, and I couldn't bring myself to disappoint her.

And there really is no reason not to be there. Mum has settled in well at Henley Hall, so I'm told every time I go. Apart from the first visit after leaving her there, when I brought as many of her belongings as I could and Mum watched me rearranging the room with a smile on her face, smiling even more when the various members of staff remarked on how stylish the room was looking when they popped in, she's been asleep whenever I've visited her this last week. Debs has also been every day. Unlike me, she has seen Mum awake. Her opinion is that Mum's getting the best care from some fabulous nurses, and she seems more at peace in Henley than she did in our dining room.

That part of her report comes with a sharp pang under the ribs. The rest, however, leads me to think that Mum got this right. She always did know what was best, be it what options I should take for A levels or which coat to go for in the Selfridges sale, and it turns out she knew what was best here too.

My tram's delayed, so I call Debs whilst I wait. She's still with Mum and, in a whisper, tells me she's had another good day and is already fast asleep. I say I'm on my way, but Debs insists I needn't come tonight. I'll be with her all day tomorrow, and it's not like she'll be alone if she does wake up. I'm not sure at first. It's only when Debs mentions Erica is on the night shift that I agree. Erica is the perfect nurse for Mum: pleasant without being bubbly, insistent without being bossy. I remember the laugh Erica got from Mum when she came into her room as I was reorganising the furniture and called me the Marie Kondo of the care-home world, and I know Mum would be singing her praises if she could.

Since I'm not visiting Mum tonight, I make the decision to turn back. A cocktail or two to lull me into a soupy state of calm before the weekend is just what I need. I won't stay late. A few drinks and an early night before seeing Mum in the morning. Perfect.

Maureen's plan was to go for cocktails at Drenched, but when I get there, the tiny bar area is packed with suits pressed against each other in a grey blur of frustration as they wait their turn. Olivia and Maureen are nowhere to be seen.

The ball of dread in my stomach has already formed before I ring Olivia.

'Where are you? I've come back to find you.'

'Brilliant,' Olivia shouts above the clatter of the pub. 'Drenched was packed, so we gave up and came to The Wishing Well instead.'

'Oh. Is Alec there?' I have to ask.

'Yeah, but it's packed in here. The bar's three deep. I'll get your drink now, and you come and join us at the table. He won't even notice you're in. Not that it matters, though. Right?'

'Right. Listen, it's getting late, I think I'll—'

'Too late,' Olivia interrupts. 'You've signed up now. Get in here.'

I walk into the busiest Friday night I've ever seen in The Wishing Well. Olivia and Maureen spot me and beckon me over to the table. Just before I move towards them, I dare to take a look towards the bar. The mangle of bodies in front of me do a funny thing at that moment: they rearrange themselves so a space opens up from my feet all the way to the bar, where Alec happens to be looking up whilst pulling a pint. The gap closes within seconds, but it's too late. We've seen each other.

I'm working my way towards the table to make my excuses to leave, hoping I can get back out before he notices me again when I feel a tap on my shoulder.

'Hello.'

He's sweaty and has brought the smell of ale with him from behind the bar, but he's also smiling.

I'd punch myself for making such a mistake coming in here if it didn't hurt so much already.

'Hi. Sorry, just leaving.'

'Don't do that. You've just got here. It's good to see you out. I take it this means your mum's on the mend?'

'I've got to go, Alec. Excuse me.'

He doesn't budge. I try and fail to find a path through the crowd to get past him.

'Wait up. You don't need to avoid coming in here because of me.' He says it as though it would be ridiculous of me to avoid him after four and a bit dates.

'I'm not.'

'Good. You're OK, then?'

'I'm fine.'

I spot my opportunity to bolt for the door and take it without looking back.

'You idiot,' I shout out loud at myself when I've turned the corner. It was only four and a bit dates. No big deal.

But that's all it took.

Now I know: it hurts too much to see him. I can't let it happen again.

I wake after a pathetic night's sleep to a beautifully clear early-spring morning, and set off to see Mum. The sun is finally managing to infiltrate the air with warmth, and, outside Henley Hall, nature is celebrating. Neat rows of young daffodils lining the driveway dance in the gentle wind, birds swoop in and out of the eaves, singing joyfully to each other. Behind the hall, a column of budding oak trees lean into each other like old friends.

Placed in such a beautiful frame, it's impossible to imagine anything other than nice things happening at Henley Hall. It's easier here to push thoughts of Alec away. Thinking of the walk I plan to take with Mum and the afternoon tea to follow, I sweep up the stairs to her room with my smile in place for the forthcoming hours.

Erica's coming out of the bedroom as I get to it.

'Good morning,' she says, her voice lilting with cheeriness despite the night shift she's just pulled.

'Hi. How's Mum?'

'Your mum's a dream, honey. Slept all night. If only my other patients were as easy.'

'That's great. She awake now?'

'Nope. Still in the land of sweet dreams. Lucky her.'

I'm about to smile and share some further pleasantry with Erica until I notice the snag in what she's said.

'Erica, how often has my mum been awake these last few days? She seems to be sleeping an awful lot.'

Erica tugs at the bottom of her turquoise tunic and straightens her lanyard over her bust, realising her shift hasn't quite finished yet; there's one more job she has to get through before she gets home: me.

'She is sleeping a lot, but that's not a bad thing. When she's asleep, she's not suffering. When she's asleep she gets to dream of being somewhere other than here, with someone other than me.'

'I know, I get that. It's just I'm worried about her getting enough food and drink down her if she's hardly ever awake.'

'She gets what she needs, honey.'

I expect she'll follow the remark up with some evidence, charting calorific intake or, at the very least, a list of what she's consumed over the last twenty-four hours. All Erica gives me is a knowing look and a pat on my shoulder.

Mum's room is in near-darkness when I enter. Morning is waiting patiently outside for someone to open the curtains. No wonder Mum sleeps so much if her room's left like this all day. I tug back the heavy curtains so fiercely their runners screech across the curtain pole.

Even in this vivid light, Mum appears as a small, indistinct mound on the bed. Erica's tucked the blankets right up to her armpits to keep her warm, but with all the pillows propping her up, she's slid right down under them. Her mouth is already under the duvet; if I had come much later, her whole face would have been submerged. Mum wouldn't have been able to do anything about it even if she had woken up.

I've a good mind to chase after Erica and pull her back into the room to face her mistake. Only, it's more pressing to rectify it than to chastise her about it. I tug Mum back up on the pillows, the movement waking her. I can't very well leave her to it to shout at Erica now she's up. She needs a drink and her hair brushing and her lipstick putting on. I make myself busy doing all those things, promising myself I'll speak to the manager about Erica once I get a minute.

Mum watches me under heavy eyelids as I bat around the room. I try to be cheery for her, chatting about how lovely everyone has been at work and telling her about the nice things we can do together today, but it's terribly difficult to keep it up when it becomes clear, for the first time ever, that Mum is looking at me without recognising me as her daughter.

I make the decision instantly. I've thought about this – my worst fear – a lot over the last year, wondering how I would react to it. It's so much worse than I ever imagined, like someone has taken a pair of scissors to the bond Mum and I had and cut right through it. But despite the pain, my mind is clear.

Before this moment came, I never knew if it would be better to tell her I'm her daughter and to try everything I could to get her to remember or if I should pretend it hasn't happened. The thought of Mum remembering worried me almost as much as her forgetting; she'd be beside herself if she knew she'd not been able to recognise me. It would be the worst thing this disease could ever do to her. It would be better for me to have her see me as her daughter once more, but would it be better for her?

'It's a lovely day out,' I tell her instead of reminding her who I am. 'If you like, we could go out and sit in the sun.'

Mum smiles, and we go down to the garden, just like I've planned.

Chapter Thirty-five

I make every effort to shake off the horrors of the day by the time I get to Olivia's flat. My black jumpsuit is on, I've a full face of make-up and my feet are already aching in the stiletto heels I'm wearing. From the outside, I look as I should. On the inside, I'm a mess.

Images of Mum flash into my mind every few seconds like a cruel slideshow. Mum's face as she turned to me upon waking; her eyes as they followed me round the room; her expression when I started to cry as I collected the things she'd need for our walk in the gardens. In every image there's kindness or compassion or friendliness, but it's the kind she has for everyone she meets, not the special kind reserved just for me.

Going to a party after a full day of waiting for her to see me as her Jess again and eventually having to leave disappointed seemed madness until I got back home. Given the choice between an empty house or a party where there might be enough alcohol and company to make me forget, there was only ever going to be one option.

Olivia greets me in a purple wrap dress that shows off her bump perfectly. She looks so radiant and happy, I feel guilty for showing up with my bags of misery. I force a smile onto my face, move forward to kiss both of her cheeks and make the decision to keep my misery out of her flat, to leave it on the other side of the door at least for the next few hours.

'What was with your quick exit from The Wishing Well last night?'

'Yeah, sorry. I wasn't in the mood for it being so packed.'

She bats her hand, dismissing the matter. 'Fair enough. I'm so glad you're here now. If one more of Rick's uni friends had arrived instead of you, I'd have turned them away.'

She points towards the lounge where a group of tall men are standing in a loose circle, dressed in an array of pastel oxford shirts, reminding me unpleasantly of the bedding in the nursing home.

I happily let Olivia lead me past them into her thin galley kitchen.

'Where's our lot?' I ask before helping myself to an olive.

'Our lot? Didn't I tell you? They're not coming. Maureen's caught a sick bug from one of those feral grandchildren she has to look after, and the others all have plans.'

'No, you didn't tell me. You mean it's just us and that lot in there?'

'No, silly,' she trills. 'That wouldn't be much of a party, would it? I've got a few cousins popping in and then there's − er − well, there's Michael.'

'And who exactly is Michael?'

Excitement floods her cheeks, leaving her with two pretty pink circles over her freckles.

'Just a very handsome, very up-and-coming executive at Rick's work. Poor thing's always getting his heart broken by one gold digger or another. Rick and I got to talking about him and we thought you two might hit it off.'

'Rick hardly knows me,' I tell Olivia.

'He knows you're nice, gorgeous and have been great to me these last few months, and he says Michael's great too. We thought we'd invite him round tonight and introduce you both. No pressure, of course,' she adds as an afterthought.

'No pressure? I'd say there's a fair bit of pressure, given I don't know anyone here apart from you and Rick, and I'm guessing he won't either.'

'Oh dear. Was this a stupid idea? I thought after you insisted that Alec was a bit of fun, you might fancy – well, a bit more fun. Have I got this horribly wrong?'

She looks so crestfallen rubbing her little bump through her party dress, surrounded by all her party food. What kind of monster would I be to disappoint her?

'No, it's fine. If you and Rick speak so highly of him, I'm sure he'll be lovely. I'll need a bloody big drink first, mind.'

I manage two large glasses of white wine before the doorbell goes, and Michael enters the flat. By the time he makes his entrance into the kitchen after being introduced to, and very nearly swallowed by, Rick's mates, I'm halfway down my third glass and on my way to being drunk.

'Jess, there you are,' Olivia says, as though it's a surprise I've stayed put exactly where she'd ordered me to be. 'This is Michael, a colleague of Rick's from PWC.'

'Hi, Michael.'

'Hi.'

'Michael, this is Jess, my awesome workmate. I wouldn't have got through the last few months if it weren't for her looking out for me.'

'Good work, Jess. Sounds like you've earned yourself a few drinks from our hosts. Unless you want one of these.' He pulls no less than a dozen thin cans from the Tesco bag for life he's brought with him, each one containing a different cocktail mix.

'Wow, someone means business tonight,' Olivia says, eyeing up the cans.

'Oh, I do. But here, I've got one for you too. Can't have you left out.' He passes her an alcohol-free mojito.

'That's so lovely of you. Jess, isn't it lovely?'

'Er, yeah.'

'Let me go and tell Rick what a star you are.' She squeezes past Michael on her way out of the kitchen. 'You two will be all right on your own for a few minutes, won't you?' she adds, winking at me behind Michael's back.

Without Olivia, I become shy. I turn to the window, but it's dark, and I meet Michael's eyes in the reflection. I turn back to the food, reading the instructions on packages. When I find the courage to sneak a look at Michael, I find him drumming his fingers on the worktop, staring at his trainers.

Eventually, the only course of action is to look at each other.

'You know,' he says, 'I've got a feeling you and I are being set up tonight.'

'Yeah, I'd say so. They've done a pretty crap job of hiding it, haven't they?'

'God, yeah.' He begins to laugh. 'Awful. What's with this guest list? A bunch of bladdered toffs and us two.'

'Clever, really,' I admit. 'Olivia will know there's no way I'd dream of going in there with them, so the only option I've got is to stay in here with you.'

'Same here. Rick knows full well that lot aren't my type either. I met them once before, and they were the loudest, most arrogant bunch of bores you could ever meet. Rick probably reckons if they leave us in here long enough, we'll have no other option but to fall madly in love with each other.'

'Yep. That's what Olivia will be banking on too.'

'Still, there are worse places to be left, and worse company. What do you say we make the most of our predicament and demolish this lot?' he asks, sweeping his hand around the party food and his neat line of booze. 'Will you join me in a cocktail from a can?'

'I'd love to.'

It's nice being with Michael. He's so enthusiastic about everything – 'You *have* to try this pâté, it's divine.' 'Wait until you put that morsel of black pudding in your mouth, you'll explode with happiness.' It's impossible not to join in. We end up sounding like the presenters on *Saturday Kitchen*, in fits of joy over a wedge of Brie.

And he's not hard to look at either. The more we drink and the more we laugh, the more I see it. He's nothing like Alec. Alec is classically handsome, tall and rugged whereas Michael is like a polished package of pleasant features. They don't necessarily work together to create a face people would identify as beautiful, but they are there, each working on their own. His eyelashes, for example, are black and curl at the end; when he closes his eyes in laughter or to savour whatever's in his mouth, they land on his pale skin. His mouth by itself is thin and unremarkable, but when he smiles and the deep dimples appear on either side of it, it becomes his best feature. I find myself wondering what it would be like to run my fingers over it.

'Guys, I need to get in here,' Rick says, knocking on the closed door to give us warning.

'Oh just a sec, mate. Let me get my pants back on.'

'Now where did I put my bra?' I add loudly.

'There it is, on top of the profiteroles.'

Rick comes in to find us laughing hysterically, clutching on to one another for support.

'Sorry to interrupt, but my fiancée is starving out there and can't go any longer without being fed.'

'Fiancée, oooh,' we chime in unison.

'Bloody hell, how much have you two had to drink? And where's all the food?'

We're ushered out of the kitchen by Rick and told to join the others in the lounge so he can propose a toast.

'I don't much fancy joining that lot, do you?' Michael asks.

Since we've been in the kitchen, they've started on the karaoke and are now midway through a drunken rendition of 'Sex on Fire' by Kings of Leon. It's not a performance I've any desire to set eyes on.

'Not one bit.'

'Come in here, then.' He opens the door to Rick and Olivia's bedroom.

I hesitate. So far, Michael's given no sign to suggest he's attracted to me. There's been no flirtation from either of us. His suggestion to go in the bedroom is most likely nothing more than a plan to get away from Rick's mates.

If I'm wrong, would that be so bad?

Michael's nice, attractive and I've already thought about touching him. Why shouldn't I have some fun with him? Why not take the opportunity to forget everything for a few hours?

Not a month, not six dates, not even one. Just tonight.

I've learnt my lesson. I went too far with Alec. We thought we knew what we were doing, but mistakes were made. Going to Leeds and meeting his family was a mistake. Letting him meet Mum was a mistake. Telling him about Huntington's was a mistake. I let him in. I let myself think I was being sensible by establishing our rules, but with every new rule I made for Alec, I was shattering the rules that really mattered one by one until there was nothing to keep us from each other.

I'll never let that happen again. I know I won't. But the closeness, the contact; I miss it. When Alec and I slept together, there were blissful minutes when nothing existed apart from his touch. When I lived for nothing more than the sensation of being with him.

I could do with some of that tonight, more than ever, and here's someone who might be able to give it to me. No swapping of numbers. No follow-up date.

Just tonight.

'OK,' I agree. He takes my hand and leads me into the room, shutting the door behind us.

He gets it all wrong. Instead of turning on the bedside lamp or even lighting one of the dozens of candles Olivia keeps around the room, he flicks on the switch for the overhead light. It's so bright it creates an immediate hangover. It's the kind of light that magnifies everything it touches. I cover my nose, sure that he'll be able to see my blackheads from his position in the bed.

And that's another thing: he's *in* the bed. Not on it, in it, with the covers pulled up to his chin. He looks like a little boy waiting to be tucked in by his mother, and I wonder for the first time all evening how old Michael is.

'You getting in?'

'Not yet.' I stay perched on the end of the bed, back as straight as a ruler.

'Right, no point me staying in here alone, is there?' he asks, ever the sulking boy now, and gets out of the bed to sit next to me.

'Have you not enjoyed tonight?' he asks, picking up a piece of my hair and stroking its end.

This close, the realisation hits. He's going to kiss me, and I don't want him to. The only person I want to kiss, the only person I'll ever want to kiss, is Alec. My future's not going to be peppered with meaningless trysts like the one Michael thinks he's going to have with me after all. If there's no Alec, there certainly isn't going to be anyone else.

'Tonight's been fun,' I say, hoping he'll notice the blandness in my voice.

My coolness doesn't work. My words are all the encouragement he needs. He pounces, shoving those thin lips against mine. Before I have the chance to pull back, his tongue is poking into my mouth, hard and thin. He flicks it in and out like a snake.

How stupid to imagine I'd ever be able to feel the same excitement that came over me when I kissed Alec and to find that same disconnection from everything else that came with it. This kiss repulses me. I push him away.

'I'm sorry, I can't.'

'What do you mean you can't? You're single. I'm single. Rick said you were looking for a bit of fun, that's the only reason I bothered coming tonight.'

'Did he? Well, Rick doesn't know what he's talking about.'

I'm out of the room before he has a chance to say anything else. I never want to see him again. But Michael isn't ready to let the matter drop.

'Frigid bitch,' he shouts after me.

I leave the flat, slamming the door as hard as I can. The taxi I booked isn't due to arrive for another hour, so I set off walking, my disgust at Michael, and at myself, a shield against the near-freezing night late March is still capable of producing.

The whole way home, I cry for what I had with Alec, for what I've lost.

Chapter Thirty-six

'What were you thinking?' I ask Olivia on Monday morning when she comes to my desk, head bowed in shame.

'I'm so sorry. Sounds silly now, but I was trying to cheer you up. I thought, after all the stress you've had with your mum, you could do with some excitement. Rick swore Michael was a lovely guy.'

'Oh yeah, he was a real charmer.'

'I still can't believe Rick thought to set you up with him. He was a complete prat after you left, got utterly off his face, threw up in the sink and ended up passing out in the bath. What's worse is that it wasn't a one-off; Rick admitted he's behaved like that at dozens of parties they've been to. He's on a final written warning at work about his conduct. We've completely fallen out about it.'

'Don't fall out with him on my account. I was mad as hell with you both on the night, but I'm over it now.'

'Really? I don't see how.'

Yesterday sneaks its way into my mind, despite the promise I made waking up this morning to leave the memory at home, to shut it up and close the curtains around it so no one else could see.

I offer Olivia a shrug instead of an explanation and tell her I've got a busy morning to get back to. Olivia, too relieved at being let off the hook to press the matter, agrees we should do some work and leaves me to it.

Alone at my desk I try to keep the memory at bay by concentrating on sorting the mail, but it's too strong. Before long, it roams free, pushing aside any other thoughts into the dark corners of my mind.

I'd woken late, lazy under the heavy warmth of my duvet until my unwelcome, pointless hangover woke up for another round and became impossible to ignore. Strong coffee was needed, and I padded to the kitchen to make it. Sitting at the table, I expected a hot rage to appear over the party and Olivia's clumsy set-up, but I couldn't rouse myself to think about it at any length, let alone care enough to build up to any sort of feeling about the matter. It was as if it never happened.

That's the thing about Huntington's: under its darkness, everything else becomes invisible, swallowed whole by the blackness until it's as if it was never there at all.

How could my mind worry about something as small as Olivia's failed set-up when Mum had failed to recognise me just hours before?

That I thought about.

It dawned on me whilst draining the last of my coffee: Mum was getting lost in the nursing home. Away from her surroundings, away from me, Mum was struggling to hold on to her life. At home, Mum had never looked at me like I was a stranger. At home she always had a smile, or when she couldn't muster that, an intensity in her eyes reserved just for me. At Henley Hall, amongst so many strange people, I'd become just another face, no more special than any of the other kindly nurses caring for her with smiles plastered on their faces throughout the day.

But Henley Hall was not a prison. There was no agreement saying once I'd put her in, I couldn't take her out. Somewhere amongst the shiny pages of their official brochure, I'd read that trips out of the home were encouraged as long as the resident was fit and able.

An afternoon back at home was exactly what Mum needed to jolt her back into herself. We could sit in the kitchen with the doors open, listening to Adele or, if she was too cold, we could watch a film in the dining room. There would be no pressure; I wouldn't even make a meal. Instead of giving her a pureed version of a Sunday roast, and watching her expectantly as she struggled to get it down, we'd have milkshakes instead. Everything would be easy. Normal.

And then she would remember me.

As far as I could see, the only flaw in the plan was getting Mum from Henley Hall and back again. I could take her car there, but I wouldn't be able to look after her on the drive. I'd need to be in the back with her, making sure she was OK. Debs had been visiting every day this week, and it didn't seem fair ringing to ask for help on the one day she'd made plans with her own family. A taxi could work, but if the driver was averse to taking wheelchairs or they were late when Mum was ready to go, there was the potential for my plan to be ruined. I couldn't let that happen when there was another option.

I picked up my phone and scrolled through my contacts until I found her number.

'Hello?' she asked when she picked up the phone on my third attempt at getting through.

'Auntie Sarah?'

'Jess?'

'Yes – er, hi. How are you?'

'Oh, I'm OK.'

Taking my call had flummoxed her more than it had flummoxed me to make it. I'd made a point of never asking her for anything after she backed away from us, and Sarah had long grown used to not hearing my voice – or Mum's – on the other end of a phone. I cut straight to the matter.

'I was just wondering, seeing as it's a Sunday and you've not seen Mum this month yet, if you were planning on visiting her today, and if you were, if you could do me a favour?'

'Oh right. Well, to be honest, my darling, I wasn't planning on it, no.'

'Is there any way you could change your mind and come?'

'I could, if I'm allowed. I wasn't sure she would be able to have visitors now. I'd thought it might be family only.'

'No, she can have as many visitors as she wants.'

'Oh, well, that's great.'

'It is. So you'll come today, then?'

'I – I suppose I could.'

'Perfect. I'm actually planning on taking Mum home for the afternoon; you wouldn't mind giving us a lift from the nursing home, would you?'

Before she could question the plan, I gave her the address of Henley Hall and the time she needed to be there.

I decided to arrive half an hour before Sarah to tell Mum of the plan and get her ready to leave.

When I got to Henley Hall, Nina Lew was hovering in the entrance, her hair in a less severe bun than normal given that it was the weekend. I wasn't sure whether I needed to ask permission from her specifically, but still, I outlined my plan and tried to ignore the growing crease between her brows as I did so.

Despite her reservations that it was too soon to take Mum out, that it might end up doing more harm than good, that it had the potential to unsettle her, I pressed ahead with the plan, because, after all, last time I saw Mum she didn't know me, and nothing was more important than making sure it didn't happen again.

Mum wasn't in her room. A nurse I didn't recognise poked her head round Mum's door a few minutes after I'd entered to tell me that Yolanda had taken her for a walk around the grounds since it was warm out.

It was the first time I'd been in Mum's room alone. Looking around it in her absence only confirmed what I'd worked out a few hours ago: this room wasn't Mum's. It wasn't anyone's. We'd tried to fill it with familiar things, but it still belonged to the hall, not Mum.

In the corridor, I could hear soft footsteps and the muted scrape of wheels against the wooden floor. Mum's door opened a fraction before shutting again. It swung open for a second time, this time more firmly, and Yolanda rushed to press her bum against the door to stop it from closing.

'Here, let me help.' I reached for the door holding it in place whilst Yolanda wheeled Mum straight past me and to the window.

I waited for Mum to turn her head towards me, but she remained perfectly still, her head down in between her shoulders, hunched like an old lady. It was as if I wasn't there.

Yolanda moved around the room taking out a peach fleece blanket and Mum's gloves from under the wheelchair, putting them back in the wardrobe, oblivious to her stillness.

Disappointment entered my body like cigarette smoke, clouding and polluting what I hoped would be a happy moment. I took a few deep breaths to clear it out and went over to Mum.

'I've got a little surprise for you,' I said, kissing the top of her head before moving to the front of the wheelchair to squat down in front of her.

That's when I saw it for a second time.

She didn't recognise me.

It wouldn't matter where we were. I looked into those blank, tired eyes and knew Huntington's had done its work, severing the thread that had held us together for twenty-eight years once and for all.

I couldn't bear to see it. Mumbling some excuse to Yolanda, I bolted from the room, hurling myself down the stairs, desperate to feel the pull of my leg muscles taking me away from this.

At the bottom of the stairs, I crashed into Sarah, interrupting her conversation with Nina.

'Watch where you're—' she began to chide, but when she turned to see it was me, her hand flew from where she'd been rubbing her shoulder towards me. I leant away from her touch, and, without apologising for hurting her, carried on towards the door.

'Jess, what on earth's happened?' she shouted after me.

'If you bothered to visit, you'd fucking well see for yourself,' I shouted back before sprinting down the driveway.

Sarah meets me at lunchtime in the Costa next to the Arndale centre. The memory has been such a pest all morning, running loose around the office, I decide it's better to let it come out with me in the hope that, once dealt with, it won't bother me again.

The text I sent her mid-morning was graciously replied to within minutes. She agreed to meet me for a coffee and an apology.

I'm not just mortified on my own behalf for my behaviour, I'm mortified on Mum's behalf too. She would be livid if she knew I'd spoken to her friend – to anyone – so rudely. If Mum were able to chastise me, it would come with a demand I make the matter right again.

'Hi, Jess.' She jumps the queue to join me at the till. I smile apologetically to the two men behind me.

'Hi. What can I get you?'

'Water, please.'

'You sure?'

'Yes.'

This is going to be harder work than I thought. A latte would mean she was happy to see me. A cup of tea, ready to listen. Water: she's pissed off.

We sit on stools overlooking Exchange Square. Sarah secures the clasp on her Burberry handbag and places it on the floor, hooking one of the straps around her foot in case a ruffian comes in for a mocha and decides to make a grab for it.

'Sarah, I want to say how sorry I am for the way I spoke to you yesterday.'

'No need to apologise, well, maybe a little, but I didn't come for that. I came because I'm worried sick about you. After you ran out, I went up to see your mum. I had no idea it had got so much worse. You know, I don't think she recognised me at all, Jess.'

She begins to cry. I pass her a napkin and wait whilst she rubs the rough material over the thinning skin around her eyes.

'Does she still recognise you?' she asks.

'Not anymore.'

A fresh batch of tears arrives. I wait for them to pass.

'You poor thing. I can't even begin to think what it must be like. To see what's happening to your mum and to know the same will happen to you. And to face it alone—'

I'm about to tell her I'm not alone – I've got Debs and Olivia. I'm also about to tell her I don't allow myself to worry about what might happen to me whilst Mum needs

272

me so much. Only, there's no time to say anything before Sarah speaks again.

'Well, you're not alone anymore. I'm here for you. I mean it. I've been a coward, too afraid of illness and seeing your mum getting worse. I'm ashamed of myself. But, I tell you, after seeing you yesterday in such a state, I'd stare anything in the face if it meant I could help you. So I'm here. I'll be here as long as you need me.'

She puts her water down, and I cover her in a hug.

'Thank you, Auntie Sarah. Thank you so much.'

She hands me a napkin and sits with me until I stop crying before hopping off her seat, scooping up her Burberry bag and ordering us two hot chocolates and a couple of blueberry muffins as her first act of support. We both know they won't help anything, but they're worth having all the same.

Chapter Thirty-seven

A pile of days stack up where I avoid seeing Mum, relying on Debs to pay the visits and report back to me. When Debs calls me after we've barely crossed paths for weeks and asks if I fancy coming round to hers for tea, I'm not surprised. She informs me that, after failing to get our acts together, Lauren and I *will* be going out for a drink afterwards. What she omits to say is, before we do, I'm going to receive a good talking-to.

I'm glad. If my own guilt isn't enough to get me back in front of Mum and her empty eyes, maybe an extra serving of it from Debs will do the trick.

Friday brings with it the start of an early heatwave forecast to last the whole weekend. Didsbury village grows thick with groups of friends and couples determined to make the most of the unseasonably hot temperatures. Savvy afternoon drinkers must have filled the outside seating of the numerous bars hours before. Crowds spill onto the pavements, and, in the case of The Slug and Lettuce, halfway across the road. There's a cacophony of beeping horns and loud banter that's pleasantly familiar, pulling up memories of weekends where I'd be amongst the crowds, drinking Pimm's with my group of friends or sitting on a wall with a date, sharing a bottle of wine before heading to one of the local restaurants. It's nice to be out in it again, even if I am just passing through on my way to the bus stop.

The only path to my stop without having to walk in the middle of Wilmslow Road is through a tight square of four dolled-up girls in their late teens, all wearing pretty floral jumpsuits. Personally, I think my outfit of jeans, white lacy top and pale-blue cardigan is much more suitable for the evening. Once the sun disappears, the temperature is going to plummet. Soon they'll be contending with goosebumps and blue skin.

I smile, say, 'Excuse me, ladies' in a faux cockney accent, and they politely part to let me through.

I manage to get a window seat on the half-empty bus, and I spend the journey staring at a blue sky, which would be the exact same shade as my cardigan, if it weren't beginning to darken at the edges. Maybe Mum's sitting at her window right now, watching the darkness close across the sky like a pair of curtains. There's a comfort in that: both still together under the same sky.

Before I get to Debs's front door, a smell of meat and onions attacks my nose.

'Hi.' Lauren is standing on the doorstep, vape between her lips.

I try not to wrinkle my nose at the violent smell of Debs's home cooking, so heavy and at odds with the light spring evening, but must fail, as Lauren begins to laugh.

'Something smells good,' I say.

'Don't. Mam's doing her nut in. Says she knew she should have gone out to pick up a quiche Lorraine. Who wants to eat steak pie in this heat?'

'I for one love a good steak pie, whatever the weather.'

'I'm not sure you'll be saying that when you discover how hot our kitchen gets.'

I follow her through the lounge and sitting room to the kitchen at the back of the house, the smell intensifying with the opening of each door.

'Hi, Debs,' I say to her backside, as she struggles to get her pie out of the oven. When she straightens up, beads of sweat are running down her cheeks, creating stripes in her make-up.

'Hiya, love. Sorry about the heat. I don't know what I was thinking, putting the oven on when that blasted sun already makes a furnace out of the kitchen. Do me a favour and help Lauren take the chairs outside, will you? We're dining al fresco tonight,' she says whilst giving a jaunty little wiggle of her hips.

'Lovely. It all smells wonderful. Perfect choice.'

'Hmm. Gravy in a heatwave. Just what I fancy,' Lauren agrees.

'Oh, piss off you two and get yourselves outside,' Debs says, batting us away with her tea towel.

Lauren brings a bottle of wine and three glasses out once we've trudged to and from the kitchen bringing out the chairs, a fold-up decorating table, tablecloth, cutlery and bowls of mashed potato, carrots and cabbage.

'It's stifling out here,' I say, taking off my cardigan and pulling my skinny jeans away from my sticky thighs, admitting the girls in the jumpsuits knew what they were doing.

'I know. Total heat trap. It's great, apart from when you need to do anything other than lie still. Wine?'

'Please.'

We say cheers and fall into a comfortable, friendly silence. It's strange; we barely know each other. Apart from tonight, I've met her only once before. But Lauren knows all about my life from Debs, like I know all about hers. It's allowed us to skip the getting-to-know-each-other phase and land here. I sip my wine with my eyes shut, looking forward to going out with her later.

'Here we are.' Debs joins us in her small back garden struggling to hold an overflowing pie tin with gravy seeping down the sides onto her oven-gloved hands.

'Looks amazing,' I say genuinely, my stomach remembering this week's diet of crisps and Frosties.

It's good, the kind of home-cooked meal I'd expect from Debs. Whilst Lauren and I eat, she barely touches her food, concerning herself with forcing second helpings of pie and mash onto our brimming plates. Neither Lauren nor Debs starts any other conversation apart from the in-between-mouthfuls one about the food, and I imagine this is how all their meals take place.

Once Debs has finished shuffling her meal around her plate, she orders Lauren to take everything in and start the washing-up. As Lauren passes her mum, they exchange a look and I catch a flicker of understanding cross Lauren's face before she disappears inside.

'I know what you're going to say,' I begin, grabbing the conversation out of her control before she has chance to start. 'I should be seeing Mum more often. I know I should. It's just so hard. I've been convincing myself it doesn't matter anyway, not now she has no idea who I am. But I know that's wrong. I can't keep obsessing over what I've lost, not when she's still here, and there's still a chance to spend time with her. So I'm going to visit her first thing tomorrow.'

'That's good, but, listen, whatever happens, you can't beat yourself up about finding it hard. Of course it's hard. It's bloody awful. If you need a few days away from it, that's perfectly understandable.'

'Thanks, Debs. I can't tell you how much easier you being there for Mum makes all this.'

Debs wriggles in her seat like she's suddenly noticed she's sitting on a sharp object.

'I'm glad. Just going to get us some water. Back in a sec. Must have put too much salt in the pie.'

'OK, thanks.'

Bless Debs. Always looking after everyone else. When she gets back out, I'll pour her a glass of wine and we'll talk about something nice like Tom Hardy or the new Aldi opening next week.

The sun is beginning to disappear behind the trees at the back of the house. Soon, it will be too cold to sit out. I point my face to the sun, closing my eyes as I take in the last of the rays. Out of nowhere, Alec appears in my mind. I picture him climbing the stairs at Henley Hall, walking the corridor to Mum's room and swinging open the door. Only, instead of finding Mum, he finds me. He places himself in front of me, smiling and saying my name. But his smile, his happiness is sharply pulled off his face and is replaced by a contorted grimace of misery when it becomes clear I don't recognise him.

I open my eyes against the image and reach for my cardigan, noticing how cold it's become. If Alec had stuck around, that would have been his fate. Just as Mum's life is mine in the future, if I'd have let myself end up with Alec, my life now would have been a mirror image of the life he would have been bound to lead. Thank God he escaped it.

'You OK, Jess? You've gone pale.' Debs has returned to the garden without my noticing and places a concerned hand on my shoulder.

'I'm fine. Here have some wine.'

'Later. There's something I need to speak to you about first.'

'It's so sweet of you to look out for Mum the way you do, but I promise I'm back on track. I'll see her tomorrow and will bloody well force myself to deal with whatever's thrown at her. I have to. She's my mum and that disease is not going to make me miss out on spending any more time with her.'

'That's good. Although, I never thought for a second it would be any different. You're doing a grand job. It's not that I want to talk to you about.'

'Oh?'

'Jesus, this is hard. I'll just say it, shall I? Ever since your mum went into Henley Hall, I've been able to spend more time with the family, with Ray in particular. Obviously, I've been worried sick about your mum and you, but the thing is, having the time to be with Ray again has been good for us. It's made us realise that maybe our relationship isn't as dead in the ground as we'd thought.'

'You're getting back with him?'

'I am,' she replies defiantly. 'We've been married a hell of a long time, and we both agree it would be mad to let each other go, not when there might be a chance of us being happy together again.'

'But I thought you didn't want him anymore. That's what you said.'

'Well, yes, and I'm not saying it's perfect now, but me ending it forced us into talking again. About what didn't work. And about what did. We've been married a long time, and there's been a lot of good in those years. I was too hasty to throw them away. We're going to try again.'

'That's great, if that's what you want.'

'It is.'

'OK, then. If you're sure, I wish you luck.' Ignoring the wave of sadness crashing round me, as Debs pursues her happiness in a way Mum and I will never be able to, I give her a hug and rub her sticky back. 'I should go help Lauren tidy up so we can get out for this drink.'

I get off my chair and pick it up, ready to take it back in with me.

'Wait. There's more.'

'More?'

'It's just that, now I'm no longer your mum's carer and since Ray's retired, we've got to talking about where exactly we should have this fresh start. Ray's always wanted to spend his retirement somewhere hot. He has arthritis, you see, and there's nothing like the Mediterranean heat to calm it down. If we sell this place, he reckons we'll be able to scrape enough together to get us a nice little flat by the sea. I wasn't sure at first, but the children have all been so supportive about it, and I do think it'll do us the world of good.'

My stomach twists. 'What are you telling me, Debs?'

'We're thinking of moving to Spain.'

I drop the chair I'm holding, and it lands on the flags. 'Wh – what?' I struggle to ask, my throat feeling like there are hands around it squeezing so tight I can't breathe.

'I'm moving, love,' she repeats. 'Probably not for a good while – we've got to put this place on the market, convince someone to see past three decades of clutter and buy the place and find somewhere suitable for us in Spain – and certainly not before your mum – well, until, you know,' she stutters, missing out the crucial word. 'But one day we hope we'll be able to make it happen. You understand, don't you?'

I understand she's moving on from us. She's doing what she thinks is best to make her life happy. Soon she'll be gone, and I'll still be here. This is my life now. People come into it and they leave again. Everyone moves forward, and I stand still watching them go.

'Sounds great,' I tell her, unable to smile as I do.

She doesn't notice; she's too busy crumpling in relief.

'Thanks, love. To be honest, I've been dreading telling you. Lauren reckoned I should just keep quiet about it all until everything had gone through and we were ready to go, but I couldn't do that. Couldn't sneak around, concealing what we were planning. I said you'd rather know – and you would, wouldn't you?'

Lauren comes back into the garden, a fresh layer of make-up on her face.

'I've told Jess. And she's made up for us. I knew she would be.'

Lauren grins. 'Thanks for being so great, Jess. Mam's been worried sick you'd think she was turning her back on you. She won't be going for ages yet, your mam might not even be – you know. Anyway, it's not like Spain is the other side of the world, and there's always a Skype or a phone call when you need her, isn't there?'

'That's right. And our Lauren will still be here. You'll be such firm friends by the time I'm off, you won't think to miss me.'

Lauren holds out her hands and I take them. 'You're right. I'm delighted for you. Mum will be too. If you'll excuse me, I've suddenly come over a bit funny. Must be the heat. I need to get going.'

I'm standing up Lauren by leaving, failing to take the step forward to become friends. But what's the point? I've just lost the mother, why put myself through the agony of letting the daughter in only to lose her too when life pushes her forward?

I drop Lauren's hands and walk back into the kitchen, weaving my way through Debs's house, stubbing my toe on a hoover and crashing into a door in a bid to be outside, away, alone.

Chapter Thirty-eight

The heatwave continues throughout the weekend. Swarms of people will be leaving their homes to congregate in the parks and beer gardens in and around Manchester. I could join them, giving my pale legs their first outing of the year. I could, like everyone else, scoff at how crazy a bit of sun sends us all, whilst tilting my head back with my sunglasses on, a glass of something icy in my hand, remembering again how much I love hot days like this.

Instead, when I wake up on Saturday morning in a fug of sweat and sadness, I close every curtain in the house and set up camp on the double bed in the spare room under the seventies ceiling fan Mum never got round to removing. The blades don't turn nearly fast enough to offer any real comfort, but the weak breeze it offers is better than the suffocating stillness of the other rooms.

There's a stale smell of sheets left too long unused. A fine film of dust covers my fingers when I run my hand over the duck-egg-blue cover. I can't remember the last time this room was used. Never by Debs: when she stayed over, her place was next to Mum. If she were able to manage some sleep, it would be in the chair by her bed. I suppose the last person to use the room would have been Sarah, when she'd had too much on a Friday night.

There was a time when this room was often in use. If not by Sarah, by one of my friends staying over, or used by me and whatever boyfriend I had at the time whom Mum liked enough to deem worthy of staying the night.

Lying here, the silence of the house becomes more stifling than the heat. I long to be away from it. I should get up and go and see Mum, but I'm not strong enough for that yet. Not ready for her not to recognise me. I stay where I am, promising myself I'll go in a few hours once I've cooled down.

The fan begins to groan from use after so long. It needs to be switched off or it will overheat. I get up to stop it and don't sit back down. I take a quick shower, not bothering to wet my hair, pull out a semi-crumpled khaki T-shirt dress and bronze flip-flops and go downstairs. The garden's looking as unappealing as ever, more so under the accusing glare of the sun. I make do with sitting in the kitchen with the doors open, reading an old magazine Debs or one of the carers left behind.

There's a knock on the door just before noon. Some of Mum's equipment is still to be collected. I pass the dining room and look in at the empty hospital bed that someone else needs now Mum has no use for it. I've never before wished for something so hateful to stay with me.

'What are you doing here?' I ask the man who definitely isn't here to take Mum's bed away.

Alec takes off his sunglasses and fills his face with a smile.

'I've come to see how you are,' he says. No embarrassment about turning up uninvited. No ill feeling left over from the last time he was here.

'Can I come in?' he asks.

I'have haven't done any cleaning since Mum left. The hallway has become a dumping ground for my clothes, the kitchen floor is covered in stains and there are dirty dishes covering every surface.

'I guess.'

The best course of action is to lead him through the house and back out again into the garden. It's as bad as inside, but at least it doesn't smell.

'What's going on?' I ask once he's perched on the garden wall. 'I'm not sure why you're here.'

'OK, time to come clean,' he says. 'I've been texting Olivia a fair bit ever since your mum went into hospital. I wanted to know how you were, to make sure you were doing OK. Olivia's only ever told me the bare bones, about your mum going into the home, you being back at work. She hasn't said anything else, except that it's been hard for you. When I saw it was so lovely this morning, I thought of you. I got this idea we could hang out. I know you can't do a relationship, and it's not about that. I thought we could go back to being two people enjoying having nice chats once in a while, like we were before. What do you think?'

I think here's my chance to finally put an end to this, to close up at least one tear in my broken heart for good.

'That's sweet,' I tell him. 'I can't stop looking at your legs in those shorts, though. We're never going to go back to being two people having nice chats again.'

'Can you try to stop? I won't look at your waist in that dress if you keep your eyes off my legs.'

'It's not going to work, Alec. I'm flattered you came, and I know you're a good person to have around, but I can't.'

He breathes out a long line of air. I catch a faint smell of toothpaste and think of how perfect his teeth are. 'OK. I figured you'd say that,' he says. 'Still, I had to ask. If there were a chance you'd want me around and I never offered my services, as it were, I'd have hated myself. Here, this is for you.'

He bends round and picks up a small bag by his side. I hadn't noticed him carrying it in.

'What's this?'

'I bought it for you after your mum went into hospital. I was going to give it to you when I came round that night to make you dinner but never got the chance. I couldn't face taking it back. It needs a good home.'

I open the bag to find a troll with fuchsia-pink hair under a woolly hat, wearing a ski jacket and boots.

'A little reminder of our trip to the Lakes,' he says.

I remember the troll collection I had as a girl. The one I built up over the years. The one I treasured above everything else. I never told him that, did I?

'I love it so much,' I say quietly. I don't want to cry in front of him, so I cough and walk back into the house.

'You are so lovely,' I tell him once he's followed me back to the front door. 'If only everything was different.'

'If only it was.'

'Can you do me one thing, Alec?'

'Name it.'

'Stop texting Olivia and start looking for a girlfriend.'

'I don't know—'

I lean up to kiss his cheek one last time.

'For me?'

Chapter Thirty-nine

True to her word, Debs keeps seeing Mum every day while she wraps up her life with us. It's almost as if nothing's changed. We speak all the time; she never fails to text me to tell me when she's setting off to see Mum, and the odd occasion when we're there together at Henley Hall she's just the same as she was when she shared our home six nights a week.

In front of Mum she never mentions her plans to leave – she must figure there's no point. But there are times on the phone or on the way out of Mum's room she'll tell me about a flat they've seen on the Costa del Sol or a house that's sold for a good price on their street. I pretend to be pleased, and she pretends it's no big deal – nothing's going to happen for ages – but we both feel it. We're careering towards an ending – our ending. The only difference is Debs wants it, and I want to scream for it to stop.

What's worse, the only person I could go to for sympathy is hardly ever awake for me to talk to.

Mum's tired all the time now. By the time I get there in the evenings, she's always tucked up in bed. All I can do is hold her hand and be thankful that in sleep, at least, she appears to find some peace.

Life carries on like this for weeks. I become so worried I'll never see Mum awake again, I decide to take a day off work to see if I can catch a window of wakefulness.

I visit on a Thursday afternoon. It's a fine, dry day, and I'm heartened to see a dozen or so residents enjoying the garden with their relatives as I walk up the driveway. If Mum is up to it, I could bring her out here to join them.

After signing in, I scan the visitors' logbook for signs of Debs. There she is. Signed in at 9 a.m. Signed out at 9.45.

Grateful she's gone and I'll have Mum to myself, I take the stairs to her room. I'm excited to see her. If she is sleeping, at least I'll be able to stick around long enough to see her wake up.

The room is surprisingly light when I enter it. One of the nurses has pulled the curtains back and opened the window to let the warm breeze in. Instead of being in bed like I'd expected, Mum is dressed in the leggings and cardigan I bought her and sitting in the chair by the window, looking down on the garden.

'Hi, Mum. You're looking very well today.'

'Oh she is, she is.' Yolanda's happy voice rings out from the bathroom, and she enters the room smiling. 'We're having a good day today, aren't we, Susan?'

'That's great.'

I crouch down next to Mum to give her a kiss on her cheek, and the most amazing thing happens: she smiles at me. Not the polite smile Mum has for everyone she comes across, but the smile she reserves for me, the one that makes her eyes watery. She knows me.

'Hi, it's me. It's your Jess,' I tell her over and over, my arms thrown around her bony frame.

'Go easy,' Yolanda says, appearing at my side. 'I think you might be squashing her.'

I release my grip immediately. 'Sorry, Mum.' Then turning to Yolanda, I ask, 'What does this mean?'

'It means she's having a very good day, and you should make the most of it.'

'I will. Fancy a walk, Mum?'

We spend the afternoon amongst the flowers. A soft wind breathes lavender-scented air over our faces, and the sun strokes our cheeks with its gentle heat.

I tell her about Olivia's pregnancy, about Alec's visit and the troll, about everything nice I can think of. Mum watches me the whole time, her hand at her throat resting on the necklace I gave her for Christmas. I find myself resting my hand in exactly the same spot on top of my own necklace.

When Mum finally shows signs of growing tired of my inane chattering, I stop, and she closes her eyes. In seconds, she's sleeping. It's too nice to take her back to her room. I park her wheelchair next to Maggie's bench and sit with her, holding her hand.

A man joins me whilst his two children bound around the garden like puppies let off their leashes. In between yelling at them to stay off the flowerbeds, he strikes up the typical conversation between relatives of the home's residents about our loved ones. His father, he tells me, has been in Henley Hall for six years, ever since his dementia made it unsafe for him to remain at home. Surprised, I ask if his father has enjoyed living here for so long. He laughs before telling me his father adores being here, and often seems much more at peace than he ever did back in his own house.

I look at Mum sleeping and think how her being here was her wish, her decision. She chose this place for herself, and I understand her choice now. Mum believed her final years here would be more peaceful than if she stayed at home. I do hope she's right.

Yolanda comes to find us when it's time for Mum to eat. I wake Mum and take her to the dining room. Yolanda insists on feeding Mum herself instead of letting me do it, and I begrudgingly agree. Yolanda is the nurse, after all. Mum struggles to keep the puree Yolanda gives her in her mouth long enough to swallow it. It's hard to watch her struggling so much, but Yolanda insists she is getting enough of it down her to give her the nutrition she needs.

By the time she finishes and is back in her room, Mum is pale and waxy with tiredness. Yolanda and I put her in her bed, and I know, just like every other evening, she's going to sleep for hours.

'Goodnight, Mum,' I say. I place a kiss on her forehead and pull away to find her looking right at me.

'I love you so very much,' I tell her. I don't know how many good days we'll have left, but I know I have to use every one of them to let her know how loved she is. 'You're the best mum I could ever have wished for.'

She smiles and closes her eyes. I stroke her hair until she's asleep.

On the way out, I thank Yolanda and promise to visit in the day as much as I can from now on. The afternoon has done us both the world of good.

The phone call comes while I'm at work the following day.

'Miss Hyland?'

'Speaking.'

'This is Nina Lew from Henley Hall. I'm ringing to let you know we've had to call an ambulance for your mum. We're a little concerned about her breathing, and we'd like to get her checked out.'

'Oh God, is she OK?'

'Yes. We've just noticed a change in her, and she has a slightly raised temperature, so we're erring on the side of caution and sending her to hospital. Are you able to meet her there?'

'Of course. I'm coming straight there now.'

I look around the office for Jane. She's locked in a fraught-looking conversation with her husband in the glass-box conference room in the middle of our floor. Usually, I'd leave her to it when she's alone with Mr Lewis, but now I burst into the room giving them no chance to throw a professional conversation over their argument.

'Sorry to interrupt. My mum's in hospital. Can I go?'

'Oh dear. Yes, go, go,' Jane orders.

Mr Lewis opens his mouth to speak, but Jane cuts him short by raising her hand.

'Don't even think about work. Go and be with your mum.'

She gives me a hug and pushes me towards the lifts.

In the taxi on the way to the hospital it occurs to me I'm less frightened than the last time I was hurtling towards Manchester Royal Infirmary. I've already seen the tubes piercing Mum's skin. I've heard the irregular bleep of the machines surrounding her. I know there will be a night on a chair that will leave me stiff all over, a greasy breakfast and the rushed, comforting words of doctors in scrubs on their ward rounds.

A crisis to face but a familiar one at least.

'Drop me here, please,' I tell the taxi driver, knowing exactly where to go this time.

Mum, I know, won't be in the A & E waiting room. If it is pneumonia she's got again, there'll be no time to wait. They'll already be working on her, trying to get her stable. I don't bother to look around, going straight to the hospital's main reception instead.

'Can you tell me what ward I can find Susan Hyland on? She was brought in by ambulance about half an hour ago.'

Impressed by my efficiency, the receptionist matches it by pulling herself to her computer, a roll of stomach flab spilling on her desk as she does so, and quickly typing in the relevant information.

A crease appears on her otherwise neutral face as she reads whatever is on the screen.

'Take a seat in the waiting area and someone will come to find you soon.'

This is new.

Unsure what it means, I take the only available seat next to a mother and her fidgeting toddler. Within minutes, a neat nurse in a senior dark-blue tabard calls out my name.

'Hello. Can you come this way, please? Dr Thornley is just finishing up with a patient but will be down to speak to you shortly.'

Dread rises up from my toes like pins and needles, spreading through my body until I can't focus on anything else.

'What's going on?'

'This way, please.'

I'm led down a quiet corridor and into a small, dimly lit cubbyhole of a room. There are three armchairs in different primary colours surrounding a low, circular table with a box of tissues placed perfectly in the middle. On the wall is an abstract picture of a lily.

Once I take a seat on the yellow chair, the nurse shuts the door, leaving me alone. I haven't seen much of Manchester Royal Infirmary, but I know for certain this is the worst room in the entire hospital.

A soft knock twenty minutes later confirms what I already know. A doctor with good news wouldn't knock so gently. A job in the NHS doesn't usually leave time for such politeness. A doctor with a patient on the mend would stride in, give their report and be off on their way.

The door opens slightly and a young man with a thin beard pops his head into the gap.

'Hi. I'm Dr Thornley. Can I come in?'

An odd question considering this is his hospital, not mine. 'Yes.'

Rather than the scrubs I'd grown used to seeing the doctors up on the intensive care unit wearing, this doctor is dressed in a slim-fitting suit and impossibly shiny black loafers. He looks like a teenage boy dressed for his first day at work, thinking he's the business thanks to the shopping trip his mum took him on. How dare he look so shiny, so fresh, when he's surrounded by illness?

'I'm afraid the news isn't good,' he says sitting opposite me on the red chair. 'Your mum's presented with significant breathing problems caused by acute respiratory failure. At the moment, we're struggling to get her stable and are growing concerned. I have to ask, are you aware your mum has a DNR on her file?'

'A DNR?'

'Do not resuscitate.'

'Oh that. Yes, I am.' Mum told me about it a few years ago when it became clear the time would come for me to be in charge of her medical decisions. Any talk of end-of-life seemed so unnecessary back then, something to push to the back of my mind. I did just that, only now those letters are back, and I see for the first time their significance. Those three letters have the power to end Mum's life.

'Can I see her?' I ask.

'Of course, I'll take you up now.'

I'm led back to the intensive care unit. Mum looks as diminished as she was the last time she was here in the midst of all the medical equipment. There are new things too, machines she didn't need before and a stillness to her that snatches my breath away.

'Oh, Mum.' I take her hand and rest my head on the scrap of pillow next to her that isn't covered with wires.

I don't move for hours. I whisper in her ear all my favourite memories of us together, and I tell her I love her over and over. We're not interrupted. We don't need anything else. The hospital ward fades until it's just the two of us.

It's only when a solid alarm sounds that I lift my head up to see what's happening. Dr Thornley softly moves across to the machine making that awful sound and presses a button to silence it.

'I'm so, so sorry,' he says.

I put my head back where it belongs and stroke her hair.

'Oh, Mum.'

Chapter Forty

The dress she's picked out for me is awful.

Green and blue. Floaty. Floor length. Happy. I've been standing in her room looking at my reflection in her full-length mirror for ten minutes now, and I'm still no nearer to knowing why she wanted me to go to her funeral dressed like a mermaid.

But her instructions were clear. Debs gave me the letter two days after she died, following up that evening with a text message all in capitals, shouting at me to make sure I read it.

I opened the envelope with a thick film of fear wrapped round my heart. I was only just managing to grip on to the edge of daily life, keeping busy and out of the house by working my way through the endless jobs a death brings about. Another letter like the last one she wrote me would be a boot stamping on my fingers, making me lose my grip altogether and fall into the darkness below.

But Mum knew what I needed. Instead of an outpouring of her love for me, she had given me a short letter and a long list. It was written at a time when her handwriting was steady and her mind was on practical matters.

Dear Jess,
I've been putting together a list of things you'll need to take care of when I'm no longer around. Sorry to be

morbid, but I want to be organised, and I'd hate to think you'd be struggling because I shied away from dealing with this.

There should be enough here to get you through everything you'll need to do after I'm gone. Make sure you ask for help if you need anything. Debs seems like a decent enough sort. If she's still around, I'm sure she'll be happy to help.

Love you,
Mum xx

I smiled when I read the bit about Debs – how right she was – then turned to the list, a gloriously practical list to get me through the days ahead. Amongst orders to cancel direct debits, inform the insurance about her death and see the solicitor about her will, there were instructions about her funeral. Nothing too big; funeral to be kept to a maximum of thirty minutes; entrance song to be 'The Time of My Life' from the *Dirty Dancing* soundtrack; only close friends and family for the crematorium; wake to be held at Didsbury cricket club because it has a nice outlook and good parking.

The only request I've struggled with is the one that's ended in me looking ridiculous for my mum's funeral.

In the list, Mum had written:

No drab mourning clothes for the funeral. Bright colours only. Please wear the green dress you'll find hidden at the end of my wardrobe, past my coats. I saw it online in the Ted Baker sale a few weeks ago and thought of you. It'd be nice for you to have a chance to get all dressed up for once. You'll make people smile by looking so lovely.

All morning I've deliberated about wearing it, but when the doorbell rings at eleven, I forget all about the dress, or about any of the meticulous plans I've been executing on Mum's behalf this last week. I step out into a light downpour to greet the two funeral directors. They offer their condolences, and like every condolence offered since Dr Thornley's, I receive it numbly and insincerely.

I nod at the neighbours. Like a scene from *Coronation Street* – one I never expected would happen in real life – they have come out onto the street to pay their respects and line up on the pavement, their heads bent. I thank them with a nod as I edge closer to the cars.

I don't look at the first one in the procession – the one holding Mum. Instead, I duck into the second car and order the driver to set off without delay.

Mum wanted Auntie Sarah, Debs and her cousin Joe to be in the funeral car with me, but it was the one request of hers I refused. This is a journey I want to make with her only. Mum and I, one last time.

Considering how few people were in Mum's life at the end, there's a pretty decent funeral party waiting for her at the church. For the first time all morning, tears leak out of my eyes. I don't expect them, so am not quick enough to prevent it happening. I've planned for the worst bits of today, tried to assign my strength to those moments. I had no idea how overwhelmed I'd be to be surrounded by kind faces.

There's Auntie Sarah, sticking out in a red trouser suit, sitting in a pew with a group of Mum's old colleagues from the optician's; Mum's cousin Joe and his wife; Erica and Nina from Henley Hall; Debs and Lauren; a large group of Mum's uni friends; some older women next to Sarah whom I've never seen before and guess must be Mum's former patients; and, finally, the girls from my office, sitting uncomfortably at the back, pulling at their black outfits.

I must have forgotten to let them know about the dress code. Poor Jane. She's decked herself out as Jackie Onassis, with a black box suit and hat complete with a fine veil over her eyes. Used to being admired for her ability to dress so perfectly, she must be mortified at coming to an event dressed so inappropriately. I catch her flashing jealous glances at Sarah and smile apologetically at her from the back of the church as I wait for Mum to be led in.

Once the pallbearers settle Mum's coffin on top of their shoulders and I'm directed to stand behind it, ready to enter the church, I push any worries about Jane's wrath out of my mind. 'The Time of My Life' strikes up, and I step forward, ready to say goodbye to Mum.

I don't give the eulogy. If Mum had wanted me to do it, I figure she'd have asked me to. She'd likely even have told me what to say about her. That she remained silent on that matter was her final kindness to me. There's no way I'd be able to stand up next to her coffin and keep the pain tucked away whilst speaking of her life.

Instead, I ask Sarah to do it.

She's been willing to do so much since Mum passed away. Every day she's been round at the house, taking unpleasant jobs off my hands and, best of all, constantly talking about Mum, sharing memories, keeping her in the house. Her way of making amends, I suppose, for all the lost time.

I don't ask Sarah what she's going to say beforehand. As she stands behind the pulpit, smoothing the creases on her jacket, it occurs to me I probably should have checked. Mum made it clear she didn't want Huntington's interfering with her funeral. The bastard had taken her life. It had no right to take her funeral too. I can't remember if I made that clear to Sarah. She starts to speak, and I think I'm going to be sick. I grab on to the end of the pew with both hands and scrunch my eyes shut.

'Susan Hyland touched so many lives before hers was cruelly taken from us.'

Oh no.

'To me she was a savvy and intelligent business partner, a fellow mother, who always had the best advice to give, and a wonderful, absolutely bonkers friend.'

There's a small, shy laugh from the congregation behind me. It's enough to make me open my eyes again.

'Ever since Jess kindly asked me to speak today, I've been racking my brain to find the words to sum Susan up in a few, short minutes. How do I express what a marvellous friend she was to me, what an amazing mother she was to Jess and how much she meant to us all? How do I fit that into one speech? It's impossible. I'll be talking about Susan for the rest of my life, and it still won't be enough. So, last night, I made a decision: I can't possibly tell you everything good about her in a few minutes, so, instead, I'll tell you about the opening night of our optician's practice.

'As you can imagine, that night was a very exciting moment in our careers. We'd worked so hard to get to that point, and it's fair to say Susan went a little overboard, hiring caterers, buying a magnum of champagne and spending two hundred and fifteen pounds on balloons. I still remember the exact cost of those balloons, because, at the time, I couldn't get over how ridiculous an amount it was to spend when you're starting a business from scratch. Safe to say, I put myself in charge of budgeting from that moment on.'

More laughter, louder this time. I join in too.

'There we were in our new premises, dressed up to the nines, ready to meet our future customers, only for no one to show up, because, well, who goes to the opening of a new optician's? I was gutted, and if I'm honest, infuriated that my new business partner had wasted so much money. But, rather than despair, Susan told me not to worry – we'd have an opening week rather than an opening night. All that first week, anyone who stepped through our door was given a glass of Moët, a plate of canapés and was sent away with a gold balloon. Word spread and we quickly became the most popular optician's in the area. Many of those first clients, falling in love with Susan's generosity and sense of fun, are still with us two decades later. Some of them are even here today.

'Susan was a fun-loving, kind and very wise woman, who brought so much joy into the lives of everyone she met.' Turning to the coffin, she wipes away the first tears that have fallen since she began. 'I'll miss you more than you can ever know, dear, dear friend.'

Leaving the pulpit, Sarah walks over to the coffin and rests her hands on it for a few moments, her head bent, before walking back to her pew. I signal for her to come and sit at the front with me instead. I spend the rest of the service with her arm around me, my head on her shoulder.

We don't let go of each other until we've taken Mum to the crematorium, until we've said goodbye for the final time, and we're back in the car on the way to the wake.

'I can't go in,' I tell her, once she's stepped out of the car and is waiting for me to join her.

'Yes, you can. This is the last bit now. Once you've shown your face, had a drink and something to eat, it's over, and you get to go home.'

Home is an even more frightening prospect than the cricket club. I get out of the car, determined to stay here as long as I can.

Sarah sits me down in a quiet corner before going to get us a drink and checking on the progress of the hot buffet that needs to be served shortly. Everywhere I look, I'm met with sympathy, the kind that screws a face up like a crumpled napkin. I turn my gaze to my lap instead.

'So sorry for your loss,' says a familiar voice struggling to mouth such uncomfortably unfamiliar words.

Lauren shuffles up next to me on the worn velvet sofa. There's a wide-eyed look of panic meshed together with her sympathy, giving her usually placid appearance a frantic edge. I want to calm her down, to help her gain control over her face.

'Thanks. And thanks for coming. How are you?'

'Oh, I'm OK, thanks. More importantly, how are you?'

'You know.'

'Yeah,' she agrees, before the lie forces her to look away. Of course she doesn't know. Lauren's still got a mum, after all.

'Where's your mum?'

'She's over there, chatting to some of your mum's colleagues, although she's desperate to come over here and be with you. She thought she'd let you see family and friends first.'

'As far as I'm concerned, she is family. Please ask her to come over.'

The second Lauren gives her the go-ahead, Debs abandons her conversation, slams her white wine on the bar and hurries over.

'You've done so well today, love. Your mum would've been so proud of you.'

'Would she?'

'Of course she would. You're a credit to her. You always have been.'

'Thanks, although I've not really done anything to be proud of.'

'Yes, you have. You've given her the perfect send-off for a start.'

'I suppose. Sarah's the one to thank for that. It was her eulogy that made the funeral special.'

On cue, Sarah arrives back with two gin and tonics and takes her seat on the other side of me. The two women exchange tight-lipped smiles before turning their attention back to me.

'The buffet looks good. It'll be ready in a minute. I'll get you a plateful. You must be starving,' Sarah says.

'You must remember to keep your strength up,' adds Debs. 'Tell you what, I'll come round tomorrow and bring you a few meals you can shove in the freezer.'

'How nice of you,' Sarah replies in my place, 'but I doubt there's any space left in the freezer. She's got enough to keep her going for weeks already.'

Mum would be delighted to know I've got Debs and Sarah fussing over me like two mother hens. I daren't tell either of them I've no appetite.

Debs's face falls, her jowls making her look like a sad dog.

'Maybe you could bring something fresh round tomorrow night, and we can all eat it together,' Sarah offers.

'I'd love to. Let me know what you fancy. Anything at all.'

'Thanks, Debs.'

I sip my gin and tonic as they continue to outdo each other with offers of generosity. By the time Sarah leaps up to fill a plate with quiche and sausage rolls for me, I've been promised a weekly meal at each of their houses, a delivery of fresh food every time Debs goes to Aldi and a cookery course by Sarah to remind me how to batch cook instead of relying on eggs on toast every evening.

Under their watchful eyes, I pick at a few crisps and the pastry of a sausage roll. A few other mourners approach the table to offer their condolences, and I thank them, making sure I ask each of them a few questions about themselves, even if I've not the foggiest idea who they are.

It's exhausting.

Eventually, people begin to leave. There's apologetic talk of rush hour and picking up children from school. The day is coming to an end. I'd woken up this morning craving this moment, but, now it's here, I hate it. Today was a day for Mum. Tomorrow won't be. Or the next day. Tomorrow everything returns to normal, and I'm not ready for that.

Sarah offers to come back to the house with me, but I tell her to get back to her own house, that she's done enough today. Debs invites me to spend the night with her. I insist there's no need. I shoo them both out the cricket club and into taxis, promising I'll go straight home too when I've made sure everything has been settled behind the bar.

Only, I won't go home. I can't. The house is haunted with grief, and I'm terrified of it.

I'd have gone with Debs if I thought tea, television and her boxroom were enough to get me through tonight. They're not. Nowhere close.

All day I've played my part like an actress in a film. I've stuck to the script and stayed in character until the final scene. Now it's over, now the camera isn't rolling, I need something for me. Something that isn't tainted with the expectation of grief. Something that lets me escape, just for tonight.

My taxi arrives a few minutes after the others leave. I get in and give the driver an address. An address where I hope I'll find the person I need more than anyone. Alec's address.

Chapter Forty-one

It's as if the rules I've created for myself these last few years and – with the exception of a few weeks – have vigilantly stuck to never existed. I saunter through the open gates of Alec's complex, ring his buzzer and climb the stairs without any hesitation. I know full well what I'm after, and it doesn't bother me one bit.

I knock on his door with the confidence of a long-term girlfriend, adjusting my boobs in the mermaid dress as I wait for him to open up.

It's the boxes piled up behind him that stop me in my sultry tracks.

'Hello. What an unexpected surprise.' I've baffled him with my outfit, my face, my very presence at his door. His face struggles to settle on a suitable expression. In the end his lips draw together in a wobbly, uncertain line.

The weight of the mistake I've made presses down on my shoulders. I reach for the doorframe to steady myself against it.

'I shouldn't have come.'

'OK.'

'Sorry, bye.'

He lets out a laugh that isn't really a laugh at all, more a tiny piece of pain caused by the bizarre situation I've just created.

'Bye, then.'

I wait for him to close the door. He's fed up with my crap. If he wasn't, he'd ask why I'm here. He'd at least try and coax me into coming in. No, he's utterly finished with me. He might not want to say as much, but he doesn't need to. The boxes say it for him. He's going home. Back to Leeds and back to her.

I almost feel sorry for his weakness. Until I realise it's not weakness at all, but his best option. He and Ellie can have a long, safe, somewhat bland life together, but one they can fill with children and the solid certainty of good health. A life with Ellie versus a life with me. It's not even a contest.

So why won't he close the bloody door? Why stare at me with those ridiculous eyes of his that pull out every emotion I've got left like two magnets?

He keeps it up until I feel a snap. The heart I've tried so hard to keep intact breaks apart right in front of him.

The pain of it is overwhelming, sending me to the floor. I try desperately to find a way to get some of it out of me, but there's nothing I can do. I can't even scream. I open my mouth but nothing comes out.

'What's happened? What's happened?'

I want to answer him, to let him help me, but it hurts too much to speak. Instead, I throw up over his shoes.

It takes a long time for the pain to subside enough to work out I'm in Alec's lounge propped up against the wall, cushions against my back. There's a gentle pressure against my thigh. I look down to see Alec's hand rubbing it slowly, rhythmically. For a while, I just watch the movement, each slow stroke slowing my breathing down until I'm ready to look up at him.

He's staring ahead, his eyes fixed on nothing. He's sweating. Beads of it make his hair stick together in clumps across his forehead. The sweat he's already pushed off his face makes the rest of his hair stick up. Troll hair. He's given himself troll hair. I'd smile if it weren't for the paleness of his skin or the tears leaking from his eyes.

'I'm so sorry.'

I make him jump. His hand jerks off my leg, and I wonder how long we've been sitting like this.

'Will you please stop saying sorry to me.'

'Sorry.'

'Nothing to be sorry about. Do you think you can tell me what's happened?'

I start to cry again, but the tears are gentler this time. Once I'm sure they don't have the power to knock me out again, I manage to say it. 'Mum's funeral was today.'

'Oh, Jess. What I wouldn't do to take away your pain.'

He pulls me to him, squashing me against his chest, and I remember why I'm here. Alec *can* take away this pain, at least for a little while. It would be so easy for him to do. All it would take would be for him to start kissing me.

I know if I asked, he'd do it. Despite the hurt I've caused him, despite Ellie, despite being the most decent person I know, he'd do it.

I stay silent. I try to find comfort instead from the citrus smell of his shower gel, from his fingers smoothing my hair, from the warmth of him, from how solid he feels compared to the weightlessness of my own body. It's not enough.

I pull away from him and stumble until I'm standing.

'What are you doing?' he asks, getting up from the floor.

'I really shouldn't have come here. It's not fair of me to expect anything from you. Especially now,' I say, wafting my hand around his near-empty lounge. 'I'm happy for you, by the way.'

'You are?'

'Yeah. And I don't blame you. I'm sure you'll be able to make it work with her.'

'Jess, what are you on about?'

'You going back to Ellie. For what it's worth, I think you're making the right choice.'

'Interesting . . . I'm not going back to Ellie, by the way. I'm moving to a house share in Chorlton, closer to a new bar I'm going to be managing, but I'll take your opinion on my future with Ellie on board.'

'You mean you're not—'

'No, I'm not.' He keeps his face serious, but his voice is amused. I cast off my composure like a coat that's become unbearably stifling to wear and throw myself on him. My lips press against his so violently, he tries to pull back, but I lock my hands around his head to keep him in place until I've lost myself in him.

I keep going, my body so tightly pressed against his it's almost painful. And he lets me. He squeezes me back, pushes his tongue deep into my mouth.

It's not enough. Why isn't it working?

We continue for a while, but it's clear I'm still me and he's still him. I've not gone anywhere. My mother is still dead, and all I'm doing now is making a prat of myself in front of the man I love.

I pull away, my gaze falling to the gold, strappy sandals I've been wearing all day, noticing how swollen and red my feet look in them.

'Look at me,' he says.

'I can't.'

'Yes, you can.' He hooks a finger under my chin, and pulls my face up to meet his. 'See, there you go. Now, whatever you came here for tonight, I'll give it you. No questions. But before you throw yourself at me again, if that's what you want to keep doing, can I make a suggestion?'

'Go on.'

'How about we make a new rule for tonight?'

'What kind of rule?'

'A rule that allows me to take care of you, without worrying about what it means, where it's going to lead. Do you think you can let me do that?'

All that kissing must have made me weak. There's no way I could muster the energy to sleep with Alec. It's an effort to even remain standing up.

I lean against him, letting him wrap his arms around me.

'I'd like that.'

Chapter Forty-two

The flat is quiet when I wake up. I'm in the middle of the lounge on a makeshift bed of sofa cushions, a wrapped-up towel for a pillow and a duvet without a cover. The cushions are narrow, and I'm sure I've slept alone. There's a fog-covered memory of Alec busying himself putting it together last night whilst I sat on the floor, my back against the wall, watching him. I check underneath the duvet and find I'm wearing one of his T-shirts over my knickers. I vaguely remember him sorting that out for me too. Sitting up, I spot the mermaid dress folded into a neat square on top of one of the piles of boxes. His work.

Alec must be asleep in his own room. But then it feels late, like I've slept a good chunk of the day away. The flurry and excitement of a spring morning has calmed now. All that's left is the occasional bird calling out and the constant thrum of a drill in the distance.

I roll out of the bed onto the floor and slowly push myself up into an aching standing position. Last night I was so desperate to sleep, I couldn't care less where I did so. I would happily have lain down on the wooden floor as long as doing so meant I could finally close my eyes. Now, muscles aching, I begrudgingly wonder why Alec didn't give up his bed to me instead.

I march to his room craving more sleep, better sleep, but I'm stopped in my tracks when I see the sleeping bag folded up in the middle of his room where his bed used to be. I was given the superior sleeping option last night, after all.

He's not in the bedroom, and there's no noise coming from the bathroom or the kitchen: Alec isn't here.

I return to the lounge and walk over to the window, pressing my head against it, my arms wrapped around my boobs to keep out the cold. It's raining outside, making an already dank outlook even bleaker. There's an identical block of flats to Alec's and a small, uninviting square between them with two benches facing each other in the middle, seeing as there's nothing else for them to point to. The mist from my breath begins to cloud the window and block the view. I don't bother to wipe it away.

Alec returns to find me with my head still pressed to the glass, eyes shut. I think I might have been dozing because hearing my name on his lips startles me, and when I turn to him, I feel disorientated, like I've been spun round too many times in a game of pin the tail on the donkey.

He holds up a cardboard tray with two paper cups in it and a paper bag before disappearing into the kitchen. When he reappears, he hands me a napkin with a warm croissant on it and a cappuccino.

'Hope you don't mind slumming it,' he says by way of apology. 'I wasn't expecting visitors. Everything I own is either packed up in these boxes or waiting for me in the new house, and that includes plates, I'm afraid.'

'It's fine.' I smile weakly, remembering the identical breakfast we shared the first morning I was in this flat.

We eat in silence, both concentrating on directing any stray flakes of pastry onto the napkin and not his immaculately clean floor. I should ask him when he's meant to be out, if I'm holding him up, if I should leave, but it's impossible to find the energy to speak, and I don't want to hear the answers.

'Come on,' he says after taking the napkin and the empty coffee cup off me. 'It's freezing. The landlord's a miserable bugger. My tenancy officially ran out yesterday, and even though he's letting me stay on an extra day until I can move into the house, he's already turned the heating off. There's only one way I can think of to warm up.' He takes my hand and leads me back to the bed he made for me. After he climbs in, he holds the duvet up for me to join him. Not thinking once about what doing so might mean, I follow him in. We wind ourselves around each other to keep out the cold. For a little while, I lie there waiting to see what Alec does next. It's not a nervous waiting, more a detached curiosity. If he kissed me, I'd kiss him back. If he lifted the T-shirt I'm wearing over my head, I'd let him. If he rolled on top of me, I'd put my arms around him and pull him down. If he did nothing at all, I'd lie next to him and listen to him breathe, just as I am now. But as his heat spreads across my body, I become so drowsy there's only one thing that can happen.

I wake to feel him still wrapped around me. It's almost dark in the flat. The rain is coming down more heavily now, in thick, silver sheets that insulate the apartment like tin foil. I stay where I am with my eyes shut. It's warm and quiet and safe, and I don't ever want to move.

'Hi,' he whispers.

'Hi. How long have you been awake?'

'A while.'

I turn to find him propped up in bed, the arm not still wrapped under me supporting his head. There's not a trace of tiredness in him. He studies my face, his eyes narrowed ever so slightly. I could stay exactly where I am until I fall back to sleep, but not Alec. He's ready for something else. With a groan, I realise why he's watching me so intently: he's waiting to see what I do next.

Go, probably. It's what I should do. I should thank him for last night, for letting me in, get myself back into the green dress and leave.

Instead, I ask him about the new job.

Evening passes with slices of conversation and slices of silence. At some point he opens one of the boxes and finds a bottle of red. We drink it slowly from the bottle, alternating sips.

In the talking moments, I mainly sip my wine and listen. Alec is as careful as I am not to stray close to conversations with the potential to hurt me. It's another rule – an unsaid one – that my life, for now, is in this flat and nowhere else. Neither of us can mention my life outside these walls.

We stop talking around ten. It feels like three in the morning. Alec puts the empty bottle on the windowsill and ushers me back into bed.

I haven't cleaned my teeth since yesterday morning, nor brushed my hair. What's left of my make-up will be halfway down my face by now. I must look repulsive. Alec doesn't seem to care very much. He asks if he can stay with me tonight. I tell him I'd like that.

The following morning, once I'm out of the much-needed bath Alec painstakingly filled for me with kettles of water, and am standing in front of him in a towel, Alec breaks the new rule.

He needs to be out today. Another man will be moving into the flat this afternoon. As soon as we woke up, Alec extracted himself from the tangle we'd slept in, reclaimed his body as his own and set to tidying away the debris of our time together, repacking and recleaning.

Our time has come to an end.

'Have you thought about what you're going to do now?' he asks, looking behind me at the path of wet footsteps I've created over the floor.

'I'll go home. Debs and Sarah will be worried about me. I'm sure they'll be round at some point.'

I haven't checked my phone since the funeral. I can just imagine the missed calls stacking up and the panicked voice messages after two days of not knowing where I am. I'll have to ring both of them as soon as I get back.

'That's good. I'm glad they'll be there to look after you. I didn't mean today, though. I was thinking further on.'

'I suppose I'll have to start thinking about going back to work at some point.'

'No. I don't mean that, either. God, are you doing this on purpose? I'm talking about those plans of yours to see the world. You always said you couldn't do that whilst your mum needed you. I was wondering if, now, it's something you might be thinking about.'

It hasn't occurred to me once. I'd always told myself Mum was the tie that bound me to the small life I was leading and once that tie was cut, that's when I'd be free to go off and explore the world without anything to pull me back. Now I'm not so sure. Maybe it was more than Mum. I've never admitted it, but maybe I'm more attached to this life that I have than I thought. Right now, the idea of being completely alone, thousands of miles from Debs, Sarah and Olivia terrifies me. I always thought, apart from Mum, I was alone. Now she's gone, I can see that's not true. My friends – our friends – have held me up these last few weeks, and I am so grateful for them.

I begin to cry.

313

'Hey, it's all right.' Alec is in front of me, wiping my face with his thumbs before wrapping me up in him. 'You don't have to decide anything yet. The world will wait for you.'

'I know. And maybe I would be making plans if I wasn't so—' I pause.

'So what?'

'So terrified. I'm so used to seeing myself as my mum's daughter. Huntington's was about Mum. It was her battle, not mine. That's what I made myself focus on. Now—'

I can't carry on. I'm drowning. My throat burns; I can't get enough oxygen down it; the tears that come are too big, too heavy. They take over everything. I'm in the middle of Alec's empty lounge, and I'm drowning. I gasp and flail, but the harder I try to suck in air, the more painful it is.

Alec puts his hands firmly on my shoulders.

'Look at me. Look at my face, Jess. You're all right. Here.' He hands me the paper bag that held the croissants. 'Breathe into this. Big deep breaths. Think about nothing else but your breathing. In and out. In and out.'

I do as he says, not believing at all that a paper bag is going to be enough to save me, but the pain does begin to lessen its grip and my breathing begins to calm. I notice how low my towel has slipped and tug it back into place. I'm able to step away from Alec's horrible, frightened eyes and return to the bathroom, lock the door behind me and splash cold water on my face.

'Can I come in?' Alec asks.

'No.'

'OK, that's fine. Just tell me you're OK, and I'll leave you to it.'

'I'm not OK at all. I'm the most selfish person in the world. My poor, lovely mum has gone, and all I can think

314

about is myself. How I'm next. How scared I am. How unfair it is.'

'Keep breathing, Jess. Big, deep breaths, just like before. And you listen to me. You are the least selfish person I've ever met. Bloody hell, you've almost shut down your life to protect anyone else from touching on the pain you've felt looking after your mum. You're willing to live alone out of this obsession of yours to contain your disease. That's not selfish. It's stupid but not selfish.'

I get off the edge of the bath and open the door when I'm sure I can face him without crumpling again.

'Alec, I've messed you about so much. That was selfish.'

'Do you think you can get dressed now?' he asks gently.

'Yeah, I'll get out of your hair.'

The only item of clothing I've got is my mermaid dress, and I can't put myself back into it. Alec lends me a clean T-shirt and a pair of shorts. I look ridiculous, but it's better than the alternative.

'Oh,' he says when I reappear in the hallway in his clothes. 'I was going to ask you to do one thing for me, but I'm guessing you don't want to hit central Manchester in that get-up. I'll drop you home. Could you meet me at The Wishing Well one last time in a few hours?'

I almost say no, but it's the one last time that does it. I don't want the last time Alec sees me to be like this. I want to say goodbye to him properly. It's the least I can do.

'OK.'

'He's in the back waiting for you,' the barman with the ginger hair says when I get to The Wishing Well. 'Go on through.'

I'd hoped this would be a farewell drink. Instead, I walk round to the other side of the bar, through the hidden door at the end and into the stockroom.

It's dark inside. The only lighting comes from the tea lights dotted around the room on shelves and surrounding a seating area Alec's created using upturned crates covered in an array of beer mats and coats. He motions for me to take a seat next to him. On a crate in front of him there are two glasses of champagne.

'What's all this?'

'An idea I wanted to run past you,' he answers, handing me my champagne.

'Another one?' I ask, remembering the last time I was in this room.

'This one will be better, I promise. This one starts with me telling you I love you.'

'Alec, don't.'

'Hear me out, will you? I know you don't want me to love you because you don't want me to suffer watching Huntington's take hold of you.'

'Exactly.'

'Then you have no idea how much I've fallen for you. If part of being with you means watching you disappear one day, so be it. There will never be anyone I'll ever want to spend my life with apart from you.'

'You don't know that.'

'Oh yes I do. You've made me love deeper than I ever knew I could. What we have, Jess, this is it. This is what I came here looking for. I know there are going to be challenges ahead, and the chances are I'm going to have to live part of my life without you in it, but I'm OK with that. I'll be OK with the dark times too, because the life we have together is going to be filled with so many thousands of bright moments. We can be so happy together. Don't you want that?'

'More than anything. The thing is, that darkness you talk about; you haven't seen it. Not really. I have, and I won't lead you into it. You don't know what it's going to be like, Alec.'

'Nor do you. You can't predict the future. Right now, your mum's fate looks like it's going to be yours, but anything can happen. Amazing advances are happening with Huntington's. By the time it starts on you, there may be a way to stop its severity. You just don't know. We could decide to be together only for me to fall ill a few months down the line. No one can say for sure what's coming. All we can do is keep loving each other one day at a time. So here's my idea. Are you ready?'

I'm crying, heavy tears that plunge down my face and run in rivers down my neck.

'I'm ready.'

'Jess, will you go out with me? Not for a month, not for a year, but for as long as we've got?'

Chapter Forty-three

Two and a half years later

There's nothing else but the pain. It's there even before I am, waiting for me to enter back into it on waking. Muscles throbbing, head thumping, nausea malevolently pushing the two ill-advised beers I drank last night back to the surface.

There's a scuttling noise by my ear, far too loud and purposeful for the middle of the night.

'Shut up,' I tell it.

'Good morning to you too. What bag did we pack the ponchos in? It's bloody pouring down, and Pepe's going to be here any minute to get us moving.'

'Is it three already?' I ask, groaning.

'Yep. Bet you're glad you had those Coronas now, aren't you?'

I shouldn't have touched the stuff. Since landing in Cusco airport three days ago, I've been worn down with altitude sickness. It would have been unpleasant enough if we'd have stayed in the city and stuck to the cheap hotel room we booked. Trekking up the Andean mountains on the Inca trail towards Machu Picchu in the thin air has nearly finished me off.

Yesterday we covered ten kilometres over twelve hours. We hiked through jungles and archaeological sites, up steps and over steep hills. All the time it felt like I couldn't get enough air to my lungs. Every ten minutes or so I would have to grind to a halt, winded by the exertion.

Under Pepe's patient guidance, we reached our third camp before nightfall, with the faint outline of Machu Picchu visible through the haze.

Alec and I agreed; pain aside, it had been one of the best days of our lives. Triumphant and filled with beauty. It was the kind of day we came here searching for. Looking at the mountains, knowing how far we'd come, was a moment to celebrate. So when Clifford, the father of the family of Americans hiking with us, pulled out two six-packs of Corona and offered them around, I didn't hesitate.

Now, I wish I'd been as sensible as Alec and taken a cup of Pepe's tea instead. Every guidebook I'd read warned about the perils of alcohol when struggling with high altitude. Two Coronas and Alec needed to carry me into the tent.

'Ponchos, Jess?'

'Right. I think they're in the front pocket of my backpack.'

Alec turns his torch in my direction and finds the two clear, plastic ponchos we bought in Cusco and hoped we wouldn't need. I slip further into my sleeping bag as he wrestles himself into one.

'Ta da!'

Reluctantly, I pull the sleeping bag down and sit up to take a look at him.

I have to laugh. 'Well, don't you look a treat?'

'I know. Here, put yours on.'

It's freezing in the tent. Instinctively, I look through my backpack for the thick jumper and woolly hat I packed, but I remember how humid it's going to get when the sun comes up and opt for a T-shirt, thin fleece and chino shorts.

'Gorgeous,' Alec tells me when I do as much of a turn as the two-man tent will allow in front of him when I'm ready, the poncho crunching noisily around me like a packet of crisps. 'I'm so glad this is going to be the look we'll be capturing in our pictures when we get to Machu Picchu.'

'Me too.' I imagine the photos to come of the two of us beaming into Alec's phone. Two dorks at the end of their journey, eyes squinting against the sun, arms round each other, laughing. We'll put those photos in a frame, hang them around the house in Leeds we moved into a year ago, when we decided we wanted to be closer to Alec's parents so they could help us when we needed it, and look back on them, remembering this day.

If only it hadn't started with a hangover.

There's a polite coughing outside the tent, almost inaudible under the pounding of rain on the canvas roof. But we're expecting it and have been listening out. Alec opens the tent to find Pepe standing with two tin cups of coca tea, a special Peruvian tea using leaves from the coca plant, which he's sworn is the remedy for each of the various ailments that have befallen our hiking party these last three days.

'Good, you're ready. Drink this to prepare you for the journey. We've got six kilometres to cover before daybreak. We leave in ten minutes.'

Alec takes the tea off him, grimaces after taking a sip from one cup and hands the other to me. 'Ready?'

'Ready.'

We reach Machu Picchu as the sun is rising. Pepe tells us out of all the hundreds of groups he's brought here, our group have turned out to be one of the most proficient. We've made record speed, apparently. Of everything we've seen and done in South America these last three weeks, it's been this hike in the dark, in the torrential rain, that I've been most proud to accomplish.

Mum would have been proud too. The provision she left in her will to be spent only on travelling was her final nudge towards the life she wanted for me. A big life like this.

There's already a queue at the entrance to the ancient site of Machu Picchu when we arrive. Soon, it's going to be swarming with tourists; we'll have to wait our turn to take the iconic picture of the site with Huayna Picchu Mountain in the background. I tap my foot on the dusty ground, impatient to be let in and to experience it as a tranquil sanctuary, not a tourist hot spot.

Alec puts his arm around my shoulders. 'How're you holding up?'

'Great. You?' I ask, pretending the hangover has disappeared when really it's knocking against my skull.

'Great. Knackered, but we can sleep later, right?'

'Right.'

The queue slowly winds towards the entrance, and Pepe makes sure he's at the front of our party to guide us through smoothly.

Once inside, he tells us not to follow the other early arrivals heading up to the popular photo spots. Instead, he leads us into the heart of the abandoned citadel. We follow him in silence, listening intently to his quiet voice as he narrates our way around. His knowledge of and respect for the Incas is woven into the hundreds of facts he regales us with.

We have two hours at the site before we have to leave. After an hour or so, he asks us what we would like to do. We all agree we have to take the pictures of us looking down on the citadel before we go. Pepe takes us up the steps to the Gatekeeper's Hut where we'll be able to take the 'classic photos'.

By this point, May-Louise, the American mum, and her daughter Reece are busting for the loo. They ask Alec and I if they can go ahead of us and take their pictures first. We end up waiting behind them and another two families not on our hike, who managed to convince us they should go on ahead too.

I stand behind them, running my hand through my hair, gently pulling out the knots that have formed in the course of a morning's trek in heavy rain.

Alec grabs my hand when it swoops down and holds it in both of his.

'Do you want to go and sit down somewhere? We've taken enough pictures. We don't need to take this one.'

Every step of our journey, Alec's worried about me, always on the lookout for signs all is not well. With the ticking time bomb of Huntington's in my head, it's no surprise, but I wish the shadow we live under would disappear for one day. One perfect day like this.

I pull my hand out of his. 'Of course we do. I promised Debs I'd email a picture of us at the top, and that's what I'm going to do.'

'Come on, then, we're up next.'

We give Alec's phone to Pepe and stand off to the side of the shot so he can capture the scene as well as us. I wonder if secretly he hates this part of the job. If I held anywhere as sacred as Pepe holds this place, I'd take issue with it being reduced to an image on an iPhone.

'Three, two, one, smile.'

Alec doesn't look at the camera; he leans forward to kiss my cheek instead.

'Ah, the lovebirds,' Pepe says. 'Beautiful.'

'Not a bad honeymoon picture,' Alec whispers to me, before moving away to let the couple behind us take our spot.

I think back to our tiny wedding a month before. I remember it now as a circle. A circle of our closest friends and family surrounding us. All those smiling faces, and in the middle of them, with the biggest smile of all, him: my husband.

'Wait a second,' I say, pulling him back.

'We should probably move.'

'I know.' I turn my back to the line of tourists and look towards the mountains. 'I just want to take this in a little longer.'

'OK.'

I stand still. Alec is by my side. We don't know what's coming next, when Huntington's is going to appear in our lives. I might reach the same age as Mum before my symptoms begin to show, which gives us time for many more days like this. Or it might come sooner. Most of the time that terrifies me. It terrifies us both.

But right now there's nothing. Just me and Alec and the green slopes of the Andes spreading out before us.

I turn away from it, to Alec. The last year has brought more lines to his face and the first grey to pollute his black hair. I reach up to kiss his cheek.

'That's Machu Picchu done, then.'

He closes his eyes, exhausted but smiling. 'Yeah. We did it, Jess.'

'We did. Where now?'

Acknowledgements

First and foremost my immense thanks go to Rachel Neely, for the support and vision that helped turn *One Month of You* into the story you've just read and for being the kind of editor any writer would dream of working with.

I've been lucky enough to work with not one but two editors, who have invested their time, effort and immeasurable talent into this book.

Thank you to Katie Brown for being a cheerleader for this story from the start and providing so much invaluable input.

My thanks go to the team at Trapeze. I couldn't have asked for a better experience and for better people to work with.

This book started with a competition. Thank you to eharmony and Trapeze for coming together to create the Write Your Own Love Story competition in 2018. Without that opportunity, I don't know if I'd have had the courage to begin this story. Thank you to the judges for believing in it and making my writing dreams come true.

Warmest thanks to the Huntington's Disease Association for taking the time to answer my questions during the early stages of writing Jess and Susan's storyline.

Writing a novel is a funny business, which, by necessity, involves long periods of time alone on a laptop. I never imagined through my laptop I would find my way to the greatest, funniest and most helpful writing group there is. Thank you to everyone who makes up the mighty VWG. Your friendship, advice and encouragement means so, so much, and I'm eternally grateful.

Special thanks to Jenny Ireland and Sally Beare, who read early drafts and helped develop Alec's character in particular.

Thank you to the groups I've had the good fortune to be part of in the run-up to publication, especially @DebutsUK2021 and Debut 21.

I'm very lucky to have some lovely friends, who have been amazing these last few years and have made writing this book a joy. Thank you to Gemma, Nat, Kathryn, Isla, Laura, Helen and Nic and, of course, Gill. For all your excitement and support, thank you to my wonderful group of Culcheth friends.

Thank you to my brilliant family for the encouragement you've always given me and for making me believe I could do whatever I set my mind to. I remember my dad taking me into Bolton town centre every fortnight to buy the latest *Point Horror* – my love of books started at home and it's led me here.

And last but definitely not least, my biggest thank you goes to Mark, Max and Sophie – this book is for you.

Credits

Orion Fiction would like to thank everyone at Orion who worked on the publication of *One Month of You* in the UK.

Editors
Rachel Neely
Katie Brown

Copy-editor
Marian Reid

Proofreader
Clare Hubbard

Editorial Management
Jo Whitford
Charlie Panayiotou
Jane Hughes
Claire Boyle

Audio
Paul Stark
Amber Bates

Contracts
Anne Goddard
Paul Bulos
Jake Alderson

Design
Debbie Holmes
Joanna Ridley
Nick May
Clare Sivell
Helen Ewing
Rachael Lancaster

Finance
Jennifer Muchan
Jasdip Nandra
Ibukun Ademefun
Rabale Mustafa
Sue Baker
Tom Costello